Praise for the authors of

Double the Pleasure

Lori Foster

"Lori Foster writes about real people you'll fall in love with."

—Stella Cameron

"You can pick up any Lori Foster book and know you're in for a good time."

—Linda Howard

Deirdre Martin

"[Martin] can touch the heart and funny bone."

—*Romance Junkies*

"Ms. Martin always delivers heat and romance."

—*Contemporary Romance Reviews*

Jacquie D'Alessandro

"Romance at its enchanting best."

—Teresa Medeiros

"A prediction: In the years to come, Jacquie D'Alessandro will become a household name for lovers of the romance genre."

—*Midwest Book Review*

Penny McCall

"McCall is quickly making a mark on the romantic suspense landscape."

—*Romantic Times*

"Sure to get your pulse racing."

—*Romance Reviews Today*

Double the Pleasure

Lori Foster

Deirdre Martin

Jacquie D'Alessandro

Penny McCall

BERKLEY SENSATION, NEW YORK

THE BERKLEY PUBLISHING GROUP
Published by the Penguin Group
Penguin Group (USA) Inc.
375 Hudson Street, New York, New York 10014, USA
Penguin Group (Canada), 90 Eglinton Avenue East, Suite 700, Toronto, Ontario M4P 2Y3, Canada
(a division of Pearson Penguin Canada Inc.)
Penguin Books Ltd., 80 Strand, London WC2R 0RL, England
Penguin Group Ireland, 25 St. Stephen's Green, Dublin 2, Ireland (a division of Penguin Books Ltd.)
Penguin Group (Australia), 250 Camberwell Road, Camberwell, Victoria 3124, Australia
(a division of Pearson Australia Group Pty. Ltd.)
Penguin Books India Pvt. Ltd., 11 Community Centre, Panchsheel Park, New Delhi—110 017, India
Penguin Group (NZ), 67 Apollo Drive, Rosedale, North Shore 0632, New Zealand
(a division of Pearson New Zealand Ltd.)
Penguin Books (South Africa) (Pty.) Ltd., 24 Sturdee Avenue, Rosebank, Johannesburg 2196, South Africa

Penguin Books Ltd., Registered Offices: 80 Strand, London WC2R 0RL, England

This book is an original publication of The Berkley Publishing Group.

Cover art by Daniel O'Leary.
Cover design by Richard Hasselberger.
Interior text design by Kristin del Rosario.

PRINTING HISTORY
Berkley Sensation trade paperback edition / December 2008

Library of Congress Cataloging-in-Publication Data

Double the pleasure / Lori Foster . . . [et al.].—Berkley Sensation trade pbk. ed.
p. cm.
ISBN 978-0-425-22406-9
1. Erotic stories, American. I. Foster, Lori, 1958–
PS648.E7D68 2008
813'.01083538—dc22 2008037184

PRINTED IN THE UNITED STATES OF AMERICA

10 9 8 7 6 5 4 3 2 1

Contents

Deuces Wild

Lori Foster

To Kathy Andrico, photographer, reader, and friend. I appreciate all you do and all that you contribute, not only to me personally but to the entire romance community.

You're the best!

One

Dexter Winston paced across the floor, but Hart, his twin, didn't let him go far. When he turned, Hart was right there, black eye flinching, a purpling bruise on his forehead, and determination in every line of his body.

He wanted an answer.

Blocking Dex's restless pacing, Hart said, "Quit trying to think of reasons to refuse, will you? It's not like we haven't fooled people before."

"Our family, as a joke."

"And girls, to see if we could."

Knowing those youthful antics weren't among his finer moments, Dex scowled.

"Oh gawd, don a hair shirt, why don't you?" Hart laughed at his reaction. "It's not like we switched beds or anything."

No. They'd fooled girls to see if any of them could tell them apart. Unfortunately, they couldn't.

Ever.

You'd think the inherent intimacy of dating a person would

enable a woman to know the difference, but . . . "We haven't duped neighbors," Dex pointed out. "We haven't duped"—he gestured—"*everyone.*"

"Think of it as a challenge." Hart plopped down on Dex's sofa and spread his arms out along the back. These days, he was more muscular than Dex. Harder edged. And he had those very distinguishing bruises.

It all seemed so obvious to Dex. "It'll never work."

"All you need to do is hang out at my place, reply to my e-mails, and go through the snail mail, let me know about anything important . . ."

"And if you get a commission?" Dex asked. "Am I supposed to paint it for you, too?"

"Hell no." Hart snorted. "Not that you couldn't, but your work is too damn morbid. Folks would either catch on that it wasn't me, or they'd think I went off the deep end."

Cursing low, Dex strode into his kitchen and grabbed a soda. Automatically, he got one for Hart, too.

As twins, they shared not only looks, but tastes and talents, too. Either of them could have chosen a career in writing, or art. But Hart was right—Dex was far more somber, bordering on pessimistic. Hart enjoyed life more. He played harder and took greater risks just for the joy of it.

The total opposite, Dex stayed holed away in his office, glued to his computer while he created his stories. As a published novelist, he relished his privacy.

As soon as Dex seated himself beside his brother, Hart started in on him again.

"I have to do my training out of town. Not only is this an opportunity to get in with an excellent camp, but SBC promoters will be visiting."

"To hand out contracts?" Hart was a great fighter, but he wanted to be great in the Supreme Battle Challenge.

"Possibly. I don't know for sure. But if I stuck around here to train, the family would show up and start badgering me for details. Joe especially."

"Or Cole, or Chase. Somehow they always know when family stuff goes down." Dex shook his head. "Nothing ever stays secret with the Winstons."

"Even if they don't catch on that I'm training, there'd be questions about my bruises."

Dex lifted his drink. "Nah. Most would figure a woman popped you for being a jerk."

Rather than dispute that, Hart shrugged at the possibility. "If I'm going to give my all to the big opportunity, then, Dex, I need your help."

Dex didn't know enough about the professional side of mixed martial arts fighting to be sure, but he assumed the training would take months. "I am not you."

Hart looked him over. "Close enough. I'm a little more bulked up now, but thanks to our sparring matches, you're still plenty fit."

They were both runners, both natural athletes, and both blessed with the Winston physique—or so their cousins always claimed. Joe especially seemed to gather attention for his physical presence. But then, Joe worked at it.

If you looked around the family, it appeared to be an inherent trait. The men were tall and naturally strong. Even into their advanced years—a description Hart liked to apply to Joe, just to see him riled—they retained their muscular forms.

"I've only lived in my apartment for six weeks now, and I've been so swamped, I haven't really made friends with anyone yet. Thanks to your last deadline, you haven't visited me there, so no one knows I have a twin brother."

All true, but still . . .

"We look enough alike," Hart continued, "that as long as you're in the right place and cop the right attitude, no one will question it." He chugged back half the soda, belched, and then, with an annoying, cocky grin, said, "The fact that we're both currently unattached makes it easier. Just think if I had a steady girlfriend you had to appease."

Appease? Dex rolled his eyes. "I'd definitely tell you no." Hart's preferences in female company were not his own.

His brother laughed. "You could use a hot date, man. It'd do you good."

"News flash, brother: I don't need your leftovers. I can get my own dates."

"Yeah, I know." Hart gave him a look. "But you *won't*."

Exasperation prompted Dex to a verbal challenge. "How do you know? You think I keep you informed of my every move?"

That got Hart's interest in a big way. "You sly dog, have you been holding back on me? C'mon, brother, spill it. Who is she?"

Knowing Hart wouldn't relent, Dex slumped into his seat. "No one."

"Yeah, that's what I thought." Disappointed, Hart settled back. "Know what your trouble is?"

"I have an annoying twin brother?"

"Yeah, but other than that." With a friendly punch to Dex's shoulder, Hart said, "You're too damn particular. Every date doesn't have to lead toward a serious relationship."

"Yeah, well, tell that to the women. One date usually gives them all kinds of ideas." And that did pose a problem, because Dex had an aversion to theatrics. Why couldn't he meet an upfront, honest, independent woman who wanted him, enjoyed his company, and shared his likes and dislikes—but didn't act like she *needed* him? "It can get insufferable."

Watching him, Hart said, "But that's not what bothers you, is it?"

Cradling the soda can against this abdomen, Dex shrugged. The biggest problem was his own disappointment, but he saw no reason to get into it with Hart.

As usual, ignoring Hart didn't slow him down.

"I know, and I understand, because I want the same thing."

"Yeah?" Dex took the bait. "And that is?"

"A real connection. Not just perfect sex—though I have to admit, really great sex makes it almost worthwhile." He winked before turning serious again. "I'd like to think if I ever find the right woman, she'll know the difference between you and me right off."

Dex gave him a bemused stare. Hart was such a die-hard bachelor that the idea of him settling down seemed ludicrous. Many ladies had tried to get him to commit, but they'd all failed.

Dex, on the other hand, wanted hearth and home—with the right woman. Like Hart, he needed her to separate him from his brother, to see him as an individual. He had a very specific idea of the woman he wanted, and so far, no one even close had shown up.

And that's what she'd have to do: show up.

Other than family gatherings, he didn't expend much effort socializing. There were so many plots and characters in his head that he couldn't seem to drag himself away from his computer long enough to dedicate the time necessary to finding that perfect significant other.

Disgusted with his own thoughts, Dex shook his head. "You were the one just saying we're enough alike that we *should* fool everyone."

"Sure," Hart said. "Everyone other than *the one*. When I find her, that's how I'll know she's right."

Sounded like a good plan to Dex—if the right one ever presented herself.

Done with that topic, Dex got the subject back on track. "So why don't you just tell everyone you're fighting? I think it's cool. And the sport suits you, anyone can see that." It took an extreme sport to satisfy his extreme brother.

"It'd suit you, too, if you'd shake off the fictional world long enough to do more than fill in as a sparring partner for me."

"No thanks. It's hard enough for me to type with bruised knuckles. I don't want to try it with anything else damaged." Dex enjoyed watching mixed martial arts, MMA, competitions, and he especially enjoyed sparring with his brother; the physical exertion left him feeling alive.

But not in the same way that writing did. He took real satisfaction in typing "the end" to a world of his own creation.

Grinning, Hart flexed his bruised knuckles. "It's addictive. I love everything about it."

Dex shrugged. "You've always been more competitive than me."

"Ha!" Hart gave him *the* look. "That's bullshit and you know it. You're competitive."

"I let you win when we spar, don't I?"

"You let me?" Laughing, Hart grabbed him and put him in a headlock. For a few minutes, they scuffled as they'd done when they were young. They almost knocked over the coffee table and a chair.

Dex laughed so hard, he couldn't get many insults out, but he did manage to say, "That's the best you've got?"

"I'm trying not to maim you, idiot."

"Wuss." Dex tried to free himself and couldn't, and finally said, "Uncle!"

"Oh yeah!" Hart lunged to his feet. "Victory is mine."

Sprawling onto his back on the floor, Dex said, "We haven't done that in ages."

"Five years ago, on our twenty-first birthday." Hart plopped onto the couch, reminiscing with a smile. "We knocked over a lamp and Mom had a fit."

"Then Joe grabbed us both and threw us in the pond."

Together they laughed some more. "God, that water was freezing."

Dex sat up, elbows on his knees, and pressed his brother again. "We have a tight family, Hart. When are you going to tell them you're fighting?"

"I'm not."

"What do you mean, you're not?" Dex couldn't believe his

brother expected to keep something so monumental a secret. Not from *their* family. "Everyone will be majorly pissed when they find out."

"The fights are preliminary. And if I fuck it up and get an old-fashioned ass whooping, I'll never hear the end of it and you know it."

"No way will that happen."

"Besting a book geek doesn't mean I'm invincible."

"Book geek?" Dex feigned a renewed attack.

Hart held up his hands. "A joke, that's all. I'll take it back if you let me rest in peace."

"Wuss," Dex said again. But he had a lot of faith in his brother's abilities. They'd started wrestling in a kids' club when they were barely out of diapers. In junior high, Hart added boxing to his mix of sports, and Dex chose track to help build his stamina. They often intertwined, with Hart running alongside Dex, and Dex sparring with Hart. But they each had their preferences.

Hart just kept improving, and during high school he was a three-time state wrestling champion. Thanks to those skills, he got a full college ride, and then went straight into Brazilian Jiu-Jitsu.

For a few years he'd been competing in matches at local gyms, and he'd racked up an impressive record. Now he was ready for the next big step, possibly a career-altering step—and he had cold feet?

Disgusted, Dex walked to the couch and stood before his brother. "You're good and you know it."

Hart's mouth tightened. "Maybe. But there's good, and then there's *good*. Anyone can lose, so that doesn't bother me. I just don't want to get annihilated."

Dex laughed. "Stop being a baby. If you weren't ready, you wouldn't be given a shot."

"They like my wins."

"TKOs," Dex said, nodding. Not only did Hart have a lot of wins under his belt, most were knockouts.

Looking smug, Hart said, "They're calling me The Finisher."

"Huh." Dex held up a hand. "See, that beats Knucklehead, doesn't it?"

Hart threw a pillow at him. "I'm still going to wait until after I see how I do in this trial bout to tell everyone."

After tossing the pillow back to the couch, Dex pointed out the obvious. "They will not be happy that you let them miss it."

"Yeah I know." His mouth quirked. "But God, can you imagine all the Winstons crowding into the gym? The roar would be deafening."

"Likely." The males of the family were of the boisterous variety. Alphas, all of them. Overwhelmingly so, sometimes. "So we're talking a month, right?"

Hart gave his attention to finishing his soda. "It could run a little longer."

"Hart."

"I can't give you a definite time frame." And with a straight face, he said, "You're a writer, you can work anywhere, damn it."

Dex knew it was a facetious comment. Most people thought he sat at home and watched sports while drinking beer and eating chips. But Hart, more than anyone else, knew just how hard he worked at his career. He understood the deadlines, the research and edits, the endless appearances and other promotional chores.

"You're between books, right?"

Reluctantly, Dex nodded. "Yeah. But I'm under contract, so I'd planned to get started on another book real soon."

"You always do a ton of research first. Use the computer at my place for it. You can be me, and get work done at the same time."

Glad that his brother hadn't asked what the next book would be, Dex agreed. "I guess that'd be all right. But it's under duress, and in case anything comes up, you better be accessible by phone."

"I'll keep my cell charged and check it on a regular basis." With that settled, Hart got to his feet. "Help yourself to my wardrobe, drive my car, and accept any commissions that sound interesting, but with the caveat that I'm booked for at least a month, and can't start until after that. And, brother, relax. This'll be fun. I guarantee it."

So why did Dexter have his doubts?

On his way out, Hart winked. "Who knows? Maybe you'll get inspiration for the next bestseller."

The first week wasn't so bad. After moving in and setting up all his files for the next story, Dexter went about familiarizing himself with his brother's neighbors. He didn't want to be taken off guard if he should know someone who approached him. Hart helped, but not much. The time he'd spent at the apartment had not been used to socialize. He was far too busy with his training.

With reluctance Dex met the neighbors face-to-face over the next few days, but none of them seemed aware that he wasn't Hart. They greeted him amicably, were social and totally obtuse to the deception.

That is, until Dex met the slight female across the hall from Hart.

Seeing her, Dex stopped dead in his tracks. *Wow.* Why had Hart not mentioned her? She came up the steps with her head down as she perused her mail. That gave Dex an opportunity to look her over.

When she felt his stare, she looked up in surprise, and then nodded her head in a reserved show of politeness. "Hello."

Smiling, Dex indulged an interested double take. "Hello yourself."

She faltered, gave him a long look followed by several questioning and maybe worried glances.

Fumbling over her reaction, Dex toned down his smile and his obvious interest. "Everything okay?"

She blinked. "Oh, sure. Yes." But she frowned and gave him another quick look before blushing and darting into her apartment. "Have a good day." She shut her door.

Dex stood there, half smiling, curiosity growing. She was skittish, but cute, with red hair and very piercing green eyes. Thanks to his brother's rundown on the apartment complex's inhabitants, he knew the only redheaded female had to be Christy Nash.

But he didn't know much else about her. Hart had only mentioned her once, and he hadn't described her that well. He hadn't told Dex about her long auburn hair, her incredible green eyes. He hadn't mentioned that she was so pretty, or so petite, or so sweet on the eyes.

Sometimes Hart could be such a dunce.

Over the next few days, Dex got to know Christy better. They met at the mailbox and the front door of the complex, and once he ran into her doing laundry. He'd watched with interest as she rushed to put her lacy, colorful undies at the bottom of the basket.

Because most of the women he met were pushy to the point of annoyance, he found her modesty adorable.

It didn't take long for Dex to discover that Christy left the apartment each morning around nine and returned around six. She appeared prompt and well organized. Since he was the same, that part of her personality appealed to him, too.

With the knowledge of her routine in hand, Dex was determined to get to know her better. He made a point of returning from jogging right at six, and his timing couldn't have been more perfect. As he loped into the parking lot, she was just getting out of her car.

He paused, giving her the opportunity to do the same.

Eyes wide, she stared at him.

At all of him.

Her gaze darted from his face to his sweaty chest, then down to his abdomen, and farther down to his legs before creeping slowly back to his chest and lingering there.

She definitely liked what she saw.

And for Dex, her appreciation was both flattering and frustrating—because she thought he was Hart.

Had his damned brother flirted with her after all? It didn't seem likely, not when Hart had struggled to remember her name.

Dex inhaled deeply to catch his breath. Her eyes widened. He smiled. "Hi again."

Jerking her attention to his face, she blinked fast and stopped with a slight puzzled frown. "Since when did you start jogging in the evening?"

The question threw Dex. Pulling his limp T-shirt from the back waistband of his shorts, he used it to swipe the sweat from his brow and buy himself some time to think.

Did Hart have a specific routine that he hadn't mentioned? Probably. This half-baked plan had been flawed from the get-go.

Too late now to correct a mistake.

Dex shrugged. "It seemed a good day for it."

Brow pinched, she glanced around at the hot pavement, the still-blistering sun and cloudless blue sky. "It's probably high eighties."

"I won't melt." In fact, he enjoyed the exertion and fresh air. His research had stalled, especially for his female protagonist, and Dex blamed the unfamiliar surroundings and subterfuge.

"If you say so." Her gaze drifted over him again.

Dex liked the way his brother's little red-haired neighbor looked at him.

She remained quiet, but she didn't leave. They stood there in the hot lot, quiet, uninterrupted.

"Christy?" he said, enjoying the sound of her name. "Something bothering you?"

"What?" Her startled green eyes met his. "No, of course not. It's just that you always jog at the crack of dawn when it's cooler."

Figures Hart would forget to tell him that. But a more pressing issue caught Dex, and he narrowed his eyes at Christy. "You noticed that, huh?"

As soon as he said it, she blanched, and Dex wondered if Hart had talked with her during his early morning jogs, making his comment bizarre.

Instead, bright color flushed her cheeks and she forced a grin, at the same time lifting her chin with bold regard.

Shy, but not a coward. Another appealing trait.

"You caught me," she said. "Yes, I've watched you coming and going. My window faces the lot."

"And you've watched me from the window?" He'd love that idea—except that meant she'd been eyeballing his brother, not him.

Her chin firmed. "Come on, Hart, don't make it sound so pathetic. You're easy on the eyes and you know it. Given half a chance, most women would watch you."

"Is that so?" Both of Dex's brows lifted. He'd never expected such a ballsy comment from her. Her honesty was refreshing, but startling. She was an enigma, for sure. "Well . . . thank you."

"You're welcome."

They stood there in the parking lot, gazes locked, until she suddenly cleared her throat. "Well, you might not mind the heat, but I *am* melting, so it's time for me to go in."

Dex noted her suit, and the dampness on her brow because of it. She was all prim, buttoned up, and suffering for it. "Those are pretty stifling duds for summer. Where do you work?"

As she hitched the strap of a large purse over her shoulder, her mouth pinched. "You've forgotten, huh? That shouldn't surprise me."

Oh hell. If Hart knew, why hadn't he told him? "I'm sorry." And he was. His brother couldn't be expected to think of every scenario that might occur, but with this particular woman, Dex wanted to be informed. "It's just . . ."

She waved a hand, laughing without humor. "Don't worry about it, Hart. It was a quick conversation, easily forgotten."

Hoping that was true, which would mean there'd been little conversation, and therefore little interaction between Hart and her, Dex prompted, "So why don't you refresh my memory."

"I'm a secretary for the middle school. Yes, the teachers are off for summer break, but my job runs year-round."

"A school secretary." Dex surveyed her again from head to toe and decided the job suited her. There was a definite understated quality to her demeanor.

It teased him.

Even the very school-worthy clothing couldn't hide the tantalizing curves of her slight, slender frame. The damp heat had urged her long red hair into ringlets and enhanced a fair sprinkling of freckles over the bridge of her nose and soft cheekbones.

Half under his breath, Dex said, "I don't remember anyone at my school looking like you."

She shot a disbelieving look his way. "Thank you." Then she faltered. "I think. I mean . . . was that a compliment?"

Smiling at her uncertainty, Dex lifted one shoulder. "It was a complimentary male observation."

"Oh. I see. Then . . . thank you." She fanned herself. "This heat is sweltering, huh?"

"Yeah." He smiled knowingly. "Let's head in." Gesturing for her to precede him, Dex trailed behind and drank in the back view of her rounded butt in the slim-fitting skirt.

Very nice.

Damn it, he needed to ask Hart just how far his involvement went with this woman before he dared to go any further himself.

At her door, she whipped around to face him, hands clasped together, expression watchful. "So." Her smile flickered with cautious hope.

Nice lips. Nice nose, too. And damn, but he'd never considered freckles so sexy until seeing them on her.

Before he could think better of it, Dex said, "Want to go for a swim later?"

Her reaction was more appropriate for a request to donate a kidney. She blanched, backed into the wall, and started visually dissecting him again.

Running a hand through his sweat-damp hair, Dex sighed, wondering how he'd blundered this time. He waited for her to refuse.

Instead, with a lot of skepticism, she asked, "Why?"

"Why what?"

She rolled her eyes. "Why do you suddenly want to swim with me?"

No, she was not a woman to give expected replies. He stared into her eyes. "You look hot."

Her jaw went slack. "I look . . . ?"

With no intention of clarifying that double entendre, Dex added, "A swim would be . . . nice. It would refresh us both." And then he could see more of her, as in every curve, every freckle, lots and lots of soft skin.

Beneath the starchy blouse, her chest expanded on a deep breath. "No." She exhaled. "Sorry. Busy."

"You are, huh?"

She nodded hard and fast. "Very."

"Got a big date?"

Scoffing, she said, "No."

He couldn't help it. He stepped closer to her. "Got a fiancé? A steady guy?"

She frowned. "No."

"Good." The sooner she understood his interest, the easier it'd be for both of them.

Eyes wide and hands behind herself, Christy fumbled with her lock and opened her door, then practically fell inside. Again somewhat hopeful, she said, "Another time, maybe?"

"I'll hold you to that."

She started backing farther in. "Okay then. I'll . . . see ya."

"Count on it."

As she eased the door shut, her confusion was plain to see. Hart hadn't come on to her.

At all.

She couldn't understand why he was coming on to her now.

And truthfully, Dex couldn't say what it was about her that got to him. Maybe it was the need for a distraction as he struggled with his plot. Maybe it was the sheer boredom of being out of his own place, and stuck in Hart's.

And maybe it was the long bout of self-imposed celibacy.

But maybe, just maybe, it was that Christy Nash was the most appealing woman he'd met in a very long time.

Right before the door shut, she said, "Enjoy your swim."

Oh yeah, he definitely would. After that tantalizing exchange, he needed a dip in the cool water of the pool. Unfortunately, her window didn't face the right way, so she wouldn't be able to watch him. Of course, he could make a trip around front for . . . something. Now that he knew to watch her window, he'd enjoy her reaction to seeing him in trunks.

Suddenly being at Hart's didn't seem so bad after all. He was still stuck on the final details of his story, but it no longer bothered him so much.

Christy Nash shut her apartment door and collapsed against it, her eyes closed and her heart racing. In her mind's eye, she saw Hart's face, his sculpted cheekbones, that straight nose, sensual mouth, and sinfully sexy eyes.

He had the darkest, thickest lashes she'd ever seen on man or woman. They framed clear blue, intelligent eyes that suddenly saw her.

Not just a glance at her for polite purposes.

But *really* saw her, almost *through* her, to her soul. Based on his very knowing gaze, she would bet money that he knew her heart pounded and her pulse raced.

What in the world had happened?

Had the universe tilted? Since when did Hart Winston, hunk extraordinaire, give her any notice, or talk to her beyond a perfunctory hello, or ask her to *swim*?

Never.

Not once.

Regardless of how obvious she'd been in her dogged pursuit of him.

Maybe he'd hit his head or something, because there was a definite, although indefinable, difference to him now.

The second she'd laid eyes on him, she'd noticed it. It was there in the tilt of his head, the deep thought in his startling blue eyes, the way he walked, the way he smiled.

And oh yeah, the way he looked at her.

So different in so many ways, and it . . . fascinated her. As if he hadn't been potent enough already, he now assaulted her senses like a double dose of a powerful aphrodisiac.

Insane!

Biting her lip, Christy wondered if she dared find a reason to meander over to the pool. If she could get one quick look at him all wet, wearing only snug trunks that would hug his lean hips and his . . . Oh boy. That'd be enough fodder for a dozen fantasies.

Not that she needed help in that department. She had it so bad, she already dreamed of him every night.

Well, okay, not *him*. She didn't know Hart Winston well enough to dream about him, the man. But she wasn't blind, so she'd had plenty of fantasies about his gorgeous body and overwhelming sex appeal.

Perhaps she'd just sort of feel him up . . . no, feel him *out* on this new friendly mood of his.

Yes, that's what she'd do.

She'd make the attempt to get to know him, and maybe this time he'd be more receptive. Her birthday was in a few days. Maybe she'd even be able to ask him out to celebrate with her. And maybe he'd accept.

It couldn't hurt, right?

Or could it?

Two

That night, Dex called Hart and got his voice mail. Frustrated, he left a message asking about Christy Nash. He wanted details, damn it. Specifically, he needed to know how far his brother's relationship with her had extended.

While he was out the next morning, two calls came in. One from a woman named Lisa, who said to Hart, "We need to talk. Call me."

Huh. Dex wasn't about to return that call, but he made a note to let Hart know.

Not long after that, Hart called, too, saying on the answering machine, "Christy who? That little red-haired puritan? I must be thinking of the wrong woman. You can't be talking about that skinny schoolteacher with freckles, right? Christy Nash. Call me back, Dex. I think I have the names mixed up or something."

After all that, Hart hung up.

Annoyed, Dex returned the call—and again had to leave a message.

"Yes, damn it. Christy Nash, your neighbor. She's right across the hall from you." Could Hart have really been so oblivious to her? Impossible to imagine, given her effect on him. "She's petite, you ass, not skinny. And her freckles are damned cute. *And* she's a secretary at the school, not a teacher."

God he sounded defensive. Dex hesitated, but decided to come clean with his brother. "Before I make a move"—or more of a move, really—"I have to know if you've ever been involved with her. I'm guessing not, but I want to know for sure, so call me back, and soon. I don't want to wait."

If Hart was so oblivious to her, that'd sure make his pursuit easier. No way would he play trade-off with his brother.

Hart returned his call within an hour, and because Dex was eyeball deep in research for the novel, he was available and, after a glance at the caller ID, picked up on the second ring. "Hey."

"You have *got* to be kidding me."

Knowing his brother well, Dex said simply, "Nope. She's hot."

"She's my *neighbor*, Dex! As in, she's right across the hall."

"Thought you hadn't noticed that."

"I noticed that she's far too close for comfort."

Ah. So it wasn't that Hart had missed Christy's sex appeal, only that he was too chickenshit to take a risk on failure.

But Dex was not his brother. "Proximity is a convenience."

"Maybe for you, since you don't actually live there!"

Relishing Hart's reaction, Dex said, "It's a moot point now."

"You dirty dog." Hart's tone held no real anger. "Don't you dare get me entangled in some damned female drama just so you can walk away and leave me with a pissed-off neighbor."

Relief sank into Dex's bones. He settled back in his seat and smiled. "So you haven't been involved with her in any way?"

"Propinquity aside, when would I have had time?"

Satisfaction stirred Dex's imagination. "Good." Now that he knew the facts, he felt free to go after Christy full force—just one more thing to make clear. "You never will be involved with her, Hart. Got it?"

There was a moment of silence, and then: "Ah hell. You're going to do this, aren't you?"

"Damn straight." And he could barely wait.

Hart warned him, "You can't tell her that you aren't me."

"Not just yet, no." It'd be tricky, but Dex felt sure that it'd be okay. Just as he wrote his books by figuring out plot turns along the way, he'd figure this out, too.

His confidence inspired Hart to laugh. "Oh, this is going to be good. I hope I'm there when you start explaining. I mean, women are real understanding about being deceived, aren't they?" He laughed again. "They love that shit."

"Hart—"

"She'll probably be amused when she finds out that you're not me, that you deliberately duped her, that she called out the wrong man's name during—"

"Shut up, Hart."

"Now, Dex, don't get surly."

He was hot, not surly. And anxious. And done talking to his brother. "I'll handle it. That's all you need to know." And somehow, he would. Dex didn't know the particulars yet, but he'd find a way to make Christy—he liked that name, he really did—understand. After all, what difference did it make the name he used?

She didn't have a history with Hart, so it shouldn't matter.

Yeah, and he almost had himself convinced of that when he remembered his brother's other caller.

"By the way, Lisa called and needs to talk to you."

"You didn't answer?"

Sensing his brother's urgency, Dex raised a brow. "No, why?"

"Avoid the calls. Don't pick up."

Uh-oh. This didn't sound good. "Hart . . ."

"Look, it's no big deal, all right? She was a . . . mistake, that's all."

Right. Dex didn't really need to ask, but he did anyway. "What kind of mistake?"

"The kind that's not my usual type."

"Meaning she's not stacked, not dumb, or not gullible?"

"All of the above. Hell, if anything, she's . . . plain. But she caught me in a moment of weakness, and I slept with her."

Sounded to Dex like Lisa had a moment of weakness, too. "And now you won't return her calls?"

"Don't act all righteous with me. I told her upfront that I wasn't looking for a relationship. She said she wasn't either. It happened—but it's not going to happen again."

"You're a real asshole, you know that?"

"Course I do. And she'll catch on quick enough if you avoid her calls."

"Fine. I'm sure you can handle your own love life."

"Right now, with all this training, I don't *have* a love life. Enjoy yourself with Christy—but don't you dare leave a mess for me to clean up!"

Since he didn't plan to involve Hart beyond the use of his name, it wouldn't, shouldn't be a problem. Dex went to bed that night thinking of her, anticipating the moment when he made his big move.

Sometime during the night he worked out the particulars on his next novel—and named the female protagonist Christy.

Despite the possible pitfalls ahead, Dex fell asleep with a grin.

For the next few days, Christy saw Hart often. She couldn't be positive, but it seemed that he timed his jogging to meet her as she returned from work. When she checked her mailbox before work, he checked his. He chatted her up at length, always crowding her personal space by standing just a little too close, touching her in gentle, careless ways meant to be friendly but seeming very intimate, too.

He tucked her hair behind her ear, held her shoulder whenever she had moments of doubt about his motives, tweaked her chin when teasing her . . .

All in all, he seduced her.

Good grief, had the man forgotten that she'd thrown herself at him?

Apparently.

Or maybe he'd been so indifferent to her, he hadn't even noticed her less-than-subtle attempts to get closer to him.

She didn't know what to think. Physically, she still wanted him, a lot. And in fact, now that she knew him better as a person, she wanted him more than ever.

There was just something about him that drew her. He was incredibly gorgeous and sexy, but she liked his scent, too, the sound of his laugh, that teasing twinkle in his eyes.

Christy shook her head. She had to test the waters, had to find out why he had a sudden change of heart.

With a plan in mind, she deliberately left the school fifteen minutes late that Friday.

Would Hart still be around? If so, then she'd assume he'd waited for her, and she would proceed accordingly.

Watching, hopeful, Christy pulled into the apartment parking lot. Her heart pounded when she spotted Hart sitting on the front steps in casual conversation with Mel, one of their neighbors.

He'd waited.

And not only that, he looked relaxed and friendly—which was out of the norm—whenever Mel intruded.

Not that she blamed Hart. Mel could be overbearing with his lewd jokes and too loud voice. Oh, Hart was always polite; she couldn't be attracted, even physically, to an obnoxious person. But the way Hart smiled now, the ease of his relaxed posture, told her that Mel's behavior didn't bother him at all.

And that was another major difference.

Hart seldom relaxed. He was always on the go, rarely hanging around his apartment except in the evenings, to sleep. He did his painting at a studio, but Christy knew that only took up a small portion of his day. Usually he stayed busy with athletics, or women, or a combination of the two.

Seeing Hart sprawled out on the steps, just chatting, was . . . unique. And appealing.

She liked this new layer to him. A lot. But it was still unsettling.

The way he lounged back, braced on his elbows with his long legs stretched out, led her to believe he'd been there awhile.

Probably fifteen minutes or so.

Damn the man, he made no pretense of doing anything other than waiting for her.

Even from a distance, she appreciated the sight of his long, strong body. Muscles bunched in his arms and thighs. Dark chest hair narrowed down to a thinner line bisecting his hard abdomen.

Her heart beat a little faster.

Hart was a dark man, not overly hairy, but he left alone the gorgeous body hair God had given him. No waxing or laser hair removal for him. No sir.

She imagined that dark hair would be crisp to the touch, a nice contrast to his hot, sweat-damp skin.

Dark sunglasses hid his eyes from her, which might make her plan easier. His direct gaze sometimes left her tongue-tied. Not seeing his deep blue eyes would take off some of the pressure.

As she got out of the car and started toward him, he said something to Mel. The neighbor smiled, waved at her, and went inside. Christy forced her feet to keep moving.

"Hey Hart."

"Christy," he murmured.

The way he said her name left her stomach tingling. Today she wore a blouse and pencil skirt with open-toed heels. Though she couldn't see his eyes, Christy *knew* he looked her over—and liked what he saw.

She cleared her throat. "Mel left in a hurry."

"I told him I was waiting for you. He's loud, but not insensitive."

Her mouth fell open. "You told him—"

By coming to his feet, all hot, muscled six feet two inches of him, he effectively cut off her thoughts.

"How'd your day go?"

Before he could muddle her further, Christy blurted, "It was boring and hot. I'm ready for a dip in the pool. What about you?"

In the way of a predatory animal, Hart went on alert. She saw it in every line of his body: the anticipation, the desire.

Lord help me.

He moved closer and his voice lowered. "I'm ready when you are."

The murmured words covered more than a swim, but Christy pretended not to notice. "Great. You go on ahead. I'll change, grab some towels, and join you there in a few minutes."

"Why don't we meet in the hall and go out together?"

No, if he did that, she wasn't sure they'd make it to the pool. She didn't want to be too close to her apartment when they were both in skimpy suits. "That's all right. It'll take me longer to change and check my missed calls and . . . everything. You go on and I'll come out the back entrance." She glanced down at him, then cleared her throat. "You could probably swim in those shorts. There's not much more to them than trunks."

His mouth curled. "Yeah, but I'm sweaty, so I'll change." He pulled off the sunglasses, giving her the full effect of his gaze, then touched her cheek in that now familiar way. "Don't take too long."

"I won't." She stepped back, breaking the contact, and hurried into the apartment building. Hart didn't follow.

He remained on the steps, watching her.

And that unnerved her more than anything else could have.

Praying the water would be brisk enough to cool his need, Dex deposited his wallet, cell phone, and keys on a bench and dove into the pool. Staying submerged, he swam to the other side. When his head broke the surface, he realized no one else was at the pool.

He'd be alone with Christy.

That morning, after screening more calls from Hart's mysterious Lisa, he'd written twenty pages. He'd called Hart to tell him of

Lisa's persistence over the past few days, but his brother remained unfazed by the woman's determination.

Too pleased with his own writing progress to dwell on Hart's romantic entanglements, Dex dismissed thoughts of the woman—and concentrated on Christy instead.

This particular book was, for the first time, heavy on romance, light on suspense. It was a deliberate move on his part, a slant he'd wanted to take for a while, and this particular plot lent itself to the more emotional angle.

For months he'd had it all worked out, except for the female lead. She'd eluded him—until now.

Until Christy.

Inspired by her, his female protagonist was a woman in jeopardy—who looked just like Christy.

Hot, but sweet.

Bold, but classy.

She was smart, and vulnerable. And somewhere in the book, the bad guys would *almost* get her, until the male protagonist saved her.

Until he *had* her.

The tepid water refreshed Dex, but didn't do jack about his edgy anticipation. He went to the deep end, braced his arms along the edge of the pool, and tried to relax while he waited. All the while his mind buzzed with thoughts of her, of how she'd look and what he might do, what she might want him to do.

Finally Christy stepped into view.

A fine tensing of his muscles, a constriction in his gut, told Dex he had it bad.

As a twenty-six-year-old man, he'd had plenty of women in a variety of ways. He'd had hot sex, emotional sex, and kinky sex. He'd been with woman he liked, and women he only lusted for, in extended relationships, casual dates, and one-night flings.

None of them were right, and none of the women made him feel the way Christy did.

Wanting her like this, feeling so in tune with her, was crazy but exhilarating, too.

Without makeup her lashes were a medium brown, her lips a natural pink. She wore a cover-up over her swimsuit with her legs bare except for the flip-flops on her feet. A breeze lifted her long, loose hair, sending one silky tendril past her mouth. Under the bright sunshine, the coppery lock looked iridescent.

Gathering the mass of red curls into one fist, Christy held it behind her head. The pose wasn't deliberately provocative, but Dex's libido didn't seem to care.

"Feel good?" she asked, meaning the water.

"Getting there," he replied, meaning he wanted her to lose the cover-up and get in with him.

He wanted to look at her, touch her. And more.

After dropping two beach towels beside his belongings, she stepped out of the sandals, unzipped the terry cloth robe, laid it aside, and—more or less—presented herself to him.

Seeing so much smooth, soft skin, Dex straightened from his slouching position.

Her two-piece would be considered modest by most standards, but compared to her school suits and prim blouses, it revealed a lot—in a good way.

Red with small white polka dots and ruffles around the bra top and bikini bottom waistband, the vintage-style suit looked great on Christy.

He liked it.

He liked *her*.

Her petite body sported some tantalizing curves, with B-cup-sized breasts and flaring hips filling out the material of the swimsuit. Dex made note of her sleek thighs, her very appealing belly.

Her pale skin made her look more delicate, and he saw that the freckles were limited to her face, nowhere else.

At least nowhere that he'd seen yet.

Ah hell. If she didn't join him in the pool soon, ice water wouldn't do him much good.

"Dive in."

She surprised him by doing just that. No easing in with ladylike reserve for Christy. Nope. Her splash soaked his head and made him laugh.

She surfaced right in front of him, a smile already in place.

The drenching left her lashes spiked, and her long hair floated on the surface of the water around her.

She pushed it away from her face, closed her eyes, and sighed. "It feels great."

Oh yeah. Great. Hot.

Without thinking it through, Dex leaned down and kissed her smiling lips. The second their mouths touched, he knew he was a goner. It was a perfunctory kiss, nothing more, out in the open, in broad daylight, with no other body parts touching.

And he wanted to explode.

Until Christy plunged backward so fast she lost her footing and went under.

Cursing himself, Dex caught her arms and hauled her up until her face was above the water. "You okay?"

Sputtering and gasping, she braced her hands on his forearms. When she caught her breath, she said, "*What's up with you*?"

"Lust?"

She coughed again. "Okay, but . . . *why*?"

He lifted a brow.

"Why are you acting so different?"

Dex closed his eyes and wondered how to reply. The idea of going with the deception no longer seemed like such a great idea.

At his hesitation, she pushed. "You *are* different, Hart. In a million and one ways."

He opened his eyes and snared her in his gaze. "We don't know each other well enough for you to say that."

"Ha. You might not know me but I've been . . ." She clammed

up, then eased away from his hold and went to the pool ledge, where it was shallow enough for her to stand on her own.

"You've been what?" Dex swam over to her. "Watching me through windows?"

"That, and more." Her chin went up. "You already know I've been obsessed with you."

His heart dropped to his knees. "Obsessed?"

"Just stop it." She slapped water at him, drenching his face. "You can't be that blind."

No, but apparently Hart could be. "I'm sorry." And he was. She looked hurt, and that hurt him.

Folding her arms over her chest, she turned very defensive. "So what happened? Why the sudden interest in me? Did you get dumped by a hottie? The painting business is slow and you're bored? What?"

At this point, he hated to be dishonest with her. "I don't know what to say."

Her face fell. "I was hoping you'd say that you liked me."

"I do."

She snorted and started to turn away.

"Don't." Dex caught her arms. "I like you a lot, Christy. I like your suits, and your hair, and your name."

"My name?"

"I like the way you smile and the way you watch me, I like your scent, and I like . . . everything."

Still frowning, she softened, and said again, "My name?"

"It suits you." Dex cupped the back of her head. "Your red hair suits you; your green eyes suit you. Your job is definitely you. And all together . . . it's a real nice package."

"You never thought so before."

Damn, it was tough talking when all he really wanted was to kiss her, deeper this time, hotter and longer. "There are . . . explanations. Things I can't go into right now. But"—a small truth wouldn't hurt—"I'm not the same man you knew before."

"No kidding. Everything about you is different."

Dex tilted his head and studied her. He remembered Hart's requirement—being able to tell them apart. "You really think so?"

"Yes."

He drew her closer, close enough that their bodies touched from chest to knees. Looking at her mouth, he asked, "How?"

She nodded, licked her lips—and Dex's phone rang.

"Damn." Only his family, his agent, or his editor ever called his cell. "It could be important."

"Okay."

He didn't want to break the moment, but he had no choice. "Sorry." Releasing her, he hoisted himself out of the pool, strode to his belongings, and snatched up the phone.

"Hello?"

"I think I've broken a damn rib."

Hart. "Are you serious?"

"Feels like it, but I'll live. Actually, I'm loving this shit. Awesome workouts. Terrific practices. Dean Havoc is visiting and he's teaching me some supersick leg kicks."

Dex shook his head. No doubt his brother had collected a lot more bruises. "You're a masochist."

"Maybe. So how's it going for you? Why aren't you inside, writing up a storm?"

"You're interrupting."

"The writing? You mean you took your laptop outside?"

Dex rubbed his brow. "No."

"Then what?"

"None of your business."

Laughing, Hart said, "Ah, gotcha. Moving fast, aren't you? Oh well, sorry about that."

While they spoke, a family of five joined them at the pool. The mother and father turned loose three kids, all boys, who launched into the pool like wild monkeys on a rampage.

Dex's gaze went to Christy, and he found her smiling at the kids.

It didn't matter when the largest boy, who was probably eight, did a cannonball and soaked her, or when the other two immediately crowded into her space and started asking her an endless stream of questions.

The very genuine smile remained on her face, and it warmed Dex.

So she liked kids.

Probably pets, too.

Was there anything unappealing about the woman?

The phone beeped, and Dex told Hart, "Hang on, I'm getting another call."

This time it was his editor, and she had some publicity travel to discuss. The publisher wanted him to fly to New York to meet some buyers. Unable to think beyond the moment, Dex said, "I'm sure I can work it out."

"Great." The editor wasn't done. "One more thing. The book club wants to do a feature on you. Can you do an interview?"

Ah hell. "When?"

She said, "Now?" with a cajoling tone in her voice. "And before you start groaning, I know it's short notice, but I just found out about it myself. It's a great opportunity."

"I don't know . . ." Dex looked at Christy, and watched her throw a ball for the boys. They "fetched" it the same way rambunctious puppies would. "I have plans."

"Thirty minutes, Dex. That's all they need."

"And they need it now?"

"The interviewer can call you in half an hour."

He didn't want to, but this was his career, so . . . "All right, sure. I suppose I can make the time."

She thanked him, and Dex clicked back over to his brother. "You still there?"

"Yeah, but now I need to go."

"More workouts?"

"At this time of the day? Nope. I've got a date with a sizzling hot woman, and I don't want to keep her waiting."

"What about Lisa?"

"I told you—that's over." Hart hesitated. "Why, is she still calling?"

Dex rolled his eyes. "You should call her back."

"Maybe. After I get home, I'll think about it." Hart always moved fast. "Gotta go. Have fun."

"Yeah, you, too."

After Dex disconnected the call, he noticed that more people were at the pool, including Mel, and another family with kids. Mel called out to him and waved.

Christy had already left the pool and dressed in her cover-up, and was busy drying her hair.

She had her head down, and it worried Dex.

Resigned to major disappointment, he approached the patio chair where she sat.

Before Dex could say anything, she blurted with forced enthusiasm, "I'm starving. You want to go grab some dinner?"

Damn, damn, and double damn.

Standing in front of her, he touched her chin and lifted her face. "I would love to, but I can't. Something's come up."

Her mouth flattened. She drew in a deep breath and dredged up a smile. "Okay. No problem."

There were too many people around for him to do too much explaining. "How about a rain check?"

"Sure."

Her cavalier attitude was a sham and Dex knew it. "Christy—"

Mel chose that inauspicious moment to join them. He barely said hello before launching into a loud, jovial conversation on the weather. His paunch hung over the front of his baggy trunks and his breath smelled of beer.

Dex hated the intrusion, but he knew Mel meant no harm. The guy struck him as socially inept, but not deliberately rude.

When he finally took a breath, Christy had half turned away, already escaping, and said, "I'll see you guys later. I have some errands to run."

She was gone too quickly for Dex to object.

Watching her hasty retreat, he decided that he'd take care of the interview, then he'd go to her apartment to explain. Hopefully they could pick up where they'd left off.

Dex wandered Hart's apartment in restless frustration. It was late, but he couldn't sleep. He'd knocked on Christy's door a couple of times, but she hadn't answered. When he checked the lot, he saw that her car was there.

Was she in the apartment, but ignoring him? He didn't think so. She didn't strike him as the type to play games.

Restlessness clawed at him. He wrote for a while, getting nearly an entire chapter written before his brain cramped and thoughts of Christy took over again.

It amazed Dex that he'd gotten so much done, but then it had always been that way with his writing. When scenes came to him, he could write anywhere.

Still, he preferred his own desk, his own computer, his own . . . atmosphere of oak furniture, cream-colored walls, and corduroy upholstery.

He lived in casual, tidy comfort reminiscent of the home they'd grown up in. Hart, on the other hand, had the quintessential bachelor's pad. It screamed seduction. Dex looked around in renewed amazement.

Big-screen TV.

King-sized bed.

Surround sound stereo system.

Sleek leather furniture.

Dexter felt like a different man just being here. He didn't like it. He didn't like subterfuge.

To distract himself, he took an extra long shower in hopes that the warm water would relax his muscles and make him sleepy. But given his thoughts on Christy, what he wanted from her and the ways he wanted to touch her, he still felt coiled too tightly as he stripped down for bed.

He crawled under the sheets, turned out the light, closed his eyes—and his cell phone rang.

Hoping it might be Christy, he fumbled quickly to retrieve the phone.

"Hello?"

"Where the hell have you been?"

Frowning at his brother's tone, Dex glanced at the clock on the bedside table. It was after midnight. "Do you know what time it is?"

"Yeah, I do, but apparently your little redhead doesn't care."

Little redhead? Dex sat up and dropped his legs over the side of the bed. "What are you talking about? What's going on?"

"She doesn't have your phone number, dumbass. She has *mine*."

Oh hell. Dex hadn't even considered that, but it didn't take him long to add it all up. "Since she thinks I'm you . . ."

"Bravo, Einstein. She's called my cell *three* times now."

"Three times?" What in the world could Christy want this late at night that would warrant multiple phone calls? Dex was pondering that when something else occurred to him. "You said you barely know her, Hart, so why the hell does she have your cell number?"

"It's not what you're thinking, that's for sure! Hell, you should know I don't give out my cell number."

"Not to Lisa, anyway, huh?"

Hart ignored that jibe. "It has to do with the apartment complex. We all shared contact numbers in case of emergencies. They're *not* supposed to be used for personal reasons, though."

"Ah." Wincing, Dex asked, "And her reasons were . . . personal?"

"I'll let you be the judge." And then, in a high-pitched, theatrical voice, Hart said, "*I know this might take you by surprise, but I want you. I want you a lot.*"

Three

Flushed, stiff-lipped, and narrow-eyed, Dex said, "Come again?"

"That's what she said, my man. Straight out and to the point. *To me*. Or rather to you, but since she called my phone, I'm the one who answered."

Coming off the bed, Dex paced to a window and looked out at the dark night. His brain churned, and his libido rejoiced. Combined, it caused a near dizzying effect. "When was this?"

"The last call was a few minutes ago."

Hmmm . . . "I knocked at her door earlier and no one answered."

"That's because our girl is out on the town, tying one on."

Oh shit. Dex ran a hand over the back of his neck. "Alone?"

"She called me, didn't she?"

Dex wasn't bored now. He wasn't sleepy either. "Did she say anything else?"

"You sitting down, bro?"

One hand braced on the windowsill, Dex lied. "Yeah."

In that same falsetto voice, Hart shared the rest. "*I'm not usu-*

ally so forward, but you haven't given me any choice. I know I'm not the type of woman you're usually with. But the things I want to do to you . . ."

Dex swallowed. "Damn."

"Amen, brother." Hart inhaled. "There's more."

The shock wore off, replaced with heated urgency. "Let's hear it."

"*Lights on. Naked. Flesh on flesh, for hours and hours. I'm going to drive you wild. You'll love it, and beg for more.*"

Recognizing those words, Dex straightened away from the window. "Wait a damn minute."

"You're finally catching on, right?"

He knew those words by heart because . . . "That dialogue is straight out of one of my books!"

Hart snorted. "Yeah, I know. I read it. If you check out my bookshelf, you'll find a copy."

"Hang on." Flipping on lights as he went, Dex charged from the bedroom to the living room. He dropped the phone on a sofa cushion, went to his brother's bookcase, and found every book he'd ever written on display. On the bottom shelf he found it.

Sure, his books were mostly gritty suspense, but what was a good suspense plot without a relationship on the line? He always put a hot romance in every book. Hell, they were some of his favorite scenes, which was why his current book had more focus on the romance than ever before.

Pulling out *To Die For*, written under his pseudonym, Dex Baxter, he flipped through the pages until he found the scene on page 280. There, midway down, the heroine pressed herself to the good guy and whispered those exact words against his mouth.

Book in hand, Dex strode back to the sofa. He sat down and read to himself.

You are so gorgeous, I want to start at your ears, and work my way down. I want to eat you up. All of you.

Then I want you to eat me, too.

A flash of heat went over Dex. He couldn't believe this.

She'd plagiarized him.

To his damned brother.

And *still* it turned him on.

Dex snatched up the phone. "How far did she go with it?"

"All the way, brother." Hart's voice roughened. "All the way."

Dex swallowed. "I don't believe this."

"Well, let me tell you, after her 'come and get me' spiel, I felt molested—and I had one hell of a time explaining to her why I wasn't hightailing my sorry ass to the bar to pick her up."

Like a ton of bricks, the complications flattened Dex. "She wanted you to come to her?"

"No, you dolt. She wanted *you* to. But I tried your phone twice and you didn't answer."

Damn, damn, damn. "Must have been when I was in the shower."

"Long shower." Hart gave a nonchalant whistle, then caved. "I have to use that shower, you know. I hope you didn't defile it."

"Fuck off. I had a lot to think about, that's all." Dex groaned. Now he had even more to consider. Christy had to be feeling rejected and confused by his mixed signals. "Son of a bitch."

Hart tsked. "You should be thanking me, you know."

"*Thank* you?" Dex glared at the phone. "For what—getting me into this tight spot?"

"No, for covering your ass after you didn't answer the phone." Hart laughed. "I told her I'd call her right back, thinking you'd be the one to call her, but when I couldn't reach you, I did the deed myself and told her, with utter sincerity, that it was killing me, but she sounded drunk and I couldn't take advantage of her in such a vulnerable state."

Relief took out his knees and Dex dropped back against the sofa cushions. "Good call. Did she buy it?"

"Meaning you *would* have taken advantage?"

"No!" Dex knew his brother was only ribbing him, so he drew a steadying breath. "Of course I wouldn't have. But I would have gone and picked her up."

"Me, too. I'm not without some gallantry, you know." He paused for effect. "I sent a cab."

"She accepted?"

"Yeah." Hart laughed before going back to the fake and annoying voice that sounded nothing like Christy at all. "*I appreciate all the trouble you're going to. If it wasn't my birthday, I wouldn't have gotten drunk, and never would have called you.*"

"Her birthday?" Dex blew out a breath. "Worse and worse." Now he knew why she'd asked him out to dinner, but instead of sharing the special day with her, he'd done that damned impromptu interview.

Hart wasn't done. "*I might regret it in the morning, but right now, I can't help myself. I think about you all the time.*"

Silence fell between them. Dex didn't know what to say, and Hart was no doubt grinning at his discomfort. "You still there, brother?"

Dex nodded. "Yeah." But his brain scrambled as he tried to figure out how to proceed.

"Good, because she wanted to know why we aren't interested."

"I am," Dex growled, coming to his feet to pace again. "You aren't."

"Yeah, but she's used to me, and I've been so busy finishing up my commissions while training, that I might have bordered on rude on a few occasions."

"Jerk."

"Yeah, well, usually I'm friendlier. You know that."

He knew it only too well, especially where it concerned women. "Trust me, I'm glad you weren't friendlier to her."

"Me, too, all things considered. But I think we've confused the hell out of her. Poor girl."

"What did you tell her?" Dex suddenly realized he was naked and went into the bedroom to find his boxers.

"I told her that I was real interested and first thing in the morning, I'd prove it—which means you have to prove it so I'm not made out as a liar."

Awkwardly pulling on his shorts, Dex said, "I can't just pounce on her in the morning. You said it yourself—I can't take advantage of something she said while drunk. Hell, she might not even remember the call."

"Doesn't matter. You will remind her, nicely if need be, because if she does remember and you don't say anything, she's really going to feel like hell."

Dexter froze. "Yeah, when you're right, you're right."

"And when it comes to women, I usually am. Right, that is."

"Let me think." Dex knew he had to say something to Christy. After all, she'd stolen his words, propositioned his brother, and intrigued Dex in the bargain. That was more than any woman had accomplished in a long time. "All right. I'll bring it up."

"This soap opera is getting more interesting by the moment." Hart made no bones about enjoying his brother's predicament. "Make any excuse you want, Dex, but give her your number. If she calls to proposition me again, I'm not sure I can stay so detached."

"The hell you say!"

"Hey, don't blame me. Until now, I didn't realize she was so sexy, or so into me."

"*She's not.*"

Hart laughed. "Come on, brother, you have to know that if she's intrigued you, she's intrigued me, too."

Tense with antagonism, Dex squeezed the phone. "Why don't you track down Lisa and bestow your obnoxious charm on her instead?"

"Actually, I've been thinking about that." Hart paused a thoughtful moment before continuing. "I'm going to take care of Lisa later. But as for Christy . . . being the generous sort, I'll give you first shot with her. Just don't blow it."

With those lame words of caution, Hart hung up, leaving Dex to scowl at the phone. He and his brother were best friends, and Hart was quickly making a name for himself as an MMA fighter.

But if Hart tried to cozy up with Christy, Dex would kick his ass, plain and simple.

He knew his brother would never do that. He knew that, despite his womanizing ways, Hart had a deep core of morality, most especially when it came to family.

But still, Dex couldn't shake his anger over the thought. And that, more than anything, proved he was completely gone for a woman . . . who thought he was his brother.

A beam of early morning summer sunlight climbed the wall, slipping in through a part in the curtains.

The second Christy rolled to her back, she remembered.

Everything.

Her confusion over Hart's bizarre turnaround, her rejected dinner invitation, and then her ridiculous pity party.

She'd gone out on her own with the idiotic notion of celebrating her birthday with or without an escort. She'd taken a cab to the least objectionable club she knew, sat alone in a corner, and . . . drank.

Oh God. She *never* drank. Not like that. Not until last night.

Humiliation weighed on her, and she covered her face. Like a volcanic eruption, her brain throbbed, her stomach heaved, and her eyeballs burned.

She would never drink again.

But just thinking of the fruity wine pushed her already rebellious stomach over the edge. She rolled off the side of the bed and raced into the bathroom with barely enough time to reach the toilet.

Her knees landed on hard tile, she pushed up the seat, hung her head, and . . .

Oh God, oh God, *oh God.*

She was ten times an idiot for doing this to herself.

When the nausea finally abated, Christy slumped back against the cool tub and wondered if a woman could will death upon herself.

It'd have to feel better than this brain-numbing mortification and sick-all-over malaise.

But the minutes passed, and other than increased agony in her brain and stomach, nothing happened.

Forcing herself up, Christy turned on the shower, stripped off her T-shirt and panties, and climbed under the chilly spray. It helped the tiniest bit to make her feel more human, and cleared away a few cobwebs.

Coffee was next on the list and she managed that without another trip to worship at the porcelain god.

No way could she consume food.

But she did drag a comb through her wet hair and brush her teeth. Lacking interest, she found scruffy blue jean shorts and an old, loose T-shirt that said, "Be Poor. It's Cheaper."

No way was she messing with a bra, and she didn't have the energy to hunt up sandals.

Awake, dressed, and as presentable as she could make herself under the effects of a raging hangover, she faced the inevitable.

She'd called Hart late at night, and he'd sounded half-asleep. Maybe he wouldn't even remember the call.

Doubtful.

When she'd started detailing her fantasies for him, he'd become a lot more alert.

He'd also sounded like his old self, not the new Hart that she'd started to like. A lot. Maybe even . . .

No. Getting drunk and acting the fool was bad enough. She would not play at melodrama, too.

At this point, all she could do was make her excuses and pray that her asinine behavior would inspire him to avoid her as he always had in the past.

A glance in the hallway mirror showed she looked worse than ever. Deep circles shadowed her red-rimmed eyes. Her fair skin looked even more pasty than normal. Her hair hung long and lank. Her lips were pale.

But hell, given what she'd done last night, who gave a flying flip how she looked?

Not Hart. Until recently, he'd never had more than a polite greeting for her, and only when she'd trapped him long enough to give the greeting first. Whatever strange turn he'd taken . . . well, her inebriated antics of the night had surely killed that.

Why did he have to be the sexiest man she'd ever laid eyes on?

Enough. Barefoot, determined, resolute on her course, Christy opened her door and stepped out into the hall. She hesitated only a moment before crossing over to Hart's apartment to give three sharp raps on the door.

She would do this and get it over with. She would apologize, laugh it off, and suggest they both forget about it.

In mid pep talk his door opened, and there he stood.

Six feet, two inches of pure sexified hunk. Christy put a hand to her stomach. *Oh wow.* He smelled like a man fresh out of bed, all sleep rumpled and warm, bristly jawed, dressed only in unsnapped jeans, and as beautiful as a man could be.

It wasn't fair.

Her tongue stuck to the roof of her mouth.

Hart's thickly lashed eyes were heavy, either from sleepiness or suggestiveness. Christy was too hungover to tell.

After one long look that didn't seem the least repulsed, he leaned on the doorframe and murmured, "Good morning."

Her jumpy stomach dropped to her shaky knees. Not good. "Uh . . ."

He smiled.

Oh Lord. If she fainted dead away, what would he think? No, she wouldn't do that. She'd humiliated herself enough for one lifetime.

Bracing a hand on the doorframe, she said again, "Uh . . ."

"You woke me." He gave a sexy stretch of muscles and long bones, then smiled at her again. "Want to come in for some coffee?"

Her head bobbed, but her feet wouldn't move. Damn it, he'd always had this awful effect on her, but in her weakened condition, it was so much worse.

Since the day she'd first met him, his good looks had drawn her. Combined with his sincere attention and openness of late, she didn't stand a chance. In a very short time, he'd become the total package.

His astounding appeal, as much as the alcohol, had prompted her late-night call. Or maybe it was more of a plea. That part wasn't entirely clear. All she knew for sure was that she'd called him and humiliated herself.

"Take a breath, Christy."

Her infatuated gaze went to his chest, and then slipped down to his unsnapped jeans.

Her heart stopped. They hung low on his lean hips, showing off a good bit of muscled abdomen bisected by a happy trail that disappeared down . . . *there.*

Lord help her. She dragged her attention back up to his face and tried to keep it there. It felt like her eyes crossed with the effort.

His gaze darkened and his smile went crooked. In a gentle voice that seduced, he said, "It's really okay, you know."

Maybe from his perspective, but not from hers.

After a fortifying breath, Christy straightened her melting bones and girded herself. It didn't matter that inky dark, tousled hair hung over his brow, or that his teasing blue eyes brimmed with male curiosity.

She had to deal with this.

He stepped aside and held the door for her. After clearing her throat, she stepped in. "More coffee might help, but I doubt it."

"Let's try a few cups and see." He walked away in a long-legged, casual stride that sent muscles moving over his back.

Christy trailed behind him, eyeing his butt encased in worn denim and his big bare feet. You'd think after seeing him in the pool, his physical appearance wouldn't have such an impact.

But just the opposite was true. The more she talked with him, visited with him, and got to know him, the more impact he had on her senses.

"Not to make excuses," she said, "but I've never drank before."

He spared a quick glance over his shoulder, one dark brow lifted. "Never?"

She shook her head, but stopped that quick enough when her brain throbbed. "Trust me, it'll never happen again, either."

This was her first time in his apartment and she looked around with curiosity. It was stylish, but somehow, it didn't suit Hart. That is, not the Hart of late. Perhaps the Hart she used to know . . .

He held out a chair at a chrome and glass table. "Now that'd be a pity."

"What would?"

His gaze locked on hers. "If it never happens again."

Pulling back, Christy faltered before forcing herself to take a seat. "You have to know how horrified I am over calling you."

His quiet, sexy chuckle teased her. "You shouldn't be. I'm flattered." He searched through cabinets as if he didn't know where he kept his own coffee. "I had a hell of a time sleeping last night, thanks to you."

Christy blanched. No way was she touching that comment. After rubbing her temples, she forced herself to continue. "Not to bore you with my excuses, but it was my birthday, I'm without a steady date, my family is touring Europe, and I indulged in a ridiculous pity party that went downhill fast."

Finally, he pulled out a can of coffee and frowned at the brand before going about his preparations. "How old are you again?"

He didn't remember that either?

"Twenty-five."

"Legal, then, right?" He didn't even look at her as he said that, choosing instead to give his attention to the coffeemaker. "You look young." He glanced back at her, then away again. "Especially without makeup. But considering your job, I assumed you were early twenties."

This was not how she'd expected things to go. He wasn't annoyed that she'd bothered him in the middle of the night, and he wasn't making a lewd acceptance of her drunken offer.

Bemused, she sat silently and tried to still the drumbeat in her brain.

When Hart finished at the sink and the coffeemaker began sputtering, he came to the table and seated himself. Slouching in his chair, he surveyed her in silence.

"This is awkward," Christy said.

"It's just coffee with a neighbor," he soothed, but the way he watched her wasn't the least bit comforting.

"Uh, no, not quite." Damn it, she wished he would put on a shirt. Or at least snap his jeans! "Look, I really only came here to apologize."

"For keeping me up all night?"

Up? The second she thought it, he grinned as if he *knew* what images crowded into her pickled brain.

She shook her head, both to clear it and to deny his assumptions. "No, I mean, sure. If it's necessary. But mostly I wanted to apologize for getting stupid drunk and bothering you. I can't say I was so out of it that I didn't know what I was doing, because the second I woke up today, it all came crashing in."

"Liquid courage." He nodded with understanding. "Most people have relied on it at least once. I take it, though, that it was something you'd wanted to say—or rather *do*—for a while?"

"No!" Heat rushed up her neck and burned her cheeks. Curse her fair skin. "That is . . ." She propped her elbows on the table and put her face in her hands. "Oh God, this is awful."

His voice softened. "Might as well come clean at this point, don't you think?"

That caused her to stiffen and she lifted her head to face him. "I am not a liar, so there's nothing to come clean about." And since that was true, she felt compelled to add, "You knew that I'd *thought* about it. I've admitted that much to you already. But no way would I have ever propositioned you like that. Not that it matters now anyway, because I have no intention of—"

"Eating me up?" He slowly came out of his seat. "Letting me eat you?"

He said that without pause, and this time the heat exploded deep inside her. Christy didn't know if she should make a run for it, jump his gorgeous bones, or do . . . nothing at all.

She opted for nothing—and they watched each other for a heart-stopping moment that almost made her stomach heave again. He stood over her, not threatening in any way, but *there*, so damn tall and imposing and impossible to disregard.

She remained seated, which felt like a supplicant position.

It sort of turned her on.

A confident half smile tipped up the corner of his mouth. He moved toward the counter, picked up a pen and paper, and scrawled down a message. Returning to her, he handed her the paper with a phone number written on it. "Next time you call me, use this number. It's my private line."

Though she had no intention of ever repeating such a farce, she accepted the paper and tucked it into her pocket. "Are you telling me that I called a business line?"

"Sort of, but don't worry about it. Just use that number from now on."

"Seriously, Hart, you don't have to worry about me bothering you."

"Seriously, Christy," he teased, "you could never be a bother." He went back to the counter. "How do you like your coffee?"

"Today?" Given everything he threw at her, she needed to clear her head and fast. "Black and strong."

"Nah, that's no good." He sized her up with a single quick glance. "You usually take cream and sugar?"

Giving up, she nodded. "Lots of both."

He poured two cups, doctored hers just right, and brought them to the table. Standing so close to her side that she felt the warmth of his bare skin and breathed in his sleepy scent, he handed her the coffee.

"Thanks." She took a cautious sip, and savored the invigorating taste.

Hart didn't move away. "We've got something going on here, don't we?"

"I don't know." To keep her composure, she stared at her cup and not at him. "You confuse me."

"Okay then, trust me. We do." He reached out and touched her chin, bringing her gaze to his. "The phone call last night doesn't change anything, except that now I know how you feel, and I'm glad."

Caught in that hot blue gaze, she stared at him.

"You do want me, right?" His gaze never wavered.

"There is *no* way you can possibly be uncertain about that."

Like the center of a flame, the blue of his eyes heated. "Good. I want you, too, so we're even. Now the thing to decide is what to do about it."

No words came to her. Jumping his bones suddenly seemed like a very good idea.

"I couldn't do anything last night," he explained, and at the same time, he threaded his fingers into her hair, lifted, let the long strands drift down. "A man does not take advantage of a tipsy woman." Gently, he threaded his fingers into her hair again, caught a fistful, and tipped her head back. "But I wanted to."

Her lips parted to accommodate her fast, shallow breathing.

"I still want to."

"Oh," she said on a long exhalation, then frowned as memories danced through her mind. All she remembered for sure was his sputtering, hesitant response to everything she said.

And his offer of a cab, which she'd accepted.

He stepped away from her, giving her the opportunity to calm her racing heart and catch her breath.

"Have you had any aspirin?"

Glad for the shift in topic, Christy shook her head. "Not yet. The idea of swallowing them . . ."

"Trust me on this, honey. Aspirin are necessary. Food, too, but I'll give you a few minutes before we tackle that issue."

Even after he left the room, his earthy, early morning scent remained, teasing her, twisting her up inside.

Carrying pills and a book, he reentered the kitchen. He filled a glass with water and brought it to her. “Take these first.”

Because she couldn’t be any more miserable, she trusted him and tossed back the pills, washing them down with the water. “Alcohol sucks. Why in the world do people drink?”

“I have no idea. It’s not something I’ve ever enjoyed to excess either.”

“What do you mean?”

“I don’t drink much.”

Okay, she was hungover, but not stupid. “I’ve seen you with a beer in your hand a couple of times now. And a few weeks ago, you were out on the balcony with a mixed drink in one hand and a woman in the other.”

He looked arrested for only a moment. “Isolated occasions.” He studied her. “Not much gets by you, does it?”

Not if it concerned him, no. But she wouldn’t admit that. “I just happened to see, that’s all.”

“I can’t think of another single woman who’s paid that much attention to what I do.”

Christy scrubbed at her tired eyes. Hadn’t she told him that she knew she didn’t compare to his usual tastes in women? “Thank you for the aspirin and the coffee. I think it’s time for me to go home to sleep off my aches and pains.”

“Sleeping alone isn’t what you need.”

She almost groaned. At the moment, it was probably all she could manage.

She was trying to think of a reply to his suggestive statement when he turned over the book and pushed it toward her.

Eyes direct and inquiring, he said, “I think drink wasn’t the only influence you had last night.”

Seeing the cover, her jaw dropped. “You took my book?”

“What? No.” He watched her too closely. “Actually, it’s my

book. It's the book you quoted from. I've read it so I recognized the words."

Could this nightmare get any worse? "Great. So not only did I beg for sex, but you know I did it using someone else's words." *Definitely* time to go. Christy pushed back the chair and got to her feet.

He reached her side in a heartbeat. "Actually, I was honored."

"Honored?" That didn't make any sense.

"And like I said, flattered. And more than a little turned on, and pretty damned hopeful that maybe you haven't changed your mind now that drink isn't influencing you."

Words escaped her. She couldn't draw air into her lungs. He was too big, too sexy, too close, too . . . much.

Of everything.

He curved his big hands over her shoulders. "I do have a stipulation, though."

Why oh why couldn't she just disappear? "Let me guess." Sarcasm saved her. A little. "No commitment. Right?"

His fingers gently squeezed—and urged her nearer to his bare chest. "Actually, I have three stipulations. And no, smart ass, that's not one of them."

How did he make "smart ass" sound like an endearment? "Three?" Was that her squeaky voice?

"You can't get angry afterward." He dropped one hot hand to her hip—which effectively stopped her heart and sent her stomach into a tumble. "You have to give me no less than three hours once we start."

Her knees trembled. Three hours? She didn't know if it was the hangover or the lust throbbing through her veins.

"That long, huh?" Her voice emerged as a whisper, but she couldn't get more than a thread of sound out of her constricted throat.

"And I want a date afterward."

Christy blinked in stupefaction. "Come again?"

"A real date. No," he said, stopping himself. "Scratch that. I want five dates."

"Five . . . ?"

"Dates," he confirmed.

Somehow he had both hands holding her hips now, and he'd drawn her so close that her pelvis pressed into his upper thighs and her breasts were squashed against his hard abdomen.

"Movie, dinner," he murmured. "Whatever suits you. Five times, Christy. Promise me."

"But . . . why?"

He leaned down—close enough to kiss her. But he didn't. Not yet. "You don't know the real me, that's why."

"I don't?"

"No." He looked at her mouth. "But I want you to."

From the time he'd moved in six weeks ago, Hart Winston had all but ignored her, and when that wasn't possible, he'd treated her with perfunctory politeness.

Now he behaved as if he wanted her more than anything. "*Why?*"

His eyes brightened. "Well, for one thing, we share similar tastes in reading material."

And *then* he kissed her.

Four

Dex held Christy close to his chest, and she felt perfect there. Her lips were soft and warm, and her heartbeat raced against him. As she went limp in his arms, he wondered just how far he'd get, right now, right this instant. He was ready. More than ready. He had enough wood to start a fire.

"Wait."

Not far at all, he realized when she pushed back, panting, red-faced again, and a little wild-eyed.

Being totally honest, he said, "I'd rather not."

"But . . . I'm a mess."

She was. Her still-damp hair hung in tangles, she had a greenish cast about her, and she looked ready to topple over.

Only, none of that seemed to matter to him. "You look great. I like the scruffy clothes. They're less intimidating than your suits."

Her laugh was genuine, but strained. "You're a terrible liar, Hart Winston. I *saw* myself. I'm not blind. And I doubt anything, much less a woman's clothes, would ever intimidate you." She straight-armed him and when he released her, she backed up several steps. "If I was considering doing this—"

"You are," he insisted.

"I wouldn't do it looking like a hungover hag."

"I *really* don't mind."

Her lip curled. "Men never do." Her chin lifted. "But remember, I want the lights on."

Thinking her too adorable, Dex gestured at the kitchen table. "If you're game for fluorescent lights, count me in."

"What?" She smothered a laugh of disbelief. "No, no kitchen tables, thank you anyway."

"So you're a traditionalist, huh? You like tidy beds?" And that made him think about beds, and the fact that he didn't want to make love to her for the first time on his brother's sheets, even if they were freshly laundered. "I can deal with that."

She put both hands over her face. She breathed hard.

Dex waited. His dick twitched.

She dropped her hands. "Actually, since we're both being so blunt, you might as well know that I'm a very conservative woman who has had sex all of three times."

"Three guys, huh?" Great. Whatever.

What the hell did he care?

As long as he didn't have to think about her with other men, it didn't matter to him.

"Three *times*." She held up her fingers. "When I was eighteen, twenty-one, and twenty-two."

He was a writer, not a mathematician, but didn't that mean . . . "You haven't been laid in *three years*?"

His awful wording—brought about by surprise—had her copping an attitude. "Yeah, unheard of, I know. I was asked to be in a museum, but I refused."

Dex's brain scrambled as he absorbed the information—*three years*—and tried to recover from his verbal faux pas. The last thing he wanted to do was insult her.

Seduce her, yes.

Entice her, definitely.

Hear her scream out as she climaxed . . . he couldn't wait.

"I'm just surprised that the male population has let a woman as sexy as you do without."

Her eyes rolled. "Yeah, that's why you've been after me so hot and heavy, huh? You were here six weeks, Hart, before you gave me so much as a second glance. Just admit that you're looking for an easy lay, and because of my phone call, I'm it."

She had to be kidding. There wasn't anything easy about this, or her. "If you'll stop and think about it, Christy, you'll admit that I was interested before you called."

Her eyes were so red, he could almost hear her blinking.

"Okay. I admit it." Her stance became more rigid. "Now tell me why."

The way she stood, arms crossed and hip jutting out, made him grin. "Okay, you want a truth?"

She retrenched. "I'm not sure."

But he was. "That book you quoted from? I wrote it."

Her chin tucked in. "No way."

"I'm the author. You obviously read me. I'm incredibly flattered."

Her arms dropped and she backed up a step. "You're making that up!"

He shook his head, all the while indulging a big, satisfied smile. "Add that to your very provocative phone call, and my already ignited interest, and yeah, you're it."

Her blank face said she couldn't quite grasp it all. "You're a *writer*?"

"Yeah." He took her arm and walked her over to his brother's bookcase. "These are all mine."

"No way," she said again.

Her disbelief felt very complimentary. "Way."

"But . . ." She snatched up a book two years old and turned on him with challenge. "Who's in this?"

"Lead characters, or the arsonist? Never mind. I'll just tell you everything about it." And he did, going over the setting, a brief recap of the plot, some of the more interesting dialogue, and lastly, the characters' names and descriptions.

Christy clutched the book to her chest. "You really wrote it?"

"All of them. And I'm working on another right now. That phone call that interrupted us in the pool?"

She stared wide-eyed at him, waiting.

"That was my editor."

She shook her head. "But you're a *painter*."

"That, too." The small fib didn't bother him. He did paint, just not for a living the way Hart did.

Slowly, she replaced the book on the shelf, and kept her back to him. "You're not only too gorgeous to be true, you're supertalented."

Because she sounded almost forlorn about that, Dex frowned at her. "I'm creative, but trust me, there's a lot I can't do."

"I doubt that." Finally she stood and turned toward him again. Fingertips pressed to her temples, she inhaled, slowly exhaled, and looked at him. "So let me get this straight. I not only got sloppy drunk and propositioned you, I did it by plagiarizing one of your works?"

"Afraid so." He cupped her jaw. "But you know what Charles Caleb Colton said."

"No, I have no idea what he said."

Grinning again, Dex recited, "Imitation is the sincerest form of flattery."

She put a hand over her mouth. "Oh God, I think I'm going to throw up."

"Seriously?" Startled, Dex took a few cautious steps away from her. "I'd rather you hit the john for that."

Waving a hand at him, she closed her eyes, waited, and finally relaxed again. "No. I'm okay." She paced away, turned back to him. "I need some time to think."

"About?"

Mouth falling open, she stared at him. "You're kidding, right?"

This time Dex laughed. "You don't need to be home alone, trust me."

"You keep saying that."

Her disgruntlement amused him. "Because if you'd trust me, this would all work out just fine."

"According to the man of fiction."

"You like my fiction." He put an arm around her and started her toward Hart's kitchen. "You'll like my reality even more, I promise."

She nearly tripped, straightened herself, and then elbowed him. "Braggart."

"You've boosted my confidence." Once in the kitchen, Dex held her chair for her. "I want you to try eating something salty. Small bites. It'll help settle your stomach."

"No, really, I can't even think about food."

He tipped up her chin. "So think about me instead."

"That's a given."

Contentment sank into his bones, and he hadn't even had her yet. Her upfront manner, in contrast to her school secretary image, appealed to him as much as her innocence and infatuation.

He poured her more coffee. "Sip on that while I make you something."

"If you're sure food won't kill me . . ."

"It won't, but if you leave me waiting for another day, the anticipation will definitely do me in."

Growing more at ease, she smiled at his quip, took a drink of coffee, and eased her head down onto her folded arms.

Constantly glancing at her, Dex made very simple canned soup and crackers. After a moment, her head still down and her eyes still closed, she said, "Okay, that doesn't smell totally revolting."

"I'm glad." He carried a tray to the table, smoothed her hair to let her know it was ready, and seated himself opposite her. "Eat slowly, just a few small bites, and see how you do."

By the time she finished, her hair had dried and her color had returned. "Better."

"Great."

She sighed, patted her mouth with a napkin. "Okay." She glanced at him. "Now what?"

"That's up to you." He was hard again and there wasn't a damn thing he could do about it. "I've been interested and willing for over a week. At the moment, I'm more than ready. But I want you to enjoy yourself, Christy, so if you need more time—"

She came to her feet. "No."

Going on alert, he stood also. "No, you aren't ready, or no—"

"I don't need more time." Her gaze stayed locked with his. "Being this close to you for so long has bothered me more than the hangover. I've always been really attracted to you. Now I . . . I like you a lot, too."

"And it's a powerful combination? I know, because I feel the same."

She started to speak, then shook her head. "I'm not going to question it anymore. If you say you want me, then that's—"

Rounding the table, Dex caught her up in his arms and kissed her. It wasn't easy, but he kept it light. "Forget anything before right now. And right now, I definitely want you. Tomorrow I'll want you. Next week I'll want you."

"Okay." Going on tiptoe, she smashed her mouth to his and devoured him.

She was so slight that it required little effort to lift her. Scooping her up, he carried her into the bedroom.

So it was Hart's bed.

So she thought he was Hart.

He was the one she wanted. Not his brother. Not anymore.

Damn it.

Furiously blocking those disruptive thoughts, Dex lowered her to the mattress and then stepped back to look at her.

The loose T-shirt had scrunched up, baring her midriff. Well-worn, frayed shorts showed off her very shapely legs. Her hair fanned out on the pillow, she squirmed, and he wanted to be all over her, all at once.

It wasn't easy to think straight. "You've yet to promise me."

Eyes half-closed, lips moist, Christy watched him with encouragement. "Promise you what?"

So tempting. But damn it, like a virgin on prom night, he needed assurances. "That you won't end up angry with me, no matter what."

Her gaze roamed over him. "Are you a lousy lover?"

Without a second's hesitation or a single qualm, Dex said, "No."

"Then I promise." She reached out to him.

Dex sucked in a breath and shook his head. "Five dates, Christy. Regardless of what happens or how you feel about me, I get those five dates."

"Five, ten, a hundred, fine, I don't care. That's later and this is now, so stop teasing me."

With her promise made, Dex told himself not to worry. As a levelheaded woman, Christy would understand his predicament.

But he made a mental note to inform his brother that all bets were off. Christy deserved the truth, so Hart could just deal with it. He'd tell her everything.

Later.

Right now, he had to have her.

Aiming for a little finesse, Dex sat beside her on the bed, smoothed back her hair, kissed her softly, and then opened the snap on her shorts.

Her belly sucked in as she held her breath. He didn't skim the shorts off her. He just opened the zipper and insinuated his hand inside. He felt the edge of her panties, went beneath them, and pressed farther until his hand cupped over her sex.

"*Hart.*"

God, if the walls had ears, his brother would never let him live this down. To keep her from calling out Hart's name, Dex leaned down and took her mouth with his own, effectively silencing her with his hand still between her thighs, his fingers barely moving.

Their tongues touched, stroked, hot and wet and exciting. Her breathing accelerated. Her hips lifted off the mattress.

He'd barely touched her, but she skyrocketed ahead of him, giving him a glimpse of what lay ahead.

Kissing her jaw, her throat, Dex worked his way down over the thin material of her T-shirt until he found her breast. Already puckered tight, her nipple pressed against the shirt. Dex opened his mouth over her, sucking gently, drawing on her, teasing with his teeth.

On a soft groan, she opened her legs more, and he took the hint, sliding his fingers between slick lips, gliding over sensitive flesh, finding and fondling her small clitoris.

"*Oh God.*"

She almost came.

Surprised, Dex lifted his head to look at her. Flushed and trembling, she looked beautiful. But he wanted to be with her when she climaxed, not just a voyeur, as pleasant as that seemed, but a part of her in every way.

Sitting up in a hurry, Dex caught the hem of her shirt and drew it away. The sight of her naked breasts and torso fascinated him. "So pretty," he whispered.

Using both hands, he cuddled her breasts, moved his thumbs over her puckered nipples. He lay down beside her and drew her right nipple into his mouth, while teasing the other with his fingertips.

Twisting and panting, Christy sank her fingers into the muscles of his shoulders, stinging a little, turning him on a lot.

She arched toward him, put a leg over his hips, and pressed against him.

A master of understatement, Dex said, "We need to be naked." Rolling to his back, he lowered his zipper and shucked off his jeans and boxers. Before he could reach for her, Christy was over him, her gaze heated, her lips parted.

"I've dreamed about this."

Ah hell. He wouldn't last, but how could he deny her?

Watching her, Dex said, "Help yourself."

She licked her lips. "Thank you." For agonizing moments, she just looked at him, her gaze so tactile that Dex felt primed and on the edge.

With tentative care, she put her hands on him, first his bare shoulders, then his chest. "No other man could look like you."

Wrong. Dex closed his eyes. His brother looked exactly like him. Most women and even some family members couldn't tell them apart.

But damn it, he couldn't think about that now.

Not with Christy's hot little hands smoothing over him, touching everywhere. He locked his jaw and did his best to let her take her time—that is, until her slender fingers wrapped around his cock.

Catching her wrist, Dex restrained her. If she stroked him, even once, he'd lose it. "That feels great, honey. Too good. We're both ready, so let's just—"

Instead of listening to him, Christy kissed his chest, down to his abdomen.

Oh hell. He wanted this first time with her to be about her, to be special for her, but he wasn't a saint. Squeezing his eyes shut, Dex knew he should stop her.

But he couldn't.

She got to her knees beside him and looked at him some more, so adoring that it humbled him.

"Lose the shorts, honey."

"Okay." But instead, she bent down again, both hands holding him tight, and her mouth slid over the head of his dick with incredible enthusiasm.

Dex almost shot off the mattress.

The feel of wet heat, soft suction, numbed his brain to immediate protests. Her movements were awkward but hungry, and in no time he shook with the need to let go.

Out of survival, he caught her head, but for the briefest moment, his control wavering, he kept her in place. Her tongue stroked him, and with a groan, he urged her to her back.

It took several deep breaths before he could speak. "You're killing me, babe."

Her eyes shone with need. "I really do want to eat you up."

Damn. "Hold that thought, okay?" Unwilling to take another chance on losing it, Dex quickly wrestled with her shorts. "You need to play fair."

"I've wanted you too long."

Not really, Dex wanted to tell her, but he couldn't, not yet. "Well, now you'll have me."

"I'm glad it took so long. You're . . . nicer now. I like you more."

Dex paused to look at her.

She smiled uncertainly. "A whole lot more."

Ah hell. He quickly cupped her face. "I like you, too. More than you can imagine. Please don't forget that."

"Why would I forget?"

He had to stop confusing her. But this was so important. "Just promise me."

"Okay. I promise." Her smile flickered. "I'll never forget."

He gave her a quick, hard kiss, and then stripped away her clothes. As soon as he had her naked, he fetched a condom from the drawer where he'd stashed them, rolled it on, and came down over her.

His hands on her thighs, he said, "Open your legs for me, Christy."

She went one further and wrapped her legs around his waist, shattering his fragile control.

Dex pushed into her, rocked his hips, and filled her. Oh yeah, this was what he wanted. This . . . and more.

Her slick inner muscles clamped tight around him.

Wanting to make it last, Dex murmured, "Easy," as he pulled out, sank in slowly again.

"No." Locking her ankles at the small of his back, Christy dug her fingertips into his shoulders. "Hard. Please."

To hell with it. Giving up, Dex took her hot, soft mouth and kept on kissing her even as he began thrusting, hard and fast, as she'd requested. Their skin grew damp, their breathing labored—and still he kissed her, drowning in her growing pleasure, the feel of her, the reality of her.

He felt her heels pressing into his back, tasted her trembling moan, smelled her heated scent, and when her contractions started, Dex let himself go.

He freed her mouth to lift his head and watch her as they both came. He saw her neck arch, her mouth open on a shuddering cry.

Beautiful. Real. And his.

Minutes later, they went limp together, and it was the most replete Dex had ever been.

Christy awoke with a long stretch and a deep groan. She felt sore in certain places, still tingly in others, and very lethargic. She didn't want to open her eyes.

But she did—and found herself alone.

Reaching out to touch Hart's pillow, she found it cool, meaning he'd been gone for a while.

Nervousness fluttered in her chest. Had she really been so wild with him?

Yes.

She had.

Falling to her back, Christy sighed. And smiled. And even laughed.

Wow. She couldn't say much more than that. But . . . *wow.*

Hart was amazing, and so considerate and gentle and . . . He was everything she'd never imagined him to be, given her first impression of his personality. But that had changed. Now that she knew him better, she wasn't surprised. He was better than her fantasies.

Better than anything she'd ever imagined.

Wondering if this was the start of a wonderful relationship, she bit her lip. He'd made her promise to give him several dates, so apparently he didn't intend to end things anytime soon.

That suited her just fine.

Wrapping the sheet around her naked body, she left the bed and meandered into his bathroom. His apartment was the same size as hers, but set up the opposite, and decorated . . . in a way that just didn't seem like the man she now knew.

Silvery gray towels and chrome fixtures dominated his bathroom. He was neat to the point of being obsessive, with not a single thing out of place anywhere.

Christy refreshed herself and, still wearing only a sheet, ventured into the rest of the apartment.

"Hart?"

No one answered. He'd left her alone in his place? Odd. But maybe he'd had an important errand to run or something. She could certainly make her way back to her own apartment without him.

Still . . . it nettled that he'd left her.

Standing in the middle of the living room, she looked around at the perfectly situated furniture with the clean lines. Everything was masculine and heavy, leather, glass, and chrome in shades of tan, black, and gray with accents of autumn red.

Slick. Modern.

So unlike Hart.

So unlike the man who had written those amazing novels.

But . . . his place did match his artwork. She'd seen many of Hart's pieces, and they were always bold and outgoing.

Such a contrast.

Suddenly Christy wanted a moment to herself. She wanted to be in her place when he returned, rather than still hanging around, forcing herself on him.

Again.

She dressed in her wrinkled clothes and made a hasty retreat across the hall. Luckily, no neighbors ventured out to catch her. She could only imagine what they'd think—and they'd be right.

Unable to wipe the smile from her face, she went into her bathroom, stripped, and stepped into the shower.

She was still rinsing off when she heard her doorbell ring.

Joy exploded inside her, and she had to struggle to calm her reaction. Though he now seemed like the most wonderful man, it wasn't that long ago that Hart had been oblivious to her. She'd be wise to keep a cool head and a cautious heart around him.

Easier said than done, given how she felt.

Within seconds Christy left the shower and was tucked into her terry cloth robe. A glance in the mirror showed the mess of her hair pinned atop her head, but when the doorbell rang yet again, she decided to hell with it. She didn't want Hart to leave.

Wearing a big smile, she opened her door.

With new familiarity and intimate warmth in his eyes, he leaned in and took her mouth in a damp, lazy, sexual kiss. Close enough that she felt the heat of his breath, he asked, "Why'd you leave?"

Flustered, Christy licked her lips, and tasted him again. "Why did *you* leave?"

He tilted his head, kissed her chin, along her jaw, and up to her ear before straightening. "Didn't you read the note I left you in the kitchen?"

"I didn't go in the kitchen."

"Oh." Languid, satisfied, he looked her over. The intensity sharpened in his gaze. "Invite me in, honey."

"Oh. Of course." She held the door wide and stepped out of his way. As he passed her, she again made note of his broad shoulders, his sturdy frame, his dark hair and indescribable scent.

Would she ever get used to him?

No. Not likely.

He glanced down at her, caught her appraisal, and something almost savage entered his beautiful blue eyes. "The note said that I'd be right back, and that you should stay in the bed, waiting for me."

Hell of a plan, if only she'd known. Christy laced her fingers together, as much out of nervousness as to keep from grabbing at him. "I didn't want to make myself at home without you there. It didn't seem right to start going through your place."

He set a bag on the floor and drew her into his arms. Broad hands opened over her back. One slid up to her nape, inciting nerve endings all along the way.

In a voice low and deep, he said, "Consider yourself invited to make yourself at home . . . wherever I am."

That confused her. Where did he plan to be other than his apartment? "Hart . . . ?"

He stepped back, leaving her cold. "I got you something."

"You did?"

"Mmm." Looking at her mouth, he smiled and reached out to trace her bottom lip with a thumb. "But damn, it's difficult to remember why I left when I come back to find you looking like this."

Christy touched her sloppy hair. "I'm a mess. Again."

Not really listening, he fingered one lapel of her terry robe. "Your skin is still damp, and from what I can tell . . ." His hand drifted down so that his knuckles brushed over her breast. His incendiary gaze came back up and locked on hers. "You're naked under that robe."

Five

In a distanced, merely polite mood, Hart could make her knees weak. Now, like this, he obliterated her self-control. To keep from throwing off the robe in advance of attacking him, she snatched the material closed around her throat. "You caught me in the shower."

"If you'd waited, we could have showered together." Not giving her time to ponder the awesome possibility of showering with him, he lifted the bag again. "Before I lose the fight and take you on the floor, let me say that I'm sorry I missed your birthday. I hope this makes up for it, at least a little."

Take her on the floor?

Christy looked down at her plush carpeting, envisioned them both naked there—but wait. He'd said more. She focused on the bag he held and something far more than sexual arousal expanded in her chest.

No way. He couldn't be that sweet. Feeling almost shy now, Christy shook her head. "You didn't know. And we've only just started . . . well, I don't know what to call it." She wrinkled her nose. "Dating doesn't sound right since we haven't been out yet."

"We're involved," he prompted, and waited for her agreement with steel determination in his eyes.

Involved. She liked how that sounded. She liked how it seemed to mean so much to him, too. "Okay."

"The fact that it's just happened is no excuse. So . . ." He reached into the bag and lifted out a medium-sized white bakery box to hand to her.

Feeling giddy and silly, Christy walked over and set it on the coffee table. She untied the string and lifted the lid. Inside was a small, fancy decorated cake, just big enough for two. The top of it read "Happy Birthday" in pink frosting.

She put a hand to her heart. "How did you manage that so quickly?" He couldn't have been gone from the apartment more than an hour or so.

Still standing where she'd left him, he watched her. "The cake was already made. I just had them write the message on top. I would have liked it to be more personalized, but that's the best I could do on short notice."

"Your best is always incredible."

Pleased with her reaction, he nodded. "I hope you've recovered from your hangover so you can enjoy a piece. It's chocolate cake with raspberry filling and vanilla cream icing."

"It sounds heavenly." And considerate, and special—like the man himself.

Until recently, Hart had hidden from her depths of thoughtfulness and layers of complicated personality. The change was sharp—and so appealing.

Much more of this, and she'd turn into emotional mush on the floor. Voice soft, weak with happiness, she murmured, "Thank you."

"I'm not done yet." He looked at her legs, showing from a part in her robe. He looked at her throat. For a moment, his eyes closed as if to regain control, then he opened them with that charismatic smile. "A birthday deserves a small gift, right?"

"Hart," she whispered, chastising him, thanking him. For some reason he winced, making her rush to explain. No one had remembered her birthday in a very long time. "You didn't have to do that."

He frowned a little and reached back into the bag. "I wanted to."

This time, he pulled out a long narrow jewelry box.

Disbelief kept Christy staring. "But . . . I don't know. I mean, we've only just—"

Taking her hand, he kissed her knuckles. That must not have sufficed, because he turned her hand over and kissed her palm, too. She felt the touch of his tongue there, then on her fingers—and between. The provocative touches started a fire in her center, making her breath heat.

"Damn, you tempt me." He nipped her palm, and pressed the box into her hand. "I hope you like it. If not, we'll return it and you can pick out something else."

Shaken by her own sexuality, wishing he'd continue and let her open the gift later, Christy gazed at him.

He stole a soft, lingering kiss from parted lips, stood back, and waited. "Open it."

So much had happened so soon, she had a hard time reconciling it all. Hart was a different person; still gorgeous and magnetic, but now he was also sensitive and so incredibly aware of her, generous not only in bed, but . . . everywhere.

Biting her lip, she loosened the shimmering ribbon enclosing the box and slowly lifted the lid. Lamplight glinted off a delicate gold and silver bracelet, enhanced with a single filigree heart, nestled on snowy white velvet.

While she sat there, numb, he took it out of the box and hooked it around her wrist.

It was so beautiful, Christy's lips parted. "It's too much."

"It reminded me of you." With two fingers beneath her chin, he brought her gaze to his. "It's delicate and sweet, but with a big heart."

She sniffled, and Hart turned grave.

"You don't like it?"

"Of course I do. I love it." Stupid, overly emotional tears stung her eyes. She hadn't expected, hadn't even considered, that he'd do something so thoughtful, or so personal. Throwing her arms around him, she squeezed him tight. "Thank you so much."

"You're very welcome." His voice was rough. The hand on her derriere was rougher. With one arm he brought her close; with the other he stole beneath the robe to exlore a bare cheek. "You have a great ass, Christy Nash."

Christy instinctively arched closer to him, drawing in a greedy breath. "Hart."

His fingers contracted on her flesh, and a second later, his mouth was over hers, keeping her silent as his fingers searched from behind. He slid teasing fingertips down along her cleft, then inward until he found her lips, damp and swollen. He pressed two fingers up into her.

She moaned, but he took the sound, holding her tight as he lifted her higher, fingered her more deeply, pleasured her. He released her mouth enough to say, "God, it's never enough."

"I know."

Less than a minute after that, Hart withdrew to open her belt, pushed the robe off her shoulders, and she was . . . naked. She might have been self-conscious except for how quickly he shed his own clothes—all the while devouring her with his eyes.

"The floor?" she asked.

"It's as far as I'm going to make it." He fumbled with a rubber, cursing softly, then took her to her knees with him.

Christy didn't mind. She was every bit as anxious as him, doubly so now that she knew he cared, that she wasn't a one-night stand for him.

Sleeping with him no longer meant indulging a fantasy; it represented the start of a relationship that felt so right, so perfect, she had to believe it was meant to be.

Kissing her, Hart eased her to her back, opened her legs, and settled between.

Arms straight, he braced himself over her. "You make this so hard."

Caught in the heat of the moment, Christy cocked her head in incomprehension. "Hart . . . ?"

He pushed into her with one solid, deep thrust.

They both went still, breath checked, bodies trembling. "It'll never be enough."

God, she hoped that was true for him—because she knew a lifetime wouldn't be enough for her.

He looked down her body to where they joined, eased out, and drove back in. She gasped. He groaned.

"Christy." He lowered himself to his elbows to kiss her, her breasts, her throat.

Christy watched his face, now taut with a nearing climax. She wrapped her legs around him, smoothed her hands over his chest. They moved together, harder, faster, and knowing that Hart watched her, that she watched him, only made it hotter.

She came first, and it was enough to push him over the edge. He gritted his teeth, put his head back, and pressed himself to her, so deep he felt a part of her.

Not until much, much later did they make it to her bedroom. And afterward, when Hart came up on one elbow and smoothed her hair, Christy said, "Stay the night with me."

Rather than look put off by her request, his eyes darkened and his mouth touched hers. "I was hoping you'd ask." He settled back down, pulled her in close to his body, and they both soon fell asleep.

It didn't seem to matter how much time Dex spent with her. He wanted her. Constantly. Not just sex, though that was as perfect as it could be.

Until Christy, he hadn't realized the difference emotion could make to sex. When deep inside her, her slick, hot muscles tugged at his cock, just as she tugged at his heart. Everything about her fascinated him: the prim clothes that cloaked a hot body, the reserved manners that disguised a wild sexuality.

Christy matched him, stayed with him every step of the way, whether things turned adventurous and kinky, or soft and lingering.

She wrenched his emotions, and turned him inside out physically.

He loved it. Hell, he loved her. Everything about her.

After pulling into the apartment parking lot, Dex turned off the engine of his car, scooped up his bag and a bouquet of flowers, and dialed his brother.

As soon as Hart answered, he said, "Today is the day."

Hart didn't take it well. "Damn it, Dex. You can't tell her. Not yet."

Holding his purchases in one hand and his cell phone in the other, Dexter kicked his car door shut and leaned back on the fender. He didn't want to go inside yet, because he knew Christy would greet him. As Hart.

With a tight hug and a hungry kiss.

And warm enthusiasm.

All for Hart.

She'd hug him and entice him—and call him his brother's name.

Enough was enough. Another week had passed and still Hart hadn't made plans to return. He couldn't take it any longer.

"Screw that," Dex told him. "I can't *not* tell her. This is getting out of hand."

"What is?"

Dex grumbled, "None of your damn business."

But Hart understood exactly what bothered Dex, and he laughed without pity. "No one told you to get too involved, butthead."

"I'm not sure I had any choice."

Hart quieted his humor. "She's that perfect, huh?"

"Yeah, she is." In every way. Even knowing he moved at Mach speed, Dex couldn't slow down. Christy was the one, and he knew it.

"Great. I'm happy she pushes all the buttons."

Dex heard the "but" coming. "Thank you."

"*But,*" Hart continued, "even paragons have vices. You haven't known her long enough to know if she can keep a secret, especially given her involvement in all this. She'll feel burned, Dex, you know that."

Know it? It ate him alive, thinking how she'd feel, how she might react. "That's exactly why I have to tell her sooner, rather than later."

"Pissed-off women are unpredictable, Dex. Most of them want to vent to other women. And as soon as she starts that, the cat's out of the bag."

"Christy is different." But saying it to Hart didn't entirely convince Dex. No, he didn't think she'd swear a vendetta for revenge, but God, he did not want her to feel betrayed, or duped. It cut him to even consider it.

"Get real, Dex. If she has even one best friend that she tells, who has one best friend that *she* tells, eventually everyone will know my private business."

Dex was just annoyed enough to say, "Big fucking deal. Your private business shouldn't be all that private anyway." In the face of his dilemma, Dex couldn't see why Hart still cared if everyone knew he fought.

"Actually"—Hart inhaled deeply—"it is a big deal. See . . . the SBC offered me a contract."

Dex almost dropped the phone. The SBC was the premier MMA fight organization, a dream come true, the ultimate goal. "A contract? You're shitting me."

"Nope." The smile came through, along with the exhilaration and satisfaction. "I've been doing pretty good."

"That has to be an understatement."

"Yeah. We had several exhibition-type bouts, without a lot of rest time in between. I'm exhausted, but hey, this is what I wanted, right? And then thanks to Havoc's recommendation, Drew Black himself dropped by to check me out."

As the president of the SBC, Drew Black was the driving force behind the sport's success. "I take it he liked what he saw."

"He's the real deal, for sure. Easy to talk to, but man, does he know his business."

"How many times did he swear at you?"

Because everyone knew Drew couldn't say three words without swearing, Hart laughed. "Let's just say he lives up to his reputation. What you see on TV is him, through and through. He told me I had some 'fucking' killer moves."

Dex laughed. "Sounds about right."

Caught up in the excitement, Hart barely drew breath before continuing. "You know Sublime?"

"Yeah, Simon Evans. Light heavyweight champ turned trainer. Who doesn't know him?"

"He trains at Havoc's gym, right? Well, he and Havoc invited me to join their team. I'm going to Havoc's gym and they'll train me for my SBC fights."

The grin came, so big and filled with pride that Dex felt like whooping. "Damn, I *told* you that you were good!"

"Yeah, you did." Hart sobered. "It's the truth, Dex, I couldn't have done it without you."

"Bullshit."

"You started out sparring with me, encouraging me. And then filling in for me so that I didn't have to worry about everyone finding out . . . it means a lot, Dex. Seriously."

Only on the rarest of occasions did Hart get overly sentimental. Usually it was at funerals, or during Christmas.

Because no one had died, and it wasn't a holiday, Dex knew just how much this meant to his brother. He was glad he'd been there to do what he could to make it easier for him. "So now you're going to tell people, right?"

"Soon." He went quiet, then said, "Can you imagine Joe's reaction?"

Their cousin Joe was fast closing in on his midforties. Not that it slowed him down any. Since marrying nearly a decade ago, he'd gotten domesticated. He'd given up some dangerous careers, and now ran a vacation lake with his wife and kids.

But in the ways that counted, Joe remained as hard-edged as ever. All the Winstons were loyal to family, but Joe especially took pride in family.

"Joe will blab to Cole and Chase and the others as soon as he knows," Dex predicted.

"And he'll probably take credit for teaching us to defend ourselves." Hart laughed. "I'm looking forward to telling them all, I really am. I just want everything official before I do, and that should be any day now."

Dex made a decision. "Fine, I'll wait. But you're on a timeline."

"I'll get it all finalized quick as I can. Scout's honor." Hart went silent a moment. "I know you, Dex. I realize this girl is important to you, so I'm sorry to leave you hanging like this."

Dex was sorry, too. He said only, "She doesn't even know my real name, Hart. But you'll like this part. She wants to know why I'm suddenly so different."

"From what?"

"You."

"But I barely knew the girl!"

Dex felt deep satisfaction in the truth. "Apparently you'd said and done enough, because she knows something is up. She can tell a difference between us."

"The hell you say."

"Scout's honor," Dex said, mocking him.

"Huh. I suppose it's possible. But I'm not entirely convinced. You're just seduced because she likes your writing enough to steal your words."

Dex grinned. "Luckily no one gives a shit what you think."

Still in a good mood, Hart laughed at Dex. "Hang in there, brother. It'll all be over with soon enough."

After they hung up, Dex started toward the apartment building, but pulled up short when he saw Christy standing there in the doorway, watching him.

Had she overheard? If so, she hid it well. But then, he'd realized right away that Christy wasn't one for fanfare or exaggerated displays.

Except in bed. Then she really cut loose.

Thoughts now diverted, he looked her over as he approached. He wanted her mouth. Again. On his, and on his body.

Heat skipped down his spine. "Hello, gorgeous."

Unaware of his inner turmoil, she smiled at him, and then at the flowers. "Been shopping?"

"I needed to pick up some supplies." He'd counted on her being a woman partial to wildflowers instead of roses. The sparkle in her green eyes made his question redundant. "Do you like them?"

"They're beautiful." She inhaled the fragrance. "Perfect."

Soft in the heart and head, Dex pulled her into a hug and turned her until they both had their profiles to the lot. "You're perfect." After a kiss that almost got out of hand, he asked, "Where would you like to go tonight?"

"Go?"

"You owe me two more dates, lady. No reneging on our deal." So far, they'd been to dinner, a club, and the theater. Not much of a social expert, Dex was already running out of places to take her.

He'd like her to meet his family. He had a feeling Christy would enjoy the whole crazy lot of them.

And speaking of family . . .

As Dex stood there with his arms looped around her, a big muscle truck pulled into the lot. When Dex glanced at the driver, he nearly swallowed his tongue.

He'd recognize that imposing visage anywhere: His cousin, Joe Winston, had come for a visit.

What the hell?

Joe got out and, seeing Dex, started in his direction.

Thinking fast, Dex turned with Christy in his arms, moving her so she couldn't see Joe. While she laughed at his antics, Dex lifted one finger and made a slice-his-throat motion at Joe.

Just that quick, Joe checked himself and veered off.

Christy glanced over her shoulder—and Joe, without missing a beat, went right on past them both and into the apartment building. He gave a polite nod of greeting, but otherwise, pretended he didn't know Dex from Adam.

Still rattled, Dex ran a million reasons through his mind why Joe might have come calling.

None of them were good.

"Did you see him?"

Dex cleared his throat. "Who?"

"The big guy who just went past us!" She shivered. "He was . . . a little scary, but in a good way."

Dex scowled at her, and that made her laugh.

"Don't get offended. Truthfully, Hart, he reminded me of you, only bigger and probably meaner."

With no idea what to say or how to handle the situation, Dex continued to scowl.

Christy sighed. "Okay, sorry." She peeked at him. "Am I forgiven?"

"You can make it up to me after our date tonight." *If Joe lets me have a date.* Why was he here?

"Actually," Christy said, oblivious to Dex's near miss, "I only owe you one more."

"One more . . . ?"

"Date, silly. The movie we rented—"

"And only half watched," he reminded her.

"Counts." She rested one hand on his chest and stared up into his eyes. "It's not my fault you have an insatiable sexual drive."

Thank God Joe wasn't hanging around to hear that. Dex lowered his voice. "It's entirely your fault. I look at you, and I want you. Hell, I think of you, and I want you."

She smiled. "Well then, if it's all the same to you, I'd rather stay home and have you all to myself."

That warmed him. "You're not hungry?"

"A little, but we could grill. I picked up steaks. And there are some good movies on tonight."

"Yeah?"

She caught the front of his shirt and began back-stepping into the building, taking him along with her. "An *Alien* movie marathon."

Dex frantically searched the interior for Joe, but he'd moved out of sight. "Sounds good to me." They even shared similar tastes in movies.

"And if we stay home," Christy said, thankfully leading him into her apartment, instead of Hart's, "you could indulge your sexual drive all you want."

Dex growled, but forced himself to think straight. "I hope you don't want those steaks anytime soon?"

She reached for his belt buckle. "I'm thinking an hour or so from now."

"Now that's my kind of date." He caught her hands. "But I need to run next door first." When she pretended a pout, he said, "Rubbers."

"Ah."

"I won't be long." He kissed her, and made himself back out the door.

Now to find Joe.

God knew he was dreading it.

Dex crept to Hart's apartment, found the door still locked, and looked around the hallways. "Joe?" He called in a barely audible whisper.

The door opened and Joe stood there—*inside* Hart's apartment. He filled the doorway, rock solid, imposing, and larger than life.

"If we're trying for subterfuge, you suck," Joe told him.

Dex grinned, he couldn't help himself. Stepping in fast and closing the door, he asked, "How'd you get in?"

"I picked the lock. It sucks, too."

Okay, shouldn't have asked. God knew if Joe wanted in, he got in. "Sorry."

He nodded toward the hallway. "Where's your lady friend?"

"She's in her apartment, just across the hall." Dex cleared his throat. "So . . . What are you doing here?"

"You first." Joe folded massive arms over a more massive chest. "Who is she, Hart? A married woman?"

"No!" Surely Joe had to know better than that. "I'd no more do that than you would."

Some of Joe's tension eased. "Engaged then?"

"Not yet." But as soon as his brother let him clear things up . . .

Joe's dark brow lifted. "Do I have to beat it out of you?"

As if he would. Not the least threatened, Dex grinned again. "She's a woman I'm seeing, that's all." He paused, shook his head. "No, that's not all. I care for her a lot. She's . . . special."

"So special that you're afraid for her to meet your most adoring cousin?" He snorted. "Try again, and this time make it believable."

Well hell. There was no way he'd be able to fool Joe. "Can I have your word that you won't tell anyone, not even family?"

"Depends." He eyed Dex up and down. "Tell me first, and then I'll decide."

Knowing that was the best he'd get, Dex said, "She thinks I'm Hart."

Joe scowled. "So you're not . . . Damn it, Dex. What are you two up to?"

Explaining would be tricky—and given Joe's expression, he'd better get to it. "She didn't know Hart very well, so we're not running a scam on her or anything like that. It's just that Hart is off doing something . . . private, so he wanted me to fill in. I did, then I met her, and now . . ." Dex shrugged. "Honestly, I think I'm in love."

After another long, intimidating stare, Joe turned and strode to the couch. He seated himself much as Hart had, with his arms along the couch back. "First, when you're in love, there's no thinking to it. So are you?"

Dex sucked in a breath. "Yes."

"Congratulations. But she thinks you're Hart?"

"Yeah." Running a hand over his head, Dex tried to explain. "It's complicated. She'd met Hart, but didn't know him, not really."

"She knows you?"

"Yeah." His frustration softened. "I think she feels the same."

"You should find out, and fast." After that bit of advice, Joe asked, "So what is Hart doing?"

Knowing it'd be pointless to try to keep it from him, Dex fessed up. "You've heard of the SBC?"

"Yeah."

"He's been training, fighting at smaller venues, but he was just offered a contract with the SBC. He doesn't want family to know until everything is finalized."

Intrigued, Joe sat forward. "No shit?"

"No shit."

"Well, I'll be damned." Joe grinned with pride, then shook his head in bemusement. "And to keep this private, you two came up with the cockamamie plan that now has the woman you love calling you your brother's name?"

Put like that, it sounded even worse. "Yeah. You won't tell anyone?"

"How you two have survived this long . . ." Joe sighed. "I won't say anything, but I suggest he tell the family, and soon."

"He promised he would."

Joe pulled a note from his back pocket. "When you get in touch with Hart, tell him he has another issue to deal with."

Reaching for the note, Dex asked, "What is it?"

"Lisa is trying to reach him."

Persistent woman. "You know her?"

"Met her once by accident. Luna and I were out, Hart and Lisa were out . . . Anyway, she remembered my name and looked me up in the phone directory."

"Damn." Dex stared at the slip of paper as if it could offer insight. In Joe's bold scrawl, he read Lisa's name and number.

Joe shrugged. "She said it's important, but Hart won't return her calls. She asked me to tell him to call her."

Frowning in thought, Dex admitted, "She's called here several times and left messages on the answering machine. I told Hart, but he says she was just a casual date."

"Casual for Hart could mean any number of consequences." He clapped Dex on the shoulder. "Tell him to call her. It's never good to piss off an impatient woman."

Given the lengths Lisa had gone to reach him, Dex felt certain Hart would take care of it right away.

"Right. I'll see to it. And speaking of impatient ladies . . ." He smiled. "I hate to rush you, Joe, but Christy is waiting for me."

"Got one waiting for me, too." He winked, proving the honeymoon hadn't worn off. On his way out the door, he said, "I look forward to meeting her, Dex. Bring her to the lake. Soon."

And that, Dex decided, was a hell of an idea.

Six

Dex watched as Christy finished off the last bite of her steak. She wore only a long T-shirt and panties, her hair loose, her face still flushed.

Even though he knew he was rushing things, he said, "I'd like for you to meet my family."

Her gaze shot to his. "Your family?"

"There are a ton of Winstons, mostly males except for the wives and a sparse selection of female offspring."

That made her laugh. "Dominant male genes, huh?"

"That's what Joe tells me."

"Joe?"

"He's an older cousin, and one hell of a character. Women meet him once, and they don't forget him." Dex didn't tell her that she'd seen him earlier.

"He sounds a little like you."

That made Dex laugh. "Ah . . . no. Not really."

"You have that impact on women. I know once I saw you, I couldn't get you out of my head."

Dex was about to groan, knowing it was Hart she couldn't forget, but then Christy continued.

"I have to admit that knowing you is so much better than just imagining you." She sat back in her seat. "So tell me more about your cousin."

An easy enough subject. "Joe's had a lot of interesting jobs—bounty hunter, bodyguard, private eye—if it's dangerous, Joe has probably done it. But since he married and settled down, he runs a vacation lake with his wife."

"Vacation lake?"

"Yeah, where you can rent boats, go fishing, swimming, that sort of thing. It's really popular and just an hour or so south of us." Dex watched her, then said, "We should go sometime."

"I'd love to." As she drank the last of her lemonade, the ice clinked in her glass. "You've never said much about your family."

Dex crossed his arms on the table. "What do you want to know?"

She shrugged. "Anything. Everything."

"I have a brother, mother, and father. All of them are pretty terrific. What about you?"

"I'm an only child. Mom and Dad invested wisely, so they were able to retire early. Now they do a lot of traveling."

"Do you miss them?"

"Sometimes, but I'm happy that they can spend their retirement doing what they love, so I don't mind too much. They're usually here for holidays, and when they can't be, they ask me to come to them, wherever they might be."

"I'd like to meet them."

"They'd love you, no doubt about it."

Love. Dex smiled at the word. "I'm getting to know you pretty good, Christy Nash."

"You think so, do you?"

"Absolutely." He lifted her wrist and examined the bracelet she now wore, and never took off. "I know that you appreciate simple jewelry."

"It's more beautiful than anything gaudy ever could be."

He glanced at the bouquet of flowers now displayed in a vase in the middle of the table. "You appear to like wildflowers just fine."

"They're my favorites."

Pleased that he'd figured that one out on his own, Dex added, "And since you wanted to stay home, I'm guessing that you aren't big on social gatherings."

"Nope." Then she turned uncertain, glancing at him with doubt. "But I know you are, so—"

"No, honey, I'm not."

She frowned. "But until recently, you were almost never here. You'd come in and immediately go back out again."

"I can explain that." She waited, and Dex said, "Later."

"Later? What's wrong with now?"

Damn, he needed this ruse to end. "Right now, the first movie is set to start." Using his hold on her wrist, Dex hauled her up out of her chair.

"But Hart—"

Dex leaned down and kissed her. "If we hurry, we can get these dishes put away without missing the opening scenes. Since tomorrow is Saturday, I vote we stay up to watch all four movies, then sleep in late tomorrow. And if you're good—"

Laughing, she slugged his arm.

"In the morning, I'll make you breakfast in bed."

"If I'm good, huh?" She put up her chin, teasing and smiling. "Well, I guess I'll just have to give it my best shot."

Catching her close and kissing her again, Dex said against her lips, "Given my personal experience in the matter, I can almost guarantee you'll be not only good, but mind-blowing."

Christy's lips parted. She swallowed. "Hart?"

Damn, damn, damn. He couldn't wait to hear her say his name. "Hmmm."

She stroked a hand down his body, teasing, coy. "I think we should tape the movies and watch them later. What do you think?"

When her hand settled over him through the material of his shorts, Dex sucked in a breath. "I think that's one hell of an idea."

Dex sat up in bed, stretched awake without waking Christy, and after picking up his jeans, crept into the kitchen. One look at the clock and he saw that they had, indeed, slept in late. It was almost ten thirty, and neither of them usually slept beyond eight.

But he'd worn Christy out, he remembered with a smile.

Or she'd worn him out.

However he looked at it, it was a night he wouldn't soon forget but wanted to repeat for the rest of his life. With Christy.

After putting on coffee, Dex noticed his cell phone that he'd left on the kitchen counter. He checked it for any missed calls, but sometime during the night, it must have died. Because the charger was in Hart's apartment, he decided it could wait. For now, he wanted to treat Christy to the breakfast he'd promised her.

He made French toast and bacon, but before he could carry it to her, she showed up in the kitchen.

Dex looked at her, and accepted his fate. Sleep warm and rumpled, red hair wild and eyes still heavy, she stole the last remnants of his heart.

Big, soft, bold emotion choked him. "Good morning."

After a yawn, she nodded and said, "That smells divine."

Even the way she yawned turned him on. "You were supposed to wait in bed so I could surprise you."

"Bed is no fun without you in it." She sprawled into a chair and propped her head on a fist.

Pouring her coffee, Dex took her words to heart and said, "Remember that, okay?"

"You want me to remember so much, I think I should start taking notes."

"Wouldn't hurt." He handed her the coffee. "Ready to eat?"

She eyed him with lascivious intent. "I'm ravenous."

"You're a hussy who needs nourishment." Dex smoothed back her hair. "And God knows I need to recoup. But I appreciate the sentiment."

"Wimp." Still sleepy to the point of looking boneless, she nursed her coffee.

"A dare?" Dex asked her. "Well, we'll see about that. *After* we've eaten."

"Promises, promises."

Dex loved her intimate teasing, and the underlying fact that she wanted him almost as much as he wanted her. "I've got the whole day reserved for you, woman. When I finish loving you silly, you'll need another night of sleep."

The *love* word gave her pause and softened her green eyes. She shivered, looked up at him, and smiled. "I can hardly wait."

Companionable conversation accompanied breakfast, and again Dex thought how easy it was to be with her. He could easily see quiet times like this becoming a cherished part of his routine.

After they'd finished, Christy said, "I need a nice, long, hot shower."

Dex checked his watch. It was almost noon. "While you do that, I think I'll head back to my place. I need to recharge my phone, check the mail, that sort of thing."

Pausing in the doorway, Christy looked at him with solemn sincerity. "We've spent a lot of time together. I know we're moving pretty fast, so if you want to be alone some . . . well, I'd understand."

Hell no, he didn't want to be alone. "Is that what you want?"

"I don't want to impose on you."

"Christy." Knowing he had to give her some facts, with or without the right name, Dex crossed the floor to her. "Truth is, honey, I'm falling for you. Hard."

Her lips parted, and her eyes filled with pleasure. "You are?"

"I enjoy every second with you. I'm happy to spend the rest of the day with you. Hell, the rest of the week would work for me. But if *you* want to be alone—"

"No." She hugged him tight, and then in a small whisper, she admitted, "I'm falling for you, too."

Over the top of her head, Dex closed his eyes, battling the need to spill his guts. *Hurry up, Hart. I need her to know.* "I'm relieved that I don't have to amp up my pursuit."

Laughing, she squeezed him hard. "You, Hart Winston, are so much more than a gorgeous face and bod."

Damn, and double damn. "I'm glad you think so." He released her with a small swat on her plump behind. "Hustle up with that shower, woman. I'll be back before you know it."

As he tried his brother's cell one more time, and had to leave another message, Hart Winston cursed. Why the hell wasn't Dex answering? Surely nothing was wrong. If anything had happened to Dex, he'd be the first to know.

But still it worried him. Even if he was intimately involved with Christy, it wasn't like Dex not to answer.

But just in case, Hart pulled into the far end of the parking lot and surveyed things. He saw his car—the car Dex had been using—parked in front of the building.

Was Dex out with Christy? If so, he could just sneak in, shower, nap, and wait for his brother to get in.

Wearing dark shades and a ball cap, Hart disguised himself as best he could.

He'd almost made it—but the second he got to the top of the stairs, Christy's door opened and, surprised to see him, she laughed. "Hart? What in the world are you doing?"

"Uh . . ." Scrambling, Hart tried to come up with something suitable.

He had nothing.

His beleaguered brain went blank. "Hi, babe."

"Babe?" She gave him a mock look of annoyance—and approached him. "I'm done with my shower."

"Yeah?" *Dex, where are you?* Hart backed up two steps. "That's . . . good."

Her smile twitched. "Are you done charging your phone?" She pulled off his ball cap.

Charging his phone. No wonder the calls hadn't gone through. Must've been a marathon in the sack for Dex's phone to go dead. Hart eyed Christy, found her cute, but just didn't see what Dex must see. "Actually," he said, trying to stall for time, "I was just about to—"

"What's the matter, Hart?" She eyed him with suspicion.

Oh hell. Going on the defense, he said, "I don't know what you mean."

"Something's going on, isn't it?"

"No. Of course not." He looked at his apartment door, willing it to open, willing Dex to materialize.

He didn't.

"If nothing's wrong, then come here." She reached for him. "I missed you."

Oh shit. Hart tried backpedaling again, but the little redhead pursued him. She backed him into a wall, glanced around to make sure no other neighbors intruded, and then she kissed him.

Really kissed him.

Tongues. Heat. Plenty of damp, hungry passion.

His sunglasses fell off. His knees—but only his knees, thank God—stiffened.

What to do, what to do? Hart kept his hands rigid at his sides and tried not to enjoy the play of her soft mouth on his.

Damn, she was good.

Wrong, in a million ways, *wrong*. Dex would kill him. But if he pushed her away, she'd think Dex had rejected her.

If he didn't . . . well, he couldn't continue this one-sided make-out with his brother's woman.

He *had* to stop this—for his own sake, if not for the sake of honor.

Hands going to her upper arms, Hart held her for only a split second, and then peeled her away.

"Wow." He cleared his throat, felt her warm little body squirming closer, and added, "That was . . . great."

She pulled back to look into his eyes. "Hart?"

He smiled—and she lurched back, stumbling away from him. "What's going on?"

Now she looked frightened, and that had never been his intent. "Nothing." He held out a hand to her. "You just . . . uh, took me by surprise."

Moving farther away, her gaze locked to his, she said, "You're not Hart."

Perceptive woman. "You don't think so?"

"I know so." She looked him up and down and glared with both fear and rage. "Who are you?"

Hart's eyes narrowed, but really, what would be the point of convincing her?

Accepting that the gig was up, Hart relaxed his stance, leaned against the wall, and crossed his arms. "Actually, I am."

She shook her head. "No."

It struck him that she truly could tell them apart. Not even knowing they were twins, she sensed a difference. "Hang tight, sweets. Don't move."

"Sweets? Babe? You are *not* Hart Winston."

He held up a finger, asking for patience. Taking the few steps necessary to his apartment door, Hart dug out his key, opened it, and saw Dex sitting at the computer.

Dex faced him in surprise. "What the hell? Hart, are you nuts? What are you doing here?"

Bracing an arm on the doorjamb, Hart explained, "Truthfully, brother, a few seconds ago I was being molested by your ladylove."

Dex's brows shot up high, then came down in icy fury. He rose out of his chair.

"Right now," Hart continued before Dex decided to attack him,

"I'm hoping for some assistance because, honestly, Dex, she noticed the difference, and it's unnerving her."

"Damn it." Dex charged forward, but before he reached the door, Christy leaned in under Hart's arm. She stared. Blinked.

"Oh shit," Dex said, then rushed forward. "Honey, I can explain."

"There are two of you."

Hart looked down at her, moved back a safe distance, and had to grin at the absurdity of it. "I'm Hart Winston." He gave a slight, mocking bow. "The guy who's moonstruck over you is my brother, Dex."

She paid him no mind at all. "Dex? So . . . you don't live here?"

Feeling invisible, Hart crossed his arms and watched.

Dex approached her with due caution. "Let me explain."

"Yeah, do."

Dex launched into speech. "Hart needed a little subterfuge and asked me to be him for a while. It wouldn't have been a problem if I hadn't fallen in love with you."

Love? Hart stopped relaxing. "I'll be damned, Dex. Declarations and all?"

Christy said to him, "Shut up." Then back to Dex, she accused, "You could have told me."

Ignoring the order to be silent, Hart said, "He wanted to; he really did. But I went on bended knee and pleaded. He's my brother. My twin. He's honor bound to keep all my secrets."

Glaring at him, Christy said, "You're so full of it. He should have told me."

"No. He should never have gotten involved with you in the first place. I told him so, but he didn't listen. I recall him saying something about being unable to resist you, and some other melodramatic crap like that."

Dex shoved Hart's shoulder hard. "*Shut up*, Hart."

Appearing somewhere between tears and explosive fury, Christy touched Dex. "So . . . your name is Dex?"

"Dexter Winston. I'm the writer, though my pen name, as you know, is Dex Baxter. Hart is the painter. Well, he's also a fighter now, which is why he didn't want anyone to know—"

"*Dex*."

He sighed. "Other than that, I haven't lied to you, Christy, I swear. Everything I said, everything I asked you to remember . . ." He drew in a deep breath, moved closer to her. "Everything I've done with you, and who I've been with you, is true."

She nodded slowly. "Odd bits and pieces are coming back to me. All that talk about how you wanted me to trust you, that you wanted me to promise not to be mad before we . . ." She glanced uneasily at Hart.

"Go ahead," Hart encouraged her. "I'm a big boy. I can take the sexual details."

Growling, Dex said, "One more word from you, and fighter or not, I will kick your ass."

Hart pretended to zip his lips, then gestured for them to continue. He had a hell of a time holding in his laughter. Dex might not realize it, but Christy was already convinced. For anyone with eyes, it was plain to see the girl was madly in love to the point she'd realized right off that he wasn't his brother.

Confusing, even to him.

But Christy knew.

And even now, with Hart standing right there, the mirror image of Dex, she paid him so little attention he could have been on Mars.

She wanted Dex—regardless of any name he used.

"I feel like a fool."

"Please don't," Dex said. "You're not a fool. I'm a bastard for not leveling with you, regardless of what my brother wanted."

Forgetting that his lips were zipped, Hart said, "He told me that he was going to tell you, and honestly, I asked for a few more days. Look at this from Dex's angle. He'd already started the charade when he met you. Then it was love at first sight, when really, who could predict a thing like that?"

Not looking at him, Christy asked, "Is your brother always this annoying?"

Dex grinned. "Yeah. But I'm not. I'm the good twin."

"That's a fact," Hart said. "He's the best of brothers. So put him out of his misery already."

She turned on him. "Oh, right. And what do you suggest? That I just forget I was duped? That I just forget it was *your* name I've been using at the most intimate times?"

"Well . . ." Hart cleared his throat. "That had to be more awkward for him than you, right?"

"Oh my God." Her eyes widened with comprehension and she glared at Hart. "Was it *you* I called the night I got drunk?"

Hart grinned—and she slugged him hard, right in the gut.

Taken off guard, he huffed, bent over, and wheezed, "Reel her in, bro. She's killing me here."

Dex wrapped his arms around Christy from behind. "I'm sorry, Christy. But I do love you. Hart's right about that. I fell in love with you almost the second I met you. I even changed my lead female character's name to yours, and that was well before we were intimate." He turned her in his arms, put two fingers under her chin. "If you'll be honest, you'll admit that you're falling in love with me, too."

"No."

Dex stiffened, and that made Hart stiffen. If Christy Nash broke his brother's heart, then to hell with her, she wasn't the right one after all.

Christy smiled up at Dex. "I'm not falling in love with you, because I'm already full-blown, madly, head over heels crazy about you."

"All right," Hart said, putting a fist in the air, relieved that he hadn't been a party to his brother's emotional demolishment.

Dex's grin came slowly. "Yeah?"

"Definitely." Christy kissed him. "Hmmm. Now that's more like it."

"Have I been insulted?" Hart asked.

"Yes." She snuggled in close to Dex's chest. "I was almost there before finding this out. But there were so many conflicting things about you . . . I just couldn't figure them out and they bothered me."

"Like what?"

She leaned back to see him. "Come on, Dex. Please tell me you're not really a chrome and leather person?"

He smiled. "Oak and corduroy."

Hart threw up his arms. "Now she doesn't like my furnishings either?"

"And you really do enjoy small talk with the neighbors, and staying home instead of going out—"

"Yes and yes."

Christy sucked in a deep breath, turned to Hart, and held out her hand. "Hi. I'm Christy Nash."

Grinning, Hart took her hand. "Hart Winston. And as the saying goes, any woman my brother loves is a woman I love. In the platonic sense, of course."

"Understood." She took Dex's hand. "Come on."

"Where are we going?"

"To my place. To talk. And maybe . . . other stuff. But talk first. There's a lot I want explained, and a lot I want to know about you, like where you live, for example. And I want to hear more about this character in the next book who shares my name."

"She's a hot redhead," Dex said.

Christy laughed, ready to drag him into her apartment.

Dex held back. "One second, honey." To Hart, he said, "You need to call Lisa."

"I will."

"No, I mean you need to call her now." He dug out the note he'd been carrying in his pocket. "Joe came by. She looked him up, Hart, just in an effort to reach you."

"The hell you say." He took the note, looked it over. "Joe was here?"

Dex rubbed his brow, and turned back to Christy. "Remember the big guy you noticed? The one—"

"Who looked a little like you? How could I forget?"

Dex grinned. "That's our cousin, Joe Winston."

As they discussed Joe, Dex and Christy went into her apartment—all but dismissing Hart from their minds.

Christy's door closed, and Hart stood there alone in the hallway, smiling, feeling pretty damn good about his awkward homecoming.

He wanted what his brother now had.

Some day.

But for right now he had the start of a new career in the SBC, and an obviously agitated woman after him. That was more than one man could handle.

What could Lisa want?

He'd call her first, and then he'd call his family.

The contracts were signed and everything was official, but Hart had a feeling he had to get his good news in now, before his brother stole the show with his own announcement.

Christy Nash would quickly become a member of the Winston clan. That's how it was in their family.

It was a pretty good place to be.

The Luck of the Irish

Deirdre Martin

One

God, the ass on him. The shoulders. The big, calloused hands and the biceps straining against the sleeves of the T-shirt. The dark, tousled hair and the unnerving directness in those sapphire blue eyes. And of course, the Irishman's easy way with words. Brendan Kelly.

Maggie O'Brien watched him surreptitiously from behind the bar at her family's pub, the Wild Hart. A revered fixture of New York's Hell's Kitchen, the pub was undergoing a face-lift. That's why Brendan Kelly was here: He and his Uncle Joe were doing the work. In the dining area, custom wainscoting and beautiful, dark maple booths were being installed. Maggie's parents knew Joe from way back; he'd emigrated from Ireland to the States the same time they had. In fact, he'd done much of the original work on the Wild Hart's interior when her parents had bought it in the late sixties. If there was one thing Maggie had learned growing up, it was how tight the Irish immigrant community was. More than half her parents' friends came from "the ould sod" as well. She wasn't surprised they'd once again tapped Joe to perform his carpentry magic.

The dining section at the rear of the pub was closed during the day while Brendan and his uncle worked. But this didn't stop Maggie's mother from making lunch for the two of them daily and expecting Maggie to serve it to them. She was, after all, a waitress in the family business, at least until she got her act together following her ugly divorce from Tom Meyers, the most charming con man on the eastern seaboard. A real wheeler-dealer, he'd crushed Maggie's heart while also managing to run through all her savings. Unlike her parents, Maggie no longer wanted to kill Tom. Mostly, she was mad at herself for being so impetuous, marrying the bastard after a six-week courtship. Two years of her life wasted. Never again, she vowed. She didn't care if she died an old woman alone in her bed: Never again would she be taken in by a charmer.

Maggie felt lucky that she had her family to come back to, no questions asked. She loved being able to work with her baby brother, Liam, the bad boy, who'd taken over from her father as bartender at the Wild Hart.

Maggie's mother bustled out of the kitchen, handing a plate of her bangers and mash over to Maggie. "Give this to Brendan," she instructed, the soft lilt of her brogue still intact after more than forty years in the States. "He looks famished."

Maggie chuckled. Everyone looked famished to her mother. "Where's Joe?" Maggie asked, holding the giant plate heaped with food.

"Out getting some more linseed oil." Her mother smiled slyly. "Don't think I don't see you looking at Brendan Kelly like he's a choice piece of meat you want to devour. What happened to that vow of celibacy you took after your divorce? You seem to have forgotten that pretty quick."

Liam laughed as he handed her a Guinness to take over to Brendan. Maggie scowled at both of them. Her mother had gotten it wrong: Brendan was the one who'd been looking at *her* for two days straight. Boldly. Appraisingly. She had a right to look back, didn't she?

Sighing with resignation, Maggie brought Brendan his food. "Lunch," she said, plunking the plate and beer down in front of him as he slid into one of the completed booths.

"Ah, thanks," said Brendan gratefully, wiping sweat off his brow in a gesture Maggie told herself was not sexy. He took a long pull off his beer. "Perfect."

"I'll put it on your tab."

Brendan laughed, gesturing at the bench across from him. "Care to join me?"

Maggie's eyes shot to the bar. Her mother had gone back into the kitchen, but of course Liam was still there, and would tease her like hell if she sat down. In fact, he was watching them right now. He looked highly amused. Maggie threw her brother her best "Mind your business" look and sat down anyway.

"I can only sit for a minute."

Brendan looked perplexed. "You've no other customers."

"So? That doesn't mean I don't have work to do."

Brendan shrugged. "Suit yourself." He cut a piece of sausage, wolfing it down. Her mother was right—he was famished after all. "Joe tells me you've just come off a bad marriage."

"What a great way to open a conversation," Maggie replied dryly. God, she'd wring the old busybody's neck when he got back. "What else did he tell you?"

"Things." Brendan looked apologetic. "Sorry if I embarrassed you."

"It's all right. Why were the two of you talking about me?"

"He was just, you know, filling me in on your family."

"He tell you anything else?"

"Well, that's for me to know and for you to find out," Brendan replied with a wink.

Maggie felt unwanted heat flash through her body. "I suppose you think that's flirtatious."

"You don't?"

"I don't like playing games," Maggie said sharply.

"Pity," Brendan murmured. His expression was semiseductive as he took another long drink of his beer, his eyes pinned to her. Maggie felt like she was sitting across from him naked. She would not be taken in by this overconfident, brazen charmer. She would not.

She tossed back her long, black hair, folding her arms across her chest. "How 'bout I find out a few things about *you*?" she challenged.

Brendan shrugged diffidently. "Feel free. I've nothing to hide."

"How long have you been here?"

"About ten years."

"Are you married?"

His eyes danced with mischief. "Why are you asking? Interested?"

"In your dreams," Maggie scoffed. "I was just wondering if you were one of those creeps who flirt with the ladies while your lovely wife slaves away at home."

"Encountered many of these creeps, have you?"

"I was married to one." Jesus, why was she telling him this? She changed the subject. "Do you ever regret coming over? I mean, the economy is booming back in Ireland, isn't it?"

"Well, it wasn't when I left," Brendan muttered.

Maggie raised an eyebrow. "Have I hit a nerve, Mr. Kelly?"

"How do you know I've got any?"

"Don't dodge the question."

"I'm not. It was just a statement of fact. When I came over here—one of the reasons I *came* over here—the Irish economy was in the toilet."

"Fair enough."

Brendan cocked his head. "You always been a waitress, then?"

"Why don't you ask your uncle Joe, since he seems to know all about me."

Brendan laughed delightedly. "You're very cheeky, you know that?"

Maggie felt another blush overtake her. *Cheeky*—not a word

you often heard American men use. Yet it was one she'd heard all her life, courtesy of her County Cork–born father. *You cheeky thing, would you ever stop giving me lip and go help your mother in the kitchen? Jaysus help me, the cheek I have to put up with, and from my own daughter.* Her father always said it affectionately; the same way this strapping, flirtatious Irishman had.

Maggie rose, unable to resist cocking her hip. "Does cheekiness bother you?"

"Not at all. Shows spirit."

"So you like spirited women."

"Yes, I do."

They were flirting. *Harmless enough*, she told herself. Didn't mean she was going to forget her vow not to be suckered.

Brendan's expression was playful as he rolled his glass of beer between his hands. "Would you like to know what else I like in a woman?"

Maggie's mouth fell open in indignation, but inside, her heart was beating wildly. "You cocky bastard!"

"I'll take it that's a no. Though you're the one who started us down this conversational road with your cheekiness." He pushed his empty plate of food aside.

"Well, we've reached a fork in that road," Maggie said stiffly as she snatched his plate, "and it's time for you to go one way and me to go the other."

"What are you afraid of?"

"I'm not afraid!" Maggie scoffed. "I'd just rather not share my 'road' with an arrogant Irishman." *Or any other man, for that matter.*

Brendan shook his head sadly. "Big mistake."

Maggie snorted. "Don't flatter yourself."

"Prove to me you're not afraid, then. Come out for a drink with me tomorrow night."

"I don't need to prove anything to *you*!" *Talk about nerve.*

"Then forget the part about proving something to me," said

Brendan, draining his beer. "Come out for a drink anyway. Tomorrow night."

"Why would I want to do that?"

"Why wouldn't you?"

Maggie, never one to resist a challenge, though in this case she knew she should, took the bait. "Where?"

"Maxie's Supper Club? Around eight?"

"Fine."

"Shall I pick you up here?"

"I know where Maxie's is. I can get there on my own."

"Suit yourself."

"See you at eight tomorrow, then." She began walking away, then abruptly turned around. "Need anything else?"

Brendan grinned devilishly, not saying a word.

Maggie whirled away from him so he couldn't see her face turn red for the third time. *Jerk*, she thought. *Arrogant egotistical swine.*

But if that were the case, why was she already looking forward to tomorrow night?

Brendan was bone tired by the time he got home, but it was the best kind of tired, the kind resulting from a hard day's physical labor well done. He said a small prayer that the red light on his answering machine wouldn't be blinking when he opened the door, but clearly, the Lord wasn't in his corner today. There it was, flashing like a beacon from hell. He closed the door, took off his work boots, and forced himself to listen to the message, more to get it out of the way than anything else. He assumed it was his brother, Connor, calling from Dublin. He was right.

"Bren, it's Connor. Again. Kudos on avoiding me; you've turned it into an art. Look, I really need to know if you're going to come home to work with me or what. You've been putting off giving me an answer for months now, and it's not fair; I've got guys here who would kill for what I'm offering you.

"So here's the deal: You've got a month to make up your mind. I'm gonna haunt you on this, because I think you're a fool if you don't come back home. Give my love to Uncle Joe. Call me, you bastard. I miss you."

Brendan groaned, deleting the message before heading into the kitchen to grab a cold one. Connor was right—he *had* been avoiding him. He'd been avoiding the whole issue, because just thinking about it kicked up so much turmoil inside him it was keeping him up nights.

Brendan could stay in the States and continue working for his uncle, who had no kids and promised the business would be passed on to him very soon; or he could go home and work alongside his brother, who was making money hand over fist in an upscale cabinetry business that had tapped into Ireland's galloping economy. Just last week, Connor had boasted about installing custom made bookcases for Bono. *You'd be an eejit to pass up this kind of money*, his brother pointed out. *Plus you'd be back home.*

Brendan closed his eyes. Home. Mum, Dad, Connor, Siobhan, nieces, nephews, friends galore that went all the way back to childhood. He visited Dublin once a year, and every time he left, it felt as if a stone was weighing down his heart. No matter how many times he said it, it was always tough to say good-bye. Then he'd get back to New York, and confusion would set in. Wasn't this home now? It felt like it. But so did Dublin.

He went back out to the living room and sat down on the couch, staring at nothing, really, rubbing his temples. Ten years ago, when unemployment was so high in Ireland people joked about it being a third world country, his uncle Joe had offered him an out. *Come to America and work for me. I'll teach you all you need to know. You can get your citizenship.* At the time, thousands of Irish were coming illegally to New York each year, getting jobs at Irish bars and in construction. The offer of being able to work legally in the "land of opportunity" was too good to pass up—plus, he loved his uncle dearly.

So he went—not only willingly, but quite happily, glad his brother didn't resent him for it. But then he wouldn't, would he? Connor always said he'd rather cut off one of his arms than leave Ireland.

"Feck," Brendan cursed softly. He was mere months away from getting his citizenship. *Months.* His uncle *had* taught him all he knew, and now he was as good a craftsman as the old man. As Uncle Joe had told him countless times down the years, Brendan was his surrogate son. The business would be his in six months or so. He'd have his own business in a city he loved, a place where he'd made a lot of friends.

Connor's offer meant going home, possibly making a lot more money than he did now. It also meant losing a second shot at citizenship if Uncle Joe died and he had no one to sponsor him if he wanted to return to the States. If the Irish economy took a nosedive, he'd be right back where he'd started a decade ago. And he'd be wounding his uncle terribly.

Brendan sighed. He needed to come clean with Joe and tell him about Connor's offer. If he did decide to take it, it wouldn't be right to just spring it on the old man at the end of the month. He owed his uncle more than that. He owed his uncle . . . everything. *Feck.*

He shook his head, his shoulders rising and falling wearily as he took a long, tired breath. He'd finish his beer, then jump in the shower and make an early night of it, since his uncle wanted to start work bright and early tomorrow. He wanted to be well rested when he went for drinks with Maggie.

Maggie O'Brien. He'd been so amused by that proud toss of her head, pretending she wasn't interested when he had felt her eyes watching him for two solid days. He hadn't been this attracted to a woman in a long time. It was probably wrong to have asked his uncle about her. Then again, she'd turned things around on him quite nicely, hadn't she? Not the type to take any guff. Beautiful as hell, acting as if she were doing him a favor by going for a drink with him. He loved the challenge that presented, the slow breaking down of her defenses to reveal the real woman. That's what he'd think about for the next few days. That's what he'd think about tonight and tomorrow. Maggie O'Brien. Period.

Two

"You're late. On purpose, I suppose."

Maggie suppressed a small smile as she slid onto the barstool next to Brendan's at Maxie's. He was right, of course. There was no way she wanted to look overeager by arriving before him, which would make her look desperate (which she wasn't), or breezing through the door right on time, which would make her neurotic. She preferred he squirm a little, perhaps worry that she'd changed her mind. Maybe that would cut his ego down a peg or two.

Brendan slid off his stool, extending a hand. "May I take your coat?"

"Yes, thank you."

Maggie shucked her jacket and handed it to him, impressed by his manners. She tried to remember the last time she was at Maxie's. It was a few years back with her loser ex-husband.

The place was packed. Some people, like her sister Sinead, felt suffocated in bars, overwhelmed by the noise and the forced intimacy with strangers, but not Maggie. She loved growing up in her parents' pub, enjoying the energy and the mix of people who walked through the door. There were so many regulars at the Wild Hart that it often felt like an extended family.

She turned to see Brendan wending his way back to her through the dense crowd, an adorable, crooked smile on his face. Her heart lurched. He was so striking that other women noticed him. It irked her, even though she knew she had no right to feel that way.

"It's packed tonight," he noted as he returned to her side.

"Always is. What made you pick Maxie's?"

Brendan grinned as he pointed to the bartender. "This man right here. I know him from Dublin. Which is why our drinks are going to be on the house, right, Aidan?"

"You're a cheap bastard, Kelly," said Aidan before extending a warm hand to Maggie. "Aidan Mullen."

"Maggie O'Brien."

"Nice to meet you, Maggie. What's your pleasure, lovely lady?"

Another Irish charmer, Maggie thought. For once she'd like to meet an Irishman who didn't lay it on thick within a minute of meeting. "A mojito, please," said Maggie.

Aidan winked at her. "A mojito it is." He turned to Brendan. "Another Guinness for you, boyo?"

"Mother's milk, as they say back home," Brendan joked, nodding yes.

Aidan leaned over the bar toward Maggie. "Don't let this one fool you. He may come across all smooth and interesting, but he's boring as one of your granny's tea parties."

Maggie laughed. "I'll keep that in mind."

She felt Brendan's palm against the small of her back, protective and proprietary, and liked it. She imagined the heat emanating from his palm leaving a burning imprint on her skin, and suppressed a shiver. God, how pathetic was she, turned on by the mere touch of a man's hand?

"There's a small table opening up along the wall there," Brendan murmured into her ear, pointing toward the back of the bar. "Let's grab it." His warm breath in her ear felt intimate, giving her goose bumps. She didn't like the way he was making her feel without even trying.

Maggie nodded silently as Brendan steered her through the crowd. She caught more women looking at him, but instead of feeling irked by it, she felt a little smug.

Brendan pulled out her chair for her, and Maggie sat down. "I see your mother taught you manners," she said dryly.

Brendan ducked his head in embarrassment. "I know; I'm a bit old-fashioned."

"It's nice," Maggie admitted. Uncomfortable, she glanced around, desperate for her drink to arrive so she'd have some kind of prop. She nearly lunged at the waitress's hand when her mojito arrived, suppressing the urge to shake her in disbelief when the waitress asked if they needed anything else in the thickest brogue she'd heard since her father's.

"Is everyone who works here Irish?" she asked Brendan after the waitress departed.

"Pretty much."

"And you know them all?"

"Pretty much."

The Irish, thought Maggie. *Such a tight-knit little group.* "Do you have any friends who aren't Irish?"

Brendan looked mildly insulted. "Of course I do."

"Well, that's good."

"Why is it good?"

"Because . . ." Flustered, Maggie couldn't provide an adequate answer. "I'm sorry. That was a dumb thing to ask."

Brendan sighed heavily. "We're not getting off to a very good start, are we?"

"Afraid not."

"Then we'll pretend we're in a movie: *Brendan and Maggie's First Date*, scene one, take two."

Maggie held up a hand. "Whoa, whoa, wait. This is not a *date*."

"Okay. Sorry. Drinks. *Brendan and Maggie's First Drink To-*

gether. Maybe we should start with a small toast," Brendan suggested.

Maggie looked skeptical. "To—?"

"Sharing the road?"

It took Maggie a minute to remember their conversation from the day before. "If that's what you want."

Brendan's face fell. "You don't seem very enthused."

"It's a weird toast."

Brendan raised an eyebrow. "I thought it was poetic. Can you think of anything better?"

Shit, she hated being put on the spot; it always made her mind blank instantly. "I guess not." She raised her glass high. "To sharing the road for a very brief time over drinks."

Brendan laughed. "Good one."

Maggie clinked her glass against his.

Brendan put his beer mug down with a resounding plunk. "So, what would you like to talk about?"

"It's your responsibility to get the conversation ball rolling," said Maggie, taking a sip of her mojito, which was god-awful. "This was your idea."

"Too true." He leaned back in his chair, curiosity sparking in his eyes. "How about I tell you what I know about you?"

Maggie closed her eyes for a moment, relishing the image of herself choking Joe Kelly until his eyes popped out of their sockets. And then she realized something. "You still haven't told me the real reason you and Joe were discussing me. Were you pumping him for information about me?" she asked coyly.

Brendan looked embarrassed and Maggie loved it, the sight of the suave, self-confident alpha male looking like he'd just been busted with his hand in the cookie jar. Brendan coughed into his closed fist. "So what if I was?"

"I can't say I'm surprised," Maggie continued breezily. "You were checking me out the minute you walked through the door of my parents' pub."

"Takes one to know one, love."

Maggie's gaze shot away as she reached for her drink, furious at her body's betrayal as she felt her face go crimson.

"There's nothing wrong with appreciating a good-looking man," Brendan continued playfully, "just like there's nothing wrong with appreciating a good-looking woman. Admit it: You'd have been insulted if I hadn't checked you out."

"I'm not an egomaniac, you know. Unlike someone else at this table."

"Let's not talk about egos. Let's have a proper conversation, Miss Maggie O'Brien."

One drink turned to two, followed by a casual dinner. Decent pub fare, but nowhere near as good as the food at the Wild Hart.

It unnerved Maggie how easy Brendan was to talk to. Once they'd gotten past their initial awkwardness, the words just flowed; but there was still something guarded about him she couldn't quite figure out. One minute, he was hanging on her every word; the next he seemed distracted. She didn't feel she could ask him about it, since she really didn't know him well.

The problem was, she wanted to. She wanted to bombard him with questions until he told her to shut up.

God, he was funny. He came from a big, boisterous, Irish family like her own, so he appreciated her stories. She could tell he loved his family as much as she loved hers, though there was a tinge of melancholy that stole into his eyes whenever he talked about them. He missed them, and he obviously missed Dublin, too. But it was also clear he loved working with his uncle, and he considered himself a New Yorker.

Brendan was the first person outside her family she spoke to at length about what had happened with her ex; that's how comfortable he made her. He seemed to genuinely want to know, and in return offered up a somewhat abbreviated (she assumed) version of his own romantic history. He told Maggie that his last girlfriend seemed more enamored with his being a foreigner than with him, seeing him as somehow exotic—until some rich guy with an apartment on the Upper East Side came along. "I make nice money," he told Maggie. "But not *that* much."

Maggie accepted his offer to walk her home. She was somewhat embarrassed that she was living with her parents in the apartment above the pub, but Brendan seemed unfazed. "That's what family's for," he told her. "To be there for each other. You'll get your own place when you've got enough saved up. I stayed with my uncle until I could afford a place of my own."

Arriving at the Wild Hart, Maggie made sure they didn't stand directly in front of the window. The last thing she needed was Liam spying on the two of them. She was sure the whole family knew she was going out for drinks with Brendan. Nothing was sacred in the O'Brien family. Nothing. Of course, why she'd told her brother in the first place was beyond her.

Brendan cocked his head in the direction of the front window. "Shouldn't I go inside and say hello to Liam?"

Maggie groaned. "God, please, no. I'm sure he told my parents we went out for drinks and they're in there waiting to pounce on me the minute I walk through the door. If we both walk in there, my father will break out his tin whistle and start playing the wedding march."

Brendan chuckled.

Maggie rocked on her toes nervously, staring down at the pavement. "So, um, thanks for the drinks."

"Still calling it that, are you? Call me mad, but it seems to me it wound up being a proper date."

Maggie didn't know what to say as she looked up at him. She did *not* want to like Brendan Kelly as much as she did. She hadn't felt this enchanted by a man since her ex wove his spell. It frightened her, considering how *that* had turned out. Her resolve to keep her eyes open and her legs closed was weakening by the second.

"So, would you like to go out again?" Brendan asked. His tone, as well as his expression, was studiedly casual.

"On a *proper date*?"

"Call it whatever you need to call it," Brendan replied flirtatiously, "just as long as you say 'Yes.' "

Maggie's head was swimming. "Listen, Brendan. I think you're great, but I really don't want to get involved with anyone right now."

"Me neither," he said. "Maybe we could just spend time together, casually. Have a bit of fun."

A bit of fun. He meant sex; of course he did. She imagined herself riding him, prompting an explosion of heat through her body.

"Casual is perfect," Maggie said briskly. *That way I don't get hurt. That way I don't risk falling for you.*

"Good. Glad we're on the same wavelength. Allow me to rephrase my question, then. Would you like to go out again *casually*?"

"Sure. Why not?"

"What's your schedule?"

"I have Thursday night off."

"Great. Think about what you want to do and we can talk about it tomorrow."

"Right," Maggie said weakly. It had totally slipped her mind that she'd see him tomorrow when he came to work at the pub. Maybe she'd make herself scarce.

She gestured feebly at the Wild Hart. "I guess I'll go in now. I'm kind of tired. Thanks for a nice . . . date."

"No, thank *you.*" He lightly put his hands on her shoulders. "You know, I've been looking at those full, beautiful lips of yours all night, wondering, 'What might it be like to kiss her?' Would you mind if I found out?"

Maggie staggered back slightly, desire gripping her like a vise. "I wouldn't mind," she whispered.

Brendan's eyes kindled with desire as he softly put his mouth to hers, taking her in his arms. Mouth to mouth, his lips scorching hers, Maggie felt herself sliding off the edge of the world. This was no "casual" kiss; within seconds it turned passionate and deep, primal. She hungered for this man as surely as he hungered for her. The way he held her so tight . . . the hard press of their bodies as he maneuvered her so she was up against the wall . . . it was intense, making her ache from a deep place that hadn't been awakened in a very long time. But she had to put a stop to it, fearful of what would happen if she let her galloping desire take over.

Reluctantly, she tore her mouth from his. "I really—I really—should go inside. You must be pretty tired, and I'm sure you have a full day's work ahead of you tomorrow."

"Yes." Brendan brushed his lips softly against hers one final time. "Sleep well, Maggie O'Brien," he said with a wink.

And then he was off down the street, leaving her alone with her confusion.

Do I know my family or what? Maggie thought to herself as she walked in the door of the Wild Hart to find her parents there as she'd predicted. Their eyes lit up when they spotted her, and within seconds they descended on her like two hawks on innocent prey. She shot Liam a dirty look, which he pretended to ignore.

"Well, how did it go?" her mother asked eagerly.

Maggie feigned innocence just to get her goat. "How did what go?"

Her mother's tongue clucked in exasperation. "You know what. Your date with Brendan Kelly."

"It wasn't a date, Mom," said Maggie. "We just met for drinks."

"You could have done that here," said her father.

"Really? So all of you could hang around and pretend you weren't watching us?"

"We'd never!" her mother insisted.

"Yeah, right."

Maggie grabbed a seat next to Peggy McKenzie, one of her mother's bingo friends from church. She'd known Maggie since she was a child. Peggy always stopped in on Thursday nights after her knitting group. Usually she sat in one of the booths in the back and chatted briefly with Maggie's mother, but since the dining area was under construction, she was forced to sit at the bar. Maggie's eyes scanned the long bar. Shit—the guy the family called "the Mouth" was here tonight, sitting on the other side of Peggy. The guy had an opinion and advice about everything.

Peggy smiled at Maggie, planting an affectionate kiss on her cheek. "Your mother tells me you had a big date tonight."

"It wasn't a date," Maggie said wearily. "It was just drinks."

The Mouth leaned over, craning his neck past Peggy McKenzie so he could see Maggie. "Be careful. Drinks can lead to other things. Love. Then the inevitable heartbreak."

"I take it you've had your heart broken?" asked Maggie, feeling like she had to ask.

"Oh yes," the Mouth said sadly.

"What happened?" Peggy asked. "Did she leave you?"

"No," the Mouth sighed. "Got kicked in the head by a horse. I haven't been able to watch the Kentucky Derby ever since."

"That's really sad," said Maggie, even though she wanted to laugh.

"You never know what's going to happen," the Mouth continued. "So just be careful."

"I will," Maggie promised. Liam walked toward her end of the bar and Maggie reached over to grab his shirt. "You," she hissed, "are going to die."

Liam shook her off. "I don't understand why," he said innocently.

"We'll talk about it tomorrow morning at breakfast, okay?"

"If you want."

"I do."

Maggie said her good nights and went upstairs. *Sleep well*, Brendan had said to her. He had to be kidding.

Three

"You wanted to see me?"

Maggie glowered at Liam as he sauntered into their parents' kitchen bright and early. This had been his ritual ever since he'd moved into his own place right out of high school: pop upstairs for a cup of coffee, shoot the breeze, then sit down with the folks to discuss the previous night's take and what needed to be ordered for the bar. Right now, their parents were downstairs talking to Joe Kelly and Brendan.

"I can't believe you told Mom and Dad about my drinks date."

"You mean your date date."

"Drinks date," Maggie said again, taking a bite of her dry toast. She was trying to drop a little weight; not that she was heavy, but her ex, Tom, had constantly teased her about "her fat, dimpled Irish ass," and she still wasn't over it. She'd never really been motivated to do anything about it before, especially since she wasn't even sure if it were true, but now . . .

"Why do you keep insisting it was a date date?" she quizzed her brother. "What's it to you?"

Liam grabbed a mug and poured himself a cup of coffee. "I'm just curious, especially since you've told anyone who'd listen that you were done with the male of the species."

"That's not true," she replied crossly.

"Anyway," said Liam, "it made Mom and Dad's day to know you were out with 'a nice Irish boy.' "

Typical, thought Maggie. Anyone with a brogue was wonderful. Maggie had no doubt that if an Irishman held up the bar, her mother would find a way to defend him: "Poor creature. I bet he never got enough love from his mammy and da."

Maggie couldn't resist digging for more info. "Other than his being Irish, is there anything else they like about him?"

"They like that he works hard, and that he's respectful of his uncle. Mom says he comes from good people."

"What, did she have the FBI run a check on his family?" She loved her mother, but Jesus God, she could be a busybody.

"Probably."

Maggie wrapped her hands around her steaming coffee mug. "Do *you* know anything about him?" she murmured.

"I thought it was just drinks." Liam said with a smirk.

"Don't bust my buns, Liam, okay? Just tell me."

Liam shrugged. "All I've heard is he's a good guy. Been here a long time."

Maggie nodded, satisfied, watching as Liam poured so much sugar into his mug she feared he might become diabetic. "Look, Mags: I know Tom burned you badly, but not all guys are conniving jerks, okay? Give Brendan a chance."

Maggie shook her head resolutely. "I'm not looking for a relationship. Just a casual dating situation."

"Then casually date him."

"And what if he ends up wanting more?"

"You mean, what if *you* end up wanting more."

"*No*."

Liam chugged down his coffee. "Why don't you just go with the flow? I know you don't want to get hurt again, but Jesus, if you try to control everything, you're going to wind up like Sinead, with her sky-high blood pressure and daily migraine."

Liam was right. But it was easy for him; he'd always been able to go with the flow. Ultracool, laid-back Liam. Sometimes Maggie envied him, and sometimes she worried about how little he seemed to want from life, perfectly content to tend bar. Not that there was anything wrong with that, but she suspected it might have to do with his always being overshadowed by Quinn. Liam had always felt he couldn't compete with his ambitious, successful older brother, so he didn't even try.

"Mags?"

"*Mmm?*" she said distractedly.

"Sorry—did I just interrupt you picturing Brendan Kelly naked?"

"You're an asshole, you know that, Liam?"

"Yeah, but you love me anyway," said Liam, draining his coffee cup before jumping up to give her a small peck on the cheek. "When are you seeing him again?"

"How do you know I am?"

"Because I popped in downstairs before I came up here and he told me you were going out again."

Maggie cradled her head in her hands. "What is wrong with you people?"

"We're Irish," Liam said matter of factly. "We never shut our cake holes. You know that."

"I swear to God, you're as bad as Mom sometimes."

"We love you, Mags. We just want you to be happy."

"I know you do," said Maggie, softening. "I'm seeing him Thursday."

"What are you two going to do?"

"Don't know yet."

He massaged her shoulders lightly from behind. "Well, whatever it is, let yourself have fun, all right? Like I said, not all of us are pricks."

"I'll try to keep that in mind."

"I'm thinking this might not have been a very good idea."

Maggie nodded in agreement as she and Brendan strolled out of a Times Square movie theater. Not wanting to go out again for drinks and dinner, she suggested they see a movie, one that had come highly recommended by her old high school friend Denise Dugan, who was happily married with three kids in Queens. It was called *This Time Around*, and it was about two old lovers who meet up again after years and rekindle their love. What Denise had failed to tell her was that the sex scenes were extremely steamy, and that the woman had a terminal brain tumor. In the final scene, she dies in her lover's arms, but only after promising him that he'd always feel her love around him. Above her own sobs Maggie could hear women all over the theater reacting the same way.

"Sorry about that," Maggie said with a sniffle. "My friend told me it was a good date movie. I had no idea it was such a downer."

"Not all of it was," Brendan noted, taking her hand.

"No."

Maggie assumed he was referring to the love scenes. She'd never felt so uncomfortable in her life, sitting there next to him as she became more and more aroused. He'd held her hand at different points during the film, and she could have sworn his grip tightened ever so slightly whenever the two lovers made love. It was so hard not to casually press the side of her leg against his, or even rest her head on his rock-solid shoulder.

Out on the sidewalk, she pressed close to him, having no other choice. The shows were just ending at all the Broadway theaters so people were pouring out into the streets. She remembered when Times Square had an exciting edge of danger and seediness. Now it was safe enough to bring kids to.

"Not what it used to be," Brendan said wistfully as if reading her thoughts.

"I know. I kind of miss its old personality."

"Too commercial now. Too touristy."

Maggie poked him playfully in the ribs with her elbow. "Says the man who was probably a goggle-eyed tourist when he arrived here."

"Actually, I wasn't. Joe made me his slave the minute I stepped off the plane."

"My parents have been very happy with the work you two are doing."

"Mmm," said Brendan, looking preoccupied.

His reaction puzzled her. She'd thought his face would light up with pride.

"You and Joe not getting along?"

Brendan squeezed her hand reassuringly. "Nah, nah, nothing like that. We've just got a lot on our plate right now, is all."

Maggie assumed he meant they had a ton of work lined up after they finished the job at the Wild Hart. "But that's good, right? Too much work is probably better than too little."

"Yes, it is. Thankfully, we've never had to worry about not having enough work lined up." His look of preoccupation returned. Perhaps feeling her scrutiny, he changed the subject. "So, what about you?"

"What about me?"

"You like your job?"

"It's okay for now," Maggie murmured. She hoped Joe hadn't told him her family nickname: "Butterfly," chosen because she'd always been flitting from thing to thing, from place to place. It was only after her marriage blew up that she realized her yen for constant movement and change had less to do with wanderlust than running away from herself. Since the divorce she was determined to stay put and figure out who she wanted to be.

Brendan, still on the thread of conversation, asked, "Is there something else you want to do?"

Should she tell him what she'd been thinking about? She decided there was no harm in it, unless he made fun of her, in which case she'd call it a night.

"I was actually thinking of going to massage school," she admitted shyly. "I've taken a couple of weekend seminars and I really liked it a lot."

"Well, if you ever need someone to practice on, feel free to let me know."

"I'll keep that in mind," Maggie said dryly.

"Please do."

"Are you this flirtatious with everyone, or am I special?" she asked casually, not quite making eye contact.

"Do you really want an answer?"

Maggie felt a soft blow to her gut. "I guess not," she said, trying not to sound like she cared.

"You're special." The quick flash of desire in his blue eyes made Maggie weak as she glanced at him. "I hope that's the answer you wanted."

"You'll never know." They were walking west. "We're not going to the Wild Hart, are we?"

"No. I thought—if you wanted—we could go back to my place. For a bit. Nothing intense, now," he hastened to assure her with the faintest hint of teasing in his voice. "Just, you know, *casual*."

"Of course. Though I have to tell you, I'm casually starving." She hadn't eaten a thing before going to the movies, and the bucket of popcorn they'd split hadn't filled her up at all.

"No worries," said Brendan. "I do have a fridge. I'm sure I can figure something out."

Brendan had a fridge, all right, but there wasn't much in it. There was an embarrassed hunch to his shoulders as he peered into it. "Well, I've got coffee, beer, some eggs, and some bacon."

"Streaky bacon, I'll bet." The kind they ate in Ireland; the only kind her parents would eat.

Brendan smiled. "We Celts are so predictable, aren't we?" He paused, his face lighting up. "We could pretend it's breakfast. I'll make us some coffee, cook up some eggs and bacon. That all right with you?"

"Sounds heavenly." Maggie crossed her arms across her chest, hoping to hide the sound of her grumbling stomach. It didn't work.

"When's the last time you ate?"

"This morning," Maggie admitted.

"That doesn't seem very bright."

Maggie hesitated. "I'm on a diet."

She wished she hadn't said it, as Brendan looked her up and down with a baffled expression on his face.

"What the hell for?"

"I just need to drop a few pounds."

"Take it from me—casually, of course—you look fine. You look more than fine. All right?" He quickly ducked his head back into the refrigerator.

"Thank you," Maggie said. A good-looking man had just told her she looked fine, the same one who told her a few nights before that he'd found her lips delectable. Maybe she did look okay.

Maggie took a step toward him. "Can I help out?"

"No. You go sit down in the living room. I'll have our breakfast fixed in no time." His expression was sheepish as he pulled ingredients out of the fridge. "I'm sorry I don't have a kitchen table. We'll have to eat with our plates balanced on our laps."

"It'll be fun," said Maggie.

And she meant it.

The food was delectable. Maggie fought the urge to wolf it down to quell the hunger that had been dogging her all day.

"Not bad for a carpenter," she teased.

"Any eejit can do a fry-up and make a pot of coffee."

Throughout their "breakfast," Maggie kept seeing the flashing red light of the answering machine out of the corner of her eye. If it were her, she would have checked it immediately. The fact that he didn't made her nervous. What if he were seeing someone else? After all, the two of them were only together *casually*. What was to stop him from seeing other women, then? It was driving her crazy.

"The light on your answering machine is blinking," she finally said.

"Mmm."

"Don't you want to check your messages?"

"Not particularly," said Brendan.

"I'm sorry," said Maggie. "I'm nosy."

"It's all right. I'm sure it's just my brother, calling from Ireland. I can ring him back tomorrow."

Maggie nodded, taking his empty plate and putting it on top of hers. "I'll just put these in the kitchen."

"I can do it," said Brendan. "You're the guest. Sit."

The guest. It sounded so formal. Maggie forced a smile and let Brendan bring the dirty dishes into the kitchen, where she heard them clink against the sink. He was back in a minute, sitting close to her on the couch.

The ensuing silence between them, while less than a minute long, felt interminable. Where were the Brendan and Maggie who had chatted their heads off in Maxie's a few nights ago? Paralyzed by thick sexual tension, that's where. She longed to just grab his face and plant one on him. But that would look desperate, wouldn't it? And forward. Damn her mother, and damn the nuns who had drilled it into her head through twelve years of Catholic school that "good girls don't." Hungry as she was to taste his mouth on hers again and to feel the hard press of his body, she was traditional enough to wait for him to make the first move.

Brendan cleared his throat. "So . . . um . . . I would love to kiss you again."

"I would like you to kiss me."

"Maybe we should wait until we've digested our food."

Maggie blinked, unsure for a moment if he was joking. But then he burst out laughing.

"C'mere, Miss Casual," he murmured.

Maggie felt her heart picking up speed as he enfolded her into a hard embrace. She wanted him to seduce her, to make every nerve in her body crackle like a slow igniting flame before bursting into fire. His mouth was already sinking into hers with a heated familiarity that made the grinding ache she'd experienced the other night return. *It's just because you haven't had a man in so long that you want him so badly*, she told herself, but she'd never been terribly good at lying. It was Brendan Kelly whose flesh she wanted to explore. Brendan Kelly she wanted to feel thrusting hard inside her until her senses shredded and the known universe shrank down to just the two of them.

He groaned into her mouth, a groan of such need that her own fevered breathing quickly turned to moans. *Please*, she thought, as one of his greedy hands fisted in her hair while the other tenderly cupped her neck, the fingers gently rubbing the nape. *Devour me*, she thought. *Possess me, tear me to pieces, eat me alive. Now.*

She heard the guttural moan of her name, and responding like the animal she wanted to be, tore her mouth from his to bite down on his hard, muscled shoulder. If he let her, she could make it hurt so good. Brendan's eyes widened in surprise, but then he followed her lead, scraping his teeth along her naked throat before his fingers greedily sought the buttons of her blouse. Their eyes met for a brief second before he laid her back on the couch and pushed her bra up, lowering his head to suckle, to lick, to nip. Wanton desire juddered through her, splintering all semblance of propriety. "You're so beautiful," Brendan whispered.

Maggie gasped, swooning at the animal gaze in his eyes as he gently lay down atop her. His hardness against her was driving her mad and she arched against him—wantonly perhaps. All she could think about now was her own greed, her own hunger. She could see him struggling for self-control as her fingernails scraped against the iron muscles of his back. *He wants to make love to me right here and now*, she thought, *and I want him to. God, please.*

But he didn't. Instead, his large, calloused hands went for the fly of her jeans. "Lift your hips higher," he whispered. Maggie, feeling like she was in a fevered dream, complied, lifting so he could hastily tug down her jeans and soaking panties. And then he was sliding down her body, gently pushing her knees apart. Maggie felt herself losing her mind as he lowered his head and put his hot, wet tongue inside her.

The pure shock of it was almost unbearable. She could not keep from bucking wildly as heat and pressure built, his tongue darting in and out of her to circle and tease before plunging deep inside her again. She was losing control quickly, guttural, animal cries pushing their way up her parched throat. Her hands clenched in Brendan's hair, holding on for dear life as her body began quivering uncontrollably. Brendan, attuned to her tortured excitement, let out a groan of his own before quickening the pace.

And then it happened; she came in a shining instant, explosion after explosion after explosion tearing through her as she screamed like an animal. Brendan Kelly, relieving the pulsing ache she'd felt ever since she'd set eyes on him. *Brendan Kelly.*

Four

"Did you enjoy dessert, Miss O'Brien?"

Maggie felt herself slowly floating back down to earth as she tugged her jeans and panties up before Brendan slid back up her body, stroking back her damp hair.

Maggie's breath was still coming fast. "That was—that was—"

"Not bad for an Irish boy?"

Maggie laughed, but then a long-buried memory came back to her, that of Sister Delphina telling her friend Carmella Bordoni she was whore for kissing her boyfriend in the hall. They were in seventh grade at the time. "Do you think I'm a slut?" she asked Brendan worriedly.

Brendan laughed with surprise. "No."

Relieved, she flicked her tongue against his ear. "Would you like me to reciprocate? After all, this is all about having 'a bit of fun,' right?" For some reason, the phrase, though she made sure it rolled casually off her tongue, made her feel bad. Maybe because it sounded cheap. She'd never been one for casual sex. Maybe she was deluding herself, but right now, nothing about this felt casual.

Brendan ran a gentle finger down her cheek. "I vote we postpone my fun till the next time."

Maggie reared back in shock. "You're kidding me." She'd never, ever encountered a man who didn't want his due after pleasuring her. Never. She felt a momentary panic; maybe he hadn't enjoyed it? Maybe it had turned him off? But no, he was still hard against her.

"Won't you get blue balls or something?" she asked queasily.

Brendan chuckled. "I'll be fine."

"But isn't what you're doing kind of masochistic?"

"I suppose." He kissed her. She could taste herself on his lips, musky, intense. "The truth is, I want an excuse for us to see each other again," he admitted. "I want to prolong this."

"Me, too. Casually, of course." Her gaze glanced off his.

"Of course."

Her fear of seeming easy was back. "Are you sure you don't think I'm slutty because I just—"

"Maggie." His touch was so tender as he cradled her face in his hands that she felt weak in the knees. "I don't know where you're getting this mad idea from."

"From Sister Delphina in seventh grade."

"Well, she can piss off, all right? You're a grown woman. There's nothing wrong with receiving pleasure. Nothing at all."

"But so soon?" she fretted. She couldn't believe how worried she was about this. How non-casually she was behaving.

"We're adults," Brendan pointed out. "On top of which, I didn't know there was any timetable for pleasure. Besides, given my sheer animal magnetism, you really had no choice."

Maggie frowned. "Egomaniac."

"I am."

"At least you admit it."

"I do."

Maggie rolled her eyes affectionately. "All you men are the same. You all think you've got some kind of mojo working, no matter what. I've seen it at my parents' pub time and time again: A guy'll come in, and he can weigh three hundred pounds, or look like he hasn't washed in days, but he still thinks he's got 'it.' "

"Yes, but in my case, I do," Brendan said with a wink.

"Did someone actually tell you that somewhere along the line?"

"No. But I can see it. From the way ladies look at me. You know, with naked hunger. The way you did the first time you saw me."

"I did not look at you with naked hunger!"

"My arse you didn't."

"Takes one to know one," Maggie replied, throwing his own words back in his face.

"I liked it, the way you looked at me that first time," Brendan admitted. "Didn't you like the way I looked at you? You did. Admit it."

"*Handsome But Delusional*: *The Brendan Kelly Story*."

"It's got a ring to it." Brendan stifled a yawn. "It's very late."

"How late?"

"Two." He paused. "You're welcome to stay here if you want. I can sleep on the couch; you can have my room. I have to be at your folks' place early tomorrow morning anyway; we could just go over there together."

Maggie looked at him like he was nuts. "Are you out of your mind? I'm living with my parents, Brendan. My still very Catholic parents. Do you want to bring down my mother's wrath on both our heads?"

Brendan sighed. "My mam is the same way."

"They're all the same way. Doesn't matter how old we are."

"I'll walk you home, then."

"No, no. I'll get a cab," Maggie insisted.

"Don't be daft. It's just a short walk. Besides, the fresh air'll do me good. I have some things to sort out about work."

Brendan hated to admit it, but the walk did him no good at all. He was more confused than ever about the choice he had to make, and the message his pain in the ass brother left him didn't help either.

"Hey, Bren, it's Connor. You're one cheap bastard, you know that? It would be nice if you rang me once in a while, you know.

"Anyway, here's a nice carrot to dangle in front of your face, just in case you haven't made your mind up yet. Guess who rang me? Colin Farrell. Yeah, that's right. He wants me to install new kitchen cabinets, and build some drawers right into the wall of his bedroom. Rich bastard; you can bet I'll charge him ten times what I'd charge someone from our neck of the woods and the eejit'll pay it, too. You come home and work with me, and this is the kind of easy money you'll see day in and day out.

"By the way, Jimmy Brown says to tell you that if you do come back to stay, he's going to kick your arse for never giving him back his Springsteen CDs.

"That's it for now. Love to Uncle Joe. Call me."

Brendan deleted the message. Kitchen cabinets for Colin Farrell, shelves for Bono—the money *had* to be unbelievable. Connor was about to buy his own house, a major miracle considering current housing prices in Ireland. *Shit.* Why couldn't this be a clear-cut decision?

Miserable, he headed to the bedroom. Despite their "casual" acquaintance, Maggie wasn't helping his clarity, either, that was for certain. He brushed his teeth and crawled into bed. He'd talk to his uncle in a few days after wrestling with the issue some more on his own. If the old man reacted by getting upset or looking betrayed, that might help sway him to stay.

"Right, then: You best tell me what's been eating at you. You've been driving me mad for days now."

Brendan felt guilty as he and his uncle slipped into one of the booths they themselves had installed at the Wild Hart, each clutching a pint and a bowl of Irish stew courtesy of Maggie's mother. Joe had wanted to sit at the bar, but Brendan persuaded him otherwise; there was no way he wanted to discuss what was weighing on his mind with Liam right there. He had big ears, that one, like every bartender he'd ever known. Also, he didn't want Maggie to catch wind of what he was about to discuss with his uncle.

Maggie. Christ. How had his feelings gone from casual to consuming so fast? Another week of spending time with her had passed so quickly he couldn't believe it. They had such an easy rhythm between them, and her beauty (every time she looked at him, even now as she took bar customers' orders and pretended she wasn't looking back at him as well, he felt as though he couldn't breathe) staggered him. Part of him wished he and Joe had never taken this job. She was doing his head in, truly.

Brendan took a sip of his beer, looking his uncle straight in the eye. He saw no point in beating around the bush. "It's Connor," he said. "He wants me to come home and work with him. Says his cabinetry business is booming. He's given me a month to decide, or the offer's off the table."

Joe sighed. "Your da told me he's been after you for ages."

Brendan blinked in disbelief. "You knew about this?"

"Of course I knew about it," Joe said with a chuckle. "Your father's been ringing me and boasting his head off about Connor's business for months."

"Why didn't you say anything?"

"Because I didn't want to pressure you. Nor do I want to do that now."

Brendan groaned. "I wish you'd told me. I feel terrible; you must think I'm a sneaky bastard, keeping this a secret from you."

His uncle reached across the table and patted his hand. "I don't think any such thing. I knew you'd come to me eventually."

Brendan ran a hand over his tired face. "Shite, Uncle Joe. I don't know what the feck to do."

"Well, which way is your heart leaning?"

It's leaning toward taking over your business because I want to stay here where Maggie O'Brien is. Wrong reason.

Brendan hesitated. "It goes back and forth. Sometimes, when I think about going home, it excites me. But then I think, working for Connor? We'd end up killing each other inside two weeks.

"And then I think, no, I want to stay here. I love New York, and you've taught me everything I know, in addition to treating me like your own son. And the business—"

"*Will* be yours," Joe finished softly. "I've told you that dozens of times." The older man looked down at his freckled hands, at the swollen knuckles and gnarled fingers. "I'm too old for this kind of work, Brendan. My hands can't take it, nor can my knees and my back. I have to retire soon before I'm crippled completely."

"Is that why it's been taking us so long to finish this job?" Brendan asked, concerned. They'd been moving at a snail's pace.

Joe leaned over the table. "No, not at all. It's because of Kathleen's food," he confided. "The longer we work here, the longer we get that fabulous grub and a couple of pints for free." Joe tapped the side of his head, pleased. "Pretty clever of me, eh?"

Brendan shook his head, amused. Leave it to Joe to figure out a way to prolong the job so he could feast on all his favorite traditional dishes free of charge.

Joe leaned back, his expression turning to one of worry. "I shouldn't have told you about how crippled I'm feeling. I'm afraid you'll feel guilted into something you might not want to do."

"You told me you weren't long for the business way before Connor ever began haunting me, so have no fears on that front."

"What is it you want, Brendan?"

Brendan laughed bitterly. "Everything."

"I'm not sure that can be arranged," his uncle said dryly. He subtly tilted his head in Maggie's direction. "Is that part of what's muddling your mind? Her mother tells me you two have been seeing each other."

"We've been seeing each other for two weeks. That's all."

Joe smiled mischievously. "Cupid only needs to shoot one arrow to make his point."

"True." He glanced at Maggie, whose back was to him as she fetched some drinks at the bar. God, the shape on her.

"I like her a lot," Brendan confessed. "But I've no idea if it would be going anywhere serious even if I stayed, so it's mad for me to even factor it into my decision."

"Does she know what you're wrestling with?"

"No, and I'm not going to tell her," Brendan said tersely. "There's no need."

"Let's say Maggie O'Brien didn't exist. Which way would you be leaning?"

"I don't know," Brendan said plaintively. "I worry that if I go home, you'll think I'm an ungrateful little bastard. You sponsored me, you taught me everything, and then what do I do in the end? Piss off back to Dublin."

Joe looked shocked. "I would never think that!" His gaze turned serious. "Listen to me, Brendan. You can't worry about me; you can't worry about Connor—it's about you and what you want. Think long and hard and be honest with yourself. That's all you can do."

"Maybe I should flip a coin," Brendan joked feebly.

"I wish it were that easy for you. Just know that whatever you do decide, I'm behind you one hundred percent, and I mean that. You've worked your arse off, Brendan. You deserve success no matter which path you choose."

"You make it sound so easy," Brendan said glumly.

"Don't I? That's because it's not me making the decision."

Maggie's mother appeared at the table. "How's the stew, boys?"

"Like heaven," Joe rhapsodized. "You wouldn't happen to have any soda bread in the back to go with it? That would make things perfect. Perfect."

Maggie's mother beamed. "Of course I do, Joe. I'll bring it right out."

She departed for the kitchen. Joe winked at Brendan. "I say we take our time finishing up here. What do you say?"

"I agree. But not for the same reasons as you."

"I think it's only fair that since you've seen where I live, I see where you live."

Maggie looked at Brendan unenthusiastically as she helped her brother lock up for the night. She'd been shocked when she'd told Brendan she had to work and he had come down to the Wild Hart and just hung around, shooting the breeze with Liam until she was done. Maybe shocked wasn't the right word; maybe *uneasy* was more accurate. The thought of Brendan passing the night with her wicked little brother, who had a lifetime of memories and stories about her, was extremely unnerving. Thankfully, there was a Blades game on the TV right above the bar, and every time she looked at Brendan, or even popped over to chat when she had a free second, he seemed to be absorbed in the hockey game. Of course, it didn't hurt that she'd cornered Liam before Brendan even came in and told him that if he told Brendan any embarrassing stories about her, she'd murder him. Liam swore he wouldn't, but a pledge from Liam was worth about as much as Monopoly money.

"Well?" Brendan pressed.

"Go on, Mags, take him upstairs," Liam urged, cashing out. "Mom and Dad are away. They'll never know you're about to sin under their roof."

Brendan laughed, but Maggie didn't think it was funny. "Have I ever mentioned how much I hate you, Liam?"

"Daily, from the time I was three." He picked up a rag and flicked it at his sister's butt. "*Go*, will you?"

Maggie smiled uncertainly. "Okay." She held out a hand to

Brendan. "Come on. Time for you to see Chateau O'Brien, I guess."

"Have fun," Liam called after them as Maggie pulled Brendan toward the steps at the back of the pub kitchen that led to the apartment above.

"Hate you," Maggie trilled over her shoulder.

"No, you don't," Liam called back at her.

Maggie looked at Brendan. "Ignore him."

Brendan just laughed.

"So, here it is," said Maggie as they emerged in the small but spanking clean kitchen, her mother's pride and joy. "The parental homestead."

"It's nice," said Brendan.

"Let me give you the grand tour. It'll only take a minute and a half, I promise."

She showed him the one tiny bathroom the six of them had had to share, the bedroom she'd shared with Sinead, her brothers' room, her parents' room.

"That's it," she said, concluding in the living room.

"I have to say," said Brendan, sitting down on the couch, "I don't know how you all lived here without killing each other."

Maggie joined him on the couch. "We came close at times, believe me." Feeling shy, she brushed her hand over his. "How much longer are you and Joe going to be working on the pub?"

Brendan looked like he was going to laugh. "A couple more weeks, I think."

"What's so funny?"

"Nothing. Why do you want to know how much longer we'll be underfoot downstairs?"

Maggie shrugged. "Just curious." She didn't want to admit that she woke up every morning looking forward to seeing him. "What's your next job?"

Brendan hesitated. “A restaurant on the Upper East Side.”

“You don’t sound too happy.”

“It’ll be all right,” Brendan murmured.

Maggie nodded as a taut silence stretched over them. *Now what?* she thought. Was she about to “sin” in her parents’ house? She’d taken him upstairs knowing she wanted him badly—but being up there with him alone felt so adolescent and furtive, especially after Liam’s teasing. It was the apartment she’d grown up in, for God’s sake. And right now, she didn’t feel like much of a grown-up, living there again.

Obviously, Brendan was clairvoyant. “You’re feeling odd, having me up here.”

“Yes,” Maggie admitted, feeling stupid. “It’s idiotic, isn’t it?”

“No, it’s sort of sweet, as long as you haven’t changed your mind about having a bit of fun.”

Maggie pressed her lips together. “I hate that expression. It makes me feel . . . like a toy.”

“You were the one who insisted you didn’t want to get seriously involved.”

“I know,” Maggie admitted.

Brendan slid an arm around her. “So, *do* you want to get involved?”

“We are involved. Kind of. Aren’t we?” Maggie hung her head miserably. “I’m so confused. Aren’t you?”

“Yes.” He drew her to him. “You’re so beautiful, Maggie. I hate the thought that that bastard of a first husband hurt you badly. I’d never hurt you. Ever.” He kissed her softly, prompting a sweet, gentle desire to course through her. She could love this man, and it terrified her. Unable to stop herself, she barely skimmed his lips with the tip of her tongue, sensing his fast burgeoning desire as he held a moan deep in his throat.

“You’re teasing me now, girl,” he breathed. “Right here under your mother and father’s sainted roof.”

They laughed together as Brendan rested his brow against hers. “What do you want to do?” he whispered.

"Right now?"

"Right this very minute. Forget all those words we've been slinging about—*casual*, *bit of fun*. What do you want right here and right now?"

"To be with you," Maggie admitted, all her fears of being hurt tiptoeing away, at least for the moment.

"But not on the family couch," Brendan chuckled.

Maggie blushed. "You must think—"

"That you're adorable. There's a little girl inside you that you don't often let out." He kissed her again. "Come with me, Miss Maggie O'Brien. I'm bringing you back to my place so I can make mad, passionate love to you. How does that sound?"

"Like a dream," said Maggie. "The best I've ever had."

Five

Maggie ached for Brendan to take her directly into his bedroom, and he did, their desire for each other like a magnet pulling them toward his bed. She was amused when he quietly closed the bedroom door. There was no one there but the two of them; the two of them and their burning need for each other.

Brendan flicked on the reading light on the nightstand, casting the small room in a dim, intimate glow. “I don’t have candles,” he apologized. “I’m sorry.”

“I don’t need candles,” Maggie said as he came to take her in his arms. “All I need is—”

Her sentence was swallowed by the greedy crush of his lips against hers. It had been so long since she’d been kissed like this, the feeling of it somehow savage yet tender at the same time. Such a long time since she’d wanted a man the way she wanted him.

His tongue probed her mouth, self-assured, teasing. Maggie felt her knees go weak. How long had it been since something like that had happened? She felt like a teenage girl getting her first taste of what it was like to be with the boy you’d been dreaming about for ages, the one you lay awake thinking about, tortured, while the rest of your house slept.

Maggie pulled back, her heart beating in her chest like the wings of a small caged bird yearning for freedom. "I need to tell you something."

Brendan looked worried. "What's that?"

Maggie blushed. "I'm a little out of practice when it comes to—you know . . ."

Brendan looked unconcerned as he tenderly rubbed his nose against hers. "You know what they say: It's like riding a bicycle. Once you learn how, you never forget. You'll be fine."

"I was never very good on my bicycle," Maggie confessed. "So you shouldn't expect much."

"If you weren't good on a bike it's because you had the wrong teacher. How 'bout I take hold of the handlebars and steer?"

Maggie laughed shakily. "Okay."

Brendan smiled, running his large, strong hands up and down her arms for a moment before putting his mouth back on hers and wrapping his arms around her. God, the heat coming off him, feeding her neediness . . . Maggie could feel her whole body beginning to pulse with energy.

"Now, then." Brendan released her a moment, his blue eyes riveted on her face as he undid the top two buttons of her blouse so he could kiss her collarbone. "I think I need to see more of you, Maggie," he murmured as he tugged her blouse free from the waistband of her jeans. "With your permission, of course."

"Permission granted," Maggie replied, breathing hard as she felt the screaming demand in her blood for more, more, more. Barely anything had happened and she was already giddy with want of him.

She was beginning to tremble now as he opened her blouse and slowly skimmed his hands down her sides. When his fingers moved to deftly unfasten her jeans, it took every ounce of her willpower not to drag him over to the bed and pull him down on top of her, raggedly trying to speak her need.

Instead, she held her breath, every muscle in her body taut with scorching anticipation as Brendan slowly lowered the zipper of her jeans, slipping one hand inside against her warm belly. His fingers toyed with the waistband of her panties a moment, his fingertips brushing low through the fabric. Maggie moaned, far past being embarrassed by her own desire.

Driven by hunger, she stepped out of her jeans, kicking them away. "Now what?" she asked hoarsely.

"Now we lie down together on my bed," Brendan instructed in a murmur. His own breath was ragged, with a darkness in his eyes that heralded possession, or so she hoped. He laid her down, his gaze watchful, unwavering, as he again put his mouth to hers. Maggie could feel her heart pounding throughout her entire body. She couldn't believe how aroused she was becoming simply by being kissed.

The room burned away. There was only her and Brendan, the soft, inviting bed, his heart hammering as hard as hers as he feasted on her mouth. He could kiss her forever, and she would never get bored. But he didn't; breathing hard, he pushed her bra up roughly, and lowered his head to sweetly torture.

An orgasm ripped through her, making her feel embarrassed at how little it took to bring her to peak. But Brendan didn't seem to care as he lifted his head to kiss her again, his tongue flicking and playing in her mouth as he paused now and then to bite her lower lip, making her cry out. Maggie arched up, pressing against him, unable to stop herself from rocking her hips. She couldn't fight the need clawing inside her any longer.

Brendan paused, rearing up to tear off his shirt. "Is any of it coming back to you now?" he teased.

Maggie giggled. "We can take the training wheels off, I think."

She watched his eyes cloud as he lowered himself to her once again, taking her in his arms. His breathing was hard and deep, a wanton impatience seeming to drive him as his hands and mouth staked their claim on her upper body. Heat was beginning to build again in Maggie's lower belly, and as she arched against him once more, she raised her arms high above her head, curling her fingers around the rungs of his brass bed. Overcome, she kept her eyes fastened to his. In movies, lovers always seemed to close their eyes. But she and Brendan didn't. It was as if neither of them wanted to miss a thing.

Brendan was wild-eyed now, a man on the edge. "I want you," he growled. "I want you so—"

"Do it," Maggie begged. "Christ, God, I can't take much more, Brendan."

Brendan groaned, hurriedly peeling off the remainder of his clothing before reaching into his nightstand for protection. Pressure was building within Maggie at the sight of his hard body. "Now," she moaned, feeling the last vestige of control leave her. "Now!"

Brendan plunged hard inside her, the raw thrust and heat of him making Maggie cry out. It had never been like this for her, ever. All she could see, hear, smell, touch, think about was Brendan, and the glorious fit of their bodies.

Gasping with pleasure, their eyes still fixed on each other, Maggie's hips met Brendan's stroke for stroke, slow at first, but then faster and faster as she clamped herself around him. Brendan kissed her sweaty forehead, and then he was pounding in and out of her, his own cries of pleasure so tantalizing to her ears she felt herself becoming aroused again. When he finally did let go, he was not alone; Maggie was right there with him, their mingled cries of pleasure turning the darkened bedroom into a place of blazing, brilliant light. Brendan Kelly, returning her to herself. Helping her heal. Showing her the way back to love, God help her.

"See, I told you it would all come back to you."

Grinning, Brendan kissed his lover's forehead. Gloriously sweaty, they were entwined in each other's arms. Maggie's response was a sleepy smile. They lay there quietly for a long time. So long, in fact, that Brendan began to worry. He'd never slept with a woman who didn't want to chat at least a little after making love.

He propped himself up on one elbow. "Are you all right?"

"Yes, of course," Maggie said, cupping his cheek.

"Why so quiet, then?"

"Can't I just enjoy lying in your arms after the sexual equivalent of the Tour de France?"

Brendan laughed. "Of course." Everything was okay, then. He lay back down, taking her in his arms.

And that's when the phone rang.

Shite. Why the hell couldn't Connor leave him alone? His brother told him he had a month to make up his mind. That meant he still had a little less than two weeks to go.

He found himself tensing against his will. He paused, waiting to hear his brother's voice through the closed door, breathing with relief when whoever was on the other end hung up. Unfortunately, Maggie had tensed, too.

"Do you have a problem with the phone?" she asked.

"No. Did you want me to jump up from bed and pick it up when we're lying here together?"

"No, but I thought it was weird when we came back here last week, and it was clear you had a message and you didn't check it out. I think it's one of the things most people tend to the minute they get home."

"I'm not most people."

Maggie looked at him with trepidation, the contentment she'd obviously been experiencing a minute ago now gone. "Do you have a girlfriend, Brendan?"

"What? *No*, don't be crazy. I told you: I was pretty sure it was my brother."

"But you didn't know for sure."

"No, I didn't. But again, would you have preferred I listened to my messages the minute we got here, rather than sweeping you off into the bedroom?"

"No," she admitted, but her expression remained somewhat tentative. "But I keep feeling like there's something you're not telling me."

"There's nothing to tell, Maggie. I just have a lot on my plate with work is all."

"Like what?" she pressed.

He took her hands in his. "Joe is thinking of retiring soon," he told her, pleased that he was able to stay within the boundaries of truth. "He's going to hand over his business to me—if I want it."

"If you want it?" she repeated, looking surprised. "I'd think that would be a no-brainer."

"You would, wouldn't you? But it isn't."

"Why?"

Brendan ran one hand down his face in frustration. "Because maybe it's not what I want to do with the rest of my life. Same as you with waitressing."

"But you seem to like it. And you said you earn a good living."

"I do, I do, but . . ." *God, Maggie, don't make me lie, please. Not while I'm holding you.* He nipped her earlobe playfully. "Can we please not talk about work now? It's not the most relaxing subject."

"You're right," Maggie conceded with a sigh. She timidly ran a hand over his shoulder. "Can we talk about us, though?"

So she is like every other woman, Brendan marveled to himself; *she needs to talk after the main event.* He'd never understand it in a million years.

"Sure," said Brendan, trying to muster some enthusiasm.

"I think what's happening between us is more than just a bit of fun, don't you?"

"Yes."

It was, but Brendan didn't want to dwell on it right now, since it only contributed to the confusion he was feeling about whether to stay in New York or go home to Dublin.

"So do you want to keep seeing each other, and see where it leads?" Maggie asked bashfully.

"Yes," Brendan said again.

"Even though you originally told me you weren't interested in a relationship?"

"You said that first, Maggie."

She kissed his mouth softly. "That was before I got to know you." She looked so relieved when he said he wanted to keep seeing her that it nearly broke Brendan's heart. How could she ever think otherwise?

He pulled her closer to him. "Do you want to stay the night? I promise I won't tell Sister Delphina."

"Who's cheeky now?" Maggie asked wryly.

"Let's just hold each other now."

Maggie looked amused. "You want me to shut up, don't you?"

Brendan chuckled. "Well . . ."

Maggie kissed him, closing her eyes as she wrapped herself tighter around him. "Thanks for the bike riding lesson."

"Anytime, love." Brendan gave her butt an affectionate little slap. "Perhaps we'll take another spin in the morning."

Brendan didn't want to admit it to himself, but his heart sank just the tiniest bit when, two days later, he arrived at the Wild Hart to work with his uncle and Maggie wasn't there. A casual check with her brother, who now wore a knowing smirk whenever they spoke, revealed that she had gone to spend the day with an old school friend of hers in Queens. Thankfully, the smirk didn't extend to Maggie's hovering mother, who was as chatty as ever. Clearly Liam had managed to keep his lip buttoned about Maggie spending the night.

"Brendan!" said Maggie's mother, looking more pleased than she should to see him. "Are you hungry? I could make you some pancakes before you start."

"I'd love some pancakes, missus," Joe chimed in, winking at Brendan.

"I'm fine," Brendan told Maggie's mother. "Thank you."

"Maggie's out seeing a friend," Maggie's mother continued.

"I already told him that, Mom," said Liam, rolling his eyes as he looked at Brendan.

"Well," Mrs. O'Brien huffed, "I just didn't want Brendan to think she was off with some other boy."

Boy. The word amused Brendan immensely. He was pushing thirty.

She patted his arm. "I'll go whip up some pancakes for Joe, but I'll make a few extra just in case you want some."

"Thank you."

Joe turned to Brendan as soon as Mrs. O'Brien was out of ear-shot. "So help me God, if we could figure out a way to make this job last a year, I'd do it." He pointed a warning finger at Brendan. "All those pancakes are mine, boyo. You got it?"

"Got it, Uncle Joe."

With that, Brendan got to work—very, very slowly.

When the time came for lunch, Joe sat in a booth with Maggie's father, while Brendan joined Liam at the bar for a quick sandwich and a beer.

"You'd best quit smirking at me," Brendan warned, "if you want to keep that face all the ladies seem to love intact."

"I'm not smirking at you," Liam insisted—smirking. "It's all in your head."

"Mmm." Brendan pointed with his beer toward the back of the pub. "So, what do you think?"

"I think you and Joe are doing a great job," said Liam without hesitation.

Less than two weeks now to decide whether he was going to leave Joe—and Maggie. Brendan couldn't pretend she wasn't a factor in the equation. He knew she shouldn't be, but he couldn't help it.

"So," said Liam, taking a long drink from a bottle of water, "you think you might be the one to catch the Butterfly in your net?"

Brendan blinked in confusion. "Pardon?"

"The Butterfly. Maggie. That's her nickname in the family."

"Ah," Brendan said knowingly. "So named because she emerged a great beauty, I take it."

Liam snorted. "*No.* We call her that because she's always flitting around, never able to settle down or make up her mind. One minute she wants to live in London, the next San Francisco. One minute she talks about becoming a social worker, the next about going to massage school. The longest commitment she ever made was to that dickhead ex-husband of hers, and look how that turned out. But you, my friend, might just be the one to get her to settle down."

Brendan forced a smile, even though he felt sick. "Right."

Maggie was a roamer. He wished Liam hadn't told him this. What was to stop her from dumping him at any moment if she became restless? That was not the type of woman he wanted to lose his heart to. Not now, with his life hanging in the balance.

There was only one thing for it. Pull away from her a little. Try to drive her from his heart and mind so things were crystal clear when he gave Connor his final answer. Liam had done him a favor. But he hated it.

Six

"What's going on? You've been acting really weird."

Eyes on Brendan as he joined her on his couch, Maggie made sure to keep her voice level, despite the fact that inside, she was feeling somewhat panicked. For close to a week now, she couldn't shake the feeling that Brendan was somehow pulling away from her. It wasn't that he was ignoring her, exactly. But he seemed distant. Distant and distracted.

Brendan puffed up his cheeks and blew out a heavy breath, his eyes not quite meeting hers.

"Brendan?"

He rubbed his temples as if trying to ward off a headache. "I'm crap with words, Maggie, so I don't know how to say this."

Maggie's guts lurched. "You're dumping me, aren't you?"

Brendan looked pained. "Maggie . . ."

"No, I get it, believe me," she said bitterly. "You got what you wanted—you fucked me—and now you're done with me."

Brendan looked at her incredulously. "It's not like that at all."

"Really? How is it?"

Maggie folded her arms across her chest, more to keep from shaking with anger and humiliation than as a gesture of closing herself off from him. Were she alone, she'd pound her head against the wall. She'd done it again—allowed herself to fall quickly and heedlessly for a rogue who, in reality, was a total *shit*. It was her own fault. She hadn't kept her promise to herself. Well, at least this time it was only three weeks of her life down the drain, as opposed to two years.

Brendan just sat there, looking tortured. *Melodramatic Irish bastard*, Maggie thought. "Let me guess," she said sarcastically. "It's not me, it's you. Maybe we can just be friends." She got up. "Spare me." Snatching up her purse, she headed for the door.

"Maggie," Brendan called out to her. "It's about those phone calls I wouldn't answer."

Maggie slowly turned around. "What about them?"

"They were from my brother. Just like I told you."

"And—?"

"He's got a cabinetry business in Dublin. He wants me to come home and work with him. He's making gobs of money. He's been pushing me for months to make a decision. Three weeks ago, he got fed up and told me I had a month to get back to him or else he'd hire someone else."

Maggie swallowed. "I see."

Brendan looked frustrated as he ran a hand through his hair. "So I've been sitting here for three weeks, trying to figure out what I want to do: go home, or stay here and take over for Joe."

Maggie felt her heart slowing sinking to her feet. "And have you decided what you're going to do?" she asked quietly.

"Yes. At least I think I have." He patted the space beside him on the couch. "Please come sit next to me. Please."

Maggie slowly walked back to him. A moment ago, the torment in his eyes had made her want to kick him. Now her heart went out to him. "Talk to me," she urged gently.

"I'm sure you know I'm falling for you, Maggie."

"Me, too." Her heart was pounding; she feared a "but" was coming. *I'm falling for you* but *I want to go home to Dublin.*

"I can't lie to you, though," Brendan continued. "I miss my family terribly."

"Of course you do," Maggie murmured. She tried to imagine what it would be like to be an ocean apart from her family and only see them once a year. It would be awful. She'd seen the toll it had taken on her parents, the melancholy and longing that often crept into their voices when they talked about "home." No matter how long they'd been in the States, Ireland would always be "home," especially after visiting.

And yet, despite the awfulness of Brendan's dilemma, Maggie couldn't stop her own feelings of selfishness stealing to the fore. *Please stay here*, she thought. *Please.*

Still, there was one question niggling at her that she had to ask. "Is it just your family that's pulling you home? Are you sure there's not—"

"There's no one. I swear to you. No one in their right mind would have me," he joked.

"I would."

"Not a second ago you thought I was a pig."

"That's before you told me what was going on, Brendan."

Brendan nodded, still looking miserable. "It's all a tangle in my mind," he continued. "My brother Connor can be an arrogant bastard. We fought like cats and dogs growing up, and even now, when we're together, we have a tendency to rub each other the wrong way, especially after we've both had a few Jamesons. But the opportunity he's offering me is golden, and for him, generous."

Here comes the but, thought Maggie. However, she sensed it was a *but* she'd like; one that wouldn't hurt her.

"But my uncle . . ." Brendan began choking up. "He saved my life, Maggie. He's been like a surrogate father to me. And the thought of up and leaving him . . ."

"Have you talked to Joe about this?"

"Of course. He tells me to follow my heart."

"And what does your heart tell you?"

"It tells me to stay for you. That we could have a future, and that at least if I take over from Joe, I'm not under Connor's thumb. I'd be my own boss." He cradled his head in his hands.

"I know I might be biased, but your decision seems pretty clear-cut to me," Maggie said carefully.

"On the employment front, yeah." He looked up at her, perturbed. "But not where you're concerned."

Maggie cocked her head, confused. "Where I'm concerned what? Does it bother you that I'm divorced?"

"No," Brendan scoffed. "Half the world's divorced. Why would I care?"

"Then what?"

Brendan scratched behind his ear distractedly. "It's something your brother Liam said."

"Oh, this should be good," Maggie said curtly. "Let's hear it."

Brendan hesitated. "Well, he told me your nickname in the family was 'Butterfly'—that you tend not to stick to things for very long. He said you're all over the place with what you want."

"So you're worried that we'll get involved and *poof*! One day I'll just be gone." Maggie felt her ire rising. "I can't believe he told you that."

"I think he told me because he likes me. He wondered if maybe I'd be the one to 'catch' you in my 'net.'"

Maggie squinted in disbelief. "He used those actual words?"

Brendan nodded.

"Sexist little bastard," Maggie seethed. "Wait until I get ahold of him."

"He'll probably kill me for telling you."

"He won't be able to kill you, because I'll have murdered him first." Maggie closed her eyes a moment, collecting her thoughts before speaking. "Listen to me carefully, Brendan." She took his large, working man's hands between her own. She loved the callused fingertips. It had been one of the things that excited her when they made love, their rough texture as they played against her own smooth skin.

"I'm not going to deny that I've spent a lot of time being confused as hell. I'm still not sure why. I think a lot of it had to do with just not liking myself."

"Why was that?"

"I don't know." She shrugged. "Lots of women don't like themselves. I don't know why." She rubbed nervous circles on the top of his hand with her thumb. "My ex was very attractive to me when he came along, because he seemed so solid and stable. He had money. He said beautiful things to me that no one had ever said before. It was a 'whirlwind romance'—passionate. As any member of my family can tell you, I've never been a great one for thinking things through, and marrying Tom was no exception. All I could think was, 'Here's something that will give me focus.'

"I dedicated two years of my life to making him happy, without a thought for myself. No wonder he told me at the end that I was boring. I was. There *was* no me; only him."

Maggie pressed her lips together. "Divorcing him was hard, and scary, but it's the smartest thing I ever did, because now I can figure myself out. What I want. Who I am."

Brendan's eyes locked on hers. "And who are you, Mags?"

"A confused woman, but one who promises you she's not going anywhere. New York is where I belong. It's where I want to build my life."

"You're certain."

"Yes. *Yes.*" She chuckled. "It's funny we're even having this talk about being a couple, considering how much I really didn't like you when we first met."

"Really?" Brendan teased. "I couldn't tell."

"I thought you were one of those silver-tongued smoothies that Ireland seems so expert at producing."

"And now?"

"Well, you are silver-tongued, but that's not what attracts me to you. It's your heart. You're a good man, Brendan. The fact that you're so handsome and so witty is just an extra perk."

"Stop flattering me. You'll give me a big head."

"Like you don't already have one." Maggie hoped it didn't seem manipulative, but she brought his hand to her cheek and held it there. "I hate pressuring you, but I really hope you don't go back."

"I told my brother I'd give him an answer tomorrow."

"But you still have a week."

"It's like an axe hanging over my head. I can't stand it. I'm giving him my answer tomorrow." There was anguish in his eyes. "Promise you won't hate me if I choose to go home, Maggie."

Hate? she thought. *No. But devastation? Possibly. Regret, too.* Not that she'd tell him.

"I promise I won't hate you. You have to do what your uncle says. You have to go with your heart." She stood. "I'll talk to you tomorrow, Brendan. And I hope . . ."

She couldn't finish the sentence.

The minute Maggie got home from Brendan's, she steamed into the Wild Hart, zeroing in on Liam, who was chatting up a very attractive blonde from his spot behind the bar.

"You!" she said, sidling right up beside the blonde. "I've got a bone to pick with you!"

The blonde looked alarmed. "Don't worry, honey," Maggie told her. "I'm his sister, not his wife—though he's already gone through two of those."

The blonde gave Liam the finger and stormed out of the bar. His mouth fell open.

"What the hell did you do that for?!"

"Why the hell did you tell Brendan the family calls me 'Butterfly'?!"

"I didn't think it was a big deal."

"You didn't think it was a big deal to plant the idea in his head that I might just up and leave on a whim?" Maggie raged.

The Mouth, sitting two stools down, couldn't help himself.

"In my opinion, butterflies are quite misunderstood. Did you know there are actually two varieties of lethal butterfly in Guatemala? Perhaps—"

"Perhaps you can butt out," Maggie snapped. The Mouth shrank back, wounded. *Shit*, thought Maggie. "Look, I'm sorry," she said to him. "I'm just trying to have a private talk with my brother here."

"In front of the whole bar!" Liam snorted.

"You listen to me," said Maggie, coming around to the back of the bar to stand toe-to-toe with her brother. "Don't you ever, ever stick your nose in my business that way again, do you hear?"

Liam held up his hands in a gesture of surrender. "Sorry."

"You better be," Maggie said with a glare.

Having gotten it off her chest, Maggie went straight upstairs to bed.

Not that she slept.

Seven

Female intuition, coupled with the fact Brendan had flat out admitted he was falling for her, told Maggie he'd be staying in the States. But you could never underestimate the pull of family; and with his brother dangling the possibility of making serious money in his face . . .

The hours ticked by until, finally, Maggie staggered out of bed, bleary-eyed and so fraught with anxiety she was nauseated, barely able to get her dry toast down.

She was downstairs in the pub before Brendan arrived solo. She wanted to be there to read his face when he came through the door after making the biggest decision of his life, one that could turn out to be the biggest of hers as well.

The door to the pub started to open, and Maggie went rigid with fear. But then Brendan stepped over threshold, beaming at her. And in that split second, Maggie knew her sleeplessness had been in vain.

Brendan threw down his bag of tools and plucked her up into his arms, twirling her around. "Well, Miss O'Brien, you're stuck with me now, whether you like it or not."

Maggie couldn't hide her happiness as he returned her to earth. "I'm so glad." She rose up on tiptoe to kiss his cheek. "How did your brother react?"

"He didn't sound as disappointed as I'd hoped."

Maggie laughed. "Joe must be ecstatic."

"He is. I actually went over to his place last night to tell him. Interrupted him watching the Mets, but he didn't seem to mind."

"Where is he?"

"He told me I needed to learn to work solo until I hire my own crew. He's sleeping in for the first time in ages. I'm glad; he needs a rest, and there's not much left to do here, anyway. I can easily finish up on my own in the next few days."

Maggie thrust her lower lip out in a pout. "I'll be sad when the job's done. It means I won't see you every day."

"That's probably a good thing." Brendan pulled her to him for a lusty kiss. "You won't get sick of me."

"Well, well, look who's here," said Liam, appearing from upstairs, a mug of coffee in his hand. He shot Maggie a nervous look. She sighed heavily and shook her head, her way of letting him know all was forgiven. "I heard from my folks you've decided to stay."

Brendan looked mystified. "Your folks—?"

"Joe called them last night after you left."

"Jesus." Brendan turned to Maggie in amazement. "There's nothing like the Irish grapevine."

Liam clamped a friendly hand on Brendan's shoulder. "We're all really glad you're staying."

"So am I. I've only got a few months to go before I get permanent citizenship."

"We'll throw you a party," said Liam. "Real Yank food: hamburgers, hot dogs—the whole shebang."

"That'd be great," Brendan said with a grin, clearly moved.

"Well," Liam sighed, "I've got to go take stock of inventory in the cellar, so you two should feel free to canoodle for a while."

"Hate you," Maggie said sweetly as her brother breezed by her with a wink. She turned to Brendan. “I guess you should get to work, Mr. Soon to Be Business Owner.”

“I need a tiny bit of fortification first.” He wrapped his arms around her, skimming his lips over hers. It was so easy and gentle; so right.

“God, Maggie,” he said, his face lighting up with elation, “it’s all going to be great, isn’t it?”

Three days later, two men walked through the door, and everything fell apart.

Eight

"Are you Brendan Kelly?"

Two men in suits had just entered the Wild Hart. Brendan shot Maggie a perplexed look before stepping forward to shake their hands. "How can I help you?"

The older of the two—thin, grey-haired, with tired eyes—flashed Brendan his badge. "I'm Agent Lehr, and this"—he pointed to the stooped, slightly dumpy man at his side—"is Agent Gilliam. We're officers of the Immigration and Naturalization Service. We'd like you to come with us. We have some questions we need to ask you."

Brendan's brows knit in confusion. "About what?"

Lehr sighed heavily. "You know what, Mr. Kelly."

"I'm afraid I don't." Brendan glanced over at Maggie. "*What* do you want to talk to me about?" Brendan asked politely. "I have a right to know."

"Your stay in this country."

"I don't understand."

"Our records show you should have gone back to Ireland years ago along with your wife."

"*What?* Look, you've made a mistake," Brendan said calmly. His eyes cut to Maggie. She'd gone ashen.

The men said nothing.

Brendan rubbed the back of his neck, trying to keep a lid on his temper. "I'll say it again: There's obviously been some kind of mix-up."

Lehr's expression was bored. "We'll discuss this down at the office, all right?"

"Are you *arresting* me?"

"You bastard," he heard Maggie growl. Brendan turned to look at her. The last thing he needed was Maggie being rude to the law. Then he realized the comment was directed at him.

"You believe *them*?"

"Go with them," Maggie hissed, her face no longer white, but red with anger. "I knew you were too good to be true. *I knew it*."

"Jesus Christ, Maggie—"

"Mr. Kelly, will you please just come with us?" Agent Gilliam said in exasperation. "We're very busy."

"Yeah, fine, I'm coming," said Brendan, thoughts stampeding through his head faster than he could corral them. "This'll all get sorted out," he reassured Maggie. "I promise."

Maggie was practically baring her teeth at him. "Ask me if I care. I don't ever want to talk to you again. Don't you ever walk through that door again, you hear me?"

"Maggie—"

It was no use. She'd already turned her back to him and was storming downstairs to the cellar. He turned back to the agents, furious with their bored expressions. *This is my life you're fucking with here*, he thought. *My life*.

"Right, let's go," Brendan said to them briskly. "I need this cleared up as quickly as possible. I've got work to get back to."

Maggie paused halfway down the cellar steps, trying to control the shaking overtaking her. *Story of my life*, she thought bitterly.

Getting screwed over by men. They're all the same. They're all the same. They're all the same.

Taking a deep breath, she continued down the steps toward her brother, who was busy taking inventory of bar stock.

Hearing her footfall, Liam glanced up with a smile, but it faded fast. "What's wrong?"

"I thought I'd come down and tell you we won't be throwing a party for Brendan anytime soon." Crates of booze surrounded them. Maggie longed to tear one open and just start hurling bottles at the wall. She'd never done anything like that before. Maybe it would be cathartic—for the ten seconds it lasted.

Liam looked mystified. "You two had your first fight already?"

"No. Let's just say he's not who he says he is. Let's just say he's a liar."

"Don't be cryptic, Maggie. Just tell me what's going on."

"Immigration and Naturalization came and took him away. Apparently, he's been living here illegally *and* he has a wife back in Ireland." She kicked at a nearby box of cocktail napkins. "Goddammit!" she yelled.

"Calm down," said Liam, staring at her like she was nuts. "Obviously, there's been some sort of screwup."

"Oh, right. And I'm a size two."

Liam frowned. "Mags, you're being crazy." He put his steadying hands on her shoulders, searching her face. "Do you think he'd be that stupid? Do you think *Joe* would be that stupid? He sponsored him so he could come here and work legally; he vouched for him to our parents."

Maggie jerked away from her brother, pushing a hand through her hair, suddenly feeling like she'd made a terrible mistake.

Liam didn't let up. "You know what? When everything gets straightened out and he walks through that door, don't be surprised if he tells you to take a hike."

Maggie stood stunned, and then shook her brother's arm to get his attention. "What are you talking about?"

"In the space of two minutes, you showed you don't trust him. The guy just decided to stay in this country to be with you and your first instinct wasn't to be supportive; it was to call him a liar. And before you say it, yeah, I know, your ex screwed you over. But it's time to get the hell over it."

Maggie felt her guts shrivel. Liam was right. She'd had a complete knee-jerk reaction. She'd been an idiot. She should have kissed him before he left with the agents and told him she'd be right here waiting for him. She should have reassured him she knew it was all a mistake. But she hadn't.

Now what?

"Eejits."

Brendan was still riled as he and his uncle walked out of the Homeland Security office. He'd called Joe as soon as he arrived and explained the situation, instructing the old man to go over to his apartment to get his passport and a copy of his application for citizenship.

After looking at Brendan's passport *and* the papers from when Joe had sponsored him, *and* his application for citizenship, Agents Lehr and Gilliam were forced to admit this was a case of mistaken identity. There must be another Brendan Kelly roaming around New York illegally. *No shit*, Brendan wanted to snarl.

His anger didn't last long since it was replaced by sorrow. He was stunned at how quickly Maggie had turned on him. That last glimpse of her face as he walked out of the Wild Hart really jarred him. It also wounded him to the core.

How could she believe the INS agents over him? Actually, he *knew* how, but still; he couldn't wrap his mind around the fact she thought him capable of deceiving her. Here he'd passed up returning home to stay with her and what had she done? Turned on him in an instant.

His uncle glanced sideways at him. "You're pretty quiet."

"Maggie was there when they came. She didn't believe me, called me a bastard, and told me she didn't want to see me anymore."

"Maybe you should cut the girl some slack," Joe urged gently.

"A bit of faith in me would have been nice," Brendan grumbled. "Don't you think?"

"Perhaps. But the good Lord's the only perfect one who walked the earth. I know Maggie. Right about now, she's choking on her words, wishing she'd reacted differently. What do you say we go over there, have a pint or two?" Joe suggested. "You two can kiss and make up."

"You don't care about us kissing and making up," Brendan scoffed affectionately. "You just want some free food."

"No, I care—but maybe not as much as I care about getting a few slices of that brown bread the missus makes." He slapped Brendan on the back heartily. "C'mon. A pint'll do you good."

"Maybe," Brendan said glumly. "But just one. Some of us have to go back to work."

Maggie wasn't there when he and Joe arrived at the Wild Hart. Brendan lingered long past the time he and Joe usually left, chatting with Liam at the bar. Both of them knew he was just waiting for Maggie to show. Finally, after two hours, he couldn't wait any longer. He said good-bye to Liam and headed home.

Maggie held her breath as Brendan emerged from the elevator and began walking toward his apartment. She'd been worrying about him all day. What if things didn't get straightened out and the INS detained him for God knows how long? What if they didn't give him a chance to prove his innocence and deported him? She'd heard lots of visitors from Ireland talk about how nasty things sometimes got when you tried to deal with immigration and security at the airports. She tortured herself repeatedly, remembering how little faith she had shown in him. She *had* to make things right. And if he didn't want to make up with her—well, she had no one to blame but herself.

She was sitting on the floor outside his door, waiting for him. A ballsy move, but then he'd said he liked cheeky women, hadn't he? She just hoped he didn't tell her to go jump in the East River.

Maggie scanned his face anxiously as he approached her. He looked surprised to see her. Not unhappily surprised, not joyfully surprised, just surprised. No scowl or frown or look of displeasure. Maggie felt her hopes begin to creep up.

She scrambled to her feet, grasping a small shopping bag she'd brought with her.

"Hi," she said nervously.

"Hi," Brendan replied, opening his front door. "Been here long?" he asked evenly.

"No."

"That's good. I'd hate to think of the woman who told me she never wanted to see me again waiting hours to see me."

Ouch. She deserved that.

"What happened?" she asked anxiously, following him inside.

Brendan's shoulders slumped. "I'm being deported tomorrow."

Maggie gasped. "Oh my G—"

"It's a joke, Maggie," he said softly.

Maggie scowled. "Not a very funny one."

Brendan shrugged, untying his work boots. "I wonder how many Brendan Kellys there are who've crept into this city illegally."

"Enough to cause you some trouble, obviously."

Boot free, Brendan headed into the kitchen. Maggie hung back tentatively in the kitchen doorway, watching as he splashed cold tap water on his face before wiping it off with the hem of his T-shirt. He moved to the fridge, pulling out bottles of water. "Want one?"

"No, I'm fine." Maggie hesitated. "Can we talk?"

Brendan tilted his head toward the living room. "Lead on."

Maggie headed for the couch. She realized she was holding on to her shopping bag for dear life. She put it down at her feet, grateful when Brendan didn't sit far away from her. Their knees practically touched as they turned slightly to face one another. Surely this was a good sign?

Brendan took a sip of water, eyebrows rising expectantly. "Well?"

"I'm so sorry," Maggie said, choking up. "I shouldn't have reacted the way I did when those agents came to talk to you. Sometimes I react without thinking."

"I've figured that out by now. But I have to tell you: It did take me back a bit. Do you really think I would ever lie to you about being here legally or about being married?"

Maggie felt two feet tall. "No." She paused. "I just told you: Sometimes I don't *think*, Brendan," she said remorsefully. "I'm working on it, though. I swear I am."

"Good." Brendan put his water down on the coffee table, the intensity of his gaze catching and holding hers as he took her hands between his. "Because trust is the foundation of everything. If you don't trust me, then we've got nothing to build on. Nothing."

Maggie flushed with shame. "I know. I can change."

"Perhaps I can help," Brendan murmured.

A smile bloomed on Maggie's face. "Perhaps you can." She dipped her head uncertainly. "So you forgive me?"

"Isn't that obvious?"

"Just double-checking."

Relief gentled her body, steady and reassuring. It was going to be okay.

Brendan peered down into the shopping bag, shaking it gently. "What have we here?"

"A present for you. Open it."

Intrigued, Brendan pulled a box out of the bag and opened it. Inside was a football, smelling of fresh leather. He turned it over in his hands.

"You're in America now, mister," Maggie teased. "That's a *real* football."

"Tell that to every other country in the world." Brendan began tossing it in the air. "So tell me: Who am I supposed to play American football with, then?"

"I'm sure my brothers would be glad to oblige."

Brendan grinned as he put the football on the coffee table. Then his arms snaked around her, holding her tight as he nuzzled his face in her hair.

"You don't ever have to worry about me lying to you," he murmured tenderly. "Or hurting you. Or pulling up stakes and going back to Dublin. I promise you."

He kissed her slow and soft, no hurry, no rush. Maggie tipped her head back so the kiss would deepen.

"I'm not going anywhere," he whispered. "You're stuck with me, O'Brien."

"There's no one else I'd rather be stuck with, Kelly," she murmured into his mouth. "Now shut up and keep kissing me."

Epilogue

"A toast to the Yank!"

Maggie grinned at the man she loved. Cheers went up and glasses clinked together as the crowd in the Wild Hart paid homage to Brendan, a newly minted citizen. As Liam had promised, he'd thrown a party for Brendan, complete with hamburgers, hot dogs, Budweiser, the works. Brendan seemed honored but overwhelmed. He didn't like being the center of attention.

Three months had passed, and they were deeply in love. No doubt that was why her mother kept leaving issues of *Brides* magazine on her bed. Maggie had applied to massage school. Brendan claimed she had a "healing touch," but it was possible he was biased. She'd never been happier in her life.

"Speech! Speech! Speech!" Liam chanted as the rest of the partygoers chimed in. Maggie looked at Brendan; smooth as he was, he looked distinctly uncomfortable. He whispered something in Liam's ear. Liam shook his head no, and Brendan rolled his eyes. He wasn't going to get out of this.

"All right, everyone." Brendan's voice rang out over the crowd.

"Liam here has put me on the spot and asked me to say a few words. I'm not one for speechmaking, so I'll try to keep it short."

"First of all, I want to thank my uncle, Joe Kelly, for bringing me over here and showing me the ropes, not only on the job, but in life." The old man's eyes began welling up, causing Brendan's to do the same. "Hey, none of that, old man," Brendan sniffled, "or you'll get me and everyone else here going."

"Next I want to thank the love of my life, the gorgeous Maggie O'Brien." Brendan waved her toward him. "C'mere, darlin'."

Blushing deeply, Maggie made her way to Brendan's side. She was so proud of him; so proud to *be* with him.

"Whether they'll admit it or not, every man dreams of two things: success and finding a smart, beautiful, witty woman to share his life with. I'm one of those lucky bastards who's been blessed with both." Brendan planted a big, exuberant, sloppy kiss on her lips before hoisting his own glass high. "To Maggie, who makes it all worthwhile!"

"To Maggie!" the crowd echoed.

Maggie took a sip of her champagne. "So, now what?" she asked Brendan, her body singing with happiness.

He put his arm around her waist, pulling her to him, tight. "Now we walk down that road you mentioned the first time we ever spoke. Together."

Your Room or Mine?

Jacquie D'Alessandro

This book is dedicated to Cindy Hwang. Thank you for including me in such a fun project! And, as always, to my wonderful husband, Joe, who makes anything and everything double fun, and to my terrific son, Chris, aka Double Fun, Junior.

One

"I have some great news, Jack."

Jack Walker's every muscle tensed. *Uh-oh.* The last time Gavin Laine, his boss and CEO of Java Heaven, had uttered those words, a month ago, they'd been followed by the decidedly *un*great news that Gavin had hired a consultant to make sure Jack and his accounting department employees all bonded with each other. Jack had been chief financial officer of the popular Southeast coffeehouse franchise for only a month at that point, and he'd thought the transition was going smoothly. Certainly as smoothly as one could expect for a department that had imploded just weeks before Jack was hired when the former CFO and controller had been arrested for fraud and embezzlement.

Good thing Jack loved nothing more than a challenge, because the department was in shambles, morale was low, and personalities were clashing. But after a rocky first few weeks, he'd hired a new controller and things were looking much improved.

Patience, however, wasn't Gavin's strong suit. He wanted everything done yesterday and had hired Madeline Price, consultant, to move things along and insure that the department bonded and resolved their issues. That was the day Jack's Java Heaven job turned hellish.

Like so many consultants Jack had been forced to deal with over the years, all Madeline Price did while racking up billable hours was talk, talk, talk, *blah*, *blah*, *blah*, and take endless notes. No doubt an X-ray would reveal a pie chart where her heart should be. It wasn't his style to sit around and *blah*, *blah*, *blah*. He much preferred to roll up his sleeves and take action.

Jack knew Madeline (or Mad Dog as he mentally referred to her) was also there to make certain good internal controls were being put into place, thus insuring that the sort of illegal activities that caused the last accounting debacle didn't happen again—something Jack frankly resented. He didn't like having someone from outside the company constantly looking over his shoulder, second-guessing and questioning all his decisions. Sure there were going to be some bumps along the way while everyone settled into their positions and became acclimated to the new CFO and controller, but nothing he couldn't handle.

As far as he was concerned, consultants could be summed up with the old joke: If you ask a consultant what time it is, he'll steal your watch then charge you fifty thousand bucks to tell you it's ten past eight. He supposed consultants could be useful in some instances, but in this case, it was nothing but interference he didn't want and a financial expenditure the company didn't need.

He'd pointed that out to Gavin, but his boss was adamant. So adamant, Jack suspected part of the reason Gavin had hired Mad Dog was that he planned to downsize the accounting department, something Jack was absolutely opposed to as he'd then be understaffed. And understaffed meant overworked employees, which meant cranky, disheartened employees, and after what they'd all just suffered, they were cranky and disheartened enough. He didn't doubt that Mad Dog was making a list and checking it twice, all to determine who the weakest links in the department might be. Who wasn't going to be a team player.

Which just pissed off Jack. They all just needed time to adjust and regroup. What they didn't need was a consultant, aka Spy Who Could Cost Any One of Them Their Job, peeking at them over the rim of her glasses.

Unfortunately, Gavin had steamrolled over all his objections, so Jack had sucked it up. But damn, it was a hard sell. Especially with a dragon lady like Madeline Price to deal with. Jack could only guess that Gavin had found the woman because he'd Googled *up-tight, frigid, unsmiling, humorless, pain in the ass consultants for hire* and her name had popped up as the number one choice.

Bad enough that he had to put up with her interference, but Madeline Price was just the sort of person he didn't like. Someone who saw everything in black or white. Everything was either totally right or totally wrong. Her way or the highway. Organized to within an inch of her life. No chances, no surprises. He'd actually possessed a few of those qualities himself not much more than a year ago, but he'd learned that life-changing events changed . . . your life. And your outlook.

"So what's this great news, Gavin?" he asked, because based on the silence that had followed Gavin's announcement, Jack knew the question was expected from him.

Gavin smiled at him across the wide expanse of glass desk separating them. A smile that was more of a showing of teeth that did nothing to allay Jack's dread. "You're signed up for a weekend away at Casa di Lago. This weekend."

Jack forced his expression to remain blank but his suspicions doubled at the mention of the well-known resort situated on the shores of Lake Lanier, about an hour and a half north of Atlanta. He knew damn well Gavin wasn't sending him to the resort for a tasting at their winery, or a massage at the spa, or a round of golf, or a meal at one of the resort's gourmet restaurants. *Wait for it . . . wait for it . . .*

Gavin didn't make him wait long. "Of course the weekend isn't just for you."

Uh-huh. He'd figured as much. *Here it comes—*

"The entire accounting department is going. For a fun-filled weekend of team building. By the time you all return to work on Monday, you'll be rested, relaxed, and fully bonded with each other."

Jack's brows rose in surprise. *Pleasant* surprise. God knows he'd expected much worse. Even though he'd have to do some rearranging of his personal schedule to get away for the weekend, this wasn't nearly as bad as he'd anticipated.

"Sounds good," he said, relaxing for the first time since Gavin had made his "great news" announcement. "Although I'm wondering about the expense."

"It'll pay off in the long run. Remember, Jack, people who have bonded work better together. And people who work better together are more efficient."

That little pronouncement sent Jack's radar whirring and knotted his stomach. He knew those words. All too well. God knows he'd heard them enough since Mad Dog was hired. They were her personal mantra.

"Madeline arranged the whole team building weekend," Gavin said.

Figures. More consultant-related money going down the tubes. But based on Gavin's determined expression and tone, his mind was set. Well, at least Mad Dog wouldn't be coming along. Thank God.

"She'll be joining the group for the weekend," Gavin added.

Jack barely suppressed a groan. And there it was. For about three seconds he'd been lulled into a false sense of security, stupidly thinking that the great news might actually not be bad. Reality had just smacked him upside the head with the force of hammer to his skull.

"Why is she tagging along?"

Gavin's expression turned inscrutable, which gave Jack's radar another jolt. He considered himself pretty adept at reading people, and in the past two months he'd picked up on a lot of the nuances of Gavin's expressions. This carefully blank look practically shouted that there was more going on than he was willing to say, which only furthered Jack's suspicions of a downsizing.

Gavin shrugged. "I want an outsider's unbiased opinion on how the group interacts. An objective rundown of the personalities. That sort of thing."

Seeing as how Mad Dog didn't even have a personality, Jack seriously doubted her ability to objectively judge anyone else's.

"Yeah, she's a frosty one," Gavin said with a chuckle, as if reading his mind.

Definitely frosty. No doubt if she were cut, little ice cubes would fall from her veins instead of blood.

"But that's what makes her good at her job," Gavin continued. "She doesn't get personally involved. It's all strictly business." He rose and walked to the door, indicating their meeting was over. "Carla will have the memo and itinerary ready shortly," he said, nodding toward his secretary's desk. "Plan to meet with me Monday to give me your impression of the weekend."

"Great. Can't wait."

Jack headed back toward his office, smiling on the outside at his staff whose desks he passed, grumbling on the inside. Damn it, he had nothing against team building, in fact he'd participated in it before and had been impressed with the results. But while it was one thing to have to reschedule his plans, having to do so in order to spend the weekend with *her*, after suffering her company all week long . . . he could sum that up in one word: *blech*.

Damn *blech* since he'd had big plans this weekend. Seriously big plans. He just hoped Claire would understand. He heaved a regretful sigh. And Sophie, too.

Two

"I'm having trouble drudging up any sympathy for a woman who's spending the weekend at the fabulous Casa di Lago," said Emma Haygood, stabbing at her Caesar salad with a plastic fork.

Madeline Price looked across the small marble-topped table at her best friend. They'd managed to meet for lunch—something they tried to do once a week, but between Madeline's rotating job assignments and Emma's crazy schedule at the local television station where she worked as a producer, it wasn't always possible. But since Java Heaven's offices were close to both the TV station and the huge food court where they now sat, they'd been able to meet more regularly.

"It would be fabulous if I were going for a round of golf, a tennis match, and a facial," Madeline grumbled, using her wooden chopsticks to pick up a stir-fried shrimp. "Unfortunately, it's going to be all work and no play."

"Surely you'll have some downtime."

"I guess. But not much. Maybe I can squeeze in a massage." Yes, a massage would be great. God knows she'd been tense lately.

Emma leaned closer and said in a low voice, "I think you should squeeze in some S-E-X."

Madeline laughed. "Oh, sure. Like that's going to happen at a corporate team building. I know it's been a long time since I've actually had sex, so my memory's a little fuzzy, but if I recall correctly, one requires a *partner.* A living, breathing partner, as opposed to a battery-operated one." Still chuckling, she popped her shrimp into her mouth.

"And that's what I'm suggesting you find." Emma waggled her brows. "Just like I did."

Madeline paused midchew, then swallowed. "What did you find?"

"A living, breathing partner." Emma heaved out a gushy sigh. "And I can sum him up in one word: *yummy.* He was all action, no talk, and just what the doctor ordered. I highly recommend a good old-fashioned one-night stand."

"When did this happen? Where? How? I thought we were on a man sabbatical." After suffering through one too many disastrous dates with men who were either boring or arrogant or commitment-phobes interested only in sex, she and Emma had decided to take a break from the singles scene and concentrate on themselves. They'd taken up jogging and signed up for a cooking class, and for a while things had gone well. She'd lost three pounds—which she gained back during the cooking class—but it was such a relief not to have to deal with dating.

Lately, however, relief had morphed into loneliness and she'd been rethinking her decision. Unfortunately, with work so busy, she didn't have the time right now to devote to a social life.

"We *were* on a sabbatical," Emma agreed. "But after six months of celibacy, I was feeling kinda stressed, not to mention horny. I met a man who lit my fire, and *whew*!" She waved her hand in front of her face. "Let me tell you, he was hot. As for when and where—last night, at the Ritz-Carlton. And as for how"—her lips curved in a slow smile—"Good lord, how *didn't* that man please me?"

A fissure of what could only be described as envy rippled through

Madeline. "Okay, I'm officially jealous. But I meant how did you meet him?"

Emma waved her fork around. "Right here. In this very food court. Yesterday. The place was packed—not an empty table in sight. Tons of schoolkids. Must have been some mega class trip downtown. There was an empty chair at my table, he asked if could join me, and . . . there you have it."

"If he was so fantastic, why was it just a one-nighter? Why not see him again?"

"He lives in New York and was here just for a few days for a conference. He flew home this morning." Emma forked up another bite of salad. "Which made it perfect—a night of great sex with no expectations, no messy relationship stuff, no awkward date. I feel *sooooo* much better. You should try it. This weekend. At the resort."

"Right. Except you're forgetting I've never been good at the one-night stand situation. The few times I've made the attempt, it just didn't work out."

"You mean you *chickened* out."

"I did not. I was just struck with shyness."

"Uh-huh. Which is secret code for 'I chickened out.'" Emma helpfully demonstrated her point by flapping her arms and making clucking sounds.

Maddie sighed. "Okay, fine. I chickened out."

"So this time don't. Be brave. Be bold. Be daring."

Could she do it? History said no, but she was so tired of being alone. "Well, if I *was* going to give it a go, who do you propose I have this steaming one-nighter with? Certainly not one of the Java Heaven people. You know I never swim in the company pool." An image flashed in her mind—of deep blue eyes, dark hair, and a sexy smile—an image she instantly banished. Why in God's name did that annoying pest Jack Walker always pop into her mind at the most inappropriate moments?

"I know, although I think it's a gray area since your tenure at any company is finite. But in this case, it's not necessary to even consider anyone from Java Heaven." Emma reached into her soft-sided leather briefcase and pulled out the newspaper. She shuffled through several sections, then handed the sports section to Maddie. "Check out the little blurb on the bottom left."

Maddie quickly scanned the brief article. "There's a charity golf tournament taking place this weekend at Casa di Lago." She glanced up. "What does that have to do with me?"

Emma rolled her eyes. "Did you not notice who's taking part in this golf tournament? Firemen. *Lots* of firemen. Hot, sexy, muscular, sexy, delicious—did I mention sexy?—firemen. At least one of whom I'm sure would be very willing and able to end your sexual drought. You'd have a great weekend, let off some steam, then never have to see him again. Take it from me—it's a perfect opportunity."

The thought of a no-holds-barred, no-commitment-required, liberating night of wild sex rushed heat through Maddie's entire body. "That sounds good," she admitted.

"Of course it does. Just a little something to take the edge off."

"Right. 'Til the real thing comes along."

"Exactly. Good grief, Maddie, you're twenty-eight years old. It's time you indulged in a one-nighter. Don't be so serious all the time."

"I'm not serious *all* the time." Yet even as she said the words, she realized that over the last few months she had been. She'd forgotten how to have fun. She'd moved into her dateless cave where aggravating men didn't exist, but neither did any potentially good men—and they had to be out there somewhere. Didn't they? Just because she didn't currently know any didn't mean they were merely urban myths.

Although one-night stands had never been her style, she clearly needed a change. Something to jolt her out of her cave. A night of hot sex would certainly do that.

"So—what are you going to do?"

Maddie grabbed a pea pod with her chopsticks. "Pack my sexiest lingerie and find a fireman to put out this damn inferno inside me."

Emma grinned. " 'Atta girl. And don't you dare chicken out. I'll expect a full report Monday. Let's meet here for lunch."

"Fine. Hopefully I'll have something interesting to tell you . . ." Her words trailed off into a low groan and she scooted low in her seat. "Damn. What's *he* doing here?"

"Who?" Emma whispered, leaning close and looking around furtively.

"Jack Walker."

Emma's blue eyes widened. "The Demon CFO of Java Heaven? Mr. Misery?"

"And Olympic gold medalist for Pain in the Ass. The very same. What are the chances he'd be here?"

"Actually, since the office is only three blocks away, pretty good." Emma leaned a bit closer. "Which one is he?"

Maddie's gaze flicked over Emma's shoulder. "Tall, dark hair, charcoal gray suit, standing in line at the pizza place."

Emma gave a surreptitious glance over her shoulder, one that turned into a double take. When she looked back at Maddie her mouth was hanging open. "*That's* the guy you've been calling *repulsive*?" Emma took another peek, and even though Maddie didn't want to look at him again, she found herself doing so. Jack was paying for his lunch, smiling at the cashier, then he laughed at something she said. He picked up his tray and found a table on the other side of the food court.

Jack Walker. Java Heaven CFO.

And currently the bane of her existence.

It was clear from her first day on the Java Heaven job a month ago that the new CFO wasn't happy she was there. Not that she cared—she was accustomed to employees giving her the stink eye. Coming on board at Java Heaven certainly wasn't the first time she'd been viewed as an interloper, a sentiment she could actually sympathize with. It was simply human nature that most people were initially resistant to change and to outsiders. She took pride in her role of helping companies run more efficiently, and early on in her career had developed a thick skin. She wasn't at Java Heaven to win any popularity contests. And besides, she certainly didn't care what Jack Walker thought of her.

"Honey, if you think that man is repulsive, you need new glasses. Stat."

Emma's voice yanked Maddie's attention back to her friend. "I didn't mean he's *physically* repulsive." Although she wished he was. It simply wasn't fair that such a pain in the butt was so extremely attractive. "But we both know the type—good-looking guy who clearly knows it."

Emma nodded. "The better looking they are, the worse they are."

"Exactly."

"Which means he must be really, really bad. 'Cause looks-wise, he's really, really good. How old is he?"

"Office scuttlebutt is that he's thirty-two."

"Perfect. Not too young, not too old, although on the young side for a CFO. He must be very smart."

"Yes. And in his case, with great intelligence comes great annoyance."

Emma laughed. "You sure he's not taken?"

"He's not married, or engaged," Maddie said, "but he's definitely a player." She'd observed a number of female employees giving Jack Walker the once-over—more than once. Although she had to grudgingly admit she couldn't blame them, nor had she seen him catch any of the ogling passes tossed his way. Still, she knew a player when she saw one. "He takes long lunches every Wednesday, often returning to the office with his tie askew. Yeah, like it isn't obvious what he'd been up to. Yesterday he came back from his Wednesday lunch with red on his collar. As if I don't know lipstick when I see it. He probably has more notches on his bedpost than an entire college fraternity. No doubt the sidewalk outside his house is littered with broken hearts."

"Well, based on looks alone, he'd be an easy man to say yes to." A gleam entered Emma's eyes and she leaned forward. "Hey—if you can't find a fireman to warm you up, why not give Mr. Gorgeous a chance?"

A wave of heat that had nothing to do with her spicy shrimp

stir-fry suffused Maddie. Get naked with Jack Walker? That sounded . . .

Absolutely terrible, screamed her common sense.

Absolutely freakin' fantastic, shouted her suddenly awake libido.

She stared across the table at Emma. "Clearly his good looks have addled your brain. Are you nuts? There are so many things wrong with that suggestion I don't even know where to begin."

"Name one."

"We work together."

Emma waved her lettuce-laden fork in a dismissive gesture. "But that's the gray area. You'll only be working together for another month."

"Yes. A month that is going to be difficult enough without adding sex into the mix. Jack already sees me as an interloper, a troublemaker, and a spy for the CEO. It does not make for a pleasant work environment."

Emma shot her a wink. "A few orgasms might change that."

Maddie's gaze involuntarily drifted to Jack, who was taking a huge bite of what looked like pepperoni pizza. He didn't carry an ounce of fat on what was obviously a very fit physique—just one more thing to dislike about him. He could eat fattening, cheesy pizza without it adhering to his ass for eight months. Damn, he even looked good when he chewed.

Just then his gaze connected with hers. And like it did every time he looked at her, for several seconds she seemed to freeze and heat at the same time—like a deer caught in the headlights while surrounded by a ring of fire. For the space of a heartbeat he seemed to still as well. The image of them, together, sharing a few orgasms, seared through her mind, stunning her. He gave her a curt nod then looked down at the book resting open on his table.

"You okay?"

Emma's voice jerked her back. "Huh?"

"You look flushed. Are you hot?"

On fire. And it was all that annoying man's fault. If she was having sexual fantasies about a man she didn't even like, it was definitely time to end her sexual drought.

"It's warm in here," Maddie said. "What were we talking about?"

"Jack Gorgeous Walker."

"Right. But you're forgetting he's also Jack Pain in the Ass Walker. Besides, the fact that he's gorgeous is half the problem. Thanks to Danny I know all too well that handsome on the outside doesn't always equal handsome on the inside." She shoved aside all thoughts of her last steady boyfriend and heaved a sigh. "Why is it that where men are concerned, there seems to be an inverse proportion of good looks to integrity: The better looking he is, the greater the chance he's an asshole?"

"Don't know," Emma said, "but it should probably be some scientific law. Like relativity or gravity."

"I suppose I have to admit—grudgingly—that Jack's intelligent and doing a good job in a difficult situation, but that doesn't mean he couldn't use some outside help. Of course, he's too arrogant to see that. Oh, sure, he'll sit across from me at a conference table and hear out my suggestions, but it's clear from his excruciatingly polite expression and the way he seems to look *through* me rather than *at* me that he's merely humoring me."

"I hate it when men do that," Emma agreed, stabbing a crouton with her fork.

"Outright hostility I can deal with, but Jack's method of hearing me but not listening to me, of looking at me but not seeing me, is so annoying."

"He's scum." Emma blew out a regretful-sounding sigh. "But damn, he is *hot* scum."

Much as she wanted to, Maddie couldn't deny it. "But in my book, *annoying* trumps *hot* every time. Plus, not only is he annoying, I simply don't understand him. Most of the executive types I've met are driven, to the point of working seventy or eighty hours a week. Jack doesn't put in a minute of overtime on Fridays."

"Probably wants to get an early start on the weekend," Emma said, crunching on her crouton.

"Oh, yeah. I pegged him as the boff-a-babe-at-lunchtime, love-and-leave-'em sort I can't stand the day I met him. Not that it matters. I only need to deal with him for another month and then I'll be gone from Java Heaven and on to my next assignment. And I'll never have to see Jack Walker again."

Emma stole another peek over her shoulder. "It is so unfair that all that lovely male pulchritude is wasted on someone so undeserving."

"Agreed." Because if he were a nice guy, she'd jump him in a heartbeat.

Yeah, her and every other woman in Atlanta. Yet clearly his annoying traits weren't hindering his success with women. Not that she was envious of his obviously active social life. Heck no. She had no desire to sleep with a bunch of different men—a preference that had led to her current sexual drought. Of course, sleeping with *one* man—a man who mattered—would be nice. But finding a man who mattered—one with integrity, and intelligence, a sense of humor, and a liking for monogamy—had proven as difficult as locating a single pearl on a fifty-mile stretch of beach.

Dating in Atlanta was brutal. While in theory a one-night stand might be good for what ailed her—and she'd definitely been tense lately—finding a man she wanted to get naked with was proving a challenge. Although the city was littered with attractive men, it unfortunately took more than looks to interest her. Still, for the purposes of a one-night stand with a sexy, golfing fireman, handsome was enough. Emma was right. She'd chickened out in the past but she wouldn't this time. After all, this weekend she was just looking for one night—not for forever.

Three

As soon as she arrived back at her office after lunch, Maddie checked her e-mail. The weekend's itinerary had arrived from Carla and she opened the attachment. Pushing up her glasses, she perused the schedule, and was surprised to see she was expected to arrive Friday evening. Her gaze skimmed lower, then fastened on the activity listed for Saturday morning. What on earth . . . ? She blinked, but the words remained, and her brows collapsed in a scowl.

"Oh, no," she murmured through clenched teeth. "Not just no . . . *hell* no."

Was this insanity Jack's idea—or Gavin's? Obviously one of them was responsible, but her money was on Jack. Anything to piss her off and make her suffer. Well, she wasn't having any of it.

With the schedule gripped in her hand, she marched out of her office and headed down the long corridor that separated the executive offices from the cubicles, wondering if steam actually spewed from her ears.

She understood the need for this team building weekend. In fact, she'd suggested it to Gavin and set up the entire thing, using Atlanta's most respected motivational team-building company. It was just what the doctor ordered to get the accounting department back on track, plus it would provide her with an excellent opportunity to make the sort of observations she needed to present her report to Gavin. He wanted the accounting staff downsized from twenty to fifteen by the end of the month and he was counting on her report to advise him as to which employees should be let go in that reduction.

But there was a huge difference between attending the weekend and *this*. She shook the itinerary and shot it another baleful look as she strode along. This other *thing* was simply out of the question.

She looked up. Jack's office was only a few doors away. Filled with grim determination, she advanced toward the door marked Jack Walker, Chief Financial Officer.

As she approached, she heard his deep voice. Pausing outside his ajar door, she heard him say, "I'm sorry, too, sweetheart . . . I know, I was looking forward to it, too." He heaved a sigh. "No, it's one of those business things I can't get out of. But I'll make it up to you." He fell silent for several seconds then gave a low chuckle. "Deal. I'm looking forward to that . . . okay, sweetheart. Talk to you soon."

Several seconds of silence followed and Madeline realized he'd ended his call. Drawing a bracing breath, she stepped into the half-open doorway. He stood with his back to her, looking out the window, his cell phone pressed to his ear. He'd removed his charcoal gray suit jacket and rolled up his sleeves. She refused to acknowledge that the rear view he was treating her to was in any way . . . a treat.

She was about to knock when he said into the phone, "Hey babe, it's Jack. Sorry I've missed you. Just calling to let you know I've gotta bail on our plans this weekend."

Madeline shook her head. Jeez, how many "sweethearts" and "babes" did he have to break dates with this weekend?

"Really sorry 'cause I was looking forward to us—"

His words cut off when he turned around and saw her standing in the doorway, hand raised and poised to knock. She froze, and for several seconds silence swelled as they stared across the expanse of his office at each other. While the rear view had been exceptionally nice, the full frontal packed a serious wallop. Six-one, broad shoulders, deep blue eyes, firm, square jaw—complete with an intriguing indent in his chin—and a mouth that somehow managed to look hard and soft at the same time. His thick dark hair looked slightly rumpled, as if he'd dragged his hands through it, an imperfection that did nothing to detract from his physical appeal. Damn it, it simply wasn't fair that he was so attractive. And such a pest.

His eyes narrowed and he said into the phone, "I'll call you later." With his gaze still boring into hers, he snapped his phone shut then set it on his desk. "Eavesdropping, Ms. Price?"

Heat flooded Madeline's face and she raised her chin. "Certainly not."

Um, actually you were *eavesdropping*, her annoyingly honest inner voice pointed out.

Okay, fine, she'd been eavesdropping. But not on purpose. It was an accidental eavesdropping. Because his door was partially open. So actually the entire thing was his fault. Based on his scowl, he wouldn't appreciate her pointing that out.

"I was just about to knock when you turned around," she said. "Do you have a minute?"

He muttered something that sounded suspiciously like *Do I have a choice?* then said, "Sure. But not much more than a minute. I have a meeting. What can I do for you?"

Drop the arrogant attitude. Then ugly yourself up. A paunch and a few hairy warts on your nose should do the trick. "Have you seen the itinerary for this weekend's team building?"

"Not yet."

She crossed the mocha-colored carpet and handed him the memo. "Read it and weep."

He gave it a brief scan. "Looks pretty standard . . ." His words trailed off and his brows jerked downward. "What's this?" He looked up at her and she knew what he'd seen.

"You're not responsible for that?" she asked.

He made an incredulous sound. "For scheduling me and you for a six A.M. orienteering session Saturday morning? Hardly. Is this your idea of a joke?"

"I know what orienteering is. Believe me, there is nothing funny about the thought of you and me stuck in the woods together with nothing but a compass and a map to guide us."

"Then clearly it's a typo."

"Heck of a typo. Who do you think they meant to send you out into the woods with? Carmen Electra?"

"I meant the entire idea of you and me doing *anything* together. Especially at six A.M."

In spite of the fact that she was equally opposed to doing *anything* with him, especially at six A.M., she took umbrage at his insulting tone. *Humph.* There were lots of men who would be damn glad to be stuck in the woods with her at six A.M. Probably. Just because she didn't know any of those men didn't mean they didn't exist. Somewhere.

"Being stuck in the woods with you isn't exactly my idea of a good time, either." She narrowed her eyes. "So this isn't your doing?"

"Hardly. Which means it must be—"

"Gavin," they said simultaneously.

"I'll take care of this." Jack reached for his desk phone and punched a few numbers. "Carla, this is Jack," he said into the receiver. "Is Gavin available?" A few seconds later, he said, "Gavin, I just saw the itinerary for this weekend's retreat. About this orienteering outing with Madeline—"

Jack's words cut off and he frowned. "But . . . is it really neces—" A long pause. "But the expense— Oh. Everyone else isn't arriving until Saturday morning." Another long pause, interspersed with a few muttered "I sees," and more scowling followed. "Yes . . . uh-huh . . . right . . . okay. I understand." He replaced the receiver and faced her.

"Well, you really told him," she deadpanned. "Way to take care of it. I don't know word for word what Gavin said, but based on your end of the conversation and your expression, I'm guessing it was Gavin's idea and that we're going orienteering Saturday morning."

"At six A.M.," Jack confirmed, looking as displeased as she felt.

"Did he say why?" Maddie asked.

"Yes. He 'senses some tension' between us and 'wants us to bond.'" His gaze practically skewered her. "What a load of garbage."

"Biggest load of garbage I've ever heard," she said, not to be outdone. "Based on your accusatory tone and expression, you clearly think this tension is my fault."

"If the shoe fits . . ."

"Did it ever occur to you that your my-way-or-the-highway attitude might be the problem?"

"Frankly, no," he said. "Because I'm not that way at all, which if you knew me even slightly you would know. And I find it very amusing that you of all people would accuse me of being so." He mimicked picking up the phone. "Hello, Kettle? Black Pot calling."

She forced herself to draw a deep, calming breath and bury her annoyance at him for being, well, so damn annoying, and at herself, for allowing him to get to her. "I'm only here to help, Jack. I'm not the enemy."

He favored her with that looking-right-through-her expression that spiked her blood pressure. Although he didn't utter a word, she could see his resentment and it really rankled. Enough for her to say, "I think I must be clairvoyant, because I can easily read your thoughts."

"Oh? What am I thinking?"

Adopting a masculine, deep voice, she said, "'She's getting paid big bucks to give answers I already know to questions I never even asked. She knows squat about my business—for cryin' out loud, she doesn't even like coffee—and I don't want her here.'"

He considered for several seconds, then nodded. "That sums it up very well. Except you left out 'and I sure as hell don't want to be stuck in the woods with her.' "

"Sorry." She shot him a fake smile. "My psychic abilities become depleted when surrounded by too much hot air and testosterone."

He matched her fake smile with one of his own. "As a consultant, you would be the expert on hot air."

"Ha ha. And don't worry about being stuck in the woods with me. I know how to use a map and a compass. Plus, unlike the male of the species, I'm not afraid to ask for directions."

"Ha ha to you, too. As for this orienteering bonding thing—it doesn't matter that we don't like the idea. Gavin wants it and that's the way it is." His gaze wandered down to her high-heeled patent leather pumps. "Are you going to be able to handle being in the woods?"

"Are *you* going to be able to handle having to ask me for help to get out of the woods?"

"I won't need to ask for help. Or directions."

"Typical. Do you know how many lost men have uttered that same statement?"

"No. But I don't get lost. I have an excellent sense of direction."

"Uh-huh. Ten bucks says you get us lost at least once."

He raised his brows, then smiled. Damn, he had a great smile. No fair. "Deal. You realize you'll never see that ten bucks."

"If I don't, it's only because you've refused to admit that we're lost."

"Noooo," he said as if she were in kindergarten. "It's because of my superior directional abilities."

"Right. Please, don't mind me. I'm just looking at the ceiling. Really. Not rolling my eyes at all."

"I promise that if I'm lost I'll admit it."

"Do you know how many lost men have uttered *that* same statement?"

He raised his hand, like a boy taking a scout's pledge. "I am a man of my word."

"Excellent. Then let's make it twenty bucks. I need a new lipstick."

His gaze dropped to her mouth, and something flickered in his eyes. Something that looked hot and raw and heated her from the inside out. Good grief, her sexual drought now had her imagining things, like a thirst-crazed person in a desert who sees a mirage of an oasis. But damn, that look affected her as if he'd actually caressed her, and she found herself moistening her lips.

And that time there was absolutely no mistaking the heat that flared in his eyes. *Whoa.* For the space of two erratic heartbeats he stared at her mouth as if she were a warm fudge brownie and he were craving sugar.

Then he blinked and shook his head, as if coming out of some sort of trance. Probably the same one that had clubbed her over the head. He obviously said something to her, because she saw his lips moving, but damned if she knew what it was. So she said the only word she could cough up.

"Huh?"

"Twenty bucks for a lipstick seems pretty steep."

"Oh? You shop for many lipsticks?"

"No, I'm just making an observation. As a fiscally responsible CFO type."

"Are you implying I'm fiscally *ir*responsible?"

"No. I'm just saying I think twenty bucks is a lot for a lipstick. But I'm not surprised, coming from someone who plans an expensive weekend bonding deal at a resort."

"Well, as a fiscally responsible consultant type, I can assure you it depends on the lipstick. Some are definitely worth it. And the weekend won't cost nearly as much as years of unproductive interactions in the workplace."

Again his gaze dropped to her lips, and for several seconds she couldn't breathe. Then he frowned and handed her back her itinerary. "If you say so. And now, if you'll excuse me, I have a meeting."

"Of course." She left his office, relieved to be away from whatever momentary madness had gripped her. She walked with her usual brisk pace back to her own office, and was halfway down the hallway when she felt the weight of someone's stare. She looked over her shoulder and nearly stumbled when she noticed Jack leaning against his doorjamb, watching her. His expression appeared to be a combination of confusion and irritation.

She resumed her pace, and realized that's precisely how she felt—confused and irritated. Why the heck had he, of all people, made her dormant hormones jump like they'd been zapped with a Taser? That was irritating. *He* was irritating.

And unfortunately, given their forced proximity during this upcoming weekend, she knew more irritation awaited her on the horizon.

Good thing she couldn't stand Jack Walker. Because if she did . . . well, *that* would be *really* irritating.

Four

By the time Jack finally arrived at Casa di Lago Friday night, he was tired, annoyed, hungry, and thirsty. Thanks to computer problems his day at work had been stressful. He'd enjoyed a light, early dinner, but then courtesy of Atlanta's notoriously heavy Friday night traffic, combined with the never ending road construction and a fender bender that blocked three lanes of the interstate, the hour-and-a-half drive to the resort had turned into a three-and-a-half-hour nightmare. All he wanted was a cold drink, some hot food, and some serious sleep.

After parking his car, he dragged his tired ass toward the resort's curved archway entrance, pulling his black carry-on-sized suitcase behind him, and in spite of his exhaustion, decided things were looking up. The grounds were beautiful, with perfectly manicured lawns and flower-lined paths, all lit by hidden lights and bathed in moonlight. The resort itself had been fashioned after an Italian villa. The pale yellow stucco exterior, dotted with elegantly curved archways and black wrought iron balcony railings, made Jack feel as if he were visiting the shores of Lake Como rather than those of Lake

Lanier. He'd visited the resort once, several years ago, and had been impressed with the service, food, amenities, and accommodations. He couldn't wait to experience them all again. Like right now.

He entered the lobby, and the soaring ceiling, golden cream marble floor, woven rugs, carved columns, tasteful artwork, and the gentle scent of fresh flowers went by in a blur. All his attention was focused on four things: register, drink, eat, sleep. In that order. Right now he was much more interested in smelling a cheeseburger than anything that sat in a vase.

He spied the registration desk ahead and quickened his steps. Another guest was registering and it looked like only one person was behind the counter. *Damn.* Hopefully the woman registering was almost done, but somehow he always ended up stuck in line behind someone experiencing a major problem of some sort that required much help and much time.

As he drew closer, he idly noted that in spite of the prim cut of the registering woman's brown suit, she had great legs. Just then she turned slightly, and his footsteps faltered as recognition hit him. He barely stifled the groan that rose in his throat. Of all people, why did it have to be *her*? Mad Dog Price was the last person he wanted to deal with now. Bad enough he'd be forced to see her in . . . he glanced at his watch. Eight hours.

He kept walking, frowning as his eyeballs again zeroed in on her legs. They were pretty spectacular. Where the hell had they come from, and how the hell had he missed them? And how unfair that they were wasted on a dragon lady. Just then she rose up on her toes and leaned forward to say something around the vase of flowers to the man behind the counter who'd stepped to the side. Jack blinked. *Wow.* Even that mud-colored suit couldn't quite hide what was clearly a very nice butt.

So intent was he on reaching his goal of the registration desk—and staring at her unexpectedly fine ass—that he didn't realize she'd turned her head. And was staring at him. Staring at her ass.

When he looked up and made that discovery, his jaw tightened with self-directed annoyance. Bad enough he'd looked at her in a way that could only be described as an ogle. *Really* bad that he'd been caught in the act.

Damn. This day was going from bad to worse.

Making sure he kept his gaze steady on hers, he offered her a nod in greeting, one she returned, then he walked between the velvet ropes that marked the line for registration.

"I can take you here, sir," said a young man with a bright smile who positioned himself before a computer next to the man helping Mad Dog. Jack moved up to the desk, parked his bag next to Madeline's, then gave the clerk his name.

"You're checking in late," Madeline said.

"I could say the same to you."

"*I* worked late."

He detected the emphasis on the *I* and gritted his teeth. So he'd left work at five o'clock. He was allowed. His reasons were none of her business. Even though his better judgment told him to shut up, he found himself saying, "Some of us have a life outside the job."

As soon as the words left his mouth, he was surprised to find himself wondering what sort of life *she* led outside work. He realized that although he'd known her for a month, he didn't know anything about her. Except that she was a thorn in his side and a pain in his ass. And really, that was all he needed to know.

"Ready for our big adventure tomorrow?" she asked.

Jack handed the clerk his credit card then turned toward Madeline. She was peering at him over the rims of her rectangular black-rimmed glasses. With her severely pulled back hair, she looked like a prim schoolmarm.

"Sure thing," he answered. "Can't wait. Really. I mean that. I'm not at all envious of the rest of the department who don't need to check in until ten A.M. tomorrow."

"I can't wait, either." She smiled and batted her eyes. "Mama needs a new lipstick."

His gaze flicked down to her mouth and his jaw tightened at the sight of her full lips. Just as he had with her legs, he had to wonder where that plump, perfectly shaped mouth had come from and why he hadn't noticed it until they'd placed their foolish bet yesterday. Right now her lips looked ripe and shiny—like a juicy peach. *Peach* . . . damn, he loved peaches. And damn, he was hungry.

A bellhop pushing a wheeled cart took charge of Jack's bag and Madeline's as well, jerking Jack's attention from Mad Dog's peachy lips. He was tempted to tell the bellhop he could handle his suitcase himself, but decided not to expend the effort. The bellhop headed toward the elevator, and Jack leaned against the counter, dreaming of a tall glass of something cold, a juicy cheeseburger, and a comfortable bed.

"You look beat up," came Mad Dog's voice. "Rough day?"

He swiveled his eyes toward her. "Gee, thanks. I might go all to pieces, what with so many compliments."

She raised one eyebrow. "Just making an honest observation. Besides, I'm sure you already get plenty of compliments."

Jack was certain that comment meant something snarky—as opposed to complimentary—but before his tired brain could figure it out, she accepted her key card from the man behind the counter. After thanking him, she said to Jack, "See you in the morning."

Morning. Right. For their fun-filled orienteering extravaganza. *Yippee*. After taking his key card, he headed toward the elevator, and was not pleased to see that Mad Dog stood before the shiny brass door. He'd hoped she'd be gone already. As he approached, the green Up arrow glowed and the door slid open. He followed her into the paneled elevator.

"What floor?" she asked as she pushed the round button with a three on it.

"Three." Great. Not only were they in the same hotel, they were staying on the same floor.

The door closed with a quiet *whoosh*, ensconcing them in the enclosed space. Soft music played. Jack noted her reflection in the shiny brass door, saw that her eyes slid closed. Clearly she was as tired as he.

"I heard a joke today," she said, her eyes still closed. "What's the definition of an accountant?"

"Just what I want—an accountant joke. Like I haven't been hearing them since the day I declared my major in college. Any chance you won't bother to tell me?"

A smile pulled up one corner of her mouth. "Nope. An accountant is someone who solves a problem you didn't know you had in a way you don't understand."

"Oh, yeah. That's a side-buster. Do you know the definition of a consultant?" Before she could answer, he said, "It's a person who you will never hear say, 'Everything looks okay to me.' "

To his surprise, she chuckled. "Guess I asked for that. What's the difference between an accountant and a vampire?"

"A vampire only sucks blood at night. Believe me, I've heard them all. Here's something else you'll never hear a consultant say—"

" 'You're right, we're billing way too much for this.' " She opened her eyes and their gazes met in the brass reflection. "I've heard them all, too."

The elevator stopped and the doors slid open. He extended his arm, indicating she should precede him, and she raised her brows. "So polite," she murmured as she exited.

He followed her, noting that she left a subtle hint of something that smelled really good in her wake. Something that smelled like . . . cookies? Damn. He loved cookies. His stomach rumbled.

"Just because I'm a bloodsucking vampire doesn't mean I don't have any manners."

"At least you admit it."

"That I have manners?"

"That you're a bloodsucking vampire."

His gaze settled on her neck and he was suddenly seized with the unwanted and inappropriate urge to nibble on that soft-looking skin to find out if she tasted as good as she smelled. "Says the consultant who admitted she'd never say 'You're right, we're billing way too much for this.' "

He checked the sign on the wall that indicated the room directions and headed to the right, noting she fell into step beside him. *Great*. Same hotel, same floor, and now rooms apparently near each other. He stopped outside room 314. "Well, good night. See you in the lobby at six."

She stopped directly across the hall, outside room 315, and looked at him over her shoulder. A tendril had escaped her severely pulled back hair and rested on her cheek, a slash of brown against pale skin that somehow made her look almost human.

" 'Night." She entered her room and the door closed with a quiet click.

The instant Jack's door closed behind him, he let out a sigh of relief. First stop was the minibar, where he helped himself to a bottle of water and a bag of peanut M&M's. After popping several candied nuts into his mouth and washing them down with a long, cool drink, he picked up the phone and ordered room service. He could almost taste that cheeseburger, fries, cole slaw, and chocolate brownie already. The turkey sandwich he'd eaten for dinner hours ago was but a memory.

The bellhop had already delivered his suitcase—talk about fast service—and he simultaneously toed off his shoes and shrugged his suit jacket from his shoulders. After tossing the jacket on the nearest chair, he slipped off his already loosened tie and flicked open the buttons on his dress shirt, all while looking over the room. Muted earth tones, brightened by attractive framed prints depicting nautical scenes, tasteful cherrywood furnishings. The best part was the king-sized bed that beckoned him like a siren with promises of a comfortable night's sleep.

Still working on his shirt, he clicked on the financial news channel, noting that the stock market had enjoyed an upswing. At least something good had happened today. Keeping one eye on the TV, and still popping M&M's, he zipped open his suitcase. Might as well unpack while he waited for his meal.

With his attention on the TV, he reached into the suitcase to pull out his favorite Braves T-shirt, which he'd packed right on top. When he looked down, he halted midchew and blinked. Instead of his T-shirt, he held a bit of black lace that looked like a . . . thong?

What the hell? He held up the wisp of material that definitely wasn't his T-shirt and frowned. Definitely a thong. Definitely sexy. Definitely not his.

He looked at the suitcase and reached for the next item. Instead of his sweatpants, he pulled out a lacy black bra that matched the thong. As if in a trance, he replaced the bra and checked out a few more items on the top. Some sort of sexy corset-looking thing. A slinky see-through number in fire-engine red. A bottle of massage oil. And a box of thirty-six condoms. A book entitled *Fifty Ways to Please Your Lover.* On top of the book was a note. Without even meaning to, his gaze scanned the brief message. *Don't you dare lose your nerve! Be brave! Be daring! Have your one-night stand with a sexy fireman and ENJOY yourself. You'll feel soooo much better. I'll want all the details at lunch on Monday. Go get 'em, girl! XOX Emma*

Wow. Somebody was expecting a sex-filled weekend. He looked closer at the bag and realized that it was identical to his, right down to the same brand name. Realization struck and he froze. The bellhop had only had two bags on his cart. His and . . .

Mad Dog's.

Holy crap. No freakin' way did this assortment of sexy goodies belong to that frosty dragon. *No way.*

He stared at the thong dangling from his fingertips. His suddenly active imagination shifted into overdrive, filling his mind with a picture of those curves hinted at beneath her prim, mud-brown skirt filling out the wispy bit of black lace. Which snapped everything male in him to attention.

This is what the icy consultant pest wore underneath those prim, boring suits? Whoa. And people thought Victoria had secrets. His gaze shifted back to the open suitcase, and before he could stop himself, he reached out and ran a single fingertip over the cup of the black lace bra.

His conscience coughed to life. *Okay, dude, hands off. Touching her underwear is just . . . wrong. What are you, some kind of perv?*

He snatched his hand away as if her lingerie had suddenly spurt flames. Of course he wasn't a perv. At least he hadn't been until he'd opened her suitcase. He was just . . . curious. And surprised. He sure as hell wouldn't have equated someone so prim with a one-night stand seeker. He'd read about the fireman charity golf tournament taking place at the resort this weekend. Clearly she had, too. Still, he would have bet his entire 401K that Mad Dog wore sensible, white cotton granny panties beneath her schoolmarm clothes. Not that he'd ever pondered her underwear or thought of her in *that* way. Hell no.

Oh, c'mon, admit it. You've thought about her in that *way more than once since you made your stupid bet. You were thinking of her in that way not twenty minutes ago when you ogled her legs.*

Okay, fine. But he hadn't known they were her legs when he'd ogled them. Or her ass.

You knew they were her lips when you ogled them, his inner voice whispered slyly.

Damn pesky inner voice. Why couldn't it lie? Just once in a while? He went to rake his hands through his hair and realized her thong still dangled from his fingers. He stared at the sexy bit of lace and groaned. He did *not* want to know this about her. Did not want to think about her wearing this under her prim and proper clothes. Think of her wearing it to entice some fireman into a one-nighter. Hell, he didn't want to think about her at all. Time to replace the panties, zip up the bag, and give her back her incredibly sexy lingerie. Yup, that was absolutely the only thing to do. Certainly better than standing here staring. And fantasizing.

Annoyed with himself, he replaced the thong and slapped down the suitcase's lid. Clearly the only reason he would, for even one nanosecond, fantasize about Mad Dog Price was because his brain was fried. He pulled the zipper closed then stepped back. *There. Done.*

Of course, this meant that she had *his* suitcase. He ran a quick mental inventory of what he'd packed and groaned. If she opened his suitcase, she'd surely have questions—questions he wasn't inclined to answer. But . . . since she hadn't knocked on his door yet, maybe that meant she hadn't discovered the Case of the Double Suitcase. Maybe, just maybe, he could get to her in time.

He grabbed her suitcase and headed toward his door.

Five

Fresh from a much needed hot shower that went a long way toward loosening the tense kinks in her neck, Maddie ran a quick brush through her damp hair then wrapped herself in the thick, luxuriously soft terry cloth robe provided by the hotel. Although she'd arrived at the resort later than she'd planned, it was still early enough to change into her Catch a Fireman Dress and scope out the bar. While she dressed, she'd peruse Emma's pep talk note and the copy of *Fifty Ways to Please Your Lover* her best friend had given her for encouragement. And hope her nerve didn't desert her.

When she exited the bathroom her gaze fell on the minibar and she realized she was hungry. *Really* hungry. The meager salad she'd eaten for dinner at her desk was long gone. Drat. Anything she ate now would permanently adhere itself to her hips. Oh, well. That's what treadmills were for.

She selected the bag of peanut M&M's and popped one in her mouth while unzipping her suitcase. If she found her one-night stand tonight she wouldn't get much sleep before her orienteering outing. *Ugh.* At six A.M. *Double ugh.* With Jack Walker. *Triple ugh.*

His words echoed in her ears. *Some of us have a life outside the job.* Arrogant ass. No wonder he'd checked in so late—probably had an entire roster of women he'd had to appease. Well, she had a life outside her job, too. One that was going to get much more exciting this weekend courtesy of some as of yet unknown fireman.

In anticipation of seeing her newly purchased lingerie, she flipped open the suitcase lid. And stared. At what had to be the rattiest looking T-shirt she'd ever seen. She could tell by the tomahawk it was a Braves shirt, but the lettering was so faded, it read 3 aves. What the heck? She moved aside the T-shirt. Okay, who had taken *Fifty Ways to Please Your Lover* and exchanged it for *How to Find Your Soul Mate*? Gone was her slinky lingerie and condoms. In their place was a huge pair of sneakers and a slim hardback entitled *Dealing with Your Four-Year-Old*.

Clearly this was the wrong suitca—

She closed her eyes and clapped a hand against her head.

Oh, God.

The bellhop must have mixed up her bag with Jack's. She slapped the lid closed and looked at the brand label. Yup. Same exact bag. Which meant that he had her bag. Her bag filled with condoms. And lingerie. And sexy reading material.

And Emma's note revealing her one-night stand plans.

Heat crept up her neck, instantly annoying her. So what if he saw all that? It was none of his damn business. She reached for the tab to pull the zipper closed, but hesitated as she recalled the titles of the two books she'd seen. Surely she must be mistaken. Compelled by a curiosity she didn't quite understand, she opened the lid again.

Clearly the man was a Braves fan, but that was hardly surprising. No, it was his reading material that had her doing a double take. She would have expected dog-eared copies of men's magazines featuring scantily clad women. Jack Walker, aka the Lunchtime Boffing Machine, certainly didn't strike her as the sort of man to read *How to Find Your Soul Mate*. Even more surprising was the guide on raising a four-year-old. Jack had a child? Based on office gossip she knew he wasn't married. She hadn't considered he'd be a father.

"It's none of my business, and who cares anyway?" she muttered, closing the lid and taking firm hold of the zipper tab. Although even as the words passed her lips, she couldn't squelch her curiosity. Those books definitely didn't fit her image of Jack Walker. Not that it mattered. She was just . . . surprised. And the sooner she rid herself of his suitcase and reclaimed her own, the better off she'd be.

She looked down at herself and grimaced. She had no desire to knock on Jack's door wearing nothing other than the fluffy robe, but neither did she want to change back into her suit. Besides, the fact that he hadn't already knocked on her door meant he probably hadn't opened her suitcase yet. Which would certainly save her some embarrassment. Not that she had anything to be ashamed of, but still. The thought of Jack Walker seeing her sexy lingerie filled her with an unsettling warmth she didn't care to examine too closely. Besides, the robe was hardly sexy—it was as see-through as cement and covered her from chin to shin.

After slipping her key card into her pocket, she headed toward the door, dragging the evil twin to her suitcase behind her. She crossed the hall and firmly knocked on the door to room 314. The door opened so quickly, she wondered if he'd been standing right there.

"The bellhop mixed up our . . ." Her words trailed off as her gaze zeroed in on the slice of bare male chest visible courtesy of his untucked, unbuttoned dress shirt. She blinked. *Wow. Nice view.* One that made her fingers itch to reach out and pull the sides of his shirt wider apart for a better look. Whatever else might be on his busy social calendar, Jack Walker's pecs and abs proved he carved out enough time to keep in shape. *Really* good shape.

A dusting of dark chest hair narrowed to an ebony ribbon that bisected his muscle-ridged abdomen then disappeared beneath the waistband of his charcoal gray pants—a deliciously masculine, yet silky looking trail she had the sudden urge to follow. With her tongue.

Yikes! Where had *that* thought come from? Obviously from the murky depths of her sexual drought, which was causing hallucinations. She tried to raise her gaze back to his, really she did, but her eyeballs seemed to have developed a mind of their own, one that wanted to continue meandering downward. Over his charcoal gray dress pants that were . . . dear God, unbuttoned. She tried to swallow, but her throat had gone totally dry. Her gaze continued downward, over his long legs, down to his black dress socks that covered his large feet. *You know what they say about men with large feet, Maddie.*

Heat whooshed through her and she managed, through sheer force of will, to yank her errant eyeballs upward. But that didn't help. Between the five o'clock shadow shading his square jaw, the way his hair was rumpled as if by a woman's impatient fingers, and his casually unfastened clothing, he looked more deliciously decadent than a triple fudge brownie. Just going by the law of averages, at some point in her life she'd most likely seen a sexier man, but darned if she could remember who that man might have been. If the CFO gig didn't work out for him, he could step in and do *People* magazine's Sexiest Man Alive issue.

Then annoyance kicked in. What the heck was wrong with her? There were tons of sexy men around. Right here in this very hotel. This very weekend.

This one standing right in front of us will do very nicely, her suddenly vocal and wide awake hormones chimed in.

Right. This one standing in front of her who was looking at her as if he'd never seen her before. Irritation rippled through her—thank God, because it managed to tamp down the lust that had grabbed her by the throat. So she didn't look all put together. So her hair was still damp and no doubt looked as if she'd stuck her finger in a light socket. So while he looked sexy and delicious, she looked like she'd been dragged behind a bus. So what? Didn't mean he had to look at her like she'd sprouted devil horns and a third eye.

His gaze, which looked oddly dazed—as if he'd just been smacked upside his head—wandered over her with a thoroughness that heated her from the inside out and made her want to squirm. He looked her over, all the way down to her bare toes, then back up. When their gazes finally met again, he said in a voice that sounded both annoyed and confused, "You're not dressed."

She wasn't sure what she'd expected him to say, but it wasn't that. In spite of her own annoyance, a whisper of amusement worked its way through. "I'm hardly naked."

Something that looked exactly like fire but surely couldn't have been flared in his eyes. His eyes, which were a really, really nice dark blue. Like a cloudless sky at twilight.

"Besides," she added, "it's not as if I had a whole bunch of wardrobe choices, seeing as how you have my suitcase." She wheeled his forward. "And I have yours."

He looked down and she followed his gaze, and realized for the first time that he held her suitcase—something she surely would have noticed sooner if she hadn't been sidetracked by the brain-cell-numbing, libido-wakening sight of his bare chest.

"I was just on my way to your room to return it," he said.

She barely suppressed a wince. Great. That meant he'd opened it. And now probably thought she was sex-crazed and desperate.

You are *sex-crazed and desperate*, her brutally honest libido informed her.

Fine. At least desperate enough to contemplate a one-night stand with a fireman to be named later. But she certainly hadn't wanted Jack Walker to know that.

Don't sweat it, her libido continued slyly. *Men view sex-starved as a* good *quality in a woman.*

Before she could kick her tongue into gear to reply, her attention was diverted by the sound of dishes clinking together. She turned and saw a young man dressed in the resort's dark green uniform approaching, wheeling a room service cart. His gaze flicked over Maddie in her robe, Jack in his unbuttoned shirt, and a knowing look gleamed in his eyes.

Great. Yet another male in the hotel who believed she was having sex. Quite annoying, especially since she wasn't. Yet.

"Would you like me to set this up on the desk, Mr. Walker?" the young man asked. "Or perhaps on the balcony? It's a nice, clear night."

Both Maddie and Jack stepped aside so he could wheel the cart into Jack's room. Something that smelled delicious and fresh off the grill wafted behind him and Maddie's knees almost buckled from the incredible aroma. She glanced at the cart and her brows shot up at the sight of the four silver-covered dishes on the table. Either Jack was extremely hungry or he was expecting company. She knew which one she'd guess. Seemed he hadn't cancelled his Friday night plans at all—he'd just relocated them. Why was she not surprised? Definitely time for her to scram before his date arrived.

Jack followed the room service guy into the room, and Maddie stepped inside, dragging Jack's suitcase behind her, telling herself it was only to get out of the hallway—not an attempt to catch another sniff of those mouthwatering smells emanating from the cart. Jack reached into his back pocket and extracted his wallet, a move that shifted his shirt open.

Oh. My. Maddie outwardly stilled at the glimpse of all that lovely muscled flesh, but inside . . . inside her heart rate sped up and her blood whooshed through her veins like bullets shooting from a gun barrel.

Jack tipped the young man, who thanked him then murmured good night to her as he exited the room. The door clicked closed behind him, leaving her alone with Jack. And their matching suitcases. And his fabulous-smelling room service. That had her mouth watering. It wasn't him and his beautiful eyes or his gorgeous body. *Nope. Not at all.* Or the intense, smoldering, and unsettling way he was looking at her. As if he were a wolf and she had a pork chop hanging around her neck.

Jack stood rooted to the spot, staring at Maddie, at a complete loss for words—at least appropriate words. Certainly *Who the hell are you and what did you do with Mad Dog?* didn't seem the right thing to say. Neither did *Wow, you're hot.*

And hot she was. So hot that when he'd opened his door and found her standing there he hadn't even recognized her at first. And who could blame him for not equating the prim, severely coiffed, modestly suited, bespectacled Mad Dog with this tousled haired, dark-eyed siren who'd clearly just stepped out of the shower and smelled good enough to nibble on?

He'd opened his door, thinking it was room service, and his first thought had been *Wow. Whoever you are, you're much better than a cheeseburger.* Then she'd mentioned the suitcase and recognition had whacked him with the impact of a brick to the head. He'd been reeling ever since. How was it possible that just letting down her hair, removing her glasses, and getting her out of those prim suits could make such a difference? She was like a female Clark Kent—get rid of the nerdy spectacles, hair, and clothes and *poof*! Superwoman was born.

And what a super woman she was. Who would have guessed she had all that silky-looking curly hair? And that her eyes were so round and large? How had he never noticed that they were the color of smooth chocolate? Wrapped up in that fluffy robe, she looked like a present, just waiting to be opened. And since she'd clearly taken a shower and he had all her clothes . . . his gaze slipped to the sash tied around her waist. That meant she probably wasn't wearing anything beneath that robe.

Damn. It was hot in here.

Her voice yanked him from his daydream and he looked away from her bathrobe to her face. She'd clearly said something to him but damned if he knew what.

He cleared his throat and said the only thing he could manage around his stupefaction. "Huh?"

"I *said* 'Here's your suitcase, may I please have mine?' " She parked his case next to the TV.

"Oh. Yeah. Sure." Jeez, he even *sounded* like he'd been clocked upside the head with a brick. He wheeled her suitcase toward her. When she took the handle, their fingers brushed, and if he'd been capable of it, he would have laughed at the sizzle that zoomed up his arm.

"Thanks," she said. Her gaze flicked toward the room service table. "Big plans tonight, I see. Well, me, too. Enjoy your evening. See you tomorrow."

Before he could say a word, she opened the door and practically ran across the hall, dragging her lingerie- and condom-filled, one-night-stand-ready suitcase behind her. He applied his eye to the peephole and watched her enter her room.

He turned and headed toward his very belated dinner. Big plans? A cheeseburger and the financial news update? He shrugged and snagged a French fry. Then frowned. *She* was the one who had big plans. Her and her glossy, curly hair and big eyes and lingerie. She was looking for a one-nighter and he didn't doubt she'd find someone willing. A sensation that felt suspiciously like jealousy but couldn't have been pricked him. He didn't care what her plans were. For all he knew she had a guy in her room right now.

That's one damn lucky guy, his inner voice informed him.

Good God, clearly he was suffering from hunger-induced insanity. Nothing his cheeseburger wouldn't cure. Sitting on the edge of the bed, he uncovered his burger and took a huge bite. It was really good, but he found himself eating mechanically, staring at the TV without seeing what was flashing on the screen. All because he couldn't stop wondering what Ms. I'm Too Sexy for My Bathrobe was doing across the hall.

Annoyed at himself, he clicked off the TV and finished his meal in silence. He'd just polished off the last of his brownie when he heard what sounded like a door opening across the hall. He strode to his own door and applied his eye to the peephole. The sex siren he'd previously referred to as Mad Dog stood in the hallway, slipping her key card into a tiny fire-engine red purse. That perfectly matched the five alarm dress clinging to a figure that needed to come with a warning sign: Dangerous Curves Ahead.

Superwoman indeed.

And one who had "big plans" tonight.

After tucking away the card, she headed in the direction of the elevator.

Where was she going? Most likely to the bar. Where there were most likely lots of firemen. Who would know something hot when they saw it.

Suddenly he didn't feel the least bit tired. No, in fact, he was suddenly in the mood for a beer. How lucky that the resort had a first-class bar.

Six

Maddie sat on a bar stool and took a sip of her wine and tried not to feel conspicuous. Engaging in a one-night stand with a hot, handsome fireman sounded great in theory, but now that the moment had arrived to actually set her plan in motion, she wasn't so sure. She could almost hear Emma making chicken noises, but she'd never actually ventured into a bar alone. Evenings at clubs were either a date or an outing with girlfriends.

The Casa di Lago's bar was crowded with both men and women, but a quick glance made it clear that the women outnumbered the men by about two to one. Clearly, she wasn't the only female who knew the resort was crawling with firemen this weekend. The air buzzed with laughter, conversation, clinking glasses, and muted jazz.

A more leisurely perusal of the crowd confirmed that there were indeed some very attractive men in the room. All she had to do now was pick out one she liked and hope the feeling was mutual. No problem. She could do this.

"Hi," said a male voice next to her. "May I buy you a drink?"

She turned. A tall, muscular, good-looking man with light brown hair and an attractive crooked smile regarded her through eyes that expressed unmistakable interest.

"I already have one," she said, so quickly the words ran together. She grabbed for her wine. "But thanks anyway." She buried her nose in her wineglass.

"Uh, sure. Have a nice evening."

He faded away into the crowd, and Maddie blew out a long breath. Okay, that didn't go particularly well, but hey, she was nervous. Next time she'd do better.

Next time arrived several minutes later in the form of another handsome, muscular man. Jeez. What did they feed these firemen that they were all so attractive? No wonder so many of them posed for calendars.

"Hi," he said, flashing her a flirtatious smile. "I'm Dave."

Something akin to panic fluttered in Maddie's chest. "Hi, Dave. Nice to meet you, but I'm waiting for someone."

He flashed her another smile. "Oh, well. Take care." He melted away and Maddie mentally thunked herself on the forehead. What was wrong with her? Both of those men were handsome and personable. Why hadn't she given either of them a chance?

Because even though you're lonely and horny, one-night stands are not your style, her inner voice informed her.

Well, hell. Much as she wished it were otherwise, she simply didn't have Emma's daring or extroverted personality. And rather than turning her on, the thought of sex with a stranger turned her into a nervous basket case. As good-looking as Dave and the other man had been, neither of them had inspired the slightest sexual tingle.

"Time to abandon this sinking ship," she muttered to herself, reaching for her wine. One last sip and she was outta here. Just then her gaze locked with that of a tall, good-looking blond guy. He stood across the room, at a small round table with a quartet of equally attractive men, all of whom held beer bottles. The blond man smiled at her, showing off perfect teeth. He really was ridiculously handsome, but for reasons she couldn't fathom, just like the others before him, he didn't light a spark in her.

Not wanting to appear rude, she offered him a return smile, yet immediately regretted it when he picked up his beer and looked as if he were about to leave his group to make his way toward her. But then his gaze shifted to a point over her shoulder. He hesitated, then shot her what seemed like an apologetic look and returned his attention to his friends.

What the heck? Before Maddie could figure out what had just happened, someone squeezed in next to her. Then a familiar voice said, "Bet your date isn't going to appreciate you smiling at that blond dude."

Maddie turned and stared at Jack. Jack, who'd buttoned up his shirt and pants—darn it—and whose presence annoyingly made her heart perform some weird swooping maneuver. No longer nervous and now concentrating on her annoyance, she treated him to a glare meant to reduce him to ashes. Instead of taking the hint, he calmly ordered a beer from the bartender then turned to her and asked, "So where *is* your date?"

Maddie narrowed her eyes. Was it possible he hadn't read Emma's note? She highly doubted it. "Not that it's any of your business, but that 'blond dude' might have been my date if you hadn't happened along. But since you opened my suitcase, I'm sure you already knew that."

For several seconds his gaze seemed to burn into hers. Then he said, "Okay, I know. I didn't mean to read the note, but in my own defense, it was just *there*. Right on top."

Well, at least he'd admitted it. So now she was *officially* mortified, which heartily irked her. She had no reason to be embarrassed.

He took a quick glance around. "Based on the number of men in this bar you won't have any trouble." His gaze flicked over her dress. "Especially in that dress."

She narrowed her eyes. "What's wrong with my dress?"

"Not a thing. You look . . . um, swell."

Maddie nearly choked on the laugh that bubbled into her throat. "Gee, thanks. Your shocked tone that I might look *um, swell* lends that compliment just an extra bit of flash. Now, if you don't mind moving along, your hulking presence is kinda cramping my style."

Clearly the man was either deaf or immune to being asked to scram, because he leaned against the bar and continued to study her, as if she were a puzzle he was trying to solve. "Now at least I understand the lingerie."

Heat suffused Maddie's face, which only served to irritate her further. "My lingerie is none of your business." She made a great show of looking around. "So where is *your* date? Surely she's missing you."

"What makes you think I have a date?"

"The room service cart with two glasses and enough covered dishes to feed an army was a good clue."

"Sorry, Sherlock, but all the food was for me. Cheeseburger, chili fries, cole slaw, and a frosted brownie." He rubbed his hand over his flat stomach. "Delicious."

"Sounds bad for the arteries." Not to mention the hips.

"Yeah." He flashed a smile. "But good for the soul."

Okay, why did *this* man's smile make her pulse misbehave in a way the handsome blond guy's hadn't? From a purely technical standpoint, the blond guy was actually more handsome than Jack. But for some inexplicable reason, Jack was the one who had her hormones in an uproar. Probably because of that accidental chest peek she'd gotten. No doubt the blond guy's chest and abs were just as nice.

We don't care, yelled her hormones. *We like Jack.*

Oh, boy. This was not good.

Plus, we already know Jack, her hormones urged. *Better to take on the devil you know.*

"Shut up," she muttered.

Jack raised his brows. "I didn't say anything."

"Sorry. I wasn't talking to you."

"Oh? Who were you talking to?"

Might as well tell him. If he thought she was crazy maybe he'd get lost. "The annoying little voice in my head."

Instead of backing away as if she were nuts, he nodded. "I've got that same little voice." Something she couldn't decipher flashed in his eyes. "I've been telling mine to shut up a lot recently, too."

Curiosity pricked her, but before she could question him, the bartender handed Jack his beer. He raised his drink and said, "To our bet. May the best man win."

She tapped her wineglass against his long-necked bottle. "Especially if he's a she."

After he took a swallow, he leaned back against the bar and again studied her. "May I be perfectly honest with you?"

"I'd prefer if you'd be perfectly absent."

Instead of looking annoyed, he smiled. "And here I thought women just wanted honesty. Except for that 'Does this make my butt look fat?' question. So . . . may I be honest?"

"Why not? Honesty from a man would be a refreshing change."

His gaze wandered down her body then back up again. "You've surprised me. Or rather, the contents of your suitcase surprised me."

"I could say the same about the contents of yours."

"Oh? What's surprising about sneakers and sweats?"

She recalled the size of those sneakers and felt her cheeks flush. "I meant your reading material."

"Says a woman with *Fifty Ways to Please Your Lover* tucked into her bag. That's much more interesting than anything in my suitcase." He nodded toward the blond guy. "You were planning to try out one of those fifty ways on him?"

"Again, none of your business."

"I know. But I'm curious, and not averse to tossing out the brutal truth. So here it is: From day one you struck me as a prim, proper, uptight, rigid schoolmarm type. What I saw in your suitcase, coupled with your obvious intent to meet someone in this bar tonight, blows all my theories about you out of the water."

"I see. Well, in light of your brutal truth, I'll return the favor. From day one you struck me as the fast-and-loose, girl-in-every-port playboy type I loathe. What I saw in your suitcase makes me wonder if you might not be quite as loathsome as I thought."

"Thanks. I think." His gaze searched hers for several seconds, then he said, "Gavin sent us here to bond, so rather than waiting for tomorrow morning, how about we start now? Since at least some of our preconceived notions about each other seem to be wrong, I vote we start all over. Not as feuding CFO and consultant, but just as . . . you and me. At work we're at odds with each other, but we're not at work now." He held out his hand and smiled. "Hi. I'm Jack Walker."

Suspicion instantly filled her. She knew damn well Jack didn't like her, yet here he was, pouring on the charm. *Why?* He had an ulterior motive, of that she was sure. But what?

Yet along with her suspicions came a heated awareness. Of him. Of the way he was looking at her. As if he were seeing her for the first time. As if he were really interested. And curious. *Just as you're curious about him.* He was undoubtedly playing some sort of game. He had to be. So why not play along? At least her curiosity would be satisfied. And if he could temporarily set aside their work-related enmity, then so could she.

She extended her hand and gave his a firm, businesslike shake. But there was nothing businesslike about the tingle that shot up her arm as his big, warm hand engulfed hers. She had to swallow to locate her voice. "Hi, Jack. I'm Madeline . . . Maddie Price."

He continued holding her hand, again looking at her with that I've-never-seen-you-before expression. She slipped her hand from his, then quickly picked up her wineglass so she didn't give in to the unnerving, overwhelming urge to touch him again. To see if another tingle would zing through her.

Deciding her best defense was a strong offense, she said, "So tell me about your reading material regarding raising a four-year-old. I didn't know you had a child."

He shook his head. "I don't. But I have a four-year-old niece. We spend a lot of time together and, well, kids don't come with instruction manuals, so I figured I'd buy one." He hesitated then asked, "Would you like to see her picture?"

Surprised, by both his answer and his offer, she said, "Sure."

He withdrew his wallet from his back pocket and slipped a photo from the black billfold. "Her name is Sophie," he said, handing her the picture.

Maddie looked down at the image of an adorable blue-eyed sprite whose grinning, dimpled face was surrounded by a halo of bright copper curls. "What a cutie," Maddie said, smiling at the photo. "She looks like a red-haired angel."

"Thanks. But don't let that angelic face fool you. She's a sweetheart, but she also has the temperament to go along with that red hair, believe me. Totally takes after my sister."

"She's a fiery redhead?"

"No, just fiery tempered. Sophie got the red hair from her dad."

She handed him back the photo. "They live in Atlanta?"

"Sophie and Claire do—Claire's my sister." A shadow fell across his features. "Claire's husband, Rob, died last year. Killed by a drunk driver."

Sympathy filled Maddie, and without thinking she reached out and touched his arm. "A close friend in college was the victim of a drunk driver. I know how painful it is. How helpless and angry you feel. I'm so sorry."

He stilled and looked down at where her fingers rested against the sleeve of his white dress shirt. It felt to Maddie as if electricity ran between them. Did he feel it, too? Several long seconds passed, then he reached for his beer and her hand slipped from his arm. After swallowing, he said, "Thanks. It's been tough on all of us, but especially on Claire. She and Rob were a perfect couple—really in love—and she's still floundering. Our dad is career army and currently based in California, so our folks are far away, and Rob's family all live in Texas. I'm the only family Claire and Sophie have here."

"So you spend a lot of time with them," Maddie said, her heart hurting for his sister who'd lost her beloved husband, and that adorable, fatherless little girl.

"As much as I can. Claire's gone back to teaching at the private school where she worked before Sophie was born. Sophie and I have a lunch date every Wednesday at her preschool daycare, and Friday nights the three of us share a family dinner. I think having a constant male figure in her life has helped Sophie a lot. At least I hope so."

Understanding struck and Maddie's hand froze with her wineglass halfway to her mouth. Long lunches on Wednesdays . . . leaving at five every Friday . . .

A sensation she couldn't name filled her. She lowered her glass, then murmured, "That's why you don't work late Friday nights."

He nodded. "I explained the situation to Gavin before agreeing to take the position with Java Heaven."

The realization that she'd made a mistake—a big mistake—slapped Maddie square in the face. One she felt it only fair to admit to. "May I be honest with you?" she asked, repeating his earlier question to her.

"Sure. Hit me with your best shot."

"Between you coming come back to the office with your tie askew after your long Wednesday lunches and leaving at the stroke of five every Friday . . . well, that's why I pegged you as a player. Which, for all I know, you may be," she added quickly. "But at least in those two cases, I misjudged you. Sorry."

"Accepted. As for the askew tie, those preschool playgrounds can get rough." He grinned, and she thanked God she was sitting down because her knees seemed to melt at the sight of that devilish smile. "Between that and the finger painting, I'm lucky to get out alive sometimes."

Finger paint . . . she recalled the red smear on his collar this past Wednesday. *Finger paint.* And she thought she'd known lipstick when she saw it. Clearly she didn't know much. Especially about Jack Walker, whose character she'd obviously grossly misjudged.

"I haven't heard any gossip about this at the office," she said.

"I haven't told anyone, except Gavin. All my energy has been spent basically in accounting triage—stopping hemorrhaging, getting the department stabilized, hiring a new controller. I haven't had the time or opportunity yet to forge any real personal relationships with the employees." He looked at her over the edge of his bottle. "Guess that's going to change during this bonding weekend."

"Yes. That was the point." She felt all her opinions about him shifting rapidly, like sand during a windstorm, and she wasn't sure she was happy about it. Disliking Jack had been uncomfortable, but she was accustomed to uncomfortable work situations. No, she greatly feared that liking him would prove even more problematic. "It was good that you and Gavin came to an agreement. I know from experience that not all bosses are so accommodating to a personal schedule."

"It was a deal breaker for me."

She raised her brows. "You would have turned down a CFO position?"

"Yes. I turned one down before I accepted Gavin's offer. Having my thirty-year-old brother-in-law—who also happened to be one of my best friends—die made me reexamine, reevaluate my life. My goals. What was important to me. For a long time my career came first. Looking back, I see I was driven to the point of letting everything else slide. After Rob died, well, everything changed. Including me."

There was no doubting his sincerity, and she could actually feel the ropes that had anchored her aversion to him slipping from their moorings. "I . . . I think it's great that you're helping your sister and are so involved in your niece's life."

"Thanks. But not all women would agree with you."

"What do you mean?"

"I have a couple of ex-girlfriends who weren't very understanding of the fact that I would take a long lunch on a weekday for a four-year-old but not for them. Or that I was unavailable Friday evenings. And sometimes on weekends as well, if Sophie had something going on at her school, or if we'd scheduled a family outing. We'd all planned to visit the zoo this weekend then catch the latest Disney flick, but I had to bow out because of the team building."

Maddie recalled the phone calls she'd overheard him making and she inwardly winced with shame for the conclusion she'd jumped to. He'd been canceling a zoo/movie outing with his sister and niece—not erotic dates with hot babes.

"And what do your current dates think?"

He gave a short laugh. "As soon as I find someone willing to take me on, I'll let you know. I can understand the frustration of not being included, and I haven't asked any women to join us on our family outings. But on the other hand, I haven't wanted to introduce anyone into our little circle until I was sure she was going to be around for a while. The last thing Sophie needs is a revolving door of 'aunts.'" He took a swallow of beer then continued, "I guess you'd be apt to take the women's side on that issue."

She shook her head. "Actually, I agree with you."

He slapped his hand over his heart and staggered back a step. "Call the paramedics. I think I'm about to keel over from shock."

She laughed. "Surely we've agreed on something before now."

He screwed up his face in an exaggerated ponder then shook his head. "Sorry. Can't think of a single time."

Maddie thought about it for several seconds and realized she couldn't think of an occasion either. They'd butted heads pretty much from moment one. "Well, clearly there's a first time for everything. I think it's very admirable that you're putting your niece's interests before your own."

"Thank you. Although you sound very surprised that I'd do anything admirable."

"I suppose I *am* surprised," she said, feeling as if she owed him both honesty and an apology. "My mom died when I was in fifth grade. It took my dad several years before he even went on a date, but once he finally started dating, he kept that part of his life separate from me and him. He didn't want me to meet someone who he might only end up dating a few times and have me wondering—or worrying—if she might become my stepmother. Now that I'm an adult, I can appreciate that he wanted what was best for me and didn't introduce me to a bunch of transient dates."

"Has he ever remarried?"

She smiled. "Yes. In fact, as we speak, Dad and Yvonne are on a two-week European cruise to celebrate their tenth anniversary."

"So happy endings *are* possible."

"In some cases, yes. Is that why you're reading *How to Find Your Soul Mate*—to find a happy ending?"

She'd asked in a slightly teasing voice, but when he answered, his gaze remained serious. "After Rob's death and my reevaluation of my own life, I realized I want to find what my sister had with Rob. What my parents have shared all these years. That special connection with one person. I'm tired of games and drama and the singles scene. After my last relationship ended, I sort of went into hibernation, and frankly, between the new job and helping out my sister, I haven't had much free time. Nor have I met anyone who interested me enough to make the effort." He drained the rest of his beer. "And I'm sure that's more than you ever wanted to know."

As recently as two hours ago, she would have sworn she knew all she wanted to know about him. But that was based on her own incorrect assumptions and wrong conclusions about him. Now she felt as if she didn't know nearly enough. As if she could sit here and talk to him for hours.

She cleared her throat. "You said that I surprised you, but I have to say . . . you've surprised me."

"Because you thought I was an arrogant, heartless prick." He said the words without rancor. Indeed, he appeared amused.

"An arrogant pain in the ass," she corrected. "Which, as far as work goes, I still think you are. But in keeping with our apparent détente, I also think you're intelligent and an excellent and fair boss to your staff."

"Thank you. As far as work goes, I think you're a nit-picking, uptight micromanager. But in keeping with our apparent détente, I also think you're intelligent and a good organizer. And that you look pretty damn amazing in that dress."

His words surprised her, but then he utterly shocked her by reaching out and brushing his fingers over the back of her hand. It felt as if a lightning bolt zoomed up her arm and spread all the way down to her toes.

"I told you all about me and the mysterious contents of *my* suitcase," he said, his gaze searching hers. "So now it's your turn. What's a nice girl like you doing looking for a one-night stand?"

She hiked up a brow. "Nice girls can't have one-night stands?"

"Sure they can." He studied her for several seconds, and she would have given a lot to know what he was thinking. "But I somehow don't think it's your usual style."

"Obviously because of the 'be brave, don't chicken out' note."

"Only partly. Even without benefit of the note, it just doesn't seem like you."

"It's not." The words slipped out before she could even think, followed by a nervous laugh. "Would you believe me if I told you I'm actually sort of shy?"

He nodded slowly then said, "Yes, I would. Not in your job, in things that you're sure of. There your confidence shows. But outside the business realm . . . yes, I can image you're often shy."

His answer surprised her. "No one believes me when I tell them I'm shy," she found herself saying. "That social situations make me nervous. That I've had to train myself not to just stand in the corner and remain silent. Force myself to talk to people I don't know. Ever since my mother's funeral, with all those people crowding around me, talking to me . . ." A shudder ran through her, one she turned into a shrug. "I was *painfully* shy then. The out of control curly hair, thick glasses, and railroad-track braces didn't help.

"But the year after my mom died, my dad gave me a camera for my birthday. It was the greatest present he could have given a shy girl because it gave me a way to communicate with people without having to make conversation. I could hide behind the lens, but still be sociable. It enabled me to fit in at school, where I joined the yearbook and newspaper staffs and photography club."

"A camera . . . that's a great idea. One I never would have thought of. Sophie isn't shy with people she knows, but she doesn't like crowds. It took her a long time to adjust to preschool. I'm going to look into a kid version of a camera for her. You didn't want to make photography your career?"

She shook her head. "I'm too practical to contemplate being a starving artist. Photography's a passion, but it's just my hobby."

His gaze skimmed over her with such unmistakable male appreciation it was all she could do not to fan herself with a cocktail napkin. "And your collection of sexy lingerie . . . is that a passion as well?"

"More of a weakness."

He shifted closer and her knee brushed against his hard thigh. "Any other weaknesses?"

Yes. Apparently tall, dark-haired, blue-eyed men. "Rocky road ice cream. Lemon meringue pie. Spicy salsa." Good lord, was that breathless sound her voice? "Not all at the same time."

He chuckled. "That's a relief. That combo wouldn't be good for the arteries or the soul."

"Or the stomach."

He casually took her hand and lightly played with her fingers. Soft strokes of his fingers over hers that made her catch her breath. "You never answered my question," he said softly.

"Question?" If he was going to keep touching her like that, he'd never get an answer. Especially since she couldn't even recall what he'd asked her.

"Why are you looking for a one-nighter? No boyfriend to take the edge off?"

Pride made her ease her hand away, and she immediately missed the sensation of his fingers on hers. "If I had a boyfriend, I wouldn't be here," she said stiffly. "You might think me a nit-picking micromanager—an assessment I disagree with by the way—but I don't cheat. I've had an unfaithful boyfriend and it's not a pain or humiliation I would subject anyone else to."

"Sorry. I didn't mean to imply you were stepping out on someone." He cleared his throat. "Your Honor, I'd like my last remark stricken from the record and I'd like to rephrase my poorly worded question."

She relaxed and gave a solemn nod. "Permission granted."

He nodded his thanks. "So why don't you have a boyfriend?"

"My last few relationships were with men who proved to be lacking in either morals, integrity, honesty, or all three. My last few first dates proved to be awkward or boring. A few months ago, I got disgusted with the games and grind of dating and basically threw in the towel."

Understanding and unmistakable interest flared in his eyes. "I see. After a few months alone, you're feeling . . . lonely. Not enough to take on a relationship with another man who'll probably just disappoint you, but enough to want a one-nighter to take the edge off the sexual frustration."

She could try to deny it, but doubted if she'd be convincing, especially when he'd nailed it so exactly. "Do you read minds?"

"No. I just guessed that's how you'd feel because it's exactly how I feel. How many months has it been for you?"

She debated lying, but in the end told the truth. "Six months. Six months, seventeen days, fourteen hours, and"—she consulted her watch—"nine minutes. Not that I'm counting."

"Well, it's been eight months, five days, twelve hours, and . . ." He lightly clasped her wrist, sending her pulse into overdrive. After checking her watch, he added, "And four minutes for me. Not that I'm counting."

Maddie opened her mouth to dispute his claim, but one look at his face, at the intensity in his eyes and the words died on her lips. Unless Jack was giving an Academy Award–caliber performance, he was telling the truth. His sexual drought was even longer than hers. Considering the fact that she felt as if her skin were too small, she had to wonder how he was faring. She moistened her suddenly dry lips. "That's a long time."

"A damn long time." He clasped her hand and lifted it to his mouth. With his gaze steady on hers, he pressed his lips against her palm. She pulled in a quick breath. His mouth looked and felt positively sinful against her skin, and oh, God, was that his tongue that just brushed over the pad of her thumb?

"I think we should fix that, Maddie," he said, his warm breath teasing the sensitive skin of her inner wrist.

The way he said her name, in that soft, deep, intimate tone, struck a chord deep inside her. One that hadn't been played in a very long time. "What do you suggest?"

He lowered her hand to his chest. The heat of him seeped into her fingers and his heartbeat thumped hard and fast against her palm. His heart was beating nearly as fast as hers. He leaned in and nuzzled her neck with his warm lips. She actually felt her eyes glaze over.

"You're looking for a one-night stand, and I've been out of commission even longer than you have," he whispered against her ear. He straightened and looked into her eyes. The fire burning in the depths of his scorched her. "I suggest we be each other's one-nighter."

Seven

Jack watched the myriad of emotions that flitted across Maddie's face. Surprise. Doubt. Confusion. Interest.

Desire.

He nearly groaned with relief when he saw that unmistakable spark in her eyes. Thank God it wasn't just him. He certainly couldn't blame her for being surprised. He sure as hell was. If anyone had told him even a few hours ago that the mere sight of Mad Dog Price would render him hard as a rock and that he'd be all but panting to get naked with her, he would have laughed himself into a seizure.

But here she was—with her hair all loose and sexy, her chocolate brown eyes lined with something smoky, her curves encased in body-hugging fire-engine red, killer heels making her legs appear three miles long, her full lips looking incredibly kissable, and smelling so much like cookies he just wanted to take a big bite. And here he was—rock hard and all but panting.

No doubt the fact that he hadn't had a woman in eight months, five days, twelve hours, and he didn't know how the hell many minutes contributed to his current overwhelming desire for her. And his suggestion that they share a one-night stand.

There were reasons, lots of reasons, why it wasn't a good idea, but damned if could remember any of them. Whatever they were, he just didn't care. Right now all he cared about was her and him and putting out this damn fire she and her lingerie and her dress had lit inside him. She wanted a one-night stand? He was more than happy to oblige. The thought of that blond guy—or any other guy in the room for that matter—spending the night with her put his teeth on edge. And if she didn't give him an answer in the next three seconds he was going to explode. He leaned forward, until only a paper-thin space separated their faces.

"Jack, I think—"

"Don't think," he whispered against her lips. Then he brushed his mouth over hers, once, twice. Her breath caught and she parted her lips. He settled his mouth on hers and in a heartbeat he was lost. She tasted so damn good. Like good wine and warm, soft woman. Their tongues tangled and he slid one hand into her silky hair, dragging her head closer. A growl of pure want vibrated in his throat and he deepened the kiss, sinking farther into the velvety heat of her mouth. He moved closer to her, pressing his erection against her thigh. She shifted her leg, and his rapidly diminishing control slipped another notch.

With an effort that cost him, he lifted his head. She looked as dazed as he felt. He prayed to God she felt as desperate as he did.

He ran the pad of his thumb over her full, moist bottom lip. "Yes or no?" he demanded in a low growl he barely recognized.

She licked her lips, a gesture that had him clenching his jaw.

"Yes," she whispered.

Jack didn't hesitate for an instant. Keeping his gaze on hers, he reached for his wallet. After tossing down more than enough to cover their drinks, he grabbed her hand and strode from the bar, heading directly for the elevators. He needed to get them back to the privacy of his room. *Now.* If he touched her before he did, he wasn't sure he'd be able to stop.

He pressed the button and the door immediately slid open. *Thank God.* He led her into the elevator then pressed the button for the third floor. Damn, he could still taste her. He wanted, needed, to taste her again. But he could wait until they were in his room.

The instant the door closed behind them he quit lying to himself and pressed her against the wall. His mouth captured hers in a demanding kiss, one she answered without hesitation. Her arms went around his neck and she rose up on her toes, straining against him. Raw need raced through him and he plunged one hand into her mass of gorgeous curls. Fisting his fingers, he urged her head back to run his lips along the fragrant curve of her neck while his other hand slid down to cup her breast. She gasped and arched against him, then lifted one leg and wrapped it around his hips, urging him closer.

With a groan he couldn't contain he flexed his hips in a long, slow thrust. Christ. He was going to lose his mind. The elevator pinged, indicating their arrival on the third floor. She moaned and slid her leg down, and with their arms wrapped around each other, still exchanging frantic kisses, they circled out of the elevator and started a halting progress down the long corridor.

"We need to lay some ground rules," she whispered against his mouth in between stumbling steps and nipping kisses.

"Fine. Good." He brought one hand forward to cup her breast. "Whatever you say."

"Ooooh," she breathed, arching against his hand. "This is only sex, Jack." She ran her tongue over his bottom lip. "Just one night, to be enjoyed here, then never mentioned again."

He skimmed one hand down her back and cupped the luscious curve of her bottom. Damn. She had more curves than a rollercoaster. Had he ever been this desperate for a woman? This hard and hot and aching? If so, he sure as hell couldn't recall the circumstances. "Fine. Good. Whatever you say."

"What happens at Casa di Lago stays at Casa di Lago."

"Come Monday morning, this never happened and it's back to work as usual," he agreed. "Can we stop talking now?"

"Absolutely."

"Your room or mine?"

"I thought you wanted to stop talking," she whispered, insinuating her hand between them to press her palm against his erection.

He sucked in a harsh breath and thrust into her hand. "Fine. Good. Whatever you say."

Her throaty laugh raised his temperature another few degrees. "Since I have a box of thirty-six condoms handy, I vote for my room."

"Right." He ran his tongue down the side of her neck. "Plus there's all that lingerie in your room." They bumped into the wall, then kept circling down the hall. He took a quick look up. They'd almost arrived. Thank God. "Please tell me you have your key ready."

"I do. No thanks to you. You're very distracting. How many hands do you have?"

"You're about to find out." He snatched the key card from her, jabbed it into the slot, turned the metal handle, then backed her into the room.

The instant the door clicked shut behind them, Maddie found herself pinned against the wall from chest to knee by Jack's very hard, very male body. His mouth came down on hers in a hard, hot, demanding kiss that left her positively woozy. Good God, the man knew how to kiss. She opened her mouth wider, wanting, needing, desperate for more.

Her impatient fingers worked on the buttons of his shirt, but before she got very far, he derailed her every thought by skimming a hand under her dress. His warm palm slid up her thigh, then lifted her leg, hooking it high over his hip.

"Black lace?" he murmured tracing his fingers over the wisp of material that comprised her thong.

"Yessss . . ." The word trailed off into a vaporous sigh of pleasure as his fingers slipped beneath the bit of lace and lightly traced her folds.

"You're wet," he murmured against her lips.

Her head lolled against the wall as he slowly caressed her with a knee-weakening circular motion. "I'm afraid you have, ahhhhh, only yourself to blame."

"I accept full responsibility."

"Good. Oh, God . . . *really* good. Now what do you intend to do about it?"

For an answer he slipped two fingers inside her and slowly pumped. Her eyes closed and a long, guttural moan rattled in her throat. She gripped his shoulders and undulated against his hand.

"Don't hold back," he urged, adding a third finger.

"I won't be able to if you keep doing that." She could barely manage the words.

"Good. Let's see how fast you can come."

She came fast. And hard. Clutching his shoulders, she arched her back and gave herself over completely to the hot pleasure thundering through her. When her spasms subsided, she leaned against the wall and fought for breath.

"Beautiful," he murmured, trailing kisses over her neck. "I call that a do-over."

"Fine. Good. Whatever you say." She gasped out his earlier words and felt him smile against her neck. "Just don't let go of me yet unless you want to peel my boneless body off the floor. My knees seem to have caught a flight to Tahiti."

He gave a low laugh, then before she'd rallied her wits, he scooped her up and walked with her toward the bed. Wow. He didn't even grunt when he picked her up. "Hey, don't hurt yourself," she murmured, wrapping a limp arm around his neck. "I'm not exactly a featherweight and I have plans for you that don't include a trip to an orthopedic surgeon."

"Glad to hear it." He stopped at the edge of the bed. "How are your knees?"

She gave her leg an experimental wiggle. "Still missing in action, but I think I can stand up. Although you probably shouldn't wander too far away. Just in case."

He slowly lowered her to her feet, dragging her body against his. "I have no intention of being any farther away than this."

"Well, okay. If you insist."

He leaned forward and his warm lips nuzzled her neck while he slowly pulled down the long zipper at the back of her dress. "As nice as this dress is, I can't wait to see what's underneath it."

"I could say the same about your shirt," she said, applying herself once again to his buttons. "And your pants."

"You first."

"I've already been first, in case you didn't notice." She looked into his eyes and caught her breath at the fire burning there. "Thank you very much, by the way."

"You're welcome. And I did notice. And I want to see it again." He slipped his fingers beneath the straps of her unzipped dress and slowly pushed the material over her shoulders.

"As much as I appreciate that, not before I take care of this," she said, tracing the outline of his erection with her fingers. "As an accountant, you should want your debits to equal your credits."

He skimmed her dress down her body, his avid gaze taking in every bit of her as it was revealed. "Right now, I'm much more interested in *your* assets." He helped her step out of the dress, leaving her wearing only her black lace thong, matching bra, and strappy heels.

His gaze roamed over her, and a thrill of feminine satisfaction filled her at his obvious appreciation. "Wow," he said, running a single fingertip along the lacy edge of her bra cup. "You do a hell of a job hiding all this beneath those prim suits you wear."

"That's the point. I'm not looking to get noticed for anything other than my job performance."

"I know a lot of women who go out of their way to use their looks, rather than downplay them."

She shrugged. "Not my style. In the workplace, I'm strictly conservative."

He reached around her and unhooked her bra with a quick flick of his clever fingers. "And in the bedroom?"

"In the bedroom . . . not so much." She slid her bra straps down her arms and tossed the garment aside.

"Best news I've heard in a long time."

He reached for her, but she slapped a hand against his chest and pushed him back a step. "Oh, no. Not until we get some of those clothes off you. I'm interested in your assets, too. Let's get rid of the footwear first."

"You always this bossy?" he asked while he toed off his shoes then pulled off his socks.

"Only when I'm impatient. And I'm very impatient at the moment."

"Well, far be it from me to argue with an impatient, nearly naked woman."

"Smart man." She made fast work of the rest of his shirt buttons then helped him shrug the garment from his shoulders. "Very nice," she murmured, trailing her fingers over his broad shoulders then molding her hands over his well-defined chest and rippled abs.

He retaliated by cupping her breasts and gently tugging on her taut nipples. "I could say the same about you."

"I'm supposed to be undressing you, Jack."

"I'm not stopping you."

No, but he sure as heck was distracting her. The man had magic fingers, and his hands were everywhere, leaving trails of fire on her skin. It required all her concentration to undo his belt, unfasten his pants, then push them, along with his boxer briefs, down his hips. They fell to the floor, and without missing a beat or a caress, he kicked them aside.

She ran her fingers along the hard length of his erection and he sucked in a quick breath. Jack Walker was definitely proof positive of that "men with big feet" theory. She wrapped her fingers around him and gently squeezed.

"I'm not going to be able to take much more of that."

For a reply she dipped her other hand between his legs and stroked while she gently squeezed him again. His eyes slid shut and he moaned. "I'm hanging on here by a thread," he warned in a rough voice.

"Let's see how much more you can take."

She pressed her lips to the center of his chest then dragged her open mouth across his firm, warm skin to his nipple. While her hands continued to stroke and caress, she circled her tongue around his nipple then drew the tight bud into her mouth. His hands sifted through her hair and his breathing grew harsh and rapid.

"That feels incredible," he said, the last word ending on a groan as her fingers circled the sensitive head of his erection where a pearly drop of fluid glistened. She dipped her finger into the warm wetness and slowly spread it around the tip while her other hand caressed between his thighs.

"That's it," he said, the words rough and his breathing ragged. Without another word he scooped her up in his arms. She kicked off her shoes and he set her on the bed with a gentle bounce then quickly peeled off her excuse for panties and tossed them aside. She'd left the box of condoms on the night table and she reached for one. The sight of him, so large and hard and aroused, filled her with a desperation she hadn't felt in a very long time.

She was about to tear open the condom package, but again he distracted her, this time by kneeling between her splayed thighs. "You're beautiful, Maddie," he said, his intense gaze hot on hers as he pushed her legs wider apart. "Really beautiful."

God knows the way he was looking at her, the way he was touching her, made her feel that way. "You're not so bad yourself—"

Her words ended on a gasp of pleasure when those magical fingers caressed her sex, gliding, delving, circling, teasing. When she was no more than a stroke or two away from coming again, he grabbed the condom and tore open the package. He rolled on the protection, leaned over her, and entered her in a single heart-stopping thrust.

Their groans mingled. "You feel so damn good," he muttered. Bracing his weight on his forearms, he withdrew nearly all the way then sank slowly into her, filling her completely. "Tight. Hot. Wet." He groaned against her throat. "Perfect."

Yes. *Perfect* was the ideal word to describe the feel of him inside her, on top of her. Maddie spread her legs wider and lifted her hips, craving more of the delicious friction of his body gliding in and out of hers. His thrusts grew harder, faster, each one seeming to touch her deeper, fill her more completely. She cried out as her orgasm exploded through her, and wrapped her arms and legs tightly around him, lost in the hot pulses of pleasure. She felt him tense, then with a harsh groan, he threw back his head and gave a final, deep thrust. After his shudders subsided, he rested his forehead against hers, their ragged breaths bouncing off each other.

Maddie lay beneath him, sated, limp, delicious aftershocks still rippling through her. His weight pressing her into the mattress felt decadent and so lovely she wouldn't have moved even if she'd been capable of doing so, which she wasn't. She wasn't sure how much time passed before he raised his head. When she felt him brush aside a strand of hair from her cheek, she forced her heavy eyelids open. And found him studying her with an expression that looked as bemused as she felt.

An unexpected tenderness suffused her, one that she wouldn't have thought to associate with casual sex. But then, she was pretty inexperienced as far as casual sex was concerned. She swallowed then reached up so her fingers could explore his features. "Okay, I want the unvarnished truth, Jack. Was that as good as I think it was?"

He turned his head and pressed a kiss against her palm. "Would you believe me if I told you I think it was even better?"

Relief filled her. "Glad to know it wasn't just me."

"Not just you," he assured her.

"Probably it was just because it had been such a long time for both of us." She studied his face in the dim light. "Right?"

She'd expected a lighthearted answer, but instead he gazed at her through serious eyes. "I don't know." He studied her for several more seconds, then one corner of his mouth quirked upward. "So I vote we do it again. Since it's now been less than ten minutes for both of us, we'll be better able to judge." He dropped a quick kiss on her lips. "What do you say?"

She gave a feigned casual shrug. "Fine. Good. Whatever you say. But I vote for doing it *two* more times. You know, double the pleasure. Just to be sure."

He heaved a put-upon sigh. "Oh, all right. If you insist. I'll try not to complain too much."

"Good. Because you know who likes a whiner?"

"Who?"

"Nobody."

He chuckled. "Let's take a shower, then you can model some of those other lingerie goodies you have in your suitcase."

"Hmmm. I have quite a bit of lingerie in there."

"And you won't catch me whining. Nope. 'Cause you know, nobody likes a whiner."

"That's right. About this shower . . ." She tickled her fingers down his smooth back to his butt, liking the heat that flared in his eyes. "I plan to get you all in a lather. In more ways than one."

"Good. Fine. Whatever you say."

Eight

Jack stomped through the damn woods, trying to concentrate on what he was supposed to be concentrating on—which was finding the various colored flags he and Maddie needed to locate on their orienteering outing so they could then make their way out of the damn woods—but he was failing miserably. The only thing he could concentrate on was the woman walking beside him.

The woman who, thanks to hours spent in sensual exploration last night, he now knew a whole lot about. And damned if he didn't like everything he'd learned.

After a leisurely shower—during which they'd both been worked into a lather in more ways than one—they'd raided the minibar. While sharing a can of peanuts and a soft drink, they'd talked about their lives and interests. Aside from the fact that she was a generous, uninhibited, and exciting lover, Maddie was smart, funny, savvy, and possessed an almost encyclopedic knowledge of movies and baseball stats. When they discovered they'd attended rival universities, a friendly debate had ensued regarding whose school was better.

He learned she was an only child and that she envied him his close-knit relationship with Claire and Sophie. That she loved animals, played a mean game of tennis, a horrible game of chess, loved shopping at flea markets, collected antique teapots, and considered her curly hair a curse—an opinion he thoroughly disagreed with. She loved to cook, hated doing laundry, adored the beach, had never been snow skiing, and hoped to vacation in Italy next year.

He'd felt completely at ease with her and more than once he mentally shook his head, unable to believe this intelligent, interesting, sexy-as-hell woman was the same person he'd dubbed "Mad Dog" and had been at odds with for the past month. With each new thing he discovered about her, he found himself wanting to know more. Wanting to know everything. It had been a damn long time since he'd felt such a connection with a woman. A connection that went beyond mere physical attraction.

Not that he could deny he found her very physically attractive. He did. Painfully so. How the hell had he missed those beautiful soulful brown eyes? That gorgeous smile? Those luscious feminine curves? He didn't know. Clearly he'd had his head in the sand. But now he knew, and he wondered how he was going to be able to forget now that their one-night stand was over.

After their can of peanuts and soda picnic on the bed, they'd made love again then fallen asleep. When the phone rang at five A.M. for their orienteering outing, he'd awakened to her snuggled against his side, one shapely thigh draped over his, her hand resting on his chest. And he'd liked the feeling. A lot. It had been a long time since he'd woken up with someone, and it brought home the realization of how lonely he'd been. How much he missed having someone special in his life. Missed being in a relationship. Being part of a couple. Caring for someone and being cared for in return.

Those feelings grew in intensity when she'd opened her eyes and greeted him with a sleepy good morning smile. And then a bout of soft, slow, morning sex—the perfect ending to what had been, as far as he was concerned, a perfect night.

He'd returned to his room to shower and dress for their orienteering outing, then met her in the lobby, where he was smacked with the realization that their night was indeed over. Maddie was all business, greeting him with a cool, professional smile, severely pulled back hair, black-rimmed glasses, and her no-nonsense attitude firmly in place. As if less than an hour ago they hadn't been naked with each other.

Which unreasonably annoyed him. During the van ride to the heavily wooded orienteering course, his common sense reminded him that that's what they'd agreed to, yet some other part of him was pissed—and incredulous—and damn it, maybe even a little bit hurt that she could so easily set aside what they'd shared. Because as far as he was concerned, what they'd shared had been . . . amazing. And certainly uncommon, at least in his experience.

"According to my calculations, the blue flag should be about four hundred yards due east," she said, pointing to the right. She paused and consulted her map. "What do you think?"

That I want to yank down your jeans to see what you're wearing beneath them. Then find out if you taste like cookies everywhere.

He raked a hand through his hair. *Damn.* This wasn't good. Why couldn't he do what she'd obviously done—enjoyed their one night together then forgotten about it?

Maybe because he'd enjoyed it so much. Too much.

"Jack? You okay?"

Her voice jerked him from his thoughts and he realized she was looking at him with a quizzical expression. He much preferred seeing arousal in her eyes. What would it take to see it there again? He didn't know, but he sure as hell wanted to find out.

He took a step closer to her and noted with grim satisfaction the desire—and wariness—that flared in her eyes. *Ah ha.* Not as indifferent as she'd like him to believe. *Excellent.* He took another step closer and had to force himself not to smile when she backed up. "Actually I'm not okay."

She retreated another step. "Oh? The sun getting to you? I have some sunscreen in my backpack."

He shook his head and kept advancing in pace with her backwards retreat. "It's not the sun that's getting to me, Maddie."

Her back hit the thick trunk of an enormous tree, stopping her. He halted a foot in front of her and planted a hand on the rough bark on either side of her head, caging her in. "*You're* what's getting to me, Maddie."

She moistened her lips, and his entire body tightened at that flick of pink tongue. "Our night is over, Jack."

"True. But I was thinking . . ." He leaned in, nuzzled the velvety soft skin beneath her jaw. Even in the woods she smelled like cookies. He leaned back and looked into her eyes. "What if we turned our one-nighter into a two-nighter?"

There was no missing the flare of interest, and arousal, in her eyes. "Well . . . we *are* staying at the resort another night," she said in a musing tone.

"Exactly. And last night was pretty damn good."

She cocked a brow. "Only pretty damn good?"

"Pretty incredibly amazing," he amended.

"You forgot spectacular."

"My bad." He stepped closer and lightly rubbed his erection against her belly. "So what do you say?"

Her eyes widened. "That you either have a water bottle in your pocket or you're really happy to see me."

He smiled and inhaled what felt like his first easy breath since he'd seen her in the lobby that morning. "I'm *really* happy to see you." He lowered his head and brushed his mouth over hers. He would have laughed at the intensity of his body's reaction to such a featherlight kiss, but he suddenly felt incapable of levity. Raw hunger sizzled through him and he settled his mouth on hers, his tongue exploring all the delicious, warm softness it had discovered last night.

She looped her arms around his neck, pressing herself against him. With a groan, he plunged his hands beneath her sweater, loving the feel of her soft, warm flesh. He filled his palms with her breasts, his fingers slipping inside her bra to tease her hard nipples.

"Jack." She gasped his name and fisted her hands in his hair. "Just how private are these woods?"

"One hundred and fifty acres of nothing but us," he assured her. "And the van won't be coming back for us for another hour."

She yanked his shirt from his jeans and skimmed her hands up his torso, shuddering pleasure through him. "Damn, I wish I'd brought a condom," she said, nipping at his neck.

He shrugged off his backpack at the same time hers hit the dirt. Then he applied himself to her jeans. "I've got one." The words came out in a rush, like his increasingly rapid breaths.

"Because . . . ?"

"Hope springs eternal."

"Ah. Have I told you that I think you're very smart?" she asked, sounding just as breathless as him, her fingers clearly as impatient as his as they attacked the button on his jeans.

"No. In fact, I think you've been more apt to call me a pain in the ass. Take off your sneakers."

"What was I thinking?" She toed off her sneakers and kicked them aside. "I should have at least called you a *smart* pain in the ass."

"Yes, you should have." He yanked her zipper then jerked down her jeans and panties with one hard tug. He felt like he'd explode if he didn't touch her. *Now.* He helped her step out of her jeans, then dropped to his knees in front of her, leaned in, and ran his tongue along the seam of her sex.

She gasped and spread her legs wider, then sifted her fingers through his hair, moaning his name as he pleasured her with his mouth and tongue and fingers. The musk of her arousal filled his head along with the subtle fragrance of . . .

"Cookies," he murmured against her thigh. "You taste like cookies. Everywhere."

"My body wash," she said, between panting breaths. "It's called Vanilla Sugar Cookie."

Damn. No wonder she smelled, tasted so good. What chance did a mere mortal male have against a woman who *bathed* in something called Vanilla Sugar Cookie? As it was, he'd never be able to eat another cookie and not think of her. Which was bad, because he really liked cookies.

He slipped two fingers inside her, thrusting in unison with his flicking tongue. He felt her body tighten, then with a long, low groan she pulsed around his fingers. As soon as her tremors subsided he slipped his fingers from her body and reached for the condom in his back pocket. She'd already gotten his zipper halfway down and he quickly took care of the rest, then shoved his jeans and boxer briefs down past his hips. He tore open the condom, sheathed himself, and sat back on his heels.

He reached for her, but she was already straddling him. She lowered herself onto him, and took him in with a slow, deep engulfment that dragged a ragged groan from his throat. Needing more of her, he shoved up her sweater, growling his approval when she jerked the garment over her head and tossed it aside. He unhooked her bra and filled his hands with her warm, soft, cookie-scented flesh, then leaned forward to draw her tight nipple into his mouth.

Gripping his shoulders, she rode him, slowly at first, then quickening her pace. Jack gritted his teeth against the intense pleasure, holding off coming by sheer will. When he felt the first pulses of her orgasm, he gripped her hips and thrust upward. His climax roared through him and for an endless moment he throbbed inside her. When his shudders tapered off, he gathered her close. She nestled against him, resting her head on his shoulder.

"*Reeeeeealy* glad you brought that condom," she said in a sleepy-sounding voice.

He brushed his lips against her disheveled hair. "Me, too. I didn't need a map and a compass to see where two hours alone in the woods with you might lead."

She lifted her head and smiled into his eyes. Such beautiful eyes. Such a gorgeous smile. Something inside him seemed to shift, like his chest had just fallen into quicksand. "Once again, the credits have exceeded the debits. I owe you one orgasm."

He smiled back at her. "Fine. Good. Whatever you say."

She laughed, and he wondered how he'd ever thought her anything other than lovely. "A very useful saying. But now that I've had my wicked way with you, I think we should find those flags."

"What for? The purpose of this outing was for us to bond." He leaned forward and circled her nipple with his tongue. "Mission accomplished."

"True. But I'm determined to find those flags then the way out of here. There's that twenty bucks I want to win from you so I can buy my lipstick."

"Your lips don't need lipstick, but okay. I'll play."

She shot him a wicked grin. "And may the best woman win."

Nine

To Maddie, who couldn't wait for the evening so she and Jack could continue their one-night stand—part two—the rest of the day seemed to drag on forever. She attended all the team building exercises as an observer, but twice joined in when they needed an extra person to even out the numbers. Through it all, she had to force herself to concentrate on the tasks at hand because her mind was filled to overflowing with thoughts of Jack.

Jack cheerfully paid his twenty-dollar debt after she led them out of the woods and to the van that transported them back to the Casa di Lago. He claimed it was all her fault he got lost, that he couldn't focus on anything other than her, a claim that made her want to drag him right back into the woods and have her wicked way with him. Again.

Throughout the day, with each new exercise, she saw how Jack and his staff interacted with each other, strategized, planned, handled problem solving, communicated, reacted to stressful situations, supported—and sometimes didn't support—each other. Things started off slow, and she sensed some initial reluctance on the part of several staff members, but as the day wore on, everyone, with the exception of a senior accounting manager named Peter Quinn, got into the spirit of the games to some degree, some more than others. The team building brought out the competitive nature of some, the sense of humor of others, the stubbornness of a few, and the thinking-outside-the-box abilities of yet others.

She jotted down her observations, trying her best not to allow her gaze to stray to Jack, but more often than not, that's precisely where she found herself looking. Even when she wasn't watching him, she was painfully aware of him. He had an easygoing, charismatic manner about him that she could see inspired respect in his staff. She'd noted as much during the previous month, but now that she was viewing him through different eyes, his leadership abilities, confidence, and commitment to his staff were crystal clear. He accomplished his tasks in the time allotted and made fair, intelligent decisions. It was easy to see he was an excellent boss, and she mentally scolded herself for allowing her preconceived notions about him to color her opinion of him so unfavorably. She normally didn't jump to conclusions about people as she had with Jack, and she wondered why she had in his case.

Because you were attracted to him from moment one and didn't want to be, her sly inner voice informed her. *So you thought the worst of him to talk yourself out it.*

Okay, that little voice was really annoying.

But totally right.

She *had* found him attractive. *Too* attractive. And hadn't wanted to. A problem that wasn't going to get any better, because she now not only found him attractive, she really liked him. A lot. Too much, she feared. He was not only an incredible lover, he made her laugh. And could converse on any subject. Heck, he was even willing to talk about chick flicks and shoes. No doubt due to his close relationship with his sister, but still—chick flicks and shoes!

Just then Jack looked up from the puzzle he and his four teammates were trying to solve. Their gazes locked and for several seconds the air around Maddie felt too thick to breathe. Something seemed to pass between them, something warm and intimate that sped up her pulse and made everything inside her turn to the consistency of warm honey. She knew in that moment that if she weren't careful, she stood in danger of falling into the emotional abyss she feared yawned before her: of caring for him, much more than she'd ever intended to.

By the time the afternoon break rolled around, Maddie could already see some new friendships forming. She purposely avoided Jack during the break, afraid that if they sat together everyone in the room would guess what was going on between them. Instead she ate her lunch at a table with Bob and Kathy Whitaker, who ran the team building program, and spent the time asking them questions, taking notes on their responses to add to her report that Gavin expected Monday morning.

Lunch was followed by more team building exercises. Maddie took copious notes on each team's dynamics, each staff member's personality, and how they responded to their tasks. Dinner was a casual outdoor cookout where the staff could volunteer to set up, cook, serve, or clean up. Maddie noted what each person volunteered for, hiding a grin at the fact that most of the men volunteered to grill the burgers and hot dogs, and none of them volunteered for cleanup duty.

Dinner was followed by a tour of the Caso di Lago winery and a wine-tasting party. Maddie mingled, making mental notes on how people reacted to each other, who interacted with whom, who kept to themselves. Jack, she noted, spoke to everyone, moving from group to group, listening and chatting with equal ease. Finally he stood before her. And smiled.

"Hi. I'm Jack Walker."

Had it only been last night that he'd said those same words to her in the bar? She was instantly reminded of the words to an old song her grandmother used to sing . . . *What a difference a day makes, twenty-four little hours.*

She smiled in return. "Maddie Price. Nice party."

He nodded, then said in a low voice, "Personally, I can't wait 'til it's over."

She raised her brows. "Hot date?"

"Very." His eyes seemed to breathe smoke. "I'm a lucky man."

"Hmmm. Yes, something tells me you're going to get lucky tonight."

He sipped his wine then said, "You've been taking notes all day."

"That's what I'm here for."

"To see how everyone is interacting with each other."

"Among other things." Anxious to change the subject, she said, "The wine is excellent."

"Yes. And you're changing the subject."

"Yes. The wine is excellent."

He studied her for several seconds and she hoped he wasn't going to question her. Per Gavin's instructions, she couldn't reveal the nature of her report. Besides, she didn't want to talk about work. Didn't want to risk having anything cast a pall on their last night together. Finally he said, "How about my room tonight?"

"Sounds good."

"Great." He shot her a wink. "C'mon over, honey. And bring your lingerie and condoms."

After the party finally broke up an hour later, Maddie remained downstairs long enough to note which Java Heaven employees returned to their rooms and who headed to the bar or lobby to continue chatting. "Don't forget, breakfast's at eight, followed by more team building," Bob Whitaker called to the departing staff.

Right. Breakfast, two more team building sessions, then by noon the weekend would be over. As would her interlude with Jack.

She hurried back to her room and changed clothes. With the resort's bathrobe wrapped firmly around her, she grabbed her supplies, checked to make certain the hallway was empty, then crossed the carpet to Jack's door. Before she even had a chance to knock, the door opened and Jack pulled her into the room. Into his arms. And laid one of those toe-curling, breath-stealing, palpitation-inducing kisses on her. When he finally lifted his head, she said, "Wow. If kissing were an Olympic sport, you'd have a trophy case filled with gold medals."

"Kissing takes two," he said, lightly scraping his teeth over her sensitive earlobe. "It's all in who your partner is. What took you so long?"

"I took a few minutes to consult my copy of *Fifty Ways to Please Your Lover.*" She leaned back in the circle of his arms and playfully waggled her brows. "I have a feeling you're going to like number twelve. And number eighteen. And number forty-six."

"Have I mentioned that twelve, eighteen, and forty-six are my lucky numbers?"

"No. But even if they weren't, I promise you, they're going to be."

He smiled into her eyes. "I think that makes me the luckiest guy on the planet."

She held up the bag she'd brought. "I come bearing lingerie and condoms."

"Excellent." He pulled her farther into the room and she noticed that like her, he wore the white terry cloth robe bearing the resort's logo. "I come bearing champagne and chocolate."

Maddie's eyes widened at the champagne chilling in a silver wine bucket on the nightstand, the pair of crystal flutes, and the gold-foil box of Godiva. "I love champagne and chocolate."

"I know. You mentioned it last night."

And he'd remembered. Everything female in her heaved a gushy sigh at the thoughtful gesture. "Thank you. Although I have it on good authority you would have gotten lucky without it."

He grinned and popped the bottle's cork. "Yeah, but maybe now I'll get *really* lucky." After pouring two glasses, he handed her one, then raised his. "To . . . surprises."

"Surprises," she agreed, and touched the rim of her flute to his.

After taking a sip, he set aside his glass then slipped his fingers beneath her robe's sash and tugged her closer, until their bodies bumped. "Whatcha wearin' under this robe?"

She set her glass next to his then tugged on the sash to his robe. "I was about to ask you the same thing."

"One way to find out."

They untied each other's sashes at the same time. He opened her robe and pushed it down her arms, where it pooled at her feet. His avid gaze took in the cream-colored lace-up corset, which she'd chosen because it made her waist look smaller than it was and her breasts larger than they were, and the matching barely there panties. When his gaze met hers, the heat in his eyes nearly singed her. "Wow."

That single word, said in that appreciative tone, made the outfit worth every penny she'd spent. She then pushed his robe off his shoulders, where it joined hers on the floor. He wore nothing but skin. And a very impressive hard-on.

"Double wow," she said. Reaching out, she ran a single fingertip down the length of his erection. "I seem to recall an imbalance between our debits and credits—something I'd like to even up. Starting with number twelve." She lowered herself to her knees and without any preliminaries drew him deep into her mouth.

Jack's eyes slammed shut as a shudder of pleasure shook him. A long groan rattled in his throat and he tipped his head back, fighting for control. Oh, yeah, twelve was definitely his new favorite number. When he'd caught his breath, he opened his eyes and looked down. The sight of Maddie's full lips surrounding him, the feel of her tongue circling, the tight draw of her hot mouth damn near made him come on the spot. He combed his fingers through her hair, watching her pleasure him, gritting his teeth to hold back the release building at the base of his spine. When he couldn't take anymore, he urged her to her feet, settled her on the bed, reached for a condom, then joined her.

"Let's make this one hell of a night to remember," he said against her lips, covering her body with his.

"Good. Fine. Whatever you say."

When Maddie entered the dining room for breakfast the next morning, the first person she saw was Jack. Heat that had nothing to do with the bright sunshine streaming through the floor-to-ceiling windows rippled through her. Their gazes locked and a kaleidoscope of images of last night flashed through her mind. Jack buried deep inside her. Over her. Under her. Making love in the shower. His soapy hands relentless, everywhere. Her hands slapped against the tiles, bending over to take him deeper. The warm water rushing over them. His dark head buried between her thighs. Feeding each other chocolates. Laughing. Sharing stories. Touching. Falling asleep in each other's arms. Her waking early. Watching him sleep while she donned her robe and gathered her belongings. Returning to her own room. Feeling its emptiness. Wishing her time with Jack wasn't over. Knowing it was.

Right. Because today it was back to business and tomorrow back to work. She needed to review her pages of notes and write her report this evening so it was ready for Gavin tomorrow. A report that she knew Jack wouldn't like, which surely shouldn't matter—their two-nighter was now officially over. But to her consternation, she realized it *did* matter. A lot.

She yanked her attention from Jack then purposely set her purse and leather portfolio on a table at the opposite end of the dining room from him, in a corner where she could observe the Java Heaven staff's interactions. After helping herself to fluffy scrambled eggs, a blueberry muffin still warm from the oven, and a glass of fresh-squeezed orange juice from the buffet, she sat and opened her portfolio. And studiously kept her gaze on her notes and off Jack.

She was working on her second cup of tea and had just jotted down an observation when a shadow fell across the table. Her heart jumped because even before she looked up, she knew it was Jack.

She raised her head and looked into his compelling blue eyes. He was dressed casually in tan khakis and a yellow polo shirt. His dark hair was slightly rumpled, as if he'd raked his hands through it. Her fingers itched with the sudden overwhelming desire to glide through those thick strands that she knew felt like raw silk.

"May I join you?" he asked.

No. Please go away. I'm terrified that I'm not a good enough actress to pretend nothing's happened between us. That I feel nothing for you. "Of course," she replied in her best businesslike, neutral tone. She closed her portfolio and picked up her teacup, more to give her hands something to do than because she wanted a sip.

"Your breakfast was good?" he asked after he'd settled himself in the chair opposite hers.

"Yes. Yours?"

"Very good." He set his hands on the table and linked his fingers. He had really nice hands. Large and strong. Capable and wickedly clever. There wasn't a centimeter of her body they hadn't explored.

"You were gone when I woke up," he said quietly, his gaze steady on hers.

Oh, God. This was going to be so much harder than she'd ever imagined. Why did something that was supposed to be so uncomplicated—just a simple one-night stand—suddenly feel so complicated? How had it happened? When?

She cleared her throat. "I didn't want to wake you. Besides, I thought it best since our two-nighter was officially over."

"No awkward farewells."

"Exactly."

His gaze shifted to her portfolio then back to her. "Maddie . . . I've suspected from the moment Gavin hired you that he's planning to downsize my department and that he wants your recommendations on whom and how many people to cut. I wouldn't ask you to break a confidence by either confirming or denying it, but I'd like you to listen for just a moment."

She nodded. "All right."

"I don't want my department cut, not by a single person. Gavin knows this and I've gone on record with him that I won't fire or layoff anyone. I've seen the same things you have this weekend. I know there are some personality conflicts, but sometimes it just takes certain people longer than others to feel comfortable. Peter Quinn, for instance. I know he can be standoffish, but he's brilliant. He may not be the most personable guy in the world, but what's important to me is that he's loyal. And honest."

He drew a long breath, then continued, "I've resented you from minute one because I viewed you as Gavin's spy. Please don't take that personally—I would have resented any consultant Gavin hired. I didn't like having someone looking over my shoulder, second-guessing me when I was doing my damnedest to pull together a department that was in shambles. I know you have a job to do, but the bottom line is this: At the risk of sounding arrogant, I know what's best for my department and it's not a smaller staff. Cutting the department won't cut the work that needs to be done, it will only dump more responsibilities on the folks who remain. Employees who are forced to work overtime and on weekends just to keep up with their workload are not happy employees. We'll end up slowly drowning. I've seen it happen in other companies and I don't want it to happen here. I want this department to not only survive but to flourish, but I need time—and my entire staff—to make that happen. We've already made great strides and it's only been two months.

"In the end, any money saved by downsizing won't be worth it because I'll have a miserable staff, which, as you know, leads to all sorts of problems. I've already told Gavin this and that any cost-cutting measures will need to come about through other channels or out of some other department. But not accounting."

Maddie pulled in a careful breath, then released it slowly. "I understand your point, but you also need to take into account that cogs in the wheel need to be fixed, or in this case let go, so the entire group doesn't suffer. And every company needs to minimize costs."

"I agree, but there aren't any cogs in this wheel. And the cost cuts won't come at the expense of my department."

"You make it sound as if it's a deal breaker for you."

"It is."

She nodded slowly then offered him a small smile. "You make a very compelling case. And your reasoning is sound."

He smiled in return. "Glad you agree." He glanced at his watch. "We're starting in just a few minutes. Thanks for listening."

"You're welcome."

His expression softened. "And thanks for a great weekend."

Her heart tripped over itself and she had to grip her teacup to keep from giving in to the powerful urge to touch him. "You, too."

With his gaze locked onto hers, he said quietly, "I know we agreed our . . . time together wouldn't go beyond last night, but just so you know, I wouldn't mind if we changed that rule. Think about it and let me know."

Without another word, he rose and walked toward the exit. She watched him leave, his last words echoing through her mind. *Think about it and let me know.*

There were lots of reasons why letting their two-nighter extend further had "bad idea" written all over it. Yup, lots of reasons. And she was going to write them down as soon as she remembered them. Then, thankfully, her brain kicked into gear.

It would make working together impossible.

Wouldn't it?

There was only sexual attraction between them.

Wasn't there?

Nothing could come of continuing their affair.

Could it?

Think about it and let me know.

God help her, she didn't know how she'd be able to think about anything else.

Ten

At one o'clock Monday afternoon, Gavin entered Jack's office. "Got a minute?" he asked.

"Sure. Have a seat," Jack said, indicating the chair opposite his desk.

Jack set aside the report he'd been reading and pulled in a bracing breath. His gut was telling him this impromptu meeting was about downsizing his department.

Gavin sat then lifted a manila folder from the top of the pile he carried. "I've spent the morning going over this report from Madeline Price. It's based on her observations of your department and includes detailed notes, most recently from the team building over the weekend."

Gavin leaned back in his chair. "I'll cut right to the chase, Jack. You need to downsize the department, from twenty to fifteen. You have two weeks to make the cuts. If you need suggestions as to who is to go"—he tapped the folder containing Maddie's report—"I'm happy to name names."

For several long seconds silence swelled between them. Jack's gaze fell on the folder and a feeling such as he'd never experienced before surged through him. A combination of anger, disgust, frustration, and betrayal all swirled with an overwhelming sense of numbness. He'd thought she'd understood—that he'd made her see reason. That she'd value and respect his opinion. Obviously he'd been mistaken. Very mistaken.

"We've discussed this before, Gavin," Jack said, his voice perfectly calm. "I feel very strongly that this is the wrong course of action. A course that's going to make my job, and my department's, extremely difficult. We simply can't operate effectively with a twenty-five percent cut in manpower. You haven't given me or my staff enough time to pull everything together. We're getting there, we've made great strides in a short period of time, but time is what we need more of."

Gavin shook his head. "Sorry, Jack. This needs to be done."

"You brought me on board to revamp a decimated department, and just when things are starting to come together, you're cutting me off at the knees."

Gavin rose, indicating their meeting was finished. "Two weeks, Jack."

Jack stood. Then nodded. "All right, two weeks. Consider this my official notice. You'll have the letter on your desk by the end of the day."

Gavin's brows rose, then he gave a hearty laugh. "I know you don't mean that."

"I assure you I do."

"I'm aware you don't like this, Jack, none of us do, but it's got to be done. I'm late for a meeting. I'll see you tomorrow."

Jack watched in silence as Gavin left the office. He wasn't sure how long he stood there while his anger and resentment and, damn it, hurt grew. But it finally reached the point where he couldn't stand still any longer. It needed an outlet, and he knew exactly who to let it loose on.

He stalked from his office and headed down the hallway, not

slowing his pace until he stood outside the small office that had been assigned to Maddie. The door was open and he strode inside, not bothering to announce himself.

She stood with her back to him, crouching next to a cardboard box into which she was placing a stack of papers. It was the first time he'd seen her since they'd departed Casa di Lago yesterday afternoon. And about the thousandth time he'd thought of her. Up until his meeting with Gavin, all those thoughts had been of missing her. Wanting more of her. Hoping she'd tell him she wanted to continue the magic and something special they'd started at the resort. Now he couldn't feel any of that for the knife protruding from his back.

"We need to talk," he said, closing the door.

She stood and turned. Her hair was pulled tightly back, her glasses framed her eyes, and a prim royal blue suit conservatively downplayed her figure. In spite of his anger, he wanted nothing more than to yank her into his arms and kiss her until they were both breathless. Pretend nothing existed except him and her. Pretend she hadn't written that damn report. Damn it, she'd gotten under his skin, and that only served to fuel his anger more. Her serious expression erased any doubt that she knew why he was there.

"Yes, I guess we do need to talk," she said. "Would you like to sit down?"

"No." His voice was steady but cold, which pretty much matched his mood since his insides felt frozen. "Are you pleased with yourself?"

Her brows pulled down. "Pleased?" She pushed up her glasses and peered at him. "Is something wrong?"

A bitter laugh escaped him. "An odd question coming from you. You knew very well what my hopes were for my position here, for my department, yet you stand there and ask me if something's wrong." The chill in his tone sliced through the room. "What did you think would be the outcome of the report you gave Gavin?"

She blinked, then her frown deepened. "Jack, I—"

"Gavin expects me to cut my department by twenty-five percent—although I'm sure you probably knew that already."

Something that looked like regret flickered in her eyes. "Actually, no. I didn't know."

"Well, now you do. And we have your report to thank. Congratulations."

Anger flared in her eyes. "If you think my report had anything to do with this, you're mistaken."

"Your report had everything to do with it, as you damn well know. Did you not hear a word I said to you at breakfast yesterday morning?"

"I heard everything you said at breakfast yesterday morning."

"But clearly it didn't make any difference to you. Which I guess means nothing that happened between us made any difference to you."

A myriad of emotions flashed across her face, too fast for him to decipher, but there was no mistaking the twin red flags that colored her cheeks. "You've come into my office, unannounced and uninvited, and tossed some pretty harsh words at me. And based on what you're saying, it's just occurred to me . . . oh. Oh my God." She pulled in a harsh breath and pressed her hand against her chest. The color that had just rushed into her cheeks drained, leaving her pale. "My God. Did you sleep with me in order to influence my report? To make it favorable to your point of view? So I wouldn't recommend downsizing your department?"

Her question so surprised him that for several seconds he couldn't even speak. Then a hurt and anger such as he hadn't felt in a long time, if ever, walloped him. A muscle ticked in his jaw. "That's what you think?"

"That's what I'm asking."

"If that's what you're asking, then this conversation is over."

"Fine by me. I'm not the one who initiated it." She nodded toward the door. "If you'll kindly leave, I'm busy."

"Leaving. Not just your office, but Java Heaven. I gave Gavin my two weeks' notice." He opened the door and walked out without looking back. He didn't want to see her reaction to the news. Didn't want to hear anything else she had to say.

He strode to his office, feeling as if he were walking through a thick fog. Damn it, he felt . . . gutted. In a matter of mere minutes he'd resigned from his job—but he had no regrets there. He'd taken a stand for what he thought was right and had no intention of compromising his integrity. What truly had him reeling was his feeling of betrayal over Maddie's report. And even worse, her belief that he'd slept with her to influence it.

Damn it, that really hurt. And the fact that it hurt really pissed him off. What the hell did he care what she thought? They'd shared a couple of hot nights and now it was over.

Yes, it was over. But he'd foolishly hoped it was just the beginning. She'd touched something inside him, eliciting feelings he hadn't felt in a very long time. The fact that he'd been so wrong about her—that she'd write that report and question his intentions, well, obviously he'd misjudged her. The only thing left to do was put her out of his mind. And his heart—where she'd unfortunately managed to burrow.

After a sleepless night spent tossing and turning, reliving every moment he'd spent with Maddie, moments he wanted desperately to forget, Jack hauled his tired ass to work Tuesday morning and immediately headed to the break room for a much-needed cup of coffee. He'd just taken his first sip when a man he didn't recognize entered the room. Jack judged him to be in his late thirties. He was well dressed and offered Jack a friendly good morning.

Since the good part was highly debatable, Jack replied, "'Morning. I don't think we've met." He extended his hand. "Jack Walker."

The man gave his hand two firm pumps. "The CFO. Good to meet you. Walter Langdon. I'm with Lazer Consultants."

Jack barely managed to hide his grimace at the name of the firm Maggie worked for. "Here to assist Ms. Price?"

"Actually I'm her replacement. I'll be taking over her office."

Jack's hand halted so abruptly midsip that some of his coffee sloshed over the rim of his cup onto the floor. Feeling as if he'd just walked into a theater in the middle of the movie, he lowered his mug to the counter and stared at Walter Langdon. "You're replacing Maddie? When did this happen?"

"Yesterday. But don't worry, Gavin's brought me up to speed on everything. The transition will be seamless."

"Why the change? Was it her idea or Gavin's?"

Walter shrugged and poured himself a cup of coffee. "I believe it was mutual." He took a sip and gave a satisfied *ahhh*. "Great coffee, but I wouldn't expect anything less from Java Heaven. Good to meet you, Jack. We'll be seeing a lot of each other over the next month." Cup in hand, Walter left the break room.

Jack stared at the empty doorway, feeling poleaxed. Which was ridiculous. He should be celebrating. No more Mad Dog Price. He'd never have to lay eyes on her again. And out of sight meant out of mind, which was great. Yeah, great. He was happy. Really happy. Happy, damn it.

Okay, maybe *happy* was too strong a word. Maybe *miserable* was better. And even though he shouldn't care, even though it didn't matter, he found himself striding toward Gavin's office. To find out what happened with Maddie. And why the new consultant thought they'd be working together for the next month when Jack would be gone in two weeks. Which Gavin damn well knew since Jack had left his letter of resignation on Gavin's desk before leaving late last night.

"Got a minute?" he asked, knocking on Gavin's open door when he arrived.

"C'mon in, Jack," Gavin said, waving him in. "Feeling better today?"

The question irked him—as if his resignation was some sort of tantrum—but he swallowed his irritation. "I feel fine. I felt fine yesterday. I just met Walter Langdon in the break room."

Gavin nodded. "The new consultant. Nice guy."

"What happened to Maddie?"

Gavin blew out a long breath and shook his head. "I'm afraid she just didn't work out."

"So her leaving was *your* idea?"

"Yes. After that report she gave me, I didn't really have a choice. She and I just weren't on the same page."

Jack's brows pulled into a frown. "What do you mean? What was wrong with the report?"

"She didn't do what I asked. She knew her objective at the team building was to recommend which employees should be cut from your department. Instead she gave me a bunch of reasons and recommendation as to why *no* cuts should be made. That's not what I hired her to do—so I asked that she be replaced with someone who could get the job done."

Everything inside Jack went still. "You led me to believe her report recommended the cuts. Named names."

"I never *said* that."

Jack tried to replay yesterday's conversation with Gavin, but his thoughts were in too much turmoil with the sickening realization that he'd made a mistake. A very big mistake.

"As far as naming names," Gavin continued, "I'm giving you first crack at it, but if you don't pick the five to go, I will."

Jack cleared his throat to loosen the tightness there. "You seem to forget that I've formally resigned. In writing."

Gavin waved his hand. "You were angry. I understand." His gaze hardened. "Just don't do it again, Jack. I don't care for ultimatums."

"I didn't give you one. I gave you my two weeks' notice. But you're right. I'd like to rescind it."

A smug grin curved Gavin's lips. "I knew you would."

"Instead, I'm resigning effective immediately." He planted his hands on Gavin's desk and leaned forward. "I'm not going to be a party to watching that department die a slow death. Good luck. You're going to need it." He turned on his heel and headed toward the door.

"You can't just walk out like this."

Jack paused long enough to say, "Yes, I can. And I have." Without another word, he strode to his office, where he quickly packed his meager personal belongings in a box then headed for the elevator. He made a mental note to contact the staff and explain, but that would have to wait until tomorrow.

Right now there was something far more urgent he needed to take care of.

Eleven

On Tuesday evening, Maddie walked the short distance from the MARTA train station to her midtown condo, relieved that the long day was over. She couldn't wait to peel off her suit, slip on her comfy pj's, plop herself in front of the TV, and drown her sorrows in the half gallon of rocky road ice cream waiting in her freezer. Her common sense knew there wasn't enough rocky road on the planet to make her forget Jack, but the misery eating at her insisted she at least try.

Jack. He hadn't been out of her thoughts for a moment. Partly because she was completely furious with him. She still seethed at the way he'd wrongly assumed the contents of her report to Gavin. But he'd also haunted her thoughts, because as galling as it was to admit, she cared for him. A lot. Too much. She didn't want to, had tried to talk herself out of it, but it was no use. In a shockingly short period of time he'd tattooed himself on her heart.

Last night, during a rocky-road marathon, she'd calmed down, and when she'd thought things through, realized that Jack clearly hadn't read the report she'd written. Since Gavin had insisted he cut the department, she grudgingly had to admit that it wasn't totally offbase for Jack to conclude that her report had recommended downsizing. Of course, she was pissed that he hadn't asked her or given her the benefit of the doubt before letting the accusations fly. He definitely owed her an apology.

Yet, after a sleepless night and difficult day, she'd concluded that she also owed him one. She'd been enraged, deeply hurt, and mortified at the possibility that he'd slept with her to influence her report. But when she recalled his face when she'd asked him, he'd looked positively stunned, then unmistakably hurt. Looking back, she could clearly see that her question had shocked him and she knew, in her heart, without a doubt, that she'd been wrong to doubt him.

Which left her with an aching sense of loss eating at her and a need to apologize. Which was why she'd spent her lunch hour at the Hallmark store, searching for the perfect card to send him. She'd finally found it and had written him a short note and included her phone number. When she arrived home she'd look up his address, slap a stamp on the envelope, and hope for the best. Maybe he would call. She prayed he would. Because if he didn't she'd have to check herself into rocky road rehab.

She turned the corner and her footsteps faltered—at the sight of Jack, sitting on the cement steps leading to her condo.

She halted and blinked, certain he was merely a figment of her Jack-saturated mind. But no, there he was. He caught sight of her and immediately stood.

She hesitated, then raised her chin and resumed walking, assuming an outward calm she was far from feeling. Part of her—the half that missed him—wanted to run to him and throw her arms around him. The other part—the half that was still pissed off—wanted to smack him upside his head with her purse.

As she approached the steps, she noticed he held a bouquet of lavender roses. Obviously a peace offering. Her missing-him half heaved a gushy sigh. Her pissed-off half stuck its nose in the air. He didn't speak until she'd climbed the steps and stood next to him on the small porch. Then he cleared his throat and offered a tentative smile. "Hi. I'm Jack Walker."

Her heart performed a rolling maneuver, one her pissed-off half steeled itself against. "Yes, I know. What do you want, Jack?"

"I was hoping we could talk. And I wanted to give you these." He held out the flowers. "The florist told me flowers mean different things. I asked him if he had any that meant 'I was an ass and I'm really sorry, can you forgive me?' and he said no. Which I think is too bad and some horticulturist somewhere really should invent a flower that says exactly that."

"No doubt it would be a big seller," Maddie said dryly.

"No doubt. I for one would have bought out his stock. But the closest he had were these lavender roses, which he said stood for sorrow. Which I have plenty of. And why they're for you."

Her heart tossed a great big bucket of cold water on her pissed-off half, which melted like the Wicked Witch of the West. Before she could say anything, he moved the flowers closer to her. "Please take them. If for no other reason than they'll have a much better life with you than they will with me. I don't know how to take care of them. Hell, I don't even have a container to put them in."

"You mean a vase."

"Right. So take pity on the poor flowers."

Unable to resist the gorgeous blooms, she accepted the bouquet. Their fingers brushed, shooting a tingle up her arm. "Thank you."

"You're welcome. Maddie, can we go somewhere and talk?"

She buried her nose in the gorgeous flowers. She'd wanted an apology and she'd gotten one. A really nice and sweet one, and an obviously sincere one. Her heart heaved out another gushy sigh.

"You can come in," she said, pulling out her key. As they walked down the hallway she asked, "How did you know where I lived?"

"A very useful device called the phone book. You should try it. Look me up. I'm listed under Doofus Who Jumps to Conclusions."

She bit the insides of her cheeks to hide the smile tugging at her lips. After they entered her condo, she led him into the kitchen. While she filled a crystal vase with water then arranged the flowers, she noted him looking around with interest.

"Nice place. Very homey."

"Thanks. I bought it last year." She dried her hands then leaned against the counter. "So what do you want to talk about?"

"Yesterday. In case you haven't gotten it yet, I'm really sorry. I hadn't seen your report, but my conversation with Gavin led me to believe you'd recommended not only that the department be downsized by twenty-five percent, but that you'd suggested who should be cut. I didn't find out until this morning that you'd actually recommended no cuts be made."

"I tried to tell you yesterday, but—"

"But I wasn't listening. I was angry and hurt and I spoke without thinking." He studied her for several seconds, then said quietly, "Thank you for taking my side."

"You need to know that I wouldn't have if I didn't believe you were right. My report was in no way swayed by us sleeping together."

"Speaking of which . . ." His gaze searched hers. "Do you honestly believe I slept with you to influence that report?"

She shook her head. "No, I don't, and I owe you an apology." She reached into her purse and pulled out the card she'd bought. "I was going to mail this to you, but since you're here . . ."

Without a word he took the card from her. On the front was a picture of a map and a compass. He opened it and she watched him read the short note she'd penned on the blank inside. *I don't need a map and a compass to figure out I was wrong. I'm sorry—I know you didn't sleep with me to influence the report.* She'd added her phone number and signed it. There was much more she'd wanted to say, but in the end had decided to keep it short and sweet. However, based on the silence swelling between them, that might not have been the wisest choice.

She cleared her throat. "I'm, ah, a woman of few words."

He finally looked up from the note. "That's okay. they're the right words."

Relief filled her and she pulled one of the lavender roses from the vase and held out the bloom to him. "Just to be totally clear—this means 'I was an ass and I'm really sorry, can you forgive me?' "

He smiled and took the flower. "Forgiven."

And with that single word, the fog of hurt and angst engulfing her lifted.

"Did Gavin asking for a replacement cause any problems for you at Lazer Consulting?" he asked.

"No. It's not unusual for consultants and executives to clash. I've already started on a new project. What about you—did you really give your two weeks' notice?"

"Yes. But then after discovering you'd left and that Gavin had led me down the garden path about your report I changed my mind and resigned effective immediately."

Maddie blinked. "Immediately?"

"I am no longer Java Heaven's CFO."

"So downsizing your department really was a deal breaker for you. You stood by your convictions, and it cost you your job."

"Well, I don't intend to remain unemployed for long. I've been thinking since I walked out Java Heaven's door and I've come up with a plan. Maybe you'd like to hear about it?" He set his rose on the counter then reached for her hands. "Maybe over dinner?"

Her heart sped up, both by the invitation and the warmth of his hands engulfing hers. "Are you asking me for a date?"

"Yes. Are you accepting?"

To her mortification, her throat slammed shut and hot tears pushed behind her eyes. Unable to speak, she nodded.

There was no missing the profound relief that filled his gaze. He cupped her face between his hands and lowered his head. Their kiss felt like a homecoming after a long, long trip. When he raised his head, she said, "I've been absolutely miserable since you walked out of my office yesterday."

"Me, too." He brushed his thumbs over her cheeks and looked at her through very serious eyes. "I think we have something special here, Maddie. I'd like to see where it goes. What do you think?"

She wrapped her arms around his neck and smiled. "Nice to meet you, Jack Walker. I'm Maddie Price. And I'd very much like to see where it goes."

Epilogue

Two months later

Jack applied the corkscrew to the bottle of merlot and flicked a glance at his kitchen clock. Maddie was due right about—

He heard the lock turning then the door opening and he grinned. The woman was almost comically punctual. She walked into the kitchen pulling her bright red carry-on suitcase behind her. He'd given her the bag after their first dinner date, telling her he didn't want to risk anyone else getting her lingerie-packed black bag by mistake.

She greeted him with a saucy smile. "Hiya, handsome. Lookin' for a good time?"

With a laugh he pulled her into his arms and gave her the kiss he'd been dying to give her since seeing her off at the airport three days ago. She'd flown to Tampa for a consulting job and damn it, he'd felt empty and lonely the entire time she was gone. He lifted her up and sat her on the counter. Stepping between her legs, he curved his hands around her bottom and pulled her closer. Until his erection pressed against the juncture of her thighs.

"Wow, seems like somebody missed me," she said, as he ran his tongue down the side of her cookie-scented neck.

"Maybe just a little."

"And maybe I missed you, too. Just a little." She sniffed the air. "Hey, it smells good in here. Like Italian food." She leaned back and looked at him in surprise. "Did you . . . *cook*?"

"*Cook* might be too strong a word. I ordered a pizza and calzone from Mario's. They're on Warm in the oven."

She wrapped her legs around his waist. "Hmmm. Wine and food from my favorite restaurant. Is this a special occasion?"

"I have some good news," he said, nipping kisses along her jaw. "I signed on a new client today."

She pulled his head back and kissed him on the mouth. "Jack, that's wonderful! I'm so proud of you." Then she shook her head and laughed. "I never doubted you'd be a success, but the irony of you being a consultant will never cease to amuse me."

He smiled and pulled her tighter against him, quickly calculating how long it would take to get her out of her prim suit, deciding it would have to wait until he told her everything he needed to first. "It's all your fault. You gave me a whole new appreciation for consultants, and I sure as hell like being my own boss." He lifted his hands to free her mass of curls from their restraints. "Of course, I consider myself an atypical consultant."

She cocked a single brow. "Are you implying that I'm typical?"

"Not in any way." Her hair cascaded around her shoulders and he sifted his fingers through the shiny strands. "Which is why I love you. Or at least one of the reasons I love you."

She went perfectly still. With his heart pounding, he looked into her eyes, trying to gauge her reaction to his admission. She looked . . . stunned. Damn. He'd been hoping for deliriously happy. These past two months had gone by in a blur, one filled with striking out to start his own company and spending every free minute with Maddie. And each minute spent with her had pushed him further into love. He'd kept his emotions in check as much as possible, not wanting to rush anything, but he couldn't hold back any longer. He knew she was The One. And it was time she knew it, too.

"You love me?" she whispered.

"I love you," he confirmed.

To his consternation, her chin quivered and a pair of fat tears rolled down her cheeks. "Oh, hell," he muttered. He reached behind her and ripped off a half-dozen paper towels. "Damn. I didn't mean to make you *cry*." Feeling helpless, he dabbed at her eyes with the huge wad of crumpled paper towels.

"I love you, too," she said, then promptly buried her face against his neck and sobbed.

Even as elation rushed through him he felt compelled to ask, "Are you sure? Because you don't seem very happy about it."

She leaned back and laughed—at least he thought she was laughing. It was kinda hard to tell with all the tears running down her face. "I'm happy," she said, kissing him. "I love you. I've wanted to say it for weeks, but was afraid I'd scare you off if I did. So I decided I'd give you one more week to tell me."

"And if I hadn't?"

"Then I was going to tie you to the bed so you couldn't escape, then tell *you*."

"You mean if I'd kept my mouth shut for just one more week, you'd have tied me to the bed?"

"Yes."

"I take it back." He nuzzled her neck. "Now will you tie me to the bed?"

She pushed at his shoulders. "You can't take it back." Suddenly she sobered. "Unless you want to."

"I don't want to."

"You're sure?"

"Positive." He cupped her face in his hands. "I think it's time you met Claire and Sophie. I told them all about you and they can't wait to meet you. Would you join us for dinner Friday night?"

Her smile could have lit a dark room. "I'd be delighted."

"And the Friday after that? And the Friday after that? And the Friday after that?"

The joy and love glowing in her eyes filled him with a happiness he'd never before known. "Sounds perfect."

"Good. What also sounds perfect is this tying me to the bed you mentioned. Would this by chance include your copy of *Fifty Ways to Please Your Lover* and some slinky lingerie?"

She leaned forward and kissed him. "Why don't you bring me to the bedroom and find out?"

He didn't hesitate. Hoisting her into his arms, he headed down the hall. "Good. Fine. Whatever you say."

Double the Danger

Penny McCall

One

Dr. Abigail West unzipped the body bag on her exam room table, expecting to see a head. She got feet. They were nice feet, good high arches, not too hairy, toe tag that read John Doe. The feet led to legs, then to knees, which led to her humming the "Dry Bones" song, and okay, the humming had a slightly violent edge to it, but she was pretty much in last-straw territory.

The eccentric, xenophobic inhabitants of Pottersville were trying to drive her away, but she'd be damned if she obliged them. The town sat less than two hundred miles from Chicago, but proximity to one of the largest, most cosmopolitan cities in the country had only made them hunker down all the more stubbornly within their buffer of corn and wheat fields. Pottersville was a glass-half-empty kind of town, and the great shopping, really huge Ferris wheel, and Oprah Winfrey in the Windy City couldn't outweigh crime, immorality, and probable atheism.

Abby hadn't been born in Pottersville; she'd come to stay with her elderly grandfather. Virgil hadn't been born there, either, but he'd lived in town long enough for some of the "outsider" to wear off. The minimal amount of grudging acceptance he'd achieved didn't extend to her, however. Worse, her point of origin was Washington, D.C., home of crooked politicians and the interns who loved them. The Pottersvillains (as she referred to them) treated her like she ranked right below Left-Wing Liberals on the list of "People Not to Associate With." They barely made conversation, let alone ventured within stethoscope range.

The surrounding community of medical professionals weren't much better. They allowed her clinic time, but they'd sent her no patients—until John Doe—and they'd stuck her with him because it was a weekend and none of the other doctors wanted autopsy duty. If she didn't do it she'd lose what little respect she'd managed to gain from a bunch of old men who were closer skill-wise to Dr. Quinn Medicine Woman than Dr. Kildare. They called the shots, though, and if the only doctoring they'd let her do was on dead people, then that's what she'd do.

She unzipped the body bag the rest of the way and froze, heart going still in her chest, breath trickling out, not believing her eyes. "Drake," she whispered, stumbling back a step or two, shocked to see the face of the man she'd once loved on a dead body that had turned up in an Illinois cornfield.

Abby didn't know how long she stood there before the truth sank into her stunned brain. She stepped up to the table again, but she didn't touch him. As a doctor, she knew death had to become a part of her professional life, but not like this. True, she'd lost loved ones, her mother most recently, but Drake was different.

They'd met in college. She'd been a freshman, he'd been a couple years ahead of her, and the attraction had been more intense than spontaneous combustion. In a matter of weeks she'd moved into his off-campus apartment, and by the time two years had passed, the idea of marriage had been cropping up in her thoughts with a regularity that should have worried a young woman who knew medical school was an all-or-nothing kind of commitment. Turned out it wasn't a problem.

A month before his senior year was over, Drake had gone on an interview. The day after graduation he'd moved out of their apartment without telling her where he was going. He'd come back once for a visit, but after that there'd only been phone calls that had gotten shorter and less frequent over the following summer. Then all contact stopped—not by her choice—and pride had finally forced her to quit reaching out to a man who never reached back.

Work had saved her sanity, if not her heart. With nothing to distract her, she'd worked her way to the top of every class. But while there'd been immense satisfaction in becoming a doctor, there'd also been a feeling of emptiness because she'd had no one to share it with.

That had changed a few months ago. She wasn't alone anymore, but Drake had always been an unfinished part of her life. Until today. She wanted to walk away, but she couldn't bear to have him treated like a slab of meat by some other doctor with uncaring hands.

"The subject has bruises and abrasions consistent with loss of consciousness, probably due to the wound just above his right temple," she said into a microrecorder, her voice firming as she tried to retreat behind clinical detachment. Tried and failed. "The wound doesn't appear to be lethal, but is the likely reason he passed out and probably died of exposure . . ." She trailed off, her hand tracing the lines on his forehead, lines that hadn't been there ten years before.

It took a second for her to notice something was wrong—or right, considering he was a lot warmer than a dead body should be. Her heart slammed into her ribs. She put on a pair of magnifying glasses and leaned close. There appeared to be fresh blood oozing from the wound, and his skin was too pink for a corpse . . .

She laid her fingers on his neck to search for a carotid pulse, and his eyes popped open. So did her mouth. Inside she was screaming but all that came out was a trickling little wheeze. She froze, pinned in place by a pair of intense, familiar blue eyes, which meant she didn't notice the rest of him until his hands closed around her throat. And then it was too late because everything went black.

Abby opened her eyes, taking a few seconds to process what she was seeing. Fluorescent lights surrounded by acoustic ceiling tiles. And they were way too close for her to be on the floor, not to mention when she inched her hand out she encountered plastic . . . she was lying on the table, on the body bag that used to hold—

"*Drake.*"

She scrambled off and there he was, larger than life. Literally. Tall and alive and bulkier than he'd been in college, with muscles on top of his muscles. He had the same black hair, though, and the same intense blue eyes. He'd never been a man she'd have called handsome, even if he hadn't developed some homicidal tendencies in the last decade.

He was a couple of days past a five o'clock shadow, there were lines of pain around his mouth, and he didn't look happy to see her. He had to have a splitting headache, but he was observing, assessing the situation. He made a slow study of the exam room in the town's one and only clinic. There wasn't much to see, but his gaze lingered on the door to the waiting room, the tiny office at one end, and the door opposite the exam room, which led out to the parking lot.

Whatever conclusions he was drawing—and any intentions he might have concerning them—his body wasn't going to be much help. He was weaving and shaky, fighting to stay on his feet.

Abby crossed her arms, her compassion tempered with ten years of simmering resentment. "At least say good-bye before you take off this time."

"I said good-bye."

"Not in so many words. But you got your message across. It just took me a while to understand it."

He absorbed that in silence for a second or two. He'd always been one to think before he spoke, and the familiarity of it hurt because there'd been a time he hadn't felt a need to guard his thoughts from her.

"What are you doing here?" he finally said.

"Shouldn't I be asking you that question?"

"No."

Abby uncrossed her arms and took a page from his book. There were dozens of things she wanted to ask, even more she wanted to say outright. It wasn't the time or place, and some of it was best left unsaid. And she still had a job to do. "You probably have a concussion," she told him, "not to mention hypothermia. Why don't you sit down and let me check you over."

"I'm fine," he said, sounding anything but.

"Okay, then you don't need me." When she went for the door, he shifted in front of it, lifting his hands in what he probably thought was a reassuring gesture. Except the last time she'd noticed his hands they'd been around her neck.

Her heart jumped into her throat, beating frantically, making it impossible to breathe. She tried to tell herself Drake would never hurt her, but the Drake she'd known was gone. In his place was a cold, hard man whose capabilities she couldn't even guess.

He pulled her rolling chair in front of the door and sat, and when he looked at her again, saw her in full panic mode, he rolled his eyes and shook his head.

If he'd put on a clown nose and danced a jig, it wouldn't have killed her fear as fast as his disdain. She sucked in a breath and tried to get a grip, which was easier than it might have been if she hadn't noticed he was wearing her partner's lab coat. It was way too small—everywhere. Which brought back more memories: those first weeks together, when they couldn't keep their hands off one another, and, even more painful, moments in the dark of night when they'd turned to each other, and along with the heat had been tenderness . . .

"I'm not going to hurt you," he said.

He already had, in the only way that truly counted. "You tried to strangle me."

"You passed out because you stopped breathing. Haven't had a lot of experience with dead people, huh?"

"You're not dead."

"You thought I was."

"Right up to the moment you wrapped your hands around my throat."

"Reflex. Fight or flight."

Abby didn't respond, her brain churning out a list of reasons a man might react the way he had. None of them were reassuring.

"Don't look at me like that."

"Like what?"

"Like I'm a disappointment."

Abby huffed out a slight laugh, feeling a surge of satisfaction when he dropped his eyes from hers. There were a lot of things she could have called him. *Disappointment* wasn't even on the list. "Why don't we discuss why you're here?"

He shrugged. "I was shot—"

"Shot?"

"And I got a little too much firsthand knowledge of the local weather patterns, but I'm fine now."

"When the sheriff found you, he thought you were dead. You would be dead if we'd had the snow we were supposed to get last night."

"Don't get all broken up about it."

"Your hands, my neck . . ."

"You stuck me in a refrigerated drawer."

"Actually you were in the walk-in freezer at the diner."

"Hicks," he muttered. "Where am I now?"

"You're in my exam room."

"In?"

"The clinic."

"In?"

She spread her hands and made the give-me-a-clue face.

"The town?"

"Oh! Pottersville."

He considered that for a split second, then said, "I'm going to need some shoes."

And pants, but Abby kept that to herself. He wasn't going anywhere in his condition.

"You have a car, right?"

"Of course, but even if I were prepared to hand over the keys, you're in no shape to drive."

"I'm not driving."

This time she had no trouble getting his inference, which brought back that pesky trickle of apprehension. "Why do you need me?"

"Whoever tried to kill me thinks I'm dead. You're the only one who knows I'm not, and you're not a very good liar. You never were. Your face," he added when she looked puzzled by his assessment.

"Why would I have to lie? And what's wrong with my face?"

"It's an open book. Giving people bad news must be hell."

"Not really, they usually know—stop smirking. People don't come to me unless they're sick, and by the time I have a prognosis, they've already figured out from the actual disease that it's probably not going to have a good outcome." She was getting defensive because a delusional former corpse had insulted her. "Look, you're not dead, but obviously your brains are scrambled."

"Is that the official diagnosis?"

"In your case, yes. You spent the night outside in subfreezing weather and you have a nice gash in your forehead."

"You mean my bullet wound?"

Mentally she was rolling her eyes. Outwardly she humored him. "Bullet wound, sure, all the more reason you shouldn't be taking a trip right now."

"What I'm thinking about is staying alive. And keeping you alive."

That stopped her.

"I'm an FBI agent," he said before she could wrap her mind around his last statement. "I can't tell you why I'm here, but now you're involved, which means when the people who tried to kill me find out I'm alive and you talked to me, they might come after you."

"To kill me," she scoffed. "You're saying somebody wants me dead.

"Possibly."

"Somebody might want me dead, and you can't tell me why."

"Yes."

"Somebody might want me dead, you can't tell me why, and you expect me to just walk out that door with you?"

"And drive exactly where I tell you to, and keep your mouth shut."

"Brain damage, definitely." She unlooped her stethoscope from around her neck, but when she reached for him, he closed his hand around her wrist, over her lab coat, and held her off.

"You need to take this seriously," he said.

"I need to check you out."

He let go of her wrist and cupped her chin, turning her face back to his. He definitely got her attention, and his mouth was moving, so he was making the most of it. She couldn't hear a word he said, though. His hand on her bare skin was shooting her pulse up so fast she went dizzy.

He let her go, rubbing his fingertips on his lab coat, which meant he'd felt that instantaneous punch of heat, too. Bad, very bad. But if he could ignore it, so could she. It took a minute, some real effort, and a hell of a pep talk, but she got herself close enough to listen to his heart, take his pulse, and look into his eyes with her penlight. Heartbeat strong and steady, pupils equal and reactive, no signs of concussion. "What's the date?" she asked him.

He gave her the correct date, including the year.

"And your name?"

Just the slightest hesitation before he lifted his foot and removed the toe tag. "John Doe," he said with the hint of a smirk.

She took the tag and tossed it in the trash. "Try again."

He bumped up a shoulder. "Drake. I'll need some clothes—"

The bells over the street entrance jingled.

He lowered his voice. "But first you're going to get rid of the patient who just came in."

Abby stared at him, arms crossed, toe tapping. "You really need to stop ordering me around." But she went to the window looking out on the waiting room and peeked through the blinds. "He's not one of my patients." Or rather not one of the people who might have been her patients, if the Pottersvillains ever put away their ten-foot poles. "I don't know him."

"Then you won't have to waste time with chitchat."

"Maybe he came to kill me," she said, voice dripping sarcasm.

Drake wasn't amused. He scowled his way across the room to lurk just out of sight of the window, peering carefully over her shoulder.

The air trickled out of her lungs because he was all but wrapped around her, which should have sent her running for cover instead of noticing how warm and solid he felt.

She concentrated almost desperately on the strange man out front. He didn't look dangerous. Average height, balding, pale and rotund with a round, pleasant, forgettable face. He wore khakis, a bomber jacket, and a concerned expression. "He doesn't look like he came to kill anyone." He looked like the Pillsbury Doughboy.

"He's not going to walk in here and kill you. He'll need to ask some questions first, find out what you know."

"I don't know anything."

"You know about me."

She looked over her shoulder. "Maybe I should call the sheriff. You claim someone shot you, and I'm supposed to report any bullet wounds. It's the law."

"You call the sheriff, there's no telling what that guy might do."

"He might not do anything. He might actually be in need of a doctor."

"We can't afford to take that chance."

"We? How do *we* know you're trustworthy?"

"I've never lied to you, Abby."

"Sure. Hard to lie when you don't say anything."

"Hard to see the present if the past keeps getting in your way."

Two

Drake clapped a hand over Abby's mouth before she could respond to his delieberate taunting.

She understood immediately and quieted. No matter what she said, she wasn't sure about the man in the lobby. She wasn't sure about him, either, Drake knew, but he'd poked at her self-respect. She wouldn't let the past get in her way again.

"Why don't you get rid of the guy in the lobby, then you and I can talk."

Abby searched his face. He forced himself to meet her eyes; he'd done a lot of things that would haunt a normal man's conscience, but leaving her was the only one he'd ever felt guilty over.

She took a deep breath and let it out, preparing herself, but Drake stopped her before she could turn the doorknob. She had an excellent mind, but she couldn't lie worth a damn. Take the smile she'd pasted on her face.

"If you go out there looking like that, he'll probably shoot first and ask questions later."

"What's wrong with the way I look?" she asked, at least having enough good sense to keep her voice down.

"Nobody smiles that wide unless they have something to hide. Or they're at the dentist."

The smile turned into a glare.

"Okay, somewhere between this face and the last one should do it."

Dr. Cranky took a deep breath and huffed it out before she went through the door.

"Can I help you?" she asked the stranger.

"I can wait until you're done with your current patient," he said with the faintest of accents, one that had Drake straining his ears instead of coming up with a plan like he should have been. But there was something . . .

"I was just catching up on my paperwork," he heard Abby say, but she looked toward the exam room door, and so did the stranger.

Drake froze. He couldn't be seen unless he moved—he hoped.

"What seems to be the problem?" Abby asked, turning the man's attention her way again.

"Killer headache," he said, attempting to look the part, but only managing to squint unconvincingly.

"There's a pharmacy down the street."

He shook his head. "It's a migraine, and I left my pills at home."

"I don't prescribe medication unless I know it's necessary."

"Sure. Of course," he said, and headed for the exam room.

Abby tried to stop him, but he was already through the door. He stopped dead when he saw Drake, then his hand snaked back, under his jacket. Drake got to him before Abby did, and while he had no idea what the other man's intentions might be, Drake's plan of action took the form of a bedpan to the face.

Migraine-guy went down, but he popped right back up, gun in hand. Drake stepped in close, blocking his right hand before the stronger could bring the gun to bear. It went flying, but Drake took a brain-jarring left to the face, which would have been bad enough by itself. With the head wound it nearly took him down. He had the guy by fifty pounds of muscle and six inches, but unless Drake passed out on top of him, his bulk wasn't going to save the day.

"Shoot him," he shouted at Abby.

She picked up the gun, holding it like she meant business. Her face said otherwise. Her face said there was no way she'd pull the trigger. The other guy jerked to a stop though, fist cocked back, staring at the gun and not seeing the face behind it. He decided not to take a chance, bolting through the emergency exit that led from the exam room to the parking lot behind the clinic.

Abby slumped back against the wall, eyes on the door in case the guy came back. Wheezing, Drake dropped to a seat on the floor.

"See?" Abby said, "you're in no shape to go gallivanting around the country." She reached for him, but he raised his hands slowly, warding her off. "I just want to help you up."

"Maybe you should put the gun down first."

She looked at her hand, clearly surprised to find she was still holding the thing. She set it carefully on the counter, slipped her arm under his, and helped him to a seat on her rolling stool. "You're not having a very good day."

"It would be better if you'd shot that guy," Drake said.

"I'm a doctor. Shooting people goes against my ethical code."

"How about dying?" he said, rolling over to pick up the gun.

Abby practically jumped out of her shoes, which would have been a real shame since they were some amazing shoes—sensible, yet they managed to make her legs look about a mile long. The rest of the package was even better than Drake remembered, her face pared down by time and experience, leaving behind strength along with the beauty. Her dress covered her from neck to knees, but it was one of those curve-hugging numbers. And there were some definite curves to hug.

He lifted his eyes, thinking if he kept them on her face he could get his mind back on his near-death experience and off the fact that he was feeling the need for a nice, sweaty bout of I'm-still-alive sex. It worked, at first. She looked all proper and doctorial, but if she let her hair down out of that ugly bun and slapped some red lipstick on that lush mouth . . .

She'd still be an albatross around his neck, at least for the short term. He had a job to do, and she was a complication he couldn't afford.

"I need clothes," he said.

"There's a general store just up the way."

Drake shook his head. "You must have something here."

She waved a hand toward a white metal cabinet across the room. "Scrubs, in case we have to do any emergency procedures."

"We?"

"I borrow office time from the doctor who owns this clinic."

Drake rolled the stool over to the cabinet and took out a pair of thin blue pants, deciding to stick with the lab coat. The arms were only three-quarter length on him, and it didn't close all the way in front, but it was heavier and warmer than the tissue paper shirt that went along with the tissue paper pants. "Where is the other doctor?" he asked, dropping the gun into his pocket so he could pull on the pants.

"At the hospital, covering for a doctor who's on vacation."

"You don't have any patients today?"

"Just you."

He smiled a little over the tone in her voice. "Sorry you didn't get to autopsy me?"

"I'm pretty sure what I would have found," she said.

It sounded like she thought there'd be something missing, too, namely his heart. But he didn't need a heart to do his job. In fact, he was better off without one. "Time to go," he said.

She stayed where she was, still looking pissed and mulish on top of it. "I'm just supposed to disappear with you?"

"It's not like I'm giving you a choice."

"Great," she said, throwing up her hands and beginning to pace. "I turned down some prestigious offers to move here, you know. I could have been working in Washington, D.C., or New York, but no, I had to come to *Pottersville.* And I didn't mind really, even when this town turned out to have an epidemic of narrow-mindedness. I didn't mind," she repeated, her voice rising in pitch and volume, "because my grandfather needs me and he's old and alone, and we're—"

"Wait, *grandfather*? I thought all your grandparents were dead."

"So did I. My mother became ill a couple of years ago. Cancer. When she knew the treatment wasn't working, she wanted me to know her father—her real father—was still alive. He left the family when she was just a baby, and when my grandmother remarried, her new husband adopted my mother. She died about a year ago and—"

"He didn't come to the funeral, but he contacted you, and you began to correspond. Until two months ago, when he asked you to come out here."

She didn't need to answer, he saw it on her face.

"Shit." He ran a hand through his hair, wincing when he grazed the wound on his temple. "His name is Virgil Mason."

Abby planted herself in front of him, jamming her hands on her hips. "What is going on?"

Drake hesitated, but there was no point in keeping the truth from her, since she was the reason he'd come to Pottersville—or half the reason anyway. "I told you I'm an FBI agent. Normally we don't handle witness protection, but the U.S. Marshall was called away on another case, and I was in the area."

Abby's mouth dropped open, and she sat down, hard, on the stool he'd vacated. "My grandfather . . ."

"Has been in the program for years. He was perfectly safe until—"

"Until I moved in with him. Which is why you're here."

"I didn't know it was you," Drake said. "I got word that Virgil's name and location had popped up on one of the wiretaps because he contacted his granddaughter. Time is always critical in these cases, so I headed here before I got the rest of the intelligence.

"I was less than a mile from Virgil's farm when somebody started shooting at me. He must have gotten in a lucky shot, because the next thing I knew my car hit the ditch then flipped end over end into a field." Drake lifted his gaze to Abby's. "Sound travels for miles in this flat country, and the gunman would've been worried about who might be coming to investigate gunshots. I guess he didn't stick around to find out if I was dead."

Abby raced into the little office and dialed her grandfather. It rang a half-dozen times before the answering machine kicked in. She disconnected and tried again. Same result. "He's not picking up," she told Drake. "You don't think . . ."

"I don't know Virgil's status," Drake said. "Was he all right when you left this morning?"

"I don't know. I was on call last night at the hospital." Keeping her medical skills up to date, since they'd actually let her work with patients. "It's an hour drive in good weather. With the snow, I decided to spend the night there."

"Then there's no telling what we'll find when we get to your place," Drake said. "Better prepare yourself."

Prepare myself? How the heck was she supposed to prepare herself when the hits just kept coming? Before she could even begin to come to terms with the fact that a corpse turned out to be her ex-boyfriend, who then came to life and tried to strangle her, the Pillsbury Doughboy had showed up and pulled a gun, which was the last thing she'd expect from a balding, pasty, middle-aged fat guy. A rolling pin, maybe, but a gun?

Drake, however, was truth in advertising, big and gruff and impatient, all muscle and no tact. He'd told her Virgil was probably dead with all the finesse of a bedpan to the face, leaving her with a hollow stomach, sweaty palms, and a general sense of unreality.

On top of all that, the hit man was still lurking in the vicinity. Drake had a bloody gash on his forehead, his hands trembled a little when he forgot to keep them fisted, and every now and then he gave his head a little shake and blinked a couple of times. Hardly surprising considering he'd been shot, nearly frozen to death, and punched several times. He was in no shape for another confrontation, but she knew he wouldn't listen to reason.

Sure enough he plucked her coat and purse off the coatrack and fished out her keys.

"I'm driving," she said.

He ignored her, easing the back door open an inch and peering out at the four-space parking lot, empty except for her Mustang.

"You're a pain in the ass, but you have good taste in cars," he said, catching her by the wrist and pulling her through the door.

There was at least an inch of slushy snow on the ground and his feet were bare, but he didn't seem to notice. He opened the driver's door, stuffed her in the backseat, and climbed in, pushing the seat all the way back.

Abby had to do something. Who knew what would happen if he passed out while driving a car through the middle of town? At the very least he'd be hurt and so would she, but the townspeople were innocent bystanders. Just because they treated her like Typhoid Mary didn't mean she wanted them dead.

She scooted forward and pressed her fingers as hard as she could against the side of his neck. The right amount of force on the carotid artery could trick the body into thinking the blood pressure was too high, resulting in a blackout. He was still woozy, so how hard could it be?

"You'd need to be a little higher and about an inch farther forward," he instructed. "If you had enough hand strength."

"I would if you weren't muscle from the shoulders up," she said, sitting back in her seat and closing her fingers over her tingling palm. "And I'm including your head."

He met her eyes in the mirror, looking amused for a split second before he turned his head and stared out the driver's side window. Abby looked too, and saw an old rust bucket of a Dodge Ram cruise by the clinic lot.

"Shit," Drake said, "we gave him time to boost a vehicle."

"That was Earl Fennimore's truck."

"I don't think Earl's behind the wheel," Drake said, starting the car and steering it out of the lot.

There was no hiding in a cherry red Mustang, but the Pottersvillains were used to seeing it—and shaking their heads in disgust over the complete impracticality of driving such a vehicle in an area where snowfalls were measured in feet. It always made her wish she was the kind of woman who used obscene gestures.

Drake surprised her by keeping to the snail's pace of a speed limit while in town, ignoring the locals but keeping an eye on the truck that had swung around to follow at a reasonable distance.

"That truck might look like a piece of junk but I bet it weighs twice as much as my car," Abby said, having visions of her Mustang crumpled up like a beer can with them trapped inside.

"It has weight, but it's not as maneuverable," Drake said as they hit the edge of town, "and it doesn't have me at the wheel." He punched the gas, the tires spinning for a split second before they grabbed pavement with a squeal of rubber and a jerk that sent the GT rocketing down the road.

Abby turned to watch the truck getting gradually smaller, but before she made it all the way to relief, Drake said, "What's that?"

She faced forward again and took a good long look out the windshield. "Snow," she said. A solid white wall of it, and Drake didn't know the roads. The car wasn't built for the weather, either, so he was forced to slow down, which put the four-wheel-drive Ram right on their back bumper.

"My grandfather told me this car would probably be the death of me."

"Get into the front seat."

"What? Why?"

"Air bags," Drake said in a tone of voice that ought to come along with an ominous sound track.

He sped up again as they hit the swirling white blizzard, the engine's throaty roar rumbling through the car as she climbed over the seat and strapped herself in. "What are you going to do?"

"This." He turned the wheel sharply to the left, putting the car into a controlled spin that left them facing the way they'd come. And then he stepped on it, the back end of the car fishtailing as he sent it hurtling toward the truck.

"You're playing chicken in this weather?"

"Yep."

"You're giving him exactly what he wants. And I'm going to die, too."

"We're not going to die. He is, with any luck. The tires on that thing are probably as worn out as the rest of it, which means they're bald."

Abby wanted to scream but she'd stopped breathing. Her hand inched over the console and closed around Drake's thigh, feeling his warmth through the thin scrub pants without being reassured in the least, because the truck was barreling straight at them, full speed, and even if he'd wanted to stop there was already a half inch of slick, wet snow between the truck tires and the pavement.

All she could see was pickup grill coming closer until it filled the windshield. Drake swerved at the last second, the Mustang's tires slipping and spinning before they caught and sent the car to one side just as the Ram swerved to the other, lost traction, and went into a slide. Its back bumper just clipped the front corner of the Mustang before its tires hit the shoulder and the front end stopped abruptly. The back end had momentum, though, flipping over and landing the truck on its roof in the ditch. The cab disappeared to the door handles, buried in a winter's worth of snow and slushy ice.

"Take a breath," Drake said.

His voice was so infuriatingly calm that she would have done the opposite just to spite him. But she sucked in some air because the edges of her vision had gone gray and it would be embarrassing to pass out and prove him right.

"You can let go, too."

She glanced over, remembered where her hand was, and snatched it back. "Excuse me," she said, going for the door handle.

He put the car in motion, steering it around so they were heading away from town again.

"We have to check on him."

"Hippocratic oath?"

"That and basic decency."

"What about your grandfather? Do you think that guy was decent to Virgil?"

It shouldn't matter. Her oath was meant to obligate her to helping people no matter what, but she'd surrender her medical license before she gave any assistance to the man who might have killed her grandfather. But . . . "If Virgil is . . . gone, why would he come after us?"

Drake shrugged. "We've both seen his face."

"So no witnesses?"

"The guy is a contract hitter. That's part of his M.O."

"You're just trying to scare me."

"You bet your ass," Drake said. "I don't know that guy personally, but he's a hired gun, and he works for Joey Pollani."

"*The* Joey Pollani?" Abby said, trying to wrap her mind around it.

"The Joey Pollani who ran Boston's crime family in the fifties and sixties," Drake said, "before he was convicted of a dozen felonies. But he's out now."

That stopped Abby for a minute. Joey Pollani was rumored to be a pretty bad guy, but that had been decades ago. "Okay, but he's old." He'd have to be at least her grandfather's age, around eighty.

"He could be drooling into his oatmeal and he'd still be the head of the family. Hell, he could be dead," Drake said. "It doesn't matter. Your grandfather was supposed to testify against Joey. There was a contract taken out on Virgil, and nothing ends a contract except the death of the target."

"You're saying my grandfather was in the Mafia?"

"I'm saying your grandfather assisted in putting Joey in federal prison for three decades. Pollani wants him dead, and he only hires the best."

She shook her head, but it was all starting to add up, and she didn't like the end product. "If he was the best, why are you still alive?" she asked, grasping for straws, hoping maybe Drake was overstating the Pillsbury Hit Man's capabilities.

"I'm pretty damn good at staying alive," Drake said. "And you better hope I'm as good at keeping you alive, because I'm all you've got."

"If you're saying that to make me feel better, it didn't work."

Three

They made the rest of the drive in silence, Abby's heart sinking when the house came into view. Virgil's farm sat on a snow-covered road about ten miles outside Pottersville. The white farmhouse with its wraparound, covered porch had seen better days. So had the big red barn, but the place wasn't home to Abby because of the paint job. It didn't look like home at all now, with no lights shining a welcome through the stormy afternoon gloom.

Drake pulled in the drive and steered the car around behind the house. The back door was wide open, and Abby was out of the car before it stopped moving.

Drake jammed it into Park and caught her in the car's headlights. "Stay here," he yelled at her.

She ignored him, taking the porch steps two at a time and barreling through the back door. Drake caught up with her just inside. This time he wrapped an arm around her waist and held on.

She stilled, met his eyes. "The hit man didn't crawl out of that ditch and get here before us," she said.

"No point in taking unnecessary risks." He flicked the light switch by the door. Nothing happened.

"Go back to the car," he ordered, and went in.

Abby followed him anyway, surprised to find it wasn't completely dark inside even after they'd left the car lights behind. There was a large country kitchen off the back door, with a sitting room at the front of the house. No moon, but a soft blue white light came in the windows from the glow given off by freshly fallen snow. Enough light to see Drake go into the front room, which gave her time to sneak up the stairs and into her grandfather's bedroom. The closet was open, the room empty. A shiver of dread ran down her spine, and she turned and raced out into the hall, running headlong into Drake.

"Christ," he said, wrapping his arms around her before they went down in a tangle, "can't you ever follow instructions?"

Abby stared up into the gloom where his face should be, nerves jumping, heart hammering, and tiny bursts of light exploding in her vision.

Drake gave her a little shake.

She wheezed in a breath, then another. "Don't grab me like that."

"I wasn't the only one doing the grabbing."

Abby realized she was plastered to him, but she didn't let go, and not because of fear. The adrenaline racing through her system was sending entirely different messages to entirely different body parts. She let her eyes drift shut so she could enjoy the feel of all that hard, resilient muscle, to let the heat of him soak into her chilled skin so she felt something besides the panic and terror of the last few hours.

It wasn't just the months of celibacy and his incredible body that made her forget everything else when she was touching him. Or the memory of what they'd once meant to one another, and the long, lonely years since he'd left her behind. The man was practically indestructible. He'd been shaky and nearly out on his feet at the clinic, but at the first sign of trouble he tapped some hidden reserve that left him rock steady and in charge. As long as she was touching him, she felt like there was hope. Of course he had to speak and ruin the moment.

"Earth to Dr. Ruth."

Doctor, right, she was a doctor, and doctors were detached, so she went for detached, unlocking her hands from around the lapels of his white lab coat. But as soon as she started to ease her body away from his and her nerves began to settle, the "Ruth" part of his comment sank in, and she stepped away fast, smoothing her dress and straightening her coat.

"Did you find anything?" Drake asked her, his voice low and amused in the darkness, and edged with something that made her glad she wasn't still pressed against him. Her self-control wouldn't have stood a chance against her need and his, too.

"No," she said, "but I only checked my grandfather's room."

Drake took her by the sleeve, not making skin-to-skin contact, for which she was grateful. He first pulled her into the guest room—closet open, nobody there—then found the same situation in her bedroom at the far end of the hall. "Kind of uptight, aren't you?" he said.

Abby let go of him, reluctantly, her gaze following his around the room. "It's called *organization*."

"It's called *inflexible*." He picked up a small music box from her dresser and looked underneath it.

"What are you doing?"

"Checking for tape outlines. You didn't used to be this anal."

"There's nothing wrong with neatness," she said, plucking the music box from his hand and putting it precisely where it belonged. She brushed by him and his laughing eyes, shut her closet door, and went to check the bathroom. She righted things as she went, and to hell with him. What mattered was her grandfather. "Virgil's not up here," she said.

"Nobody's home downstairs either."

Abby stopped where she was, one hand on the wall, trying to get a grip.

"It's a good sign," Drake said, "there's no blood and no body."

"What if—"

"He wasn't taken off-site. If Virgil had been here when that guy showed up, his body would still be here."

Abby forced herself to exhale, slowly and silently, but she didn't trust herself to speak. Knowing her grandfather wasn't dead here in the house didn't mean he wasn't dead, or hurt, elsewhere. And since Drake was her only hope of finding him, he'd need clothes.

She went into her grandfather's bedroom and pulled out boxers, blue work pants, socks, and a T-shirt, holding them out because even though she hadn't heard a sound she knew Drake had followed her.

"The pants are long enough but they're too big in the waist," he said from behind her.

She gave him the belt she'd located by feel, since the lights still weren't working and the meager illumination from the windows didn't make it into the closet. She heard a ripping noise and turned around before Drake could say, "The T-shirt is too small," getting an eyeful of his bare chest, which she'd seen before, but not while she was so needy.

The urge to run her hands over all that muscle nearly overwhelmed her. And when she lifted her gaze to his, she could see he was feeling everything she was and more, his eyes so dark and so intense that it scared her a little. She took a deep breath and turned back to the closet, proud of herself for being the one who'd pulled back first this time.

She dug through the closet, hands trembling, nerves too jangled to do more than make a good show of it. But gradually it wasn't a show, and she located a pile of long johns, which were not only stretchy enough, but warm, too. She found a shirt and tossed it to him, laughing as he struggled into it—not that the attraction was gone, but the comedy was enough to override it for the moment.

"It'll do," he said, tugging the cuffs down to his wrists only to have them spring back to midforearm.

The shirt was stretched to capacity across his chest, but Abby chose to think about his feet instead. She dropped to her knees and pulled out a pair of work boots.

Drake sat on the bed, tugged them on, and said tersely, "Pretty good fit," which was a relief since the moment he had shoes he took off to check the old stone-walled, dirt-floored basement.

Not long after he disappeared down the stairs, the lights flooded on. Abby went down to the first floor, blinking at the chaos. It looked like World War III, furniture overturned, glassware smashed. She went to close the back door, and when she turned around, Drake was holding an empty picture frame.

"What was in here?" he asked.

"A picture of me. My graduation from medical school."

"Son of a bitch." He slammed the frame on the mantel, kicking a chair out of his way so he could pace across the room.

"I'd appreciate it if you wouldn't destroy the furn—"

"He wasn't at the clinic to make sure I was dead."

"But you said—"

"I assumed . . . Never mind."

"No, keep talking. If he wasn't looking for you, then he was looking for me. Why?"

Drake took to his feet, running a hand through his hair. "I called Virgil this morning and told him I was on my way to relocate him." He turned to give her a look. "All I can say is the apple doesn't fall far from the tree."

"Meaning?"

"Virgil wasn't being what you'd call cooperative. Said he was too old to make new friends."

"I don't think age has a lot to do with it."

"Yeah, I got that. We were discussing it—"

"Meaning you were handing out orders."

Drake stopped pacing, crossing the room to loom over her. "My job is to keep him alive, and I decide the best way to do that."

Abby looked around the room. She didn't need to say what she was thinking.

"This isn't exactly the way I'd have chosen, but he's still alive, isn't he?"

"Is he?"

"Has to be," Drake said, his certainty as compelling as the logic of his explanation. "I was less than a mile from here when the hit man caught up with me, and sound carries forever in this flat country. Virgil must have heard the shooting and hightailed it out of here. When the hit man found the house empty, he must have decided he could use you to flush your grandfather out of hiding."

"Hiding?" Abby felt a breath of real hope. She righted a chair and sat. "Do you really think so?"

"It's just an educated guess," Drake said. "Pollani's guy didn't stick around to find out if I was dead or not. As soon as I was out of the picture he would have come back here to kill your grandfather. From what I can tell Virgil was smart enough to take off and stay gone." Drake dropped into the chair across the table from her, looking tired. "I wish I could say I carried out my mission, but the next thing I remember is you."

And she was right there with him, recalling how it felt to see his eyes fly open, only now it wasn't shock, it was something more like relief. That couldn't be good. "So where is Virgil?" she asked, because thinking about her feelings and where they might be leading her would be a huge mistake.

"I was hoping you'd know."

"He has a couple of friends . . ."

"We can check with them, but I doubt he'd put anyone in danger. Do you have any other ideas?"

"I haven't known him that long. I only ever saw pictures of him until he contacted me after my mother's funeral. She was the only family I had . . ." Until Virgil had called her in tears, as alone as she was, but also old and devastated at losing his only child. There'd been sadness over the state of affairs, but no bitterness or acrimony, so when Virgil had asked her to come, she had.

"That's what blew his cover," Drake said. "And when Virgil disappeared the hit man came for you. Probably figured since your grandfather was willing to risk his life to have you here, he'd give himself up to save you. He went to the clinic to get his hands on you, and that's still what he wants."

"And what do you want?"

Drake held her eyes for a long minute, and in case there was any doubt about what he wanted, he put his hands on the table and levered himself to his feet, leaning across, his face so close to hers she felt the warm wash of his breath on her skin, and it was all she could do to keep her eyes from fluttering closed while he crossed that small, heated gap . . .

But he continued to his feet and stepped away. "I think I'll take a quick look around outside," he said, the rasp in his voice giving the lie to his apparent calm. And then he was gone.

But this time he was coming back. At least temporarily.

Four

Drake went to search through the outbuildings. Abby couldn't believe Pollani's assassin hadn't done that before abandoning the farm, and if she'd deduced that much, she figured Drake must have come to that conclusion as well, which meant that he was making sure the hit man hadn't missed anything—*and* he wanted to get away from her. She couldn't blame him for that. She wanted as little to do with him as possible now that she'd had enough distance for good sense to override bad urges.

She'd changed into jeans and a scoop-neck tank with a zippered jacket over it. Then she'd straightened the kitchen enough so she could throw together a meal. They were sitting at the kitchen table, eating soup and sandwiches and not conversing. In fact, Drake had never answered her last question, which was for the best since she didn't really need to know what he wanted, at least not on the personal front. She had enough anxiety on the professional front.

"I still think we should go to the authorities," she said.

"No."

"My grandfather would have gone to the sheriff."

Drake shook his head. "He knows that would make him a sitting duck. And don't even think of it."

Abby tore her eyes off her black bag, and her mind off the possibilities it offered.

"You can't sedate me because of the concussion."

"I'm willing to risk it," she said.

"No, you're not."

She shot to her feet, and then, because she had nothing to do with the anxiety-laced energy rocketing around inside her, she started to clear the remains of their lunch away. "This is crazy," she said, reaching across the table to retrieve his bowl and plate. "My grandfather is out there, God knows where. It's snowing, he could be sick or hurt—"

"Fine," Drake said, "you can call the sheriff, but only to tell him about the accident. We need to know about the hit man."

"But—"

"If your grandfather has checked in, the sheriff will let you know, right?"

Abby throttled back on her impatience and frustration. She had to do *something*, so she went to her black bag after all and took out her cell phone. Drake lifted the old-fashioned house phone off its receiver and handed it to her instead, his fingers returning to rest next to the disconnect, ready to cut her off if she didn't follow his instructions.

"How about a little trust?" she said.

"Trust is a two-way street."

Abby picked up his soup spoon, letting the soup on it dribble back into the bowl as she looked up at him. "Do you really think you'd still be conscious if I didn't trust you?"

"Point taken," Drake said.

It was a really satisfying moment until she made the mistake of wetting her lips. Drake's eyes locked onto her mouth. Abby concentrated almost desperately on dialing the old rotary phone, zinging it around in a circle for the first digit of the sheriff's office number. By the time she was listening to the *click-click-click* of the dial making its return circle for the seventh digit, she'd managed to forget that Drake was still staring at her mouth . . . Okay, she hadn't forgotten it. How could she with her pulse pounding and her breath backed up in her lungs? But she could ignore that, right?

The sheriff's secretary, Marlene, came on the line and Abby had to think about something besides Drake and his hot eyes and even hotter body. Marlene pretty much ran the gossip mill in Pottersville. If Abby couldn't string a coherent sentence together, there was no telling what rumor would be circulating in the morning, but she'd be the star of it.

"Sheriff Hanlon?" she asked, keeping the question short and to the point, if a little breathless.

"Out with the weather," Marlene said, cracking her ever-present gum.

"Has anyone reported a truck in the ditch along the main road north of town?"

"Yeah. Earl Fennimore's truck, but he wasn't in it. Some guy from out of town, a dumb guy you ask me, since he hot-wired that piece-of-crap truck of Earl's 'stead of something worth stealing."

"Yeah, dumb," Abby said, "but they got him out, right? And he was okay?"

"Yes and no," Marlene said, further enlightenment interrupted by a staticky cop-speak conversation over the police radio before she finished with "He's out of the truck and on his way to the hospital. Heard it was touch-and-go."

"Good—I mean I'm glad they got him out. Anything else I should know?"

"Doc Weathers is on call, said to tell you to take the weekend off."

Sure, because that would be different from the way she'd spent all her other weekends since she'd come to Pottersville. "Call me if anything changes."

Marlene didn't feel a need to respond. Marlene was up-to-date on Abby's professional dilemma.

"They found the hit man. I'm going to get an update on his condition," Abby told Drake, pushing the disconnect long enough to get a dial tone, then calling the hospital. "This is Dr. West," she said when she had the emergency room nurse on the line, "can you give me the status on a John Doe who was brought in a little while ago? Put his truck in a ditch." She waited while the chart was read to her, saying a couple of "uh-huhs" before she thanked the woman and hung up the phone.

"He's not going anywhere tonight," she said. "So far he hasn't regained consciousness. He's still en route to the hospital, so they haven't finished assessing him yet, but the med techs said he took a pretty good blow to the head, and was lying in a couple feet of freezing water before they pulled him out of that ditch."

"I'd be happier if he were dead," Drake said.

"It still might come to that. He went through pretty much what you did, but he's nowhere near as physically fit. That's a clinical assessment," she added before his ego could inflate any more than it already had. "And since we're on the subject . . ." She grabbed her black bag and came toward him.

He backed off.

"I have to clean your wound and bandage it." Abby turned a chair away from the table and pushed him into it, laying out gauze, sterile water, and tape. She stood in front of him, holding a cloth under the wound while she rinsed it, dabbing lightly to remove the dried blood so she could make sure there wasn't anything foreign embedded.

"Ouch."

"Wimp," Abby said, which effectively shut him up, even though she'd meant it in a teasing way. "You could use a couple of stitches."

"No stitches."

"Don't be such a baby." She pulled out a needle, smiling when he went white.

"No stitches," he repeated through clenched teeth. "Pretend you're not a doctor and do whatever your mother would have done."

Abby took another look at the shallow furrow on his forehead, muttering, "This is way beyond kiss it and make it better."

"Too bad," Drake said, voice rough; eyes, when she met them, hot. Somewhere along the line she'd shifted to stand between his legs, and his hands were at her waist. They probably were meant to steady her.

"You can let go," she said.

His hands didn't move, and when she glanced down again, he was staring at the hint of cleavage between the zipper of her jacket and above the neck of her tank. That small patch of bare skin was tingling, and hot, and the tingling and heat were spreading, to the point where she wondered if his mouth was half as hot, and if there was a way to tactfully suggest he put it to use so she could find out. After that they'd get to *his* zipper and the bulge beneath it.

She tried to think about that bulge in clinical terms, naming the internal workings of the male reproductive system, but she wasn't just fighting her response to him, she was trying to ignore his attraction to her, not to mention their history together, and it was too much. She lifted her gaze back to his wound, slapped a bandage on it, and said, "There, just like Mommy would have done. It should be stitched, but if you don't care about having a scar on your face, neither do I."

He slid his hands up, thumbs feathering across her rib cage. "That's not what I'm worried about."

God help her, neither was she, and it was ridiculous. "Do you really think this is a good idea?"

"No," he said on a heavy sigh that told her he was every bit as thrown off as she was by the strength of the chemistry, even after a decade and a less than cordial split. "But it doesn't seem to matter."

"It has to." And she went to wash their dishes, thinking out of sight would mean out of mind. But she knew it was a hopeless cause because Drake was right. It didn't matter that he'd walked out on her ten years ago. It didn't matter that he was a completely different man now, one she didn't really know. He'd come there to save her grandfather and, misguided or not, it put him in a positive light. And she still had feelings for him. There was no point denying it to herself, but it made him that much harder to resist.

She reached up to put away the glass she'd just dried, and Drake came behind her, putting his hand over hers to help nudge it onto the high shelf.

"I can reach it," she said.

"I know."

"They why are you here? Hoping I'd be overwhelmed by your sheer animal magnetism and drag you to the floor?"

He stayed behind her, not quite touching but close enough that she could feel the heat of him on her skin, his deep voice, when he spoke, practically rumbling through her. "Did it work?"

Almost.

"I'll take that as a no," he said, "since we're still upright and clothed. But if you change your mind—"

"Just put away the damn dishes," she said, handing him the soup pan that belonged all the way across the kitchen.

"So I *am* getting to you." But he moved away, and she could breathe again.

"I'm worried about my grandfather," she said, feeling guilty because it should have been the truth instead of a smoke screen.

"Virgil isn't a fool. He's somewhere warm and safe, and we'll find him before the hit man does."

Abby turned around, resting her hips against the edge of the sink. "You sound so sure."

"I am sure."

"Good. Where do we start?"

Five

They took Virgil's truck. Abby thought it was a good idea because Virgil's friends would recognize it and maybe answer the door. Drake agreed because he wasn't expecting trouble. Even if Pollani knew his assassin was out of commission, there hadn't been time to replace him.

It never hurt to be careful, though. He was the best at what he did because he didn't take risks unless there wasn't another choice, which was why he was armed with the hit man's gun. Abby was armed with Virgil's address book, a rudimentary knowledge of the surrounding environs, and a level of optimism that never ceased to amaze Drake.

"This is it, the next driveway on the left. Delores Ridgeway." She gave Drake a meaningful look. "Virgil's *special* friend."

"Special?"

"It means exactly what you think it does."

Drake didn't spend any time with that mental picture. He was still slightly queasy from the concussion. Or maybe it was the scenery. "The house is purple."

"Wait 'til you see the owner."

Another mental picture, one that made him grin. "Is she purple, too?"

"Just her prose."

Drake got that about ten seconds after Delores Ridgeway answered her door, and he realized she was channeling Mae West.

"Well hello there, handsome," she said, leaning against the doorframe, "come on in and take your coat off. And your pants."

"I think I'll keep everything on, thanks."

"Then I guess I'll have to use my imagination," she said, sounding like a bad imitation of Mae—looking like one, too, in a leopard-print peignoir with a black feather boa around her neck. Both it and the robe were open to reveal a matching gown that showed way too much wrinkled, sagging skin, from her slack cleavage to her spindly knees and red-painted toes. Her hair was dyed blond and piled on top of her head, and she must have used a putty knife to apply her makeup, including her mascara.

She was medium height and thin as a rail, looking like she'd break a hip with the first good, strong wind. But her eyes were bright green, the mind behind them was sharp, and she made it clear that Abby wasn't her favorite person.

Drake peered around Delores, hoping like hell Virgil wasn't there, because the place looked like a yard sale, antiques jammed together with flea market junk, every flat surface crowded, and so much stuff hanging on the walls he couldn't discern the paint color. If someone unfamiliar with the place went in, he could be lost for days. "Have you seen Virgil?" he asked her.

"Not lately," she said. "But I don't have to use my imagination there. The shower massage is a different story. Ever since *she*"—Delores jabbed a finger at Abby—"came to squat on Virgil's doorstep I've been sleeping alone." She coughed, sounding like she was hacking up a lung.

"I can do something for that cough," Abby said, no doubt on principle.

"There's no cure for the common cold," Delores said with a tone in her voice that had nothing to do with Mae West. "I bet it even says that in your Jamaican medical books."

"It may not be a cold," Abby said with a snap of vindictiveness Drake enjoyed. "Could be bronchitis or strep. Or pneumonia." She looked around the dingy junkyard of a room. "There's no telling what kind of infection you might have caught. You probably need a broad spectrum antibiotic."

"If you want to do something, get your skinny ass inside and let me shut the door."

"I'll wait in the truck."

"Girl has no backbone," Delores said to Drake.

Abby turned back, said, "It's not my backbone that's the problem. I don't have the stomach for dealing with you."

Delores snorted. "That's the first time you've said anything I can respect."

"Wow, that would probably make me feel really good—if I gave a damn what you thought of me."

Delores's mouth flapped open then closed, her eyes narrowing to a line of chunky mascara.

"Virgil?" Drake asked.

"Ain't seen him in weeks," Delores said, slamming the door in his face.

"Cranky old bat." Drake followed Abby to the truck and angled into the passenger side. He would have preferred to drive, but there was no point giving her the argument she so obviously wanted. "Who's next?"

"Tell me again why this is necessary," Abby said, jamming the truck into gear and giving it way too much gas, the rear tires spinning on Delores's slick drive before they grabbed hold.

"To save your grandfather's life."

"Right, life and death." Which oddly enough seemed to calm her down. "Roy Newcomb."

They made the half-hour drive to the Newcomb place in complete silence, which would have been fine with Drake if he hadn't felt like Abby was girding herself. He'd only begun to imagine what could be worse than Delores when they pulled into the drive of a meticulously maintained farm, the outbuildings freshly painted, neat paths shoveled in the snow, everything tidy and ordered.

The house, when Drake looked in the window, was just as perfectly ordered—but then it was practically empty. Bare wood floors, no carpet, no rugs. The sitting room held a couch, a chair, and a television, circa 1955, with rounded corners, small screen, rabbit ears. Drake could see enough of the kitchen to know the appliances were aqua Hotpoint from around the same time period. And everything was spotless.

"If we put Roy and Delores together," he said to Abby under his breath, "we'd have two normal households."

"Only the inanimate parts."

"What are you doing here?"

Drake straightened and whipped around, stepping in front of Abby at the same time she shrieked and jumped behind him, one hand on his arm, the other at his waist.

"Remind me not to count on you in an emergency," he said over his shoulder.

"My emergencies usually involve blood and possible death."

"So do mine."

"Waiting for an answer here," Roy said.

Roy looked like he was waiting for Elvis. He was the right age group, and he sported Elvis sideburns and a black Elvis wig. His jeans were bell-bottoms, held up by a white belt so old the leather was cracked, and he wore his jacket with the pointed collar turned up—no sequins or rhinestones on anything, Roy being very un-Elvis-like in his dislike of embellishments.

"We're looking for Virgil," Drake said to him.

Roy crossed his arms and curled his lip, but his eyes were narrowed and he took a moment to digest that information before he said, "Don't know why you came here. Virgil used to come over and watch public television with me every Saturday night. Every Saturday night for over thirty years. Now it's 'I'm having dinner with my granddaughter' or 'my granddaughter's taking me over to see the high school play.' Fifty years in this town and he never gave a crap about the high school play until she showed up."

"Roy doesn't like change," Abby explained unnecessarily.

"I don't like you," Roy said back to her.

Drake whooshed out a breath. These people were exhausting. "I take it you haven't seen Virgil."

"Isn't that what I said?"

"Sorry we bothered you." Drake took Abby's hand and pulled her to the truck.

"Aren't you going to search the place?"

"You didn't want me to search Delores's place."

"Would you go to Delores to hide out for any length of time?"

"No, but he didn't come here, either," Drake said, mentally kicking himself for not thinking this through before. The concussion, he told himself, followed by prolonged exposure to a woman who muddled his mind—which was no excuse.

It had taken them a half hour to get to Roy's place. There was no way Virgil would have walked it, even to throw the hit man off-track, when he had a perfectly good truck at his disposal.

"Who's next?" he said to Abby, mostly because she was watching him, wondering what was going through his mind. She wasn't stupid. This type of situation was new to her, but if he gave her time to put the facts together, she eventually would.

"Delores and Roy are my grandfather's closest friends," she said, "but he's on pretty good terms with some of the people in town."

"Then we go to town."

She took a deep breath and let it out. "Okay, let's go to town.

But if you think it will be a step up from Delores and Roy, you're going to be disappointed."

Pottersville consisted of a smattering of frame homes, built in the early part of the twentieth century, surrounding a main street right out of a Frank Capra movie. Parking was angled on both sides of the street, and Drake took the first open spot he came across. Abby directed him to the general store, and everyone in town stared at them as they walked by.

"Don't see many strangers around here, do you?" Drake observed.

"No, but these people make the most of what they get."

The general store was one of the oldest buildings in town, with a creaking wood floor and barrels that once held flour and cornmeal, not to mention weevils and maggots. The owner, Mrs. Hathaway, wearing a white apron and a scowl, was at her post behind the long wooden checkout counter at one side of the store. "Don't want her kind in here," she said to Drake.

Abby threw her hands up. "*Now* what did I do?"

Mr. Hathaway appeared from out of the gloom at the back of the store, but his wife held up a hand. "Don't say it out loud, Father," she said. "It's too terrible for a God-fearing man."

"If you have something to say," Drake said, "spit it out."

"She knows what she done. Doc Weathers give her a job to do and . . ." Mrs. Hathaway shuddered, leaving the rest to imagination.

Abby had no problem making the stretch. "They think I stole a dead body," she said.

"It was me," Drake said. "I was the dead body."

"You ain't dead," Mr. Hathaway piped in.

"The sheriff thought I was."

"The sheriff don't make mistakes like that."

"He looked dead, but he really wasn't," Abby said.

“Right, you big-city folk think we’re a bunch of dumb hicks, but let me tell you, we all grew up on farms. We know dead.”

Drake would have argued some more. Abby knew it was futile. “Have you seen Virgil today?” she asked them.

“Nope.”

“Great,” she said once they were outside, “now they think I stole a dead body, and God knows what they think I’m doing with it.”

“I could tell them,” Drake said, “but then I’d have to shoot them.”

Abby let her eyes roll up, appealing to the heavens. Not that it would do her any good. First she was dropped in a town filled with the most xenophobic people on the planet, and now she was saddled with a fed who thought it was all so amusing. “I could be tending to senators and congressmen,” she said crankily. “Maybe even the president, if he happened to get shot, but I’m not good enough to lance Jonas Hadley’s neck boil. But hey, you’re enjoying yourself so it’s all worth it.”

Drake took her elbow and towed her down the walkway, looking over his shoulder, startling her out of her rant.

“What’s wrong?”

“It feels like we’re being watched.”

“We are,” she snapped. “Every backward-thinking resident of this town is staring at us like we’re zoo exhibits.” Drake had creeped her out, though. She looked over her shoulder a beat after he did, and stopped dead in her tracks, reaching out to clutch at Drake’s arm.

What?”

“That guy . . .” She pointed out the man she was talking about, but it was too late. “Darn, he turned the corner.”

“What about him?” Drake asked, not immediately thinking she was crazy, which was more than she could say for herself.

“I could have sworn it was the hit man. He’s even wearing the same clothes, khakis, bomber jacket, and he’s built like the Pillsbury Doughboy.”

“Call the hospital,” Drake said, sounding grim.

She took out her cell phone and hit the speed dial number for the hospital just as Drake took her by the elbow and urged her back to the truck. She went without objection, holding the phone to her ear.

"He's still there, and he's still in serious condition," she said a few words and a minute or two later. "I guess I'm just jumpy."

"We're both jumpy," Drake said. "There's no way Pollani could get another guy here so fast."

That made sense to Abby, so when he got out of the truck, she did, too. They made a couple more stops in town, asked the same questions they'd posed in the general store, and got the same story. "Great," she said, "nobody has seen Virgil, and everyone thinks I'm doing unnatural things with a corpse."

"I can take your mind off it," Drake said on their way out of town. "Of course, I'm the dead body, so you'd actually be proving them right."

Abby smiled back at him. There was no point letting the towns-people get to her. "Make dinner and maybe I'll consider it."

"Does peanut butter and jelly count?"

"It does if you can add some vodka," she said. "It'll be worth the hangover to forget this day."

Six

A couple of PB&Js and no vodka later, Abby announced that she was going to bed.

Drake met that declaration with a moment of silence while he directed his thoughts away from the possibility that, had there been vodka involved, she wouldn't be going there alone or going there to sleep. "I think I'll take another look around outside, just to be safe," he said.

Abby handed him the soup cans from their lunch. "There's a recycling bin in the barn."

"This is the country," he said. "There's generally a way to recycle right on the premises."

"That's right, you grew up on a farm."

"It was more like doing time." Drake secured the house and left Abby with instructions not to go outside. He didn't expect her to follow them, but the hit man was an hour away and nonambulatory, so how much trouble could she get into?

He'd done a cursory check of the outbuildings before, and no Virgil. This time he skipped the toolshed, the pump house, and the carriage house—which was about to fall down anyway—heading straight for the barn.

It wasn't huge as barns went, although the entire house could have fit inside. Drake eased the small entry door open and slipped through, stepping to one side as soon as he was in all the way. His shoulder brushed something on the wall, which turned out to be a switch. He flipped it and a couple of anemic lights blinked on high overhead, precious little illumination filtering through the dusty air.

Inside it was a fairly standard barn layout, a couple of horseless horse stalls and cowless cow stanchions on one side, bales of hay against the other wall, piled up to the rafters. In between the animal accommodations and the animal fodder were assorted barrels, power tools, and the recycling bin. Drake tossed the soup cans into the bin then stopped and went still, swearing he'd heard a faint sound just after the tinny thunks of the metal cans dropping into the plastic bin. It came from the general vicinity of the hay bales.

He marked the place, shut off the lights, and, once his eyesight adjusted, made his way almost silently to the stack of bales, inching along until he saw just a hint of light. He grabbed at the nearest bale, pulled, and a door swung open. A double-barreled shotgun pointed out of it, straight at his head.

"One move and I bust a cap in your ass."

Drake pushed the gun barrel aside with a forefinger. "Sounds like you've been watching MTV."

"I've been under the weather lately. I'm not a spring chicken you know," Virgil said testily, swinging the gun back to point at Drake. "There's nothing to do around here but watch TV. Cable's the best thing that's happened to this country, you ask me."

"Are you done?"

"Not until you tell me who you are."

"You can call me Drake. I'm with the FBI, and I'm here to keep you from getting killed because of your own stupidity."

"Prove it."

Drake brought his hand up and caught the barrel of the gun,

twisted it out of Virgil's grip, and had it pointed at him before he could do more than grunt out a breath in surprise. "If I was here to kill you, you'd be dead. Believe me now?"

"Yeah." Virgil sat down heavily, looking worn-out, which he probably was since coming so close to violent death was a lot to handle for an old guy.

Then again, he had some surprises left in him. "Nice place," Drake said, peering into a room about six feet wide that ran the length of the narrow end of the barn. There was Virgil's chair and television at one end, a cot and a small, office-size fridge with a microwave on top of it at the other end. In the middle, on the wall across from the door, was a gun rack. Virgil had all the necessities covered. The place was heated, and aside from a bit of light leakage, completely hidden by a stack of hay bales of indeterminate depth.

"If I hadn't heard you rack the shotgun," Drake said to him, "I never would have found this place."

"I may not be much good at milking cows or growing corn, but it turns out I'm handy with the power tools. I even have plumbing," he said proudly, pointing to a small door.

"Too bad you didn't put as much thought into contacting your granddaughter."

Virgil scrubbed both hands through the three-day beard scruff on his cheeks. "It's been fifty years. I didn't think Joey would care anymore."

"No expiration date on the kind of contract Joey Pollani puts out."

"Now Abby's in danger, too."

"Let me worry about that," Drake said. "You stay here, Abby and I will stay in the house—"

Virgil sat forward. "No way you're using my granddaughter as bait."

"She's perfectly safe." Drake gave him a quick rundown of the last twenty-four hours. "We have at least one more night before Pollani finds out his goon has been hurt and sends someone else."

"Drake!" Abby's shout came floating out to them.

He stepped to the barn's entry door, the sight of her silhouetted in the bright kitchen doorway giving him a tug in the vicinity of his heart. If things had worked out differently, he might have had a thousand such memories—but Abby had been focused on a twenty-four-hour-a-day career, and he'd taken a job that demanded complete secrecy. Even if they'd stayed together, there wouldn't have been many nights he'd have found her waiting for him when he came home. Hell, who was he kidding? There wouldn't have been any. "Everything is okay," he said, even though, suddenly, it felt like everything wasn't. True, Virgil was safe, but Abby had put him completely off balance. "Go back in the house."

"Your head—"

"Is fine. I'll be there in a minute."

She came to the bottom of the porch steps, then stopped.

"Jesus, doesn't she ever follow instructions?" Drake mumbled under his breath, reminding himself and his "feelings" that this was just another job. "Go back in your hidey-hole," he said to Virgil.

Virgil didn't listen to him either.

"Go in or I'll put you in."

"I'd like to see you try it." But Virgil slid back in the doorway and flipped his light off. "I'm trusting you with something more precious than my own life," he said from out of the darkness. "Don't let me down."

"The only way he'll get to her is if I'm dead." Drake shut the hay bale door and then the barn door, stopping there to watch Abby coming across the yard, foolish independence in every step. Considering the way she refused to follow his advice, there was a better than even chance all of them would wind up dead. Starting with him.

As soon as Abby saw Drake coming toward the house, she went back inside, but she still couldn't settle. The night loomed long ahead, and now that there was nothing they could do about Virgil, it was all she could think about.

"I thought you were going to bed," Drake said when he came through the back door.

Abby righted a poinsettia and scooped the spilled dirt with both hands, almost bursting into tears when she remembered how Virgil had grumbled when she'd brought it home. "It'll only die," he'd said, and now she was afraid—

Drake hauled her to her feet and turned her around, taking a long look at her face, his expression going to *oh shit* before he let her go and backed away. "You should go to bed," he said, sounding like a man who thought dealing with a hysterical woman was a fate worse than death.

"How can I sleep with my grandfather out there somewhere . . ."

"You've held it together this long, don't freak out now. There's nothing we can do tonight with the snow and the darkness."

"You're right. I'll go to bed. We can get a fresh start tomorrow morning." But she stood there, staring out into the darkness, trying not to think about Virgil, until it got to be too much and she didn't just think about him, she thought about him dead, or worse, hurt somewhere and needing her, and before she knew it she was outside, and Drake grabbed her and put her up against the side of the house, hard enough to have her wheezing in a breath, but not hard enough to shock her back to sanity.

She fought—at least she tried to fight—her way free, but Drake came up against her, hard and immoveable, and her fear ignited. She stopped struggling, looking up into his face, her eyes meeting his in the snow-lit darkness.

"Oh, hell," he said, and started to back off, but she fisted her hands in his shirt and pulled him back against her, wanting his heat, needing it to stave off the fear and the darkness. His hands lifted from her arms, up her shoulders to frame her face, and then he was kissing her, his mouth insistent on hers, and she was kissing him back, shuddering as his tongue tangled with hers, feeling a tug of need deep in her belly. Her breasts rubbed against the hard muscles of his chest, and when he slid his thigh between her legs it felt so good she moaned into his mouth and he groaned back, tearing away from her.

"It's just fear and adrenaline, and chemistry," he said, but his breathing was fast and harsh and she could still feel him against her, hard everywhere.

She unzipped her jacket and peeled it off, pulling her tank over her head, not feeling the cold, especially when he lifted a hand, his finger hot and amazing on her skin as he ran it across the top of her breast above her bra.

"Tell me to stop," he said.

She sighed heavily. "No."

"No?" he echoed, looking like someone had punched him in the gut as he started to pull away again.

"Yes, then," Abby said, grabbing his hand and pressing it to her breast.

"Yes, stop, or—"

"Jeez, who's on first?" she said, wanting to scream in frustration at finding herself in a comedy routine instead of having him inside her, making her forget everything but answering this aching need.

"I think we passed first a while ago," Drake said.

"There are three more bases."

"I'm not making that trip out here." But he kissed her where they stood, long and hot and wild, took his mouth to her neck, shoulder, and breast, pulling her bra down and sucking her nipple into his mouth, rolling it hard between his tongue and teeth.

She threaded her fingers into his hair and pressed him even harder against her, her breath coming in tight little pants, her body moving restlessly with the rhythm of his tongue. Her muscles were quivering on the edge of collapse so that when he pulled away and tried to draw her inside, she stumbled. Drake didn't miss a step, swinging her up in his arms and carrying her into the house, stopping at the nearest horizontal surface, which was the couch. He put her down, and she felt him pulling her shoes off. She was right there with him, shucking her jeans and underwear while he stripped, and then reaching for him.

He knelt beside the couch and kissed her again, and that was nice, but she wanted more. She tried to pull him close but he took her hands in one of his and held them over her head, using just his mouth on her breasts, suckling until she would have screamed if she'd had any breath left. And then he moved even lower, and she realized he'd let her wrists go because he'd scooped his hands under her backside, and took his mouth to her, his tongue rasping over sensitized flesh. She was already so close that she shot to orgasm, crying out as the waves crashed through her and left her breathless and awash in memories, but feeling like she'd been with Drake for the first time, too.

She slipped off the couch and pushed him down, kneeling astride him. She wanted to relearn every inch of him, head to toe, discover again the way his skin flushed hot and his muscles shuddered when she ran her hands over his chest, scoring him lightly with her nails. She braced her hands on either side of his head and kissed him, her mouth shifting to his neck, her breath sighing out when he caught her hips and slid into her. And began to move, slowly at first, long, smooth strokes that made her mind go blank and sent her body spiraling up, coiling to an unbearable level of pleasure until she shattered into a million tiny, searing bits. Every nerve ending soared this time as his body moved in hers and under hers, and he groaned, soul deep, pushing hard against her, muscles locked and trembling as his orgasm ripped through him strong enough for her to feel him pulsing deep inside her.

He groaned again, settling to one side. "Incredible," he said on a soft breath of air, "even if it was a mistake."

Abby was going to punch him on the arm, but ended up running her fingers over his chest, hard muscle and soft, warm skin. "I agree with *incredible*," she said, "but not *mistake*."

Drake propped himself up on one elbow and studied her face. No mystery what he was thinking.

"I just needed someone," Abby said, holding his gaze.

"And I was handy."

"You were very handy," she said, smiling at him but trying her best not to let him see that she was lying through her teeth. Oh, she had needed someone, but she couldn't imagine that someone being anyone but Drake. Yes, he'd hurt her desperately ten years ago, and yes, long-dormant feelings had roared back to life, and not just the physical kind. But he was Virgil's only hope of staying alive. And hers. He didn't need any distractions, so she did her best to lie to him, and herself, and at least he bought it, climbing over her and offering her his hand.

Abby took it, letting him help her up. The first thing she saw was Virgil's chair, and the fear and worry came roaring back to life, along with a boatload of shame. Her grandfather was missing, and what was she doing? Having sex, hot, incredible, mind-blowing . . . tawdry, stupid sex. Hell, she hadn't even bothered to take her bra all the way off. She pulled it up, grabbed her panties, and stepped into them, then her jeans. But when she started for the door, intending to get her shirt and jacket, Drake stopped her.

"You're not getting hysterical again," he said, making it sound more like an order than a question.

"No, but that doesn't change the fact that my grandfather is still out there."

"What if I told you I know where he is?"

Abby snorted softly. "You're just saying that to get me to behave."

"No—"

"How could you possibly know my grandfather is all right? You spent last night unconscious in a body bag, and you haven't been more than five minutes out of my sight since you came back from the dead. Where could you possibly have seen him, except—" Her eyes shifted in the general direction of the barn, then back to Drake's face, which was set to not-giving-anything-away until she headed for the back door.

"Shit," he said, catching her wrist, and when she resisted, he heaved her over his shoulder and carried her up the stairs, giving her a moment of concern when he faltered about halfway there. He dug up the strength to carry her into her room and dump her on her feet by the bed. "Virgil is in the barn," he said. "He has a secret room out there, electricity, water, food."

"Huh," she said, wondering, just for a second, if Drake was lying to keep her calm. It made sense, though. Her grandfather spent a lot of time out there, working with power tools, never ending up with anything useful. A secret room would explain his complete lack of end product. "You're sure it's warm enough? He's eighty years old."

"He's perfectly safe, as long as we don't give him away."

She still wanted to race out to the barn and see Virgil with her own eyes. But Drake was right, and he wouldn't rest unless she did. "I'll try to sleep if you will."

"I'll take the chair," he said, giving in quickly enough for her to guess how exhausted he must be.

"You won't get any sleep in that chair," Abby said, slipping her pants back off and climbing into bed, patting the mattress beside her. "I won't, either, if I know you're uncomfortable, and I have plans to be comatose for at least the next six hours."

Drake hesitated all of ten seconds before he climbed in beside her, still naked, curving himself around her like a big, warm, comforting blanket. Abby closed her eyes and tried to shut off her brain, and when she managed that, she tackled the harder task, which was getting her body to stop reacting to the feel of Drake against her, the memory of his mouth on her, of him stroking inside her . . . It might have been easier if he'd stayed still.

"What's wrong?" she asked the third time he shifted behind her.

"The pillow smells like you. It's . . . distracting."

"I can get you one of Virgil's pillows," she offered.

"No thanks, I know what Virgil smells like."

Seven

Abby woke up alone, sprawled facedown and drooling into her pillow, naked from a couple more bouts of mind-blowing sex with Drake during the night. She opened her eyes, then slammed them shut against the sun shining in the window like a freakishly bright spotlight. She lifted her hand to shade her face, groaning as parts of her body began to ache. But her lips curved into a smile because every twinge of pain was more than worth it because of what had caused it.

And then reality crashed back in and she shot upright, giving a little startled gasp because Drake was sitting in the chair, buck naked and not seeming to feel the chill in the air. He was just watching her, hands steepled, barely breathing. If his eyes hadn't been open she'd have taken him for dead.

"Trying to get put in the body bag again?"

"Wishing you'd had the vodka? If you were a serious drinker, last night would be a nice, permanent black hole."

She pulled the sheet up, but not because she was feeling self-conscious. "Go ahead and say it," she said, because Drake was back to FBI mode, cold, all business, focused on the life-and-death reason for being there.

"You know there's no future for us," he said. "Once I do what I came to do, I'll never be able to see you again. It'll be too dangerous."

"For whom?" She met his eyes. He was the one who looked away. "I didn't ask you for any assurances," she said. "I know where my place is, and it isn't with you."

"I just thought—"

"What? That one night with you would ruin me for all other men?"

He gave her a look.

"Okay, so it was a pretty good night. There was always chemistry between us, but chemistry isn't something you base a relationship on—even if both parties could say the word without breaking out in a cold sweat."

He looked like he wanted to refute her insinuation, but he left the past alone, just like she'd done moments before. "I came here to do a job," he said. "That comes first."

Abby didn't need to be reminded why he was there; her aching heart told her she wasn't the reason. And she wasn't about to get in his way with her grandfather's life on the line. "I don't regret anything that happened, and I don't want to forget it. That doesn't mean I'm expecting anything from you. Except for you to do your *job*."

"Okay," he said, seeming a little nonplussed, which made Abby smile a bit, and if there was some wistfulness in that smile, she was the only one who had to know.

"You were expecting tears and clinging?" she said teasingly. "Or maybe undying gratitude?"

"I can do without the tears but a thank-you would be nice."

"As I remember it, you have just as much to be grateful for."

He grinned, and it was all the more enjoyable since he did it reluctantly, and it was clear he was remembering some of the high points of their nocturnal activities. Which did nothing to facilitate her trip back to reality.

"I need a shower." She took her time getting out of bed. It wouldn't do anything good for his ego to know she was having a hard time walking.

"I could wash your back," Drake offered.

"I got the distinct impression you were attempting to set boundaries."

He didn't say anything, but when she glanced at him his eyes were on her breasts. And since he was still naked, she wasn't under any misapprehension about her effect on him. She limped the rest of the way to her dresser, got out underwear, jeans, and a sweater, and hurried out of the room before the heat of his gaze could make her change her mind and drag him back into bed with her. And it wasn't his ego she was worried about inflating. It was her hopes. Much as she hated to admit it, boundaries were exactly what she needed, and if he wouldn't set them she would.

Relationship my ass, Drake thought as he stepped into the shower after Abby was done. He could think the word, hell, he could say it—if he wouldn't have felt stupid talking to an empty room. And sure, a minute ago he'd been glad she was gone. Now he had a thing or two he wanted to say to her . . . Okay, he didn't want to say anything to her, because she'd look at him like he was crazy, and then he'd feel like an idiot. And he wasn't an idiot.

She denied that she wanted anything from him, but he'd seen the hurt in her eyes. She hadn't gotten over him, and despite what she claimed, last night hadn't been just sex. They'd made love—and he wasn't balking from the word *they*. He wasn't in a position to do more than pass through her life, though, and she had *settle down* written all over her.

It had been why he'd left ten years ago. He'd been prelaw, and bored to tears until he started taking criminal justice classes. If he'd understood himself better, had a clearer path before he met Abby, he never would have let their relationship get so . . . Hell, who was he kidding? From the moment they met, he hadn't been able to keep his hands off her, and the heat had been mutual, just like last night. But after two years with Abby, the lure of undercover work, the sexiness of cloak-and-dagger, had been stronger. He hadn't wanted to let go of her, and he'd botched it, no doubt about that, but he'd walked away.

He understood now that, somewhere in the back of his mind, he'd expected her to be waiting for him. But she'd gone ahead with her life, and he couldn't blame her. You couldn't stand still. And you couldn't go back.

He threw on the clothes she'd left by the bathroom door and went downstairs, stopping at the landing midway down. It only took him a split second to realize that the man's voice he heard belonged to Virgil. He took the remaining stairs two at a time, and there he was, sitting in the kitchen, larger than life and dumb as a fence post. "You were supposed to stay put until I came for you."

Virgil shrugged. "Ran out of kerosene for the heater about three A.M. I stuck it out for a bit, but then I figured I should get in here while it was still dark."

"You weren't supposed to think," Drake said. "You were supposed to do what I told you."

"You said the hit man was out of commission." His eyes cut to the stairs, then to Abby, keeping way too busy on the other side of the big country kitchen. "But you weren't worried about me running into the hit man, were you?"

"I'm not the one who invited her here and blew your cover."

"No, but you're the one who's taking advantage of the situation."

"If you're talking about me, stop it now," Abby said, handing Drake a plate with a mound of scrambled eggs and two pieces of toast. "I'm an adult. I make my own choices."

Virgil sputtered, his face going scarlet before he managed to get any words out. "His job is to protect me. He'll leave you high and dry when this is over."

"You mean like you did for most of my life?"

"It was exile or death," Virgil shot back. "Either way I was going to be out of your life."

"Don't you think I know that?" Abby said, some of her anger fading away. She took his empty cup and went back to the stove.

Virgil sniffed, his eyes tearing over. "Her mother—my daughter—died a while back, and Abby's father was never around. I left them to keep them safe, but if I'd known . . ." He sniffed again and rubbed his eyes. "I know she understands why I wasn't around, but . . . she calls me Virgil."

"You did the right thing," Drake said. "Give her time and she'll come around. She's not a woman who jumps into things without putting some thought into it."

"She did with you."

"Stop it," Abby said, ignoring the past yet again.

It was starting to tick Drake off. He didn't want her to get any ideas about the two of them, but she ought to at least tell him what kind of ass he was. He deserved it.

Virgil took the coffee cup she handed him and set it on the table beside his chair, next to his empty plate. "I just want you to be safe," he said.

"I can take care of myself."

"You should have let me teach you to shoot."

"She doesn't need to know how to shoot," Drake said around a mouthful of eggs and toast. "She's not going anywhere without me until this is over. I'm not going to watch out for you and leave her to get used as a hostage."

"And I don't have any say in the matter?" she demanded, hands on hips.

Virgil jumped to his feet—okay, he was almost eighty, it took him a half a minute or so, and he fell back into his chair once, but when he made it upright he went toe-to-toe with her. "I got you into this mess," he said, "I'm going to get you out."

"You're right about getting her into this," Drake snarled, dropping his half-full plate on top of Virgil's empty one, which shut the two of them up. This was supposed to be a simple assignment and it had gone all to hell. "And now you're going to shut up and let me do my job."

Virgil's face mottled red.

Abby put her arm around his shoulders. "He's eighty years old and he's worried about me," she snapped at Drake. "Is it necessary to be such a jackass to get your point across?"

"Not as long as he understands that listening to me, and doing exactly as I tell him, is the only way we're going to get through this alive. You, too."

"Got it, Captain Bligh."

"Cute."

"I'm sorry, Abby," Virgil said, "it's just I've been alone for a long time."

Abby gave him a hug and a peck on the cheek. "It's okay, Granddad."

"Did you hear that? She called me Granddad," Virgil said to Drake, and just as he turned back to Abby a shot came in the window, barely missing them both.

Virgil hit the floor.

Drake tackled Abby.

"Your job is to protect my grandfather," she said, shoving at him.

"I know that." It was his reflexes that needed to be reminded.

He climbed off her, keeping low as he went for Virgil, who was back on his feet at the fireplace, reaching for the shotgun hung on hooks over the mantel. The window by the back door crashed in, and Drake dove for Virgil, knowing he'd be too late. But Abby shot to her feet, grabbed the first thing that came to hand, which was Virgil's coffee mug, and winged it at the hit man, who was bringing his gun to bear. It hit him right between the eyes. He stumbled back, falling over the porch railing.

Drake went for the door, snatching Virgil's shotgun as he tore by, flinging the back door open but stopping inside, shoulder against the doorjamb, just the barrel of the gun inching out. He leveled it about chest-high, stepped into the open doorway, and fired off a shot, getting a little burst of satisfaction at the feel of the gun recoiling against his shoulder.

But the hit man was already down for the count, spread-eagled beside the porch steps like a homicidal snow angel. His face was covered in blood from a cut above his eyes, compliments of Abby's coffee mug, but Drake could see he had two black eyes and numerous other bruises, cuts, and abrasions. The only problem was, he was still breathing—or maybe not a problem, Drake decided, since it would have been Abby who'd killed him, and she wouldn't be too happy about that.

He propped the shotgun by the back door, took hold of the hit man's coat collar, and dragged him up the steps and into the house. Okay, he needed both hands, but he wasn't in top form just yet, and the guy didn't spare the calories.

"Recognize him?" he asked Abby as he retrieved the shotgun and came inside, kicking the unconscious man's legs out of the way so he could shut the door.

"It's the guy from the clinic yesterday," she said, "the one who tried to kill you. Pollani's assassin."

"Some assassin," Virgil said, "brought down by a woman with a coffee mug."

"I may not be able to shoot," Abby said, dusting her hands off and looking smug, "but I pitched a mean softball in high school."

Eight

Abby called the hospital and verified that the man from the truck accident had, indeed, walked out sometime during the night, then she called the sheriff. Drake tied Pollani's man to a chair, then helped Virgil board up the broken window. By the time they were done Mort Hanlon was pulling up the drive in a big white Suburban with a gold star on the door.

He climbed out, removing mirrored shades as he came up the porch steps. "You're the dead guy," he said to Drake when Abby ushered him in.

"And you're the guy who put me in the body bag."

"Yep, and I liked you better in there. You didn't cause any trouble when you were dead."

"I didn't cause this trouble."

The sheriff took a look around the room, his gaze resting for a long, silent minute on the bound man before he faced Drake again.

Neither of them offered their hands, but there was a lot of sizing up going on. The guy looked like he could handle himself, Drake decided, like he'd seen some action. "Military or big-city cop?"

"Both," the sheriff said, "now I'm home, and I'm listening."

Drake gave him a quick rundown of what had happened since the body bag, only hitting the high points—which would have all involved Abby, if he hadn't been on a mission, and if what had happened between them had been anyone's business but their own.

When he was done, the sheriff looked to her anyway.

"It happened just like Drake said." But she wasn't making eye contact and she was fidgeting, looking guilty as hell.

"I was hiding out in the barn," Virgil said, unprompted. As excuses went it got Virgil off the hook, but it had to raise even more doubt in the sheriff's mind over whether he was getting all the facts, and why he might not be.

The hit man was gagged, but he'd been making muffled noises the whole time, jerking around in his chair, trying to get the sheriff's attention so he could put his two cents in, which would take the form of him declaring his innocence.

"Shut up," Drake said, knocking him and his chair over, which did nothing for his frustration level.

Hanlon didn't spare the hit man a glance. "I'm just supposed to take all this at face value?" he said to Drake.

Drake picked up the house phone, dialed a number, and held the receiver out to Hanlon.

Hanlon took it, said, "Hello," then met Drake's eyes. "It's the FBI."

"Ask for Mike Kovaleski."

Hanlon did, listened for a moment, said, "Okay," then handed the phone back to Drake. "He wants to talk to you."

"I hear you got your nuts in a wringer," Mike said when Drake came on the line.

"By nuts I assume you mean the guy I'm supposed to be relocating. And his granddaughter."

"I sent the intel to your cell phone."

"My cell phone is with the rest of my things." Drake gave him the same rundown he'd given Hanlon, leaving out the same high points.

"Let's see if I have this straight," Mike said. "You've got a witness with a blown cover, you almost got killed, you had to call in local heat, and everyone in town thinks the new doctor's name should be Frankenstein."

"I'm not responsible for most of that."

"You put him here," Hanlon said, stabbing a finger in Virgil's direction.

"Not personally."

"My grandfather has been here a long time," Abby reminded the sheriff. "I'd imagine that was a little before Drake's time."

"You know what has to happen," Mike said. "You get on the road, hit one of the safe houses and get outfitted, then head for easy cover. I'll get back to you with the details." And he disconnected.

Drake hung up, too, fielding a look from Hanlon. Not a happy—or trusting—guy.

"Maybe I should take you in until this all shakes out."

"For what? You can't arrest me for not dying. And you can't hold me for assault. Abby is the one who actually took this guy down."

"I think we should keep that to ourselves," Mort said.

"Considering the welcome she's gotten in this town, what would it matter?"

"Can't control people's feelings. They'll warm up to her in time."

"I've been here fifty years, and I'm still waiting for the thaw," Virgil said.

"You have friends."

"Yep, the other outsiders. If this was Salem, we'd've been swinging on Gallows Hill by now."

Hanlon huffed out a breath, but he didn't refute that. "I'll lock up this guy until your friends take him off my hands."

Drake nodded. "And I'll deal with Virgil and Abby."

Drake was standing on the back porch watching Hanlon's Suburban, Pollani's guy trussed up in the back, slalom down the snowy driveway. Abby opened the door and stuck her head out. "What do you mean you'll deal with us?"

"We're getting relocated," Virgil said.

But it still wasn't sinking in. "Relocated?"

"It gets worse." Drake came inside and shut the door, looking her square in the eye as he destroyed her life. "You won't be able to work as a doctor."

Abby staggered to the chair the hit man had been tied to, dropping into it before she fell down.

"It won't be for long," Drake said.

"Just until I'm dead," Virgil put in.

"From natural causes, which is the point of relocating you."

"I'm not going." Abby pushed to her feet, feeling wobbly, but thinking no way in hell was she taking this sitting down. "I spent my entire life working to become a doctor. It's all I have, and now you expect me to give it up?"

"We'll talk about this when you can be reasonable," Drake told her.

"Reasonable?"

"Mistake number two," Virgil said, chuckling.

"You think I'm being unreasonable?" Abby demanded.

"Hanging on to something that will get you killed? Yeah, I think that's unreasonable."

"And stupid, go ahead and say it."

"Fine, I think it's stupid."

"And I think you're a jackass. You drop a bomb like that and expect me to say okay and walk away from my entire life without a second thought?"

"No, but I don't expect hysteria, either."

"Mistake Number Four," Virgil said.

"This isn't hysteria, this is anger," Abby said, crossing the room to drill a finger into Drake's chest. "I imagine you'd need a playbook to recognize most of a normal person's emotional range, but anger is something you should get."

"Let him have it, Abby."

"You can't"—poke—"just hand down orders"—poke—"and expect me to follow you"—poke, poke—"like a good little soldier."

Drake caught her wrist. "I expect you to think the situation through and do the smart thing. If you don't, they'll find you again. And next time there may not be anyone around to save you."

She wrenched her wrist free, stepping away from him. "Don't you think I know that?"

"Don't tell me you're caving in, girl."

"What choice do I have?"

Virgil scowled at her, then at Drake. "I don't have a choice," he said, "but you do."

Drake rounded on Virgil. "Not anymore. You dragged her into this, and now she's in danger. You want me to take off, I'll take off, but if you decide you need my help, we're doing this my way."

"Stop bullying him," Abby said, stepping between them.

"He's right." Virgil looked over her head at Drake. "What's the plan?"

Abby rolled her eyes. "Tell me you did not just put him in charge," she said to her grandfather.

"News flash," Drake said, "I was in charge when I got here."

Abby walked away, shaking her head. "It's my own fault," she grumbled, "I should never have unzipped that body bag. Hell, I should have refused to be coroner. I don't get to work on anyone alive around here, so why take on dead duty?"

"Your point would be?"

"If I'd refused, they would have left you in the walk-in."

"And we'd all be dead," Drake pointed out like the broken record he was.

She shot him a look, not even trying to hide what she was feeling. "Every silver lining has a cloud."

Nine

Abby packed her clothes. Virgil packed his guns. Drake disappeared with her Mustang, showing up about an hour later with an SUV the size of a tank, a cell phone clipped to the belt of jeans that didn't belong to Virgil, and a duffel with a couple of scary-looking bulges. She didn't ask any questions. There was no point since Drake had decided being in charge meant keeping them in the dark about his plans. He'd made a phone call, taking precautions to keep her from hearing even his side of the conversation, then he'd driven them into Chicago.

"Easy to get lost in a big city," he said as he pulled into the driveway of a narrow two-story brick house. "Everything's arranged. We even got you a job at the local veterinarian's office, vaccinating dogs and cats."

"You're joking, right?"

"Mike figured you were used to sticking needles in things, and at least you'll be able to keep your skills up."

"I don't think you helped your case, son," Virgil said.

"The only other job was in a meat-processing plant."

"Fine," Abby snapped, "I'll vaccinate Spot and Tabby."

Drake handed her a slip of paper. "Your new identities are on there, too. Memorize everything then burn it."

"Amy North?" she said, reading the meager information he'd provided.

"We kept it close, easier for you to get used to."

"That's insulting." Virgil chuckled, so she said, "Laugh it up, Homer."

"I thought you kept the names close so us morons could remember them better," Virgil said, not so amused anymore.

"Your file says you're an ancient history buff," Drake said. "Virgil. Homer."

Abby rolled her eyes. "Great, I can't remember a simple name, but he gets ancient history references."

"There's a contact number on there," Drake said, not looking at her. "It's not strictly protocol, but . . . if you need anything . . ."

Abby handed the paper to Virgil. "I'm sure we won't. We will have to eat, so if it's all right with you, I'll go to the market and get some things."

"Your bank accounts and credit cards aren't ready yet," Drake said.

She took the wad of cash he held out and walked out the door without a backward glance, knowing he'd be gone before she got back. In fact, she was counting on it.

The market was only a couple of blocks away, a small, neighborhood mom-and-pop place where Abby received a warmer reception as a total stranger than she'd ever gotten as a resident of Pottersville.

Still, she felt uneasy, like she was being watched. The neighborhood was working class, and it was getting on toward dinnertime, so there was a lot of traffic, auto and foot. She kept glancing over her shoulder, but she never saw anyone taking an inordinate amount of interest in her. By the time she made it to the market, she'd written off her paranoia to the general suckiness of the previous thirty-six hours. Last night had been a wonderful if poignant trip down memory lane, but otherwise people kept trying to kill her, so it was no wonder she was feeling twitchy.

Then she saw him on the other side of the market's front window, the Pillsbury Hit Man, standing at the corner like he was waiting to cross. But the Walk sign was on, and he wasn't moving.

Her blood ran cold and her breath leaked out. Somewhere she found the presence of mind to duck behind a rack of chips while she fumbled out her cell phone and speed-dialed Drake, thanking providence she'd lost that argument with herself and programmed his number in.

"It's him," she whispered when he came on the line, "the hit man."

"Can't be," Drake said, just the sound of his voice going a long way toward making her feel safe.

"If it's not him he's got a twin, same clothes, same pudgy body, same stupid expression on his face."

"Does he have two black eyes and a gash on his forehead?"

Abby's heart slammed against her rib cage, hard enough to hurt. She eased out from behind the Cheetos, just enough to see the area in front of the crosswalk. He was gone. But she was pretty sure he'd been injury-free.

"You're jumping at shadows," Drake said, correctly interpreting her silence. "It's been a hell of a two days, and now you're in a new place. Nothing's familiar and you're seeing danger where there isn't any. And maybe—"

"Maybe what? Maybe I wanted to see you again?"

"Maybe you do."

"Maybe you're a jackass," she shot back, but she was angry with herself, not him, because he was right, at least in part. She got a little spooked and she couldn't wait to call Drake. It didn't take a psychiatrist to read between the lines on that one. Then she looked over her shoulder, just by reflex, and caught a glimpse of khaki disappearing around the end of the next aisle. "Are you sure—"

"He's in federal custody," Drake said. "I got word the FBI picked him up about an hour ago."

Abby took a deep breath and quick-stepped around the end of the aisle before she could talk herself out of it, and when she didn't see him, she circled the small store, coming up empty. "Okay, I guess I'm just spooked."

"It doesn't hurt to be cautious," Drake said. "You're at that little place two blocks north of the house, right? Introduce yourself to the cashier, tell her you're new in the area, and ask her if she knows the guy. And try to relax."

"I could prescribe myself something—if I were still a doctor."

"I thought self-medicating was frowned on in the medical community."

"I was making a point."

"Buy yourself a bottle of wine," Drake suggested.

Abby disconnected—making another point. She finished shopping, and when she checked out she took Drake's advice and chatted up the cashier, describing the guy she'd seen, laughing when the twenty-year-old told her she could do better. She didn't get any meaningful answers, but it made her feel better that at least she hadn't concocted the man out of her overstimulated imagination.

Unfortunately the walk home was a repeat of the trip to the market. Same two blocks, same rundown houses, same twitchy feeling and lots of looking over her shoulder, nothing to see. She even took out her phone once, but she couldn't bring herself to call Drake again. As comforting as it would be to hear his voice, he'd know she was calling for just that reason, and she wouldn't show him that kind of weakness. So she walked a little faster, not breathing easy until she was inside with the door locked.

Virgil took one look at her and asked, "What's wrong?"

"Nothing."

"You're white as a sheet, girl."

Abby pushed away from the door, handing him one of the grocery bags. "I thought I saw the hit man, but it can't be him. I called Drake, and he told me the guy's in federal custody."

"Probably just one of the locals who looks like him," Virgil said. And then he got his guns out, two rifles and a handgun that looked to be from World War II. He checked the ammo in all of them, stuck the pistol in his belt, and propped a rifle by each door, front and back. "The safeties are off and there's a round in the chamber on all three guns," he said when he was done. "All you have to do is point and shoot."

Abby smiled and kissed him on the cheek. "Thank you for not telling me I'm just jumping at shadows." And she had to admit it made her feel better to know they had a ghost of a chance at protecting themselves. Now that some time had passed she felt silly for getting so spooked. And angry at Drake.

He'd brought them to a completely strange place and dumped them—dumped her—like so much unwanted baggage. He didn't want to hear from her, that much was obvious now. The only reason he'd left his phone number was to quiet his conscience. Clearly she was nothing more than a pleasant but forgettable interlude in the life-and-death existence he led.

Which she'd known all along. But he'd been there when she needed him, kept her from crawling out of her skin with worry and fear. She was grateful—no, she was more than grateful. A lot more. Lying about her feelings was no way to get over them. She'd done that ten years ago, told herself she'd accepted that she'd never see Drake again, all the while harboring secret hope. Well, she wasn't making the same mistake, because he was never coming back. This time he'd been nothing if not clear about that.

"One thing I can say," Virgil called to her while she was finishing their dinner dishes, "got more channels here than Pottersville."

"Hooray," Abby said, thinking, *Hah, Pottersville.* Leaving that godforsaken town and everyone in it was the real silver lining. She was probably going to be an urban legend there. The doctor who'd stolen a dead body and disappeared, never to be seen again. Parents were probably already using her to scare children into eating their vegetables and brushing their teeth. If she had a mean streak, she'd drive back there some night and—

The neighbor's dog barked up a storm, interrupting her plans for terrorizing the Pottersvillains. She dried her hands and went to the window, peeking out the side of the curtain rather than parting it in the middle. Nothing, so she went to the front. No streetlights, but she swore she saw someone lurking across the street—just a shadow that was gone when she changed angles to get a better look. She flipped the switch for their porch light, and instead all the lights in the house went out.

"Hey!" Virgil yelled from somewhere in the darkness.

"I tried to turn on the front light and I think I blew a fuse," Abby said.

"Crap."

Abby silently agreed.

"For all I know the fuse box is in Cleveland," Virgil grumbled. "And even if I find the damn box, it's probably prehistoric and we won't have any new fuses. Damn government and their damn old crap-pile houses."

Abby could hear him muttering in the dark, adding the electric company to his shit list. She groped her way to the kitchen in search of candles, but she thought she caught a flash of movement outside the window . . .

"*Uh-oh,*" she said, giving up on stealth and ripping the curtains aside just in time to see a figure round the corner of their house. That someone was wearing khakis.

"Granddad," she said across his rant. "I think we have company. There's a guy outside—"

"Well, ask if he knows where the damn fuse box is."

"I'm pretty sure he knows. I'm pretty sure he's the reason the lights are out."

There was a beat of silence, then he said, "Crap," followed by more mumbled ranting about the government and secret agents who couldn't keep a damn secret.

"Maybe we could concentrate on staying alive and leave the complaining for later," Abby snapped, mostly because she felt a need to defend Drake, which was stupid since this was at least partly his fault. She'd tried to tell him she thought they were being followed, but did he take her seriously? *No*. He accused her of calling so she could hear his voice. *Egotistical idiot*.

"This is what the guns are for," Virgil said, and she heard him cock his pistol. "Remember what I told you?"

"Yes."

"I'm in the kitchen, so I'll take the back."

Abby groped her way to the front door, swallowing hard as she picked up the rifle. "Okay, I'm by the front door."

"There's wide-pattern shot in the shells. You won't kill anybody, but if someone comes through that door he'll be digging buckshot out of his ass for days."

Actually, killing didn't sound all that wrong to her at the moment. She was tired of being afraid, and if it took a little murder in self-defense to buy her and her grandfather some lasting peace, she was okay with that.

"Step to one side of the front door and point the gun at the opening," Virgil said. "Anybody comes in, don't wait to see who it is, just pull the trigger. But no matter what you think you hear or think you see, don't fire in this direction."

"Right," she muttered, trying to make her hands stop shaking, "good safety tip."

And then all hell broke loose. The back door crashed in, Virgil's gun went off with a deafening boom. There was smoke and yelling—okay, she was doing the yelling, but so was Virgil, and since he sounded angry rather than wounded she started to calm down. Her heart was still racing, but she didn't feel like she was going to throw up any more. "Did you . . . Is he . . . ?"

"Nope, but he ain't getting up anytime soon," Virgil said, sounding pretty proud of himself.

"Uh-oh," she said, because the panicked clanging in her head had eased up enough for her to hear the front doorknob rattling. She swung the shotgun up and fired just as the door started to creak open.

"Ouch! Shit. Abby?"

She froze, her heart stopped beating, and since she wasn't breathing she couldn't speak, even if she'd been able to form words. Her eyes were working fine, though, and there was no mistaking Drake's bulk filling the doorway, even in the darkness.

"You shot me," he said.

"You're lucky she didn't kill you," Virgil said, coming into the front room. "Dumbass government employee. Why didn't you knock first?"

"Because I heard a gunshot."

"Or yell out your name."

"So the hit man could shoot me, too?"

"Now, that's downright insulting," Virgil said. "I shot the hit man, and Abby shot you. Sounds to me like we don't need you looking out for us."

"You shot the hit man?"

"Take a look out the back door."

Drake came inside, and Abby finally found her voice. "Are you all right?"

"The door took most of the blast," he said as he went by. "I caught a little buckshot but it glanced off me. I'll have a few bruises, nothing more."

Abby followed him through the house, collecting her black bag on the way. They both stopped in the doorway, looking down at a chubby, balding man wearing khakis and a bomber jacket. He was unconscious but breathing, a little blood leaking from a bullet wound on his side.

"Jumping at shadows, huh?" Abby said.

"I may have been a bit hasty about that." Drake hunkered beside the guy to get a closer look in the darkness.

"Wow, did you just admit to making a mistake?"

"I came back, didn't I?"

"Yeah, why did you?"

"Because you're not a woman who panics," he said, "and considering the way we left things, you wouldn't have called me if you didn't honestly think you saw someone threatening."

"The way we left things? The way we left things is exactly the way I expected things to be left."

"Sure, but you were pissed-off about it."

"I was angry because you were ordering us around like we didn't have any say in the matter."

"You didn't then, and you don't now."

"Yeah," she said, knowing what he meant. "That's going to be a problem this time."

Ten

Drake was trained to assess a situation, make a quick decision, and not look back. He'd looked back, but that wasn't the real reason he was angry with himself. *Why* he'd looked back was the reason. Abby had gotten to him. He'd left her behind all those years ago while he went off in search of excitement, or maybe the knowledge that he was making the world a better place. Or maybe he'd just been searching for himself—and come up empty.

Abby had been back in his life less than forty-eight hours, and her safety had become more important to him than his job. Not good. Nothing was more important to him than his job. Not even his life—hell, his job was his life. So what did it mean that he'd second-guessed himself for the first time because of her? What did it mean that he was glad to still be alive? Not that he wasn't always happy to dodge a bullet, but there was another layer to his relief this time. He was still alive to see Abby.

He pulled out his cell phone, tabling that line of thought for a more appropriate time, which, if he had any brains, would be never.

"I thought you were on your way back to D.C.," Mike Kovaleski said when he came on the line.

"I was. Had a bad feeling, so I thought I'd check the witness one last time." Mike would understand that motivation, and there was no reason for him to know about Abby's phone call. "Time I got back here," he said to Mike, cutting to the chase, "a guy had bashed his way in. Witness shot him. He's not dead, but he'll need a hospital."

"What does he look like?"

"The first guy, without the black eyes and forehead wound."

"Shit," Mike said. "Identical twin hit men?"

"Yeah, answers a few questions, doesn't it?"

"Birth records must have been doctored," Mike said. "Fucking Russia. You'll have to relocate them again. Hold tight." Drake heard some keyboard action, some muttering that had to do with "damn computers," then, "Let me contact the WitPro guys and have them put a package together." And Mike disconnected.

Drake turned around and Abby was still staring at him, arms folded, foot tapping. He couldn't see her expression, but he knew he wouldn't like it.

"You checked that guy out?" he asked her.

"Yes, and you were right about his condition. He'll need a hospital, but he's stable for the moment. The bullet went through his side, which is mostly fat. I gave him something to keep him out, but we should get him inside."

"Leave him. Mike'll send someone. I'm going to see about the power."

Of course Abby followed him out to the little enclosed porch off the back door, and of course she asked a question he didn't want to answer. "Why did you come back?"

"I told you already."

"You told your boss, and I imagine it was a reason he'd accept. I'm asking for the truth."

"I had a gut feeling," he said, which was the truth, even if the gut feeling had started when she'd awakened him from the dead—and came from somewhere north of his gut.

Abby dragged him to a stop, the warmth of her hands nearly taking him down to his knees. When he'd heard that shot he'd been afraid he was too late. He'd never been afraid like that, not for himself or any other witness he'd handled. He'd barely managed to stop shaking, and if she didn't take her hands off him he was going to gather her into his arms and then she'd know the truth.

"Drake—"

"What do you want me to say?" he demanded, angry suddenly, at her, at himself. "That I let you get to me? Is that going to change anything about this situation? You're a subject, I'm an agent."

"I don't care."

"I do."

She let go of him and sagged against the side of the porch. "And you don't have any feelings for me."

He hated the note of sorrow in her voice. It was wrong. He knew it would be better to leave things the way they were, but he kissed her anyway, poured every ounce of longing into it, feeling the fear that had brought him speeding back to Chicago drain away. Until Abby slapped a hand on his chest, and when he pulled back, she looked a bit crazed and definitely panicked.

"A hit man with a gun doesn't faze you, but when I try to kiss you, you freak out," he said.

"I understand the hit man with the gun."

He rested his forehead against hers for a moment, but when he felt her begin to tremble and understood what his indecision was doing to her, he moved away, slouching against the wall beside her. They stayed that way a couple of minutes, until Drake could feel the cold again, and even then he didn't want to move. "Maybe—"

"No," she said, pushing away from the wall. From him. "Don't make promises you won't keep." And she walked away.

If she felt half of what he did, he had to admire her strength, even as he found enough of his own to catch her before she went back inside. "We'd better announce ourselves. Virgil was still holding his pistol."

"That would solve some problems," she said.

"Maybe, but I'd rather not be buried under a tombstone that reads, 'Dumbass Government Employee.' " Even if it was the truth.

By the time Abby made it through the back door, Drake had found the fuse box, and the house flooded with light suddenly, blinding her. At least it gave her an excuse to rub her eyes before Virgil asked her what the tears were about.

"We can't stay here," Drake said when he came inside.

"Nope," Virgil shot back. "I'm done running."

"You're not done running 'til you're dead."

"I've spent most of my life cut off from everyone and everything I've ever known."

"Which is why you're still alive," Drake reminded him.

Virgil looked around. "This isn't a life, this is a place I was dumped because it was convenient for the federal government. I know you people were trying to help, and I'm grateful, but I didn't do anything wrong."

"What do you mean?" Abby asked him. "What exactly happened all those years ago?"

"I was Joey Pollani's barber," Virgil said.

Drake threw his hands up in the air and stomped away, disgusted.

"The feds came around asking questions one day, but I told them, 'I'm just a barber.' " Virgil sank into a chair, and when he gestured weakly, Abby poured him a cup of coffee and set it in front of him.

"Joey got calls at my place from time to time," he continued, "but I only heard half the conversation, and that's like reading the Bible. You can make it mean whatever you want. But the idiot kid who worked for me thought it would be exciting to testify against

Pollani, do his civic duty and all that crap. Wound up they didn't even need him to make their case, which I tried to tell the dumbass, but all Joey knew was his barber ratted him out, and since the kid didn't show up on the witness stand, Joey thought it was me."

"You're lucky they put you in the program," Drake said. "They didn't really have any responsibility since you refused to testify."

"I didn't know anything," Virgil yelled at him. "And being dumped in the middle of nowhere was no favor."

Drake looked like he was barely holding on to his patience.

Abby could understand how he felt; Virgil had been kept safe, thanks to the government, and he was still alive now, thanks to Drake. On the other hand, she could sympathize with Virgil. Being totally cut off from everyone he loved and losing what he'd worked his whole life to build must have been terrible.

"And what about Abby?" Drake asked Virgil.

"Nope, guilt isn't working this time. If they kill me she'll be safe again."

"And what happens when she gets in the way, or sees the guy who shoots you, or they kill her just because they get off on it?"

Virgil took a sip of coffee, thinking that over.

Abby wasn't going to be used like that. She went to him, crouched down in front of his chair. "What do you want, Granddad? Don't let him bully you, and don't think about me."

He simply stared at her a minute, his rheumy old eyes filling with tears. "I'm eighty years old," he said, sniffing. "I could fall down tomorrow, crack a hip, get pneumonia, and die in my bed. If I'm going out, I'll go out on my feet, damn it."

"You're sure?"

"I'm too old to start over again. I don't make friends all that easy, in case Eliot Ness over there hasn't noticed. I want to go home before I die."

She stood, met Drake's eyes. "Then you're going home."

"He'll be making the journey in a coffin in the cargo hold of an airplane."

"There has to be a way," Abby insisted. "Joey Pollani is over eighty. He probably doesn't even remember the contract."

"If he didn't remember it, I wouldn't be here."

Virgil climbed stiffly to his feet, put his arm around her shoulders. "Then we go to see Joey, talk some sense into the old bastard."

"And if he shoots first and asks questions after?"

"It'll be over," Virgil said. "One way or another."

They left almost that instant, Drake giving them just enough time to secure the house and waiting long enough for someone to collect the second hit man before he packed them into the monster SUV and headed for the airport.

There were about a million reasons why a face-to-face with Joey Pollani was a bad idea, but doing the unexpected might just save their lives. Besides, Virgil had his mind made up. Drake could relocate him anywhere in the world, but he couldn't sit on the man for the rest of his life. And he couldn't count on Abby to do it. She agreed with the old man. Drake wondered how much of it was because of Virgil, and how much was because of him.

She said she didn't want anything from him, but he'd caught her watching him, and hell, he wouldn't have noticed all the sidelong glances if he hadn't been making too many of his own. It ought to piss him off, but it didn't. And that was downright frightening.

"Do you really think this will work?" Abby asked him from the center seat of the plane, squished between the two men.

"It's a chess game. We make a move, they make a move, and in between we each try to figure out the other's strategy. Joey definitely won't be expecting this."

"And what if he is?"

Drake shrugged. "I'll deal with that when I have to."

"So you're either good or lucky?"

"It's not luck."

Virgil muttered something unintelligible, probably still stewing that Drake hadn't allowed him to bring his guns along. Flying and guns didn't mix well. Flying and concussions didn't go well, either, it turned out. No sooner had they gotten airborne than the flight attendant opened the compartment over their row to get a blanket for another passenger. One of those annoying carry-on suitcases fell out, and since Drake had insisted on the aisle seat, it hit him on the head, the zipper cutting his ear.

The flight attendant was, of course, really upset. She insisted on taking him to first class, coming back about five minutes later and bending over Abby.

"Are you a doctor?" she asked. "The man who was here—"

"The one you dropped the luggage on," Virgil said.

The woman turned red, but she kept her eyes on Abby. "Can you come up front?"

"Is he hurt that badly?"

"Well, he's bleeding and he won't let any of us bandage him."

Abby retrieved her bag, which was the only luggage Drake had allowed them and only because she'd insisted. "Watch out for my grandfather," she said quietly to the flight attendant.

"Like an eagle."

Abby went through the first class curtain, the senior flight attendant motioning her to the lavatory. Drake was sitting on the closed toilet, a wad of paper towel to his ear. There was nowhere for Abby to stand except between his legs, so she stepped inside, keeping her eyes on his ear and off his face, and his chest, and . . . everything else. She tried not to breathe through her mouth, or notice the warmth radiating off him, and when she moved his hand away from his ear she was careful not to make skin-to-skin contact.

The fact that he wasn't bleeding anymore surprised her enough that she looked him in the eyes, and then she didn't have to ask why he'd asked for her, because she felt like she'd caught fire.

"How's he doing?" the flight attendant asked.

"He just needs a bandage." Drake ran his hand under her top, careful to keep the movement out of sight. "As soon as the bleeding stops."

"Do you mind if I shut the door? The pilot says there's some weather ahead. I don't want you to fall into the aisle and get hurt."

"Fine," Abby said, praying her voice sounded steadier than her hands were proving to be. She dug through her bag, pulling out what she could only hope was gauze and tape. She couldn't say for sure with her vision blurring.

The door shut and she gave up the pretense, letting her eyes drift shut, giving in to the feel of his hand on her breast, turning the chronic ache she'd lived with the last few hours into something that rose up and filled her with need.

"We can't do this here," she said, one last grab for sanity.

"We have to."

Her eyes met his and she was in complete agreement—and already half undressed, if she could call having her shirt and bra shoved up around her neck undressing.

Drake took off even less. He helped her remove her jeans and panties, then simply unzipped his pants, pulling her down on him in one long, fast stroke that had her throwing her head back, already on the brink. He took his mouth to her breast, the roughness of his two-day-old beard a stark contrast to the moist heat of his tongue on her nipple, the hard, hot strokes of him inside her. She went over, hands braced on his shoulders for a long, stunning moment as her orgasm tore through her in delicious waves, while he kept moving, stroking her from the inside, drawing out the pleasure until all she could do was collapse bonelessly against him.

"Christ, don't move," he said, hands braced around her hips, a pained expression on his face.

"It's not me, it's the plane. Gives a whole new meaning to the word *turbulence*," she added, laughing.

And then he was moving again, whispering against her skin, "Christ, Abby, what you do to me." It was hotter this time, slower, Drake making sure she felt every inch of him moving inside her, every flick of his tongue on her sensitive nipples, every caress as his fingers moved between her legs in the same rhythm.

The didn't have a future, but Abby kept her eyes on his until he threw his head back, the muscles in his neck corded as he climaxed, and she went over, too, another, gentler orgasm that left her feeling pleasantly spent, and a little sad because she knew it was the last time.

His hands tightened on her waist when she started to pull away, but only briefly before he let her go. She dressed quickly, not looking at him, and neither of them spoke until she tried to bandage his ear.

"That's not really necessary," Drake said.

Abby picked up a wad of gauze and folded it to size, handing him the tape dispenser. "Don't even think about going out there without a bandage," she said. But she didn't meet his eyes.

Eleven

A big black Lincoln Town Car, courtesy of the FBI, took them from the airport to Sunset Hills Retirement Village, on the outskirts of Washington, D.C. Joey Pollani, they were told, was by the pool. It being December, it didn't bode well for the possibility he'd be lucid enough to call off the contract.

"Christ," Virgil said as they stepped out onto what would be a sunny patio in four or five months, "he's lost it."

Pollani, once one of the most feared mafia figures in the western hemisphere, was sitting in two inches of snow by an empty pool. He wore full winter gear, but there was a drink with a paper umbrella sitting on the table beside him.

"Doesn't say much for your chance of rejoining your life," Drake said.

"The hell it don't." Virgil shoved his way past Drake, and headed for Joey's table.

"Well," Abby said, following him, "he's bundled up, so he knows it's cold."

"I ain't crazy," Joey said in a voice that sounded like it came from the soles of his feet and bubbled its way up through a vat of wine on the way. "No crazier than the next guy at least. I should be living out my golden years in the south of Italy, but the damn feds are making me stay here as a condition of my parole."

Joey hadn't turned around, so Drake shifted to stand in his peripheral vision. "I wonder where they'll send you when they find out you ordered a hit."

Joey snorted. "Didn't order no hit."

"You did originally," Virgil said.

That got Joey's attention. He stared at Virgil for a full minute, and when he put a name to the face he grinned and said, "Well, I'll be a sonuvabitch."

"Why change now?" Virgil said.

"What name you going by?"

"Don't tell him, Granddad," Abby said.

"Granddad?" Joey shifted his gaze to Abby for the first time, then back to Virgil. "So that's what smoked you out, you old cockroach. Anyone ever tell you sentimentality's a killer?"

"The guy you sent after him is the killer," Drake said.

"Why would I bother taking out a hit on him?" Joey ground out, hooking his thumb in Virgil's direction. "He looks like he's got one foot in the grave. All I gotta do is wait him out."

"We have Igor Svetsky in custody, along with his twin brother. I'm pretty sure they'll confirm they were working for you."

"Hah," Joey said, facing forward again. "Don't know the guy, but if he's a career hitter he'll have a copy of the list."

"List?" Drake repeated.

"You think the feds are the only ones with a most wanted? Why else would you keep him in Witness Protection for so long?"

"Because you're an idiot," Virgil yelled. "I didn't do anything."

"I know," Joey said. "It was that stupid kid who worked for you."

That stopped Virgil. "You knew I didn't rat you out and you let me rot in the sticks all that time? You stole over fifty years of my life." He lunged for Joey, but Drake stepped between them.

"I was kind of busy being on trial," Joey said. "By the time the government was done deciding my living arrangements you were gone. I figured you were safer where you were."

"Dumbass government lawyers," Virgil muttered, like the whole thing was their fault.

"Since you know Virgil is innocent you can cancel the contract," Drake said to Joey.

He shrugged. "Consider it cancelled. But there's no guarantee the word will get out before one of the pros finds you."

"What about the list?"

"It's a hell of a lot easier to put a name on than take one off."

Virgil blew out a breath, sounding completely exhausted and demoralized. "So now what?"

Joey thought about it a minute, then said, "You know, there's a vacancy in this place."

Virgil snorted.

" 'Course, they got a list of people all set to move in, but might be I could work it out that your name somehow got to the top."

"What good'll that do me?"

"Nobody'll lay a finger on you if you're right next door to me," Joey said. "Besides, I ain't had a decent haircut in decades."

Virgil took a seat at the table and said, "*Eh*, I can't cut hair anymore. Arthritis."

"Could be worse," Joey said philosophically. "You coulda been hit by a bus like that kid who used to work for you. Tragic accident."

"Right," Virgil said dryly, "accident." Then he shrugged. "You want me to cut your hair, I'll cut your hair. It's your head."

Abby listened to Joey and Virgil commiserate about prostate size, sleep apnea, and the dearth of Viagra-worthy female residents at Sunset Hills. Drake had wandered off to report in; he came back about fifteen minutes later and told Virgil they were leaving.

"But I'll be back, Granddad," Abby assured him.

He waved, engrossed in his conversation with Joey, so she followed Drake around the building to the parking lot.

"He can't live here," she said, "at least not until I get a job with actual patients."

"Technically, he's still in Witness Protection."

She wasn't sure what to think about that.

Drake held the door open for her. "Consider it an early Christmas gift in return for the one you and Virgil gave the FBI. Igor Svetsky," he added when she only frowned at him, "and his twin brother, who has yet to be named."

Abby couldn't help but smile, and if it was smug she figured she was entitled to it. "I was right."

"They're from Russia," Drake said by way of agreement. "It's not that hard to bribe your way into city hall there and alter records to show a single birth instead of a multiple. Every time there was credible proof that Igor murdered someone he had an airtight alibi. Thanks to your deadly aim with a coffee mug his brother was forced to come out in the open and go after Virgil, and thanks to Virgil, we got him, too.

"We could never pin any hits on Igor, but he was suspected in at least thirty-eight, and there are probably more. We're going to be closing cases off these two for years."

"Happy to be of service," Abby said, stopping at the car.

Drake came up beside her. "What about you?"

"I'd like to stay close to Granddad. He's going to be okay, but he's eighty, you know?"

Drake nodded. "I think I can help with that." He took out his cell and called a number, handing her the phone.

"George Washington University Hospital," the voice on the other end said when she put it up to her ear. "We'd like to schedule an interview at your earliest convenience, Dr. West."

"I, uh . . . Can I call you back? I don't have my schedule handy."

"Why don't you come in now, if you're free?"

"Um . . . sure," she said because that was the easiest answer with her head spinning.

"We can fit you in anytime before five."

"That's fine," Abby said and disconnected. "They can fit me in anytime before five," she repeated, feeling a little shell-shocked. And then the wonder of it wore off and she didn't know what to feel. "Why? And how?"

"The how is Mike. He pulled a few strings."

She slapped the phone back into his hand. "I can get my own job, thanks."

Drake caught her arm when she started to walk away. "Are you going to let the FBI chase you away from what you want?"

Abby gave that all of a second's thought. "No," she said, turning into his arms and kissing him. She put body and soul into that kiss. And heart.

Drake just stood there, and when she was done he said, "my turn," and kissed her back, both hands framing her face, starting out gentle and then turning hot, drawing her in, making her give him everything she had and more. He was coming to her, that kiss said, he was offering her as much of himself as he could. But was he expecting her to be a port in the storm, a place to flop between missions, or was there a commitment in his kiss? It sure felt serious, especially when he broke off, resting his forehead against hers while they both caught their breath.

"Are you taking the interview?" he said after a moment, not letting her go but keeping his hold light enough that she could have pulled free. If she'd wanted to.

But she needed to know it wasn't just physical. "Why G.W.?"

Drake's jaw clenched, and she thought he would duck the question, but he said, "You already know the answer to that."

"I thought I knew ten years ago, too. What's different now than it was then?"

"I've been asking myself that question ever since the moment I woke up on your table. When I realized my hands were around your neck." He exhaled heavily, shaking his head. "It would have been bad enough with any civilian, but when I saw it was you . . ." His grip tightened on her. "All I can say is everything shifted."

She knew exactly what he meant. She'd felt it herself, but she was afraid to believe they could have a future together. Sure, there was heat between them and heat was good, but in order to last, a real relationship needed a nice slow, lifelong simmer. "I appreciate what you're doing for my grandfather, and I'm grateful you're giving me a chance to stay close to him—"

"It's not just him, Abby." Drake took a step away, as if he, too, wanted to be sure it was more than chemistry prompting his words. "I'd like you to live in Washington, and not just so I can stop around between cases. I'll be staying with the Bureau, but I think it's time for me to make a change."

She smiled a little. "Dealing with me and Virgil ruined you for all other witnesses, huh?"

"I think it was the body bag. I always knew death was a possible outcome, but now . . . Since you . . . We were both so young, Abby. I didn't really know what I wanted—"

"Until you went on that damned interview."

"Until then," he agreed. "You were headed to medical school, and I didn't want to get in your way. But that isn't the only reason I left. I wanted to do *something*. I wanted to feel like the world would be a better place because of me."

"It was a better place. For me."

"For me, too, but I didn't know that then. I had to take a side trip before I figured out I was already on the right road."

Tears burned behind her eyes, but she needed to know he was sure. "How can you make such a huge change in so short a time?"

He took her by the shoulders. "Two days ago when Igor shot at Virgil, I jumped in front of you instead of him. Yesterday when I came back to that house in Chicago, it wasn't because you thought you saw the hit man; it was because I couldn't get you off my mind.

Hell, letting Virgil come here was just about the worst decision I've ever made in ten years of undercover work. I did it because I wanted you to be free, Abby.

"For the first time in ten years, I'm hoping I'll have someone to come home to, and that means I'll be watching my back instead of doing my job. I won't work that way."

"So your career is over because of me."

"Because I love you."

Abby threw her arms around him, burying her face in his neck. She was beyond words, but he seemed to understand her just fine if the way he kissed her was any indication. She pulled back before they lost themselves, taking his face in her hands and holding his gaze. She wanted him to see the love shining out of her, in case her words weren't enough. "I love you, too. Still. But I don't want to get in your way."

He kissed her again, quick and hard and full of exuberance. "If you think you're in the way, you weren't listening. My career isn't over; it'll just be different. The only other thing I need is for you to be happy, too," he said, his arms tight around her. "So it'll work out really well if you land that job at G.W."

She laughed softly, leaning back to look in his eyes. "When I go after something, I generally get it."

Drake smiled, opening the car door for her. "How about I give you a ride to the hospital? D.C. traffic can be murder this time of day."